THE HUMAN COMEDY

PHILOSOPHICAL STUDIES

# Louis Lambert

*Translated by Clara Bell and James Waring*

# The Exiles

*Translated by Clara Bell and James Waring*

# Seraphita

*Translated by Katharine Prescott Wormeley*

HONORÉ DE BALZAC

I0589184

ANTIPODES PRESS
www.antipodespress.com

# THE HUMAN COMEDY

# THE HUMAN COMEDY

Cover illustration based on the artwork of Auguste Edouart.

This Antipodes edition is a republication of texts from *The Works of Balzac* published in 1899 by Little, Brown, and Company and *The Novels of Balzac* published in 1900 by Gebbie Publishing.

ISBN 978-0-9882026-7-2

# Contents

# Louis Lambert

*Et nunc et semper dilectoe dicatum.*

Louis Lambert was born at Montoire, a little town in the Vendomois, where his father owned a tannery of no great magnitude, and intended that his son should succeed him; but his precocious bent for study modified the paternal decision. For, indeed, the tanner and his wife adored Louis, their only child, and never contradicted him in anything.

At the age of five Louis had begun by reading the Old and New Testaments; and these two Books, including so many books, had sealed his fate. Could that childish imagination understand the mystical depths of the Scriptures? Could it so early follow the flight of the Holy Spirit across the worlds? Or was it merely attracted by the romantic touches which abound in those Oriental poems! Our narrative will answer these questions to some readers.

One thing resulted from this first reading of the Bible: Louis went all over Montoire begging for books, and he obtained them by those winning ways peculiar to children, which no one can resist. While devoting himself to these studies under no sort of guidance, he reached the age of ten.

At that period substitutes for the army were scarce; rich families secured them long beforehand to have them ready when the lots were drawn. The poor tanner's modest fortune did not allow of their purchasing a substitute for their son, and they saw no means allowed by law for evading the conscription but that of making him a priest; so, in 1807, they sent him to his maternal uncle, the parish priest of Mer, another small town on the Loire, not far from Blois. This arrangement at once satisfied Louis' passion for knowledge, and his parents' wish not to expose him to the dreadful chances of war; and, indeed, his taste for study and precocious intelligence gave grounds for hoping that he might rise to high fortunes in the Church.

After remaining for about three years with his uncle, an old and not uncultured Oratorian, Louis left him early in 1811 to enter the college at Vendome, where he was maintained at the cost of Madame de Stael.

Lambert owed the favor and patronage of this celebrated lady to chance, or shall we not say to Providence, who can smooth the path of forlorn genius? To us, indeed, who do not see below the surface of human things, such

vicissitudes, of which we find many examples in the lives
of great men, appear to be merely the result of physical
phenomena; to most biographers the head of a man of
genius rises above the herd as some noble plant in the fields
attracts the eye of a botanist in its splendor. This comparison may well be applied to Louis Lambert's adventure; he
was accustomed to spend the time allowed him by his uncle
for holidays at his father's house; but instead of indulg-
ing, after the manner of schoolboys, in the sweets of the
delightful *far niente* that tempts us at every age, he set out
every morning with part of a loaf and his books, and went
to read and meditate in the woods, to escape his mother's
remonstrances, for she believed such persistent study to be
injurious. How admirable is a mother's instinct! From that
time reading was in Louis a sort of appetite which nothing could satisfy; he devoured books of every kind, feeding
indiscriminately on religious works, history, philosophy,
and physics. He has told me that he found indescribable
delight in reading dictionaries for lack of other books, and
I readily believed him. What scholar has not many a time
found pleasure in seeking the probable meaning of some
unknown word? The analysis of a word, its physiognomy
and history, would be to Lambert matter for long dreaming. But these were not the instinctive dreams by which
a boy accustoms himself to the phenomena of life, steels
himself to every moral or physical perception—an involuntary education which subsequently brings forth fruit both
in the understanding and character of a man; no, Louis
mastered the facts, and he accounted for them after seeking out both the principle and the end with the mother wit
of a savage. Indeed, from the age of fourteen, by one of
those startling freaks in which nature sometimes indulges,
and which proved how anomalous was his temperament,
he would utter quite simply ideas of which the depth was
not revealed to me till a long time after.

"Often," he has said to me when speaking of his studies,
"often have I made the most delightful voyage, floating on
a word down the abyss of the past, like an insect embarked
on a blade of grass tossing on the ripples of a stream. Starting from Greece, I would get to Rome, and traverse the

whole extent of modern ages. What a fine book might be written of the life and adventures of a word! It has, of course, received various stamps from the occasions on which it has served its purpose; it has conveyed different ideas in different places; but is it not still grander to think of it under the three aspects of soul, body, and motion? Merely to regard it in the abstract, apart from its functions, its effects, and its influence, is enough to cast one into an ocean of meditations. Are not most words colored by the idea they represent? Then, to whose genius are they due? If it takes great intelligence to create a word, how old may human speech be? The combination of letters, their shapes, and the look they give to the word, are the exact reflection, in accordance with the character of each nation, of the unknown beings whose traces survive in us.

"Who can philosophically explain the transition from sensation to thought, from thought to word, from the word to its hieroglyphic presentment, from hieroglyphics to the alphabet, from the alphabet to written language, of which the eloquent beauty resides in a series of images, classified by rhetoric, and forming, in a sense, the hieroglyphics of thought? Was it not the ancient mode of representing human ideas as embodied in the forms of animals that gave rise to the shapes of the first signs used in the East for writing down language? Then has it not left its traces by tradition on our modern languages, which have all seized some remnant of the primitive speech of nations, a majestic and solemn tongue whose grandeur and solemnity decrease as communities grow old; whose sonorous tones ring in the Hebrew Bible, and still are noble in Greece, but grow weaker under the progress of successive phases of civilization?

"Is it to this time-honored spirit that we owe the mysteries lying buried in every human word? In the word *True* do we not discern a certain imaginary rectitude? Does not the compact brevity of its sound suggest a vague image of chaste nudity and the simplicity of Truth in all things? The syllable seems to me singularly crisp and fresh.

"I chose the formula of an abstract idea on purpose, not wishing to illustrate the case by a word which should make it too obvious to the apprehension, as the word *Flight* for instance, which is a direct appeal to the senses.

"But is it not so with every root word? They are all stamped with a living power that comes from the soul, and which they restore to the soul through the mysterious and wonderful action and reaction between thought and speech. Might we not speak of it as a lover who finds on his mistress' lips as much love as he gives? Thus, by their mere physiognomy, words call to life in our brain the beings which they serve to clothe. Like all beings, there is but one place where their properties are at full liberty to act and develop. But the subject demands a science to itself perhaps!"

And he would shrug his shoulders as much as to say, "But we are too high and too low!"

Louis' passion for reading had on the whole been very well satisfied. The curé of Mer had two or three thousand volumes. This treasure had been derived from the plunder committed during the Revolution in the neighboring chateaux and abbeys. As a priest who had taken the oath, the worthy man had been able to choose the best books from among these precious libraries, which were sold by the pound. In three years Louis Lambert had assimilated the contents of all the books in his uncle's library that were worth reading. The process of absorbing ideas by means of reading had become in him a very strange phenomenon. His eye took in six or seven lines at once, and his mind grasped the sense with a swiftness as remarkable as that of his eye; sometimes even one word in a sentence was enough to enable him to seize the gist of the matter.

His memory was prodigious. He remembered with equal exactitude the ideas he had derived from reading, and those which had occurred to him in the course of meditation or conversation. Indeed, he had every form of memory—for places, for names, for words, things, and faces. He not only recalled any object at will, but he saw them in his mind, situated, lighted, and colored as he had originally seen them. And this power he could exert with equal effect with regard to the most abstract efforts of the intellect. He could remember, as he said, not merely the position of a sentence in the book where he had met with it, but the frame of mind he had been in at remote dates. Thus his was the singular privilege of being able to retrace in memory the whole life and progress of his mind, from the ideas he had first acquired to the last thought evolved in it, from the most obscure to the clearest. His brain, accustomed in early youth to the mysterious mechanism by which human faculties are concentrated, drew from this rich treasury endless images full of life and freshness, on which he fed his spirit during those lucid spells of contemplation.

"Whenever I wish it," said he to me in his own language, to which a fund of remembrance gave precocious originality, "I can draw a veil over my eyes. Then I suddenly see within me a camera obscura, where natural objects are reproduced in purer forms than those under which they first appeared to my external sense."

At the age of twelve his imagination, stimulated by the perpetual exercise of his faculties, had developed to a point which permitted him to have such precise concepts of things which he knew only from reading about them, that the image stamped on his mind could not have been clearer if he had actually seen them, whether this was by a process of analogy or that he was gifted with a sort of second sight by which he could command all nature.

"When I read the story of the battle of Austerlitz," said he to me one day, "I saw every incident. The roar of the cannon, the cries of the fighting men rang in my ears, and made my inmost self quiver; I could smell the powder; I heard the clatter of horses and the voices of men; I looked down on the plain where armed nations were in collision, just as if I had been on the heights of Santon. The scene was as terrifying as a passage from the Apocalypse." On the occasions when he brought all his powers into play, and in some degree lost consciousness of his physical existence, and lived on only by the remarkable energy of his mental powers, whose sphere was enormously expanded, he left space behind him, to use his own words.

But I will not here anticipate the intellectual phases of his life. Already, in spite of myself, I have reversed the order in which I ought to tell the history of this man, who transferred all his activities to thinking, as others throw all their life into action.

A strong bias drew his mind into mystical studies.

"*Abyssus abyssum,*" he would say. "Our spirit is abysmal and loves the abyss. In childhood, manhood, and old age we are always eager for mysteries in whatever form they present themselves."

This predilection was disastrous; if indeed his life can be measured by ordinary standards, or if we may gauge another's happiness by our own or by social notions. This taste for the "things of heaven," another phrase he was fond of using, this *mens divinior,* was due perhaps to the influence produced on his mind by the first books he read at his uncle's. Saint Theresa and Madame Guyon were a sequel to the Bible; they had the first fruits of his manly intelligence, and accustomed him to those swift reactions of the soul of which ecstasy is at once the result and the means. This line of study, this peculiar taste, elevated his heart, purified, ennobled it, gave him an appetite for the divine nature, and suggested to him the almost womanly refinement of feeling which is instinctive in great men; perhaps their sublime superiority is no more than the desire to devote themselves which characterizes woman, only transferred to the greatest things.

As a result of these early impressions, Louis passed immaculate through his school life; this beautiful virginity of the senses naturally resulted in the richer fervor of his blood, and in increased faculties of mind.

The Baroness de Stael, forbidden to come within forty leagues of Paris, spent several months of her banishment on an estate near Vendome. One day, when out walking, she met on the skirts of the park the tanner's son, almost in rags, and absorbed in reading. The book was a translation of *Heaven and Hell.* At that time Monsieur Saint-Martin, Monsieur de Gence, and a few other French or half German writers were almost the only persons in the French Empire to whom the name of Swedenborg was known. Madame de Stael, greatly surprised, took the book from him with the roughness she affected in her questions, looks, and manners, and with a keen glance at Lambert,—

"Do you understand all this?" she asked.

"Do you pray to God?" said the child.

"Why? yes!"

"And do you understand Him?"

The Baroness was silent for a moment; then she sat down by Lambert, and began to talk to him. Unfortunately, my memory, though retentive, is far from being so trustworthy as my friend's, and I have forgotten the whole of the dialogue excepting those first words.

Such a meeting was of a kind to strike Madame de Stael very greatly; on her return home she said but little about it, notwithstanding an effusiveness which in her became mere loquacity; but it evidently occupied her thoughts.

The only person now living who preserves any recollection of the incident, and whom I catechized to be informed of what few words Madame de Stael had let drop, could with difficulty recall these words spoken by the Baroness as describing Lambert, "He is a real seer."

Louis failed to justify in the eyes of the world the high hopes he had inspired in his protectress. The transient favor she showed him was regarded as a feminine caprice, one of the fancies characteristic of artist souls. Madame de Stael determined to save Louis Lambert alike from serving the Emperor or the Church, and to preserve him for the glorious destiny which, she thought, awaited him; for she made him out to be a second Moses snatched from the waters. Before her departure she instructed a friend of hers, Monsieur de Corbigny, to send her Moses in due course to the High School at Vendome; then she probably forgot him.

Having entered this college at the age of fourteen, early in 1811, Lambert would leave it at the end of 1814, when he had finished the course of Philosophy. I doubt whether during the whole time he ever heard a word of his benefactress—if indeed it was the act of a benefactress to pay for a lad's schooling for three years without a thought of his future prospects, after diverting him from a career in which he might have found happiness. The circumstances of the time, and Louis Lambert's character, may to a great extent absolve Madame de Stael for her thoughtlessness and her generosity. The gentleman who was to have kept up communications between her and the boy left Blois just at the time when Louis passed out of the college. The political events that ensued were then a sufficient excuse for this gentleman's neglect of the Baroness' protégé. The authoress of *Corinne* heard no more of her little Moses.

A hundred louis, which she placed in the hands of Monsieur de Corbigny, who died, I believe, in 1812, was not a sufficiently large sum to leave lasting memories in Madame de Stael, whose excitable nature found ample pasture during the vicissitudes of 1814 and 1815, which absorbed all her interest.

At this time Louis Lambert was at once too proud and too poor to go in search of a patroness who was traveling all over Europe. However, he went on foot from Blois to Paris in the hope of seeing her, and arrived, unluckily, on the very day of her death. Two letters from Lambert to the Baroness remained unanswered. The memory of Madame de Stael's good intentions with regard to Louis remains, therefore, only in some few young minds, struck, as mine was, by the strangeness of the story.

No one who had not gone through the training at our college could understand the effect usually made on our minds by the announcement that a "new boy" had arrived, or the impression that such an adventure as Louis Lambert's was calculated to produce.

And here a little information must be given as to the primitive administration of this institution, originally half-military and half-monastic, to explain the new life which there awaited Lambert. Before the Revolution, the Oratorians, devoted, like the Society of Jesus, to the education of youth—succeeding the Jesuits, in fact, in certain of their establishments—the colleges of Vendome, of Tournon, of la Fleche, Pont-Levoy, Sorreze, and Juilly. That at Vendome, like the others, I believe, turned out a certain number of cadets for the army. The abolition of educational bodies, decreed by the convention, had but little effect on the college at Vendome. When the first crisis had blown over, the authorities recovered possession of their buildings; certain Oratorians, scattered about the country, came back to the college and re-opened it under the old rules, with the habits, practices, and customs which gave this school a character with which I have seen nothing at all comparable in any that I have visited since I left that establishment.

Standing in the heart of the town, on the little river Loire which flows under its walls, the college possesses extensive precincts, carefully enclosed by walls, and including all the buildings necessary for an institution on that scale: a chapel, a theater, an infirmary, a bakehouse, gardens, and water supply. This college is the most celebrated home of learning in all the central provinces, and receives pupils from them and from the colonies. Distance prohibits any frequent visits from parents to their children.

The rule of the House forbids holidays away from it. Once entered there, a pupil never leaves till his studies are finished. With the exception of walks taken under the guidance of the Fathers, everything is calculated to give the School the benefit of conventual discipline; in my day the tawse was still a living memory, and the classical leather strap played its terrible part with all the honors. The punishment originally invented by the Society of Jesus, as alarming to the moral as to the physical man, was still in force in all the integrity of the original code.

Letters to parents were obligatory on certain days, so was confession. Thus our sins and our sentiments were all according to pattern. Everything bore the stamp of monastic rule. I well remember, among other relics of the ancient order, the inspection we went through every Sunday. We were all in our best, placed in file like soldiers to await the arrival of the two inspectors who, attended by the tutors and the tradesmen, examined us from the three points of view of dress, health, and morals.

The two or three hundred pupils lodged in the establishment were divided, according to ancient custom, into the *minimes* (the smallest), the little boys, the middle boys, and the big boys. The division of the *minimes* included the eighth and seventh classes; the little boys formed the sixth, fifth, and fourth; the middle boys were classed as third and second; and the first class comprised the senior students—of philosophy, rhetoric, the higher mathematics, and chemistry. Each of these divisions had its own building, classrooms, and playground, in the large common precincts on to which the classrooms opened, and beyond which was the refectory.

This dining hall, worthy of an ancient religious Order, accommodated all the school. Contrary to the usual practice in educational institutions, we were allowed to talk at our meals, a tolerant Oratorian rule which enabled us to exchange plates according to our taste. This gastronomical barter was always one of the chief pleasures of our college life. If one of the "middle" boys at the head of his table wished for a helping of lentils instead of dessert—for we had dessert—the offer was passed down from one to another: "Dessert for lentils!" till some other epicure had accepted; then the plate of lentils was passed up to the bidder from hand to hand, and the plate of dessert returned by the same road. Mistakes were never made. If several identical offers were made, they were taken in order, and the formula would be, "Lentils number one for dessert number one." The tables were very long; our incessant barter kept everything moving; we transacted it with amazing eagerness; and the chatter of three hundred lads, the bustling to and fro of the servants employed in changing the plates, setting down the dishes, handing the bread, with the tours of inspection of the masters, made this refectory at Vendome a scene unique in its way, and the amazement of visitors.

To make our life more tolerable, deprived as we were of all communication with the outer world and of family affection, we were allowed to keep pigeons and to have gardens. Our two or three hundred pigeon houses, with a thousand birds nesting all round the outer wall, and above thirty garden plots, were a sight even stranger than our meals. But a full account of the peculiarities which made the college at Vendome a place unique in itself and fertile in reminiscences to those who spent their boyhood there, would be weariness to the reader. Which of us all but remembers with delight, notwithstanding the bitterness of learning, the eccentric pleasures of that cloistered life? The sweetmeats purchased by stealth in the course of our walks, permission obtained to play cards and devise theatrical performances during the holidays, such tricks and freedom as were necessitated by our seclusion; then, again, our military band, a relic of the cadets; our academy, our chaplain, our Father professors, and all our games permitted or prohibited, as the case might be; the cavalry charges on stilts, the long slides made in winter, the clatter of our clogs; and, above all, the trading transactions with "the shop" set up in the courtyard itself.

This shop was kept by a sort of cheap-jack, of whom big and little boys could procure—according to his prospectus—boxes, stilts, tools, Jacobin pigeons, and Nuns, Mass books—an article in small demand—penknives, paper, pens, pencils, ink of all colors, balls and marbles; in short, the whole catalogue of the most treasured possessions of boys, including everything from sauce for the pigeons we were obliged to kill off, to the earthenware pots in which we set aside the rice from supper to be eaten at next morning's breakfast. Which of us was so unhappy as to have forgotten how his heart beat at the sight of this booth, open periodically during play hours on Sundays, to which we went, each in his turn, to spend his little pocket money; while the smallness of the sum allowed by our parents for these minor pleasures required us to make a choice among all the objects that appealed so strongly to our desires? Did ever a young wife, to whom her husband, during the first days of happiness, hands, twelve times a year, a purse of gold, the budget of her personal fancies, dream of so many different purchases, each of which would absorb the whole sum, as we imagined possible on the eve of the first Sunday in each month? For six francs during one night we owned every delight of that inexhaustible shop! and during Mass every response we chanted was mixed up in our minds with our secret calculations. Which of us all can recollect ever having had a sou left to spend on the Sunday following? And which of us but obeyed the instinctive law of social existence by pitying, helping, and despising those pariahs who, by the avarice or poverty of their parents, found themselves penniless?

Any one who forms a clear idea of this huge college, with its monastic buildings in the heart of a little town, and the four plots in which we were distributed as by a monastic rule, will easily conceive of the excitement that we felt at the arrival of a new boy, a passenger suddenly embarked on the ship. No young duchess, on her first appearance at Court, was ever more spitefully criticized than the new boy by the youths in his division. Usually during the evening play hour before prayers, those sycophants who were accustomed to ingratiate themselves with the Fathers who took it in turns two and two for a week to keep an eye on us, would be the first to hear on trustworthy authority: "There will be a new boy tomorrow!" and then suddenly the shout, "A new boy!—A new boy!" rang through the courts. We hurried up to crowd round the superintendent and pester him with questions:

"Where was he coming from? What was his name? Which class would he be in?" and so forth.

Louis Lambert's advent was the subject of a romance worthy of the *Arabian Nights*. I was in the fourth class at the time—among the little boys. Our housemasters were two men whom we called Fathers from habit and tradition, though they were not priests. In my time there were indeed but three genuine Oratorians to whom this title legitimately belonged; in 1814 they all left the college, which had gradually become secularized, to find occupation about the altar in various country parishes, like the curé of Mer.

Father Haugoult, the master for the week, was not a bad man, but of very moderate attainments, and he lacked the tact which is indispensable for discerning the different characters of children, and graduating their punishment to their powers of resistance. Father Haugoult, then, began very obligingly to communicate to his pupils the wonderful events which were to end on the morrow in the advent of the most singular of "new boys." Games were at an end. All the children came round in silence to hear the story of Louis Lambert, discovered, like an aerolite, by Madame de Stael, in a corner of the wood. Monsieur Haugoult had to tell us all about Madame de Stael; that evening she seemed to me ten feet high; I saw at a later time the picture of Corinne, in which Gerard represents her as so tall and handsome; and, alas! the woman painted by my imagination so far transcended this, that the real Madame de Stael fell at once in my estimation, even after I read her book of really masculine power, *De l'Allemagne.*

But Lambert at that time was an even greater wonder. Monsieur Mareschal, the headmaster, after examining him, had thought of placing him among the senior boys. It was Louis' ignorance of Latin that placed him so low as the fourth class, but he would certainly leap up a class every year; and, as a remarkable exception, he was to be one of the "Academy." *Proh pudor!* we were to have the honor of counting among the "little boys" one whose coat was adorned with the red ribbon displayed by the "Academicians" of Vendome. These Academicians enjoyed distinguished privileges; they often dined at the director's table, and held two literary meetings annually, at which we were all present to hear their elucubrations. An Academician was a great man in embryo. And if every Vendome scholar would speak the truth, he would confess that, in later life, an Academician of the great French Academy seemed to him far less remarkable than the stupendous boy who wore the cross and the imposing red ribbon which were the insignia of our "Academy."

It was very unusual to be one of that illustrious body before attaining to the second class, for the Academicians were expected to hold public meetings every Thursday during the holidays, and to read tales in verse or prose, epistles, essays, tragedies, dramas—compositions far above the intelligence of the lower classes. I long treasured the memory of a story called the "Green Ass," which was, I think, the masterpiece of this unknown Society. In the fourth, and an Academician! This boy of fourteen, a poet already, the protégé of Madame de Stael, a coming genius, said Father Haugoult, was to be one of us! a wizard, a youth capable of writing a composition or a translation while we were being called into lessons, and of learning his lessons by reading them through but once. Louis Lambert bewildered all our ideas. And Father Haugoult's curiosity and impatience to see this new boy added fuel to our excited fancy.

"If he has pigeons, he can have no pigeon house; there is not room for another. Well, it cannot be helped," said one boy, since famous as an agriculturist.

"Who will sit next to him?" said another.

"Oh, I wish I might be his chum!" cried an enthusiast.

In school language, the word here rendered chum—*faisant,* or in some schools, *copin*—expressed a fraternal sharing of the joys and evils of your childish existence, a community of interests that was fruitful of squabbling and making friends again, a treaty of alliance offensive and defensive. It is strange, but never in my time did I know brothers who were chums. If man lives by his feelings, he thinks perhaps that he will make his life the poorer if he merges an affection of his own choosing in a natural tie.

The impression made upon me by Father Haugoult's harangue that evening is one of the most vivid reminiscences of my childhood; I can compare it with nothing but my first reading of *Robinson Crusoe.* Indeed, I owe to my recollection of these prodigious impressions an observation that may perhaps be new as to the different sense attached to words by each hearer. The word in itself has no final meaning; we affect a word more than it affects us; its value is in relation to the images we have assimilated and grouped round it; but a study of this fact would require considerable elaboration, and lead us too far from our immediate subject.

Not being able to sleep, I had a long discussion with my next neighbor in the dormitory as to the remarkable being who on the morrow was to be one of us. This neighbor, who became an officer, and is now a writer with lofty philosophical views, Barchou de Penhoen, has not been false to his ation, nor to the hazard of fortune by which the only two scholars of Vendome, of whose fame Vendome ever hears, were brought together in the same classroom, on the same form, and under the same roof. Our comrade Dufaure had not, when this book was published, made his appearance in public life as a lawyer. The translator of Fichte, the expositor and friend of Ballanche, was already interested, as I myself was, in metaphysical questions; we often talked nonsense together about God, ourselves, and nature. He at that time affected pyrrhonism. Jealous of his place as leader, he doubted Lambert's precocious gifts; while I, having lately read *Les Enfants celebres*, overwhelmed him with evidence, quoting young Montcalm, Pico della Mirandola, Pascal— in short, a score of early developed brains, anomalies that are famous in the history of the human mind, and Lambert's predecessors.

I was at the time passionately addicted to reading. My father, who was ambitious to see me in the École Polytechnique, paid for me to have a special course of private lessons in mathematics. My mathematical master was the librarian of the college, and allowed me to help myself to books without much caring what I chose to take from the library, a quiet spot where I went to him during play hours to have my lesson. Either he was no great mathematician, or he was absorbed in some grand scheme, for he very willingly left me to read when I ought to have been learning, while he worked at I knew not what. So, by a tacit understanding between us, I made no complaints of being taught nothing, and he said nothing of the books I borrowed.

Carried away by this ill-timed mania, I neglected my studies to compose poems, which certainly can have shown no great promise, to judge by a line of too many feet which became famous among my companions—the beginning of an epic on the Incas:

"O Inca! O roi infortune et malheureux!"

In derision of such attempts, I was nicknamed the Poet, but mockery did not cure me. I was always rhyming, in spite of good advice from Monsieur Mareschal, the headmaster, who tried to cure me of an unfortunately inveterate passion by telling me the fable of a linnet that fell out of the nest because it tried to fly before its wings were grown. I persisted in my reading; I became the least emulous, the idlest, the most dreamy of all the division of "little boys," and consequently the most frequently punished.

This autobiographical digression may give some idea of the reflections I was led to make in anticipation of Lambert's arrival. I was then twelve years old. I felt sympathy from the first for the boy whose temperament had some points of likeness to my own. I was at last to have a companion in daydreams and meditations. Though I knew not yet what glory meant, I thought it glory to be the familiar friend of a child whose immortality was foreseen by Madame de Stael. To me Louis Lambert was as a giant.

The looked-for morrow came at last. A minute before breakfast we heard the steps of Monsieur Mareschal and of the new boy in the quiet courtyard. Every head was turned at once to the door of the classroom. Father Haugoult, who participated in our torments of curiosity, did not sound the whistle he used to reduce our mutterings to silence and bring us back to our tasks. We then saw this famous new boy, whom Monsieur Mareschal was leading by the hand. The superintendent descended from his desk, and the headmaster said to him solemnly, according to etiquette: "Monsieur, I have brought you Monsieur Louis Lambert; will you place him in the fourth class? He will begin work tomorrow."

Then, after speaking a few words in an undertone to the class-master, he said:

"Where can he sit?"

It would have been unfair to displace one of us for a newcomer; so as there was but one desk vacant, Louis Lambert came to fill it, next to me, for I had last joined the class. Though we still had some time to wait before lessons were over, we all stood up to look at Louis Lambert. Monsieur Mareschal heard our mutterings, saw how eager we were, and said, with the kindness that endeared him to us all:

"Well, well, but make no noise; do not disturb the other classes."

These words set us free to play some little time before breakfast, and we all gathered round Lambert while Monsieur Mareschal walked up and down the courtyard with Father Haugoult.

There were about eighty of us little demons, as bold as birds of prey. Though we ourselves had all gone through this cruel novitiate, we showed no mercy on a newcomer, never sparing him the mockery, the catechism, the impertinence, which were inexhaustible on such occasions, to the discomfiture of the neophyte, whose manners, strength, and temper were thus tested. Lambert, whether he was stoical or dumfounded, made no reply to any questions. One of us thereupon remarked that he was no doubt of the school of Pythagoras, and there was a shout of laughter. The new boy was thenceforth Pythagoras through all his life at the college. At the same time, Lambert's piercing eye, the scorn expressed in his face for our childishness, so far removed from the stamp of his own nature, the easy attitude he assumed, and his evident strength in proportion to his years, infused a certain respect into the veriest scamps among us. For my part, I kept near him, absorbed in studying him in silence.

Louis Lambert was slightly built, nearly five feet in height; his face was tanned, and his hands were burnt brown by the sun, giving him an appearance of manly vigor, which, in fact, he did not possess. Indeed, two months after he came to the college, when studying in the classroom had faded his vivid, so to speak, vegetable coloring, he became as pale and white as a woman.

His head was unusually large. His hair, of a fine, bright black in masses of curls, gave wonderful beauty to his brow, of which the proportions were extraordinary even to us heedless boys, knowing nothing, as may be supposed, of the auguries of phrenology, a science still in its cradle. The distinction of this prophetic brow lay principally in the exquisitely chiseled shape of the arches under which his black eyes sparkled, and which had the transparency of alabaster, the line having the unusual beauty of being perfectly level to where it met the top of the nose. But when you saw his eyes it was difficult to think of the rest of his face, which was indeed plain enough, for their look was full of a wonderful variety of expression; they seemed to have a soul in their depths. At one moment astonishingly clear and piercing, at another full of heavenly sweetness, those eyes became dull, almost colorless, as it seemed, when he was lost in meditation. They then looked like a window from which the sun had suddenly vanished after lighting it up. His strength and his voice were no less variable; equally rigid, equally unexpected. His tone could be as sweet as that of a woman compelled to own her love; at other times it was labored, rough, rugged, if I may use such words in a

new sense. As to his strength, he was habitually incapable
of enduring the fatigue of any game, and seemed weakly,
almost infirm. But during the early days of his school life,
one of our little bullies having made game of this sickliness,
which rendered him unfit for the violent exercise in vogue
among his fellows, Lambert took hold with both hands of
one of the class tables, consisting of twelve large desks, face
to face and sloping from the middle; he leaned back against
the class-master's desk, steadying the table with his feet on
the crossbar below, and said:

"Now, ten of you try to move it!"

I was present, and can vouch for this strange display of
strength; it was impossible to move the table.

Lambert had the gift of summoning to his aid at certain
times the most extraordinary powers, and of concentrat-
ing all his forces on a given point. But children, like men,
are wont to judge of everything by first impressions, and
after the first few days we ceased to study Louis; he entirely
belied Madame de Stael's prognostications, and displayed
none of the prodigies we looked for in him.

After three months at school, Louis was looked upon
as a quite ordinary scholar. I alone was allowed really to
know that sublime—why should I not say divine?—soul, for
what is nearer to God than genius in the heart of a child?
The similarity of our tastes and ideas made us friends and
chums; our intimacy was so brotherly that our schoolfellows
joined our two names; one was never spoken without the
other, and to call either they always shouted "Poet-and-Pythagoras!" Some other names had been known coupled in
a like manner. Thus for two years I was the school friend of
poor Louis Lambert; and during that time my life was so
identified with his, that I am enabled now to write his intellectual biography.

It was long before I fully knew the poetry and the wealth
of ideas that lay hidden in my companion's heart and brain.
It was not till I was thirty years of age, till my experience was
matured and condensed, till the flash of an intense illumination had thrown a fresh light upon it, that I was capable
of understanding all the bearings of the phenomena which
I witnessed at that early time. I benefited by them without

understanding their greatness or their processes; indeed, I have forgotten some, or remember only the most conspicuous facts; still, my memory is now able to coordinate them, and I have mastered the secrets of that fertile brain by looking back to the delightful days of our boyish affection. So it was time alone that initiated me into the meaning of the events and facts that were crowded into that obscure life, as into that of many another man who is lost to science. Indeed, this narrative, so far as the expression and appreciation of many things is concerned, will be found full of what may be termed moral anachronisms, which perhaps will not detract from its peculiar interest.

In the course of the first few months after coming to Vendome, Louis became the victim of a malady which, though the symptoms were invisible to the eye of our superiors, considerably interfered with the exercise of his remarkable gifts. Accustomed to live in the open air, and to the freedom of a purely haphazard education, happy in the tender care of an old man who was devoted to him, used to meditating in the sunshine, he found it very hard to submit to college rules, to walk in the ranks, to live within the four walls of a room where eighty boys were sitting in silence on wooden forms each in front of his desk. His senses were developed to such perfection as gave them the most sensitive keenness, and every part of him suffered from this life in common.

The effluvia that vitiated the air, mingled with the odors of a classroom that was never clean, nor free from the fragments of our breakfasts or snacks, affected his sense of smell, the sense which, being more immediately connected than the others with the nerve centers of the brain, must, when shocked, cause invisible disturbance to the organs of thought.

Besides these elements of impurity in the atmosphere, there were lockers in the classrooms in which the boys kept their miscellaneous plunder—pigeons killed for fete days, or tidbits filched from the dinner table. In each classroom, too, there was a large stone slab, on which two pails full of water were kept standing, a sort of sink, where we every morning washed our faces and hands, one after another, in the master's presence. We then passed on to a table, where women combed and powdered our hair. Thus the place, being cleaned but once a day before we were up, was always more or less dirty. In spite of numerous windows and lofty doors, the air was constantly fouled by the smells from the washing place, the hairdressing, the lockers, and the thousand messes made by the boys, to say nothing of their eighty closely packed bodies. And this sort of *humus,* mingling with the mud we brought in from the playing yard, produced a suffocatingly pestilent muck heap.

The loss of the fresh and fragrant country air in which he had hitherto lived, the change of habits and strict discipline, combined to depress Lambert. With his elbow on his desk and his head supported on his left hand, he spent the hours of study gazing at the trees in the court or the clouds in the sky; he seemed to be thinking of his lessons; but the master, seeing his pen motionless, or the sheet before him still a blank, would call out:

"Lambert, you are doing nothing!"

This *"you are doing nothing!"* was a pin thrust that wounded Louis to the quick. And then he never earned the rest of the playtime; he always had impositions to write. The imposition, a punishment which varies according to the practice of different schools, consisted at Vendome of a certain number of lines to be written out in play hours. Lambert and I were so overpowered with impositions, that we had not six free days during the two years of our school friendship. But for the books we took out of the library, which maintained some vitality in our brains, this system of discipline would have reduced us to idiocy. Want of exercise is fatal to children. The habit of preserving a dignified appearance, begun in tender infancy, has, it is said, a visible effect on the constitution of royal personages when the faults of such an education are not counteracted by the life of the battlefield or the laborious sport of hunting. And if the laws of etiquette and Court manners can act on the spinal marrow to such an extent as to affect the pelvis of kings, to soften their cerebral tissue, and so degenerate the race, what deep-seated mischief, physical and moral, must result in schoolboys from the constant lack of air, exercise, and cheerfulness!

Indeed, the rules of punishment carried out in schools deserve the attention of the Office of Public Instruction when any thinkers are to be found there who do not think exclusively of themselves.

We incurred the infliction of an imposition in a thousand ways. Our memory was so good that we never learned a lesson. It was enough for either of us to hear our class-fellows repeat the task in French, Latin, or grammar, and we could say it when our turn came; but if the master, unfortunately, took it into his head to reverse the usual order and call upon us first, we very often did not even know what the lesson was; then the imposition fell in spite of our most ingenious excuses. Then we always put off writing our exercises till the last moment; if there were a book to be finished, or if we were lost in thought, the task was forgotten—again an imposition. How often have we scribbled an exercise during the time when the head boy, whose business it was to collect them when we came into school, was gathering them from the others!

In addition to the moral misery which Lambert went through in trying to acclimatize himself to college life, there was a scarcely less cruel apprenticeship through which every boy had to pass: to those bodily sufferings which seemed infinitely varied. The tenderness of a child's skin needs extreme care, especially in winter, when a schoolboy is constantly exchanging the frozen air of the muddy playing yard for the stuffy atmosphere of the classroom. The "little boys" and the smallest of all, for lack of a mother's care, were martyrs to chilblains and chaps so severe that they had to be regularly dressed during the breakfast hour; but this could only be very indifferently done to so many damaged hands, toes, and heels. A good many of the boys indeed were obliged to prefer the evil to the remedy; the choice constantly lay between their lessons waiting to be finished or the joys of a slide, and waiting for a bandage carelessly put on, and still more carelessly cast off again. Also it was the fashion in the school to gibe at the poor, feeble creatures who went to be doctored; the bullies vied with each other in snatching off the rags which the infirmary nurse had tied on. Hence, in winter, many of us, with half-dead feet and fingers, sick with pain, were incapable of work, and punished for not working. The Fathers, too often deluded by shammed ailments, would not believe in real suffering.

The price paid for our schooling and board also covered the cost of clothing. The committee contracted for the shoes and clothes supplied to the boys; hence the weekly inspection of which I have spoken. This plan, though admirable for the manager, is always disastrous to the managed. Woe to the boy who indulged in the bad habit of treading his shoes down at heel, of cracking the shoe leather, or wearing out the soles too fast, whether from a defect in his gait, or by fidgeting during lessons in obedience to the instinctive need of movement common to all children. That boy did not get through the winter without great suffering. In the first place, his chilblains would ache and shot as badly as a fit of the gout; then the rivets and packthread intended to repair the shoes would give way, or the broken heels would prevent the wretched shoes from keeping on his feet; he was obliged to drag them wearily along the frozen roads, or sometimes to dispute their possession with the clay soil of the district; the water and snow got in through some unnoticed crack or ill-sewn patch, and the foot would swell.

Out of sixty boys, not ten perhaps could walk without some special form of torture; and yet they all kept up with the body of the troop, dragged on by the general movement, as men are driven through life by life itself. Many a time some proud-tempered boy would shed tears of rage while summoning his remaining energy to run ahead and get home again in spite of pain, so sensitively afraid of laughter or of pity—two forms of scorn—is the still tender soul at that age.

At school, as in social life, the strong despise the feeble without knowing in what true strength consists.

Nor was this all. No gloves. If by good luck a boy's parents, the infirmary nurse, or the headmaster gave gloves to a particularly delicate lad, the wags or the big boys of the class would put them on the stove, amused to see them dry and shrivel; or if the gloves escaped the marauders, after getting wet they shrunk as they dried for want of care. No, gloves were impossible. Gloves were a privilege, and boys insist on equality.

Louis Lambert fell a victim to all these varieties of torment. Like many contemplative men, who, when lost in thought, acquire a habit of mechanical motion, he had a mania for fidgeting with his shoes, and destroyed them very quickly. His girlish complexion, the skin of his ears and lips, cracked with the least cold. His soft, white hands grew red and swollen. He had perpetual colds. Thus he was a constant sufferer till he became inured to school life. Taught at last by cruel experience, he was obliged to "look after his things," to use the school phrase. He was forced to take care of his locker, his desk, his clothes, his shoes; to protect his ink, his books, his copy paper, and his pens from pilferers; in short, to give his mind to the thousand details of our trivial life, to which more selfish and commonplace minds devoted such strict attention—thus infallibly securing prizes for "proficiency" and "good conduct"—while they were overlooked by a boy of the highest promise, who, under the hand of an almost divine imagination, gave himself up with rapture to the flow of his ideas.

This was not all. There is a perpetual struggle going on between the masters and the boys, a struggle without truce, to be compared with nothing else in the social world, unless it be the resistance of the opposition to the ministry in a representative government. But journalists and opposition speakers are probably less prompt to take advantage of a weak point, less extreme in resenting an injury, and less merciless in their mockery than boys are in regard to those who rule over them. It is a task to put angels out of patience. An unhappy class-master must then not be too severely blamed, ill-paid as he is, and consequently not too competent, if he is occasionally unjust or out of temper. Perpetually watched by a hundred mocking eyes, and surrounded with snares, he sometimes revenges himself for his own blunders on the boys who are only too ready to detect them.

Unless for serious misdemeanors, for which there were other forms of punishment, the strap was regarded at

Vendome as the *ultima ratio Patrum*. Exercises forgotten, lessons ill learned, common ill behavior were sufficiently punished by an imposition, but offended dignity spoke in the master through the strap. Of all the physical torments to which we were exposed, certainly the most acute was that inflicted by this leathern instrument, about two fingers wide, applied to our poor little hands with all the strength and all the fury of the administrator. To endure this classical form of correction, the victim knelt in the middle of the room. He had to leave his form and go to kneel down near the master's desk under the curious and generally merciless eyes of his fellows. To sensitive natures these preliminaries were an introductory torture, like the journey from the Palais de Justice to the Place de Greve which the condemned used to make to the scaffold.

Some boys cried out and shed bitter tears before or after the application of the strap; others accepted the infliction with stoic calm; it was a question of nature; but few could control an expression of anguish in anticipation.

Louis Lambert was constantly enduring the strap, and owed it to a peculiarity of his physiognomy of which he was for a long time quite unconscious. Whenever he was suddenly roused from a fit of abstraction by the master's cry, "You are doing nothing!" it often happened that, without knowing it, he flashed at his teacher a look full of fierce contempt, and charged with thought, as a Leyden jar is charged with electricity. This look, no doubt, discomfited the master, who, indignant at this unspoken retort, wished to cure his scholar of that thunderous flash.

The first time the Father took offence at this ray of scorn, which struck him like a lightning flash, he made this speech, as I well remember:

"If you look at me again in that way, Lambert, you will get the strap."

At these words every nose was in the air, every eye looked alternately at the master and at Louis. The observation was so utterly foolish, that the boy again looked at the Father, overwhelming him with another flash. From this arose a standing feud between Lambert and his master, resulting in a certain amount of "strap." Thus did he first discover the power of his eye.

The hapless poet, so full of nerves, as sensitive as a woman, under the sway of chronic melancholy, and as sick with genius as a girl with love that she pines for, knowing nothing of it;—this boy, at once so powerful and so weak, transplanted by "Corinne" from the country he loved, to be squeezed in the mold of a collegiate routine to which every spirit and every body must yield, whatever their range or temperament, accepting its rule and its uniform as gold is crushed into round coin under the press; Louis Lambert suffered in every spot where pain can touch the soul or the flesh. Stuck on a form, restricted to the acreage of his desk, a victim of the strap and to a sickly frame, tortured in every sense, environed by distress—everything compelled him to give his body up to the myriad tyrannies of school life; and, like the martyrs who smiled in the midst of suffering, he took refuge in heaven, which lay open to his mind. Perhaps this life of purely inward emotions helped him to see something of the mysteries he so entirely believed in!

Our independence, our illicit amusements, our apparent waste of time, our persistent indifference, our frequent punishments and aversion for our exercises and impositions, earned us a reputation, which no one cared to controvert, for being an idle and incorrigible pair. Our masters treated us with contempt, and we fell into utter disgrace with our companions, from whom we concealed our secret studies for fear of being laughed at. This hard judgment, which was injustice in the masters, was but natural in our schoolfellows. We could neither play ball, nor run races, nor walk on stilts. On exceptional holidays, when amnesty was proclaimed and we got a few hours of freedom, we shared in none of the popular diversions of the school. Aliens from the pleasures enjoyed by the others, we were outcasts, sitting forlorn under a tree in the playground. The Poet-and-Pythagoras formed an exception and led a life apart from the life of the rest.

The penetrating instinct and unerring conceit of schoolboys made them feel that we were of a nature either far above or far beneath their own; hence some simply hated our aristocratic reserve, others merely scorned our

ineptitude. These feelings were equally shared by us without our knowing it; perhaps I have but now divined them.
We lived exactly like two rats, huddled into the corner of
the room where our desks were, sitting there alike during
lesson time and play hours. This strange state of affairs
inevitably and in fact placed us on a footing of war with all
the other boys in our division. Forgotten for the most part,
we sat there very contentedly; half happy, like two plants,
two images who would have been missed from the furniture
of the room. But the most aggressive of our schoolfellows
would sometimes torment us, just to show their malignant
power, and we responded with stolid contempt, which
brought many a thrashing down on the Poet-and-Pythagoras.

Lambert's homesickness lasted for many months. I know
no words to describe the dejection to which he was a prey.
Louis has taken the glory off many a masterpiece for me.
We had both played the part of the "Leper of Aosta," and
had both experienced the feelings described in Monsieur
de Maistre's story, before we read them as expressed by
his eloquent pen. A book may, indeed, revive the memories of our childhood, but it can never compete with them
successfully. Lambert's woes had taught me many a chant
of sorrow far more appealing than the finest passages in
"Werther." And, indeed, there is no possible comparison between the pangs of a passion condemned, whether
rightly or wrongly, by every law, and the grief of a poor child
pining for the glorious sunshine, the dews of the valley, and
liberty. Werther is the slave of desire; Louis Lambert was an
enslaved soul. Given equal talent, the more pathetic sorrow,
founded on desires which, being purer, are the more genuine, must transcend the wail even of genius.

After sitting for a long time with his eyes fixed on a lime
tree in the playground, Louis would say just a word; but
that word would reveal an infinite speculation.

"Happily for me," he exclaimed one day, "there are hours
of comfort when I feel as though the walls of the room had
fallen and I were away—away in the fields! What a pleasure
it is to let oneself go on the stream of one's thoughts as a
bird is borne up on its wings!"

"Why is green a color so largely diffused throughout creation?" he would ask me. "Why are there so few straight lines in nature? Why is it that man, in his structures, rarely introduces curves? Why is it that he alone, of all creatures, has a sense of straightness?"

These queries revealed long excursions in space. He had, I am sure, seen vast landscapes, fragrant with the scent of woods. He was always silent and resigned, a living elegy, always suffering but unable to complain of suffering. An eagle that needed the world to feed him, shut in between four narrow, dirty walls; and thus this life became an ideal life in the strictest meaning of the words. Filled as he was with contempt of the almost useless studies to which we were harnessed, Louis went on his skyward way absolutely unconscious of the things about us.

I, obeying the imitative instinct that is so strong in childhood, tired to regulate my life in conformity with his. And Louis the more easily infected me with the sort of torpor in which deep contemplation leaves the body, because I was younger and more impressionable than he. Like two lovers, we got into the habit of thinking together in a common reverie. His intuitions had already acquired that acuteness which must surely characterize the intellectual perceptiveness of great poets and often bring them to the verge of madness.

"Do you ever feel," said he to me one day, "as though imagined suffering affected you in spite of yourself? If, for instance, I think with concentration of the effect that the blade of my penknife would have in piercing my flesh, I feel an acute pain as if I had really cut myself; only the blood is wanting. But the pain comes suddenly, and startles me like a sharp noise breaking profound silence. Can an idea cause physical pain?—What do you say to that, eh?"

When he gave utterance to such subtle reflections, we both fell into artless meditation; we set to work to detect in ourselves the inscrutable phenomena of the origin of thoughts, which Lambert hoped to discover in their earliest germ, so as to describe some day the unknown process. Then, after much discussion, often mixed up with childish notions, a look would flash from Lambert's eager eyes; he would grasp my hand, and a word from the depths of his soul would show the current of his mind.

"Thinking is seeing," said he one day, carried away by some objection raised as to the first principles of our organization. "Every human science is based on deduction, which is a slow process of seeing by which we work up from the effect to the cause; or, in a wider sense, all poetry, like every work of art, proceeds from a swift vision of things."

He was a spiritualist (as opposed to materialism); but I would venture to contradict him, using his own arguments to consider the intellect as a purely physical phenomenon. We both were right. Perhaps the words materialism and spiritualism express the two faces of the same fact. His considerations on the substance of the mind led to his accepting, with a certain pride, the life of privation to which we were condemned in consequence of our idleness and our indifference to learning. He had a certain consciousness of his own powers which bore him up through his spiritual cogitations. How delightful it was to me to feel his soul acting on my own! Many a time have we remained sitting on our form, both buried in one book, having quite forgotten each other's existence, and yet not apart; each conscious of the other's presence, and bathing in an ocean of thought, like two fish swimming in the same waters.

Our life, apparently, was merely vegetating; but we lived through our heart and brain.

Lambert's influence over my imagination left traces that still abide. I used to listen hungrily to his tales, full of the marvels which make men, as well as children, rapturously devour stories in which truth assumes the most grotesque forms. His passion for mystery, and the credulity natural to the young, often led us to discuss Heaven and Hell. Then Louis, by expounding Swedenborg, would try to make me share in his beliefs concerning angels. In his least logical arguments there were still amazing observations as to the powers of man, which gave his words that color of truth without which nothing can be done in any art. The romantic end he foresaw as the destiny of man was calculated to flatter the yearning which tempts blameless imaginations to give themselves up to beliefs. Is it not during the youth of a nation that its dogmas and idols are conceived? And are not the supernatural beings before whom the people tremble the personification of their feelings and their magnified desires?

All that I can now remember of the poetical conversations we held together concerning the Swedish prophet, whose works I have since had the curiosity to read, may be told in a few paragraphs.

In each of us there are two distinct beings. According to Swedenborg, the angel is an individual in whom the inner being conquers the external being. If a man desires to earn his call to be an angel, as soon as his mind reveals to him his twofold existence, he must strive to foster the delicate angelic essence that exists within him. If, for lack of a lucid appreciation of his destiny, he allows bodily action to predominate, instead of confirming his intellectual being, all his powers will be absorbed in the use of his external senses, and the angel will slowly perish by the materialization of both natures. In the contrary case, if he nourishes his inner being with the aliment needful to it, the soul triumphs over matter and strives to get free.

When they separate by the act of what we call death, the angel, strong enough then to cast off its wrappings, survives and begins its real life. The infinite variety which differentiates individual men can only be explained by this twofold existence, which, again, is proved and made intelligible by that variety.

In point of fact, the wide distance between a man whose torpid intelligence condemns him to evident stupidity, and one who, by the exercise of his inner life, has acquired the gift of some power, allows us to suppose that there is as great a difference between men of genius and other beings as there is between the blind and those who see. This hypothesis, since it extends creation beyond all limits, gives us, as it were, the clue to heaven. The beings who, here on earth, are apparently mingled without distinction, are there distributed, according to their inner perfection, in distinct spheres whose speech and manners have nothing in common. In the invisible world, as in the real world, if some native of the lower spheres comes, all unworthy, into

a higher sphere, not only can he never understand the customs and language there, but his mere presence paralyzes
the voice and hearts of those who dwell therein.

Dante, in his *Divine Comedy,* had perhaps some slight
intuition of those spheres which begin in the world of torment, and rise, circle on circle, to the highest heaven. Thus
Swedenborg's doctrine is the product of a lucid spirit noting
down the innumerable signs by which the angels manifest
their presence among men.

This doctrine, which I have endeavored to sum up in a
more or less consistent form, was set before me by Lambert with all the fascination of mysticism, swathed in the
wrappings of the phraseology affected by mystical writers:
an obscure language full of abstractions, and taking such
effect on the brain, that there are books by Jacob Boehm,
Swedenborg, and Madame Guyon, so strangely powerful
that they give rise to phantasies as various as the dreams
of the opium eater. Lambert told me of mystical facts so
extraordinary, he so acted on my imagination, that he made
my brain reel. Still, I loved to plunge into that realm of
mystery, invisible to the senses, in which every one likes to
dwell, whether he pictures it to himself under the indefinite
ideal of the Future, or clothes it in the more solid guise
of romance. These violent revulsions of the mind on itself
gave me, without my knowing it, a comprehension of its
power, and accustomed me to the workings of the mind.

Lambert himself explained everything by his theory of
the angels. To him pure love—love as we dream of it in
youth—was the coalescence of two angelic natures. Nothing could exceed the fervency with which he longed to
meet a woman angel. And who better than he could inspire
or feel love? If anything could give an impression of an
exquisite nature, was it not the amiability and kindliness
that marked his feelings, his words, his actions, his slightest
gestures, the conjugal regard that united us as boys, and
that we expressed when we called ourselves *chums?*

There was no distinction for us between my ideas and
his. We imitated each other's handwriting, so that one
might write the tasks of both. Thus, if one of us had a book
to finish and to return to the mathematical master, he

could read on without interruption while the other scribbled off his exercise and imposition. We did our tasks as though paying a task on our peace of mind. If my memory does not play me false, they were sometimes of remarkable merit when Lambert did them. But on the foregone conclusion that we were both of us idiots, the master always went through them under a rooted prejudice, and even kept them to read to be laughed at by our schoolfellows.

I remember one afternoon, at the end of the lesson, which lasted from two till four, the master took possession of a page of translation by Lambert. The passage began with *Caius Gracchus, vir nobilis;* Lambert had construed this by "Caius Gracchus had a noble heart."

"Where do you find 'heart' in *nobilis?*" said the Father sharply.

And there was a roar of laughter, while Lambert looked at the master in some bewilderment.

"What would Madame la Baronne de Stael say if she could know that you make such nonsense of a word that means noble family, of patrician rank?"

"She would say that you were an ass!" said I in a muttered tone.

"Master Poet, you will stay in for a week," replied the master, who unfortunately overheard me.

Lambert simply repeated, looking at me with inexpressible affection, *"Vir nobilis!"*

Madame de Stael was, in fact, partly the cause of Lambert's troubles. On every pretext masters and pupils threw the name in his teeth, either in irony or in reproof.

Louis lost no time in getting himself "kept in" to share my imprisonment. Freer thus than in any other circumstances, we could talk the whole day long in the silence of the dormitories, where each boy had a cubicle six feet square, the partitions consisting at the top of open bars. The doors, fitted with gratings, were locked at night and opened in the morning under the eye of the Father whose duty it was to superintend our rising and going to bed. The creak of these gates, which the college servants unlocked with remarkable expedition, was a sound peculiar to that college. These little cells were our prison, and boys were

sometimes shut up there for a month at a time. The boys
in these coops were under the stern eye of the prefect, a
sort of censor who stole up at certain hours, or at unexpected moments, with a silent step, to hear if we were
talking instead of writing our impositions. But a few walnut
shells dropped on the stairs, or the sharpness of our hearing, almost always enabled us to beware of his coming, so
we could give ourselves up without anxiety to our favor-
ite studies. However, as books were prohibited, our prison
hours were chiefly filled up with metaphysical discussions,
or with relating singular facts connected with the phenomena of mind.

One of the most extraordinary of these incidents beyond
question is this, which I will here record, not only because
it concerns Lambert, but because it perhaps was the turning point of his scientific career. By the law of custom in
all schools, Thursday and Sunday were holidays; but the
services, which we were made to attend very regularly, so
completely filled up Sunday, that we considered Thursday
our only real day of freedom. After once attending Mass, we
had a long day before us to spend in walks in the country
round the town of Vendome. The manor of Rochambeau
was the most interesting object of our excursions, perhaps
by reason of its distance; the smaller boys were very seldom
taken on so fatiguing an expedition. However, once or
twice a year the class-masters would hold out Rochambeau
as a reward for diligence.

In 1812, towards the end of the spring, we were to go
there for the first time. Our anxiety to see this famous chateau of Rochambeau, where the owner sometimes treated
the boys to milk, made us all very good, and nothing hindered the outing. Neither Lambert nor I had ever seen the
pretty valley of the Loire where the house stood. So his
imagination and mine were much excited by the prospect
of this excursion, which filled the school with traditional
glee. We talked of it all the evening, planning to spend in
fruit or milk such money as we had saved, against all the
habits of school life.

After dinner next day, we set out at half-past twelve,
each provided with a square hunch of bread, given to us

for our afternoon snack. And off we went, as gay as swallows, marching in a body on the famous chateau with an eagerness which would at first allow of no fatigue. When we reached the hill, whence we looked down on the house standing halfway down the slope, on the devious valley through which the river winds and sparkles between meadows in graceful curves—a beautiful landscape, one of those scenes to which the keen emotions of early youth or of love lend such a charm, that it is wise never to see them again in later years—Louis Lambert said to me, "Why, I saw this last night in a dream."

He recognized the clump of trees under which we were standing, the grouping of the woods, the color of the water, the turrets of the chateau, the details, the distance, in fact every part of the prospect which we looked on for the first time. We were mere children; I, at any rate, who was but thirteen; Louis, at fifteen, might have the precocity of genius, but at that time we were incapable of falsehood in the most trivial matters of our life as friends. Indeed, if Lambert's powerful mind had any presentiment of the importance of such facts, he was far from appreciating their whole bearing; and he was quite astonished by this incident. I asked him if he had not perhaps been brought to Rochambeau in his infancy, and my question struck him; but after thinking it over, he answered in the negative. This incident, analogous to what may be known of the phenomena of sleep in several persons, will illustrate the beginnings of Lambert's line of talent; he took it, in fact, as the basis of a whole system, using a fragment—as Cuvier did in another branch of inquiry—as a clue to the reconstruction of a complete system.

At this moment we were sitting together on an old oak stump, and after a few minutes' reflection, Louis said to me:

"If the landscape did not come to me—which it is absurd to imagine—I must have come here. If I was here while I was asleep in my cubicle, does not that constitute a complete severance of my body and my inner being? Does it not prove some inscrutable locomotive faculty in the spirit with effects resembling those of locomotion in the body? Well, then, if my spirit and my body can be severed during sleep, why should I not insist on their separating in the same way while I am awake? I see no halfway mean between the two propositions.

"But if we go further into details: either the facts are due to the action of a faculty which brings out a second being to whom my body is merely a husk, since I was in my cell, and yet I saw the landscape—and this upsets many systems; or the facts took place either in some nerve centre, of which the name is yet to be discovered, where our feelings dwell and move; or else in the cerebral centre, where ideas are formed. This last hypothesis gives rise to some strange questions. I walked, I saw, I heard. Motion is inconceivable but in space, sound acts only at certain angles or on surfaces, color is caused only by light. If, in the dark, with my eyes shut, I saw, in myself, colored objects; if I heard sounds in the most perfect silence and without the conditions requisite for the production of sound; if without stirring I traversed wide tracts of space, there must be inner faculties independent of the external laws of physics. Material nature must be penetrable by the spirit.

"How is it that men have hitherto given so little thought to the phenomena of sleep, which seem to prove that man has a double life? May there not be a new science lying beneath them?" he added, striking his brow with his hand. "If not the elements of a science, at any rate the revelation of stupendous powers in man; at least they prove a frequent severance of our two natures, the fact I have been thinking out for a very long time. At last, then, I have hit on evidence to show the superiority that distinguishes our latent senses from our corporeal senses! *Homo duplex!*

"And yet," he went on, after a pause, with a doubtful shrug, "perhaps we have not two natures; perhaps we are merely gifted with personal and perfectible qualities, of which the development within us produces certain unobserved phenomena of activity, penetration, and vision. In our love of the marvelous, a passion begotten of our pride, we have translated these effects into poetical inventions, because we did not understand them. It is so convenient to deify the incomprehensible!

"I should, I own, lament over the loss of my illusions. I so much wished to believe in our twofold nature and in Swedenborg's angels. Must this new science destroy them? Yes, for the study of our unknown properties involves us in a science that appears to be materialistic, for the Spirit uses, divides, and animates the Substance, but it does not destroy it."

He remained pensive, almost sad. Perhaps he saw the dreams of his youth as swaddling clothes that he must soon shake off.

"Sight and hearing are, no doubt, the sheaths for a very marvelous instrument," said he, laughing at his own figure of speech.

Always when he was talking to me of Heaven and Hell, he was wont to treat of Nature as being master; but now, as he pronounced these last words, big with prescience, he seemed to soar more boldly than ever above the landscape, and his forehead seemed ready to burst with the afflatus of genius. His powers—mental powers we must call them till some new term is found—seemed to flash from the organs intended to express them. His eyes shot out thoughts; his uplifted hand, his silent but tremulous lips were eloquent; his burning glance was radiant; at last his head, as though too heavy, or exhausted by too eager a flight, fell on his breast. This boy—this giant—bent his head, took my hand and clasped it in his own, which was damp, so fevered was he for the search for truth; then, after a pause, he said:

"I shall be famous!—And you, too," he added after a pause. "We will both study the Chemistry of the Will."

Noble soul! I recognized his superiority, though he took great care never to make me feel it. He shared with me all the treasures of his mind, and regarded me as instrumental in his discoveries, leaving me the credit of my insignificant contributions. He was always as gracious as a woman in love; he had all the bashful feeling, the delicacy of soul which make life happy and pleasant to endure.

On the following day he began writing what he called a *Treatise on the Will;* his subsequent reflections led to many changes in its plan and method; but the incident of that day was certainly the germ of the work, just as the electric shock always felt by Mesmer at the approach of a particular manservant was the starting point of his discoveries in magnetism, a science till then interred under the mysteries of Isis, of Delphi, of the cave of Trophonius, and rediscovered by that prodigious genius, close on Lavater, and the precursor of Gall.

Lambert's ideas, suddenly illuminated by this flash of light, assumed vaster proportions; he disentangled certain truths from his many acquisitions and brought them into order; then, like a founder, he cast the model of his work. At the end of six months' indefatigable labor, Lambert's writings excited the curiosity of our companions, and became the object of cruel practical jokes which led to a fatal issue.

One day one of the masters, who was bent on seeing the manuscripts, enlisted the aid of our tyrants, and came to seize, by force, a box that contained the precious papers. Lambert and I defended it with incredible courage. The trunk was locked, our aggressors could not open it, but they tried to smash it in the struggle, a stroke of malignity at which we shrieked with rage. Some of the boys, with a sense of justice, or struck perhaps by our heroic defense, advised the attacking party to leave us in peace, crushing us with insulting contempt. But suddenly, brought to the spot by the noise of a battle, Father Haugoult roughly intervened, inquiring as to the cause of the fight. Our enemies had interrupted us in writing our impositions, and the class-master came to protect his slaves. The foe, in self defense, betrayed the existence of the manuscript. The dreadful Haugoult insisted on our giving up the box; if we should resist, he would have it broken open. Lambert gave him the key; the master took out the papers, glanced through them, and said, as he confiscated them:

"And it is for such rubbish as this that you neglect your lessons!"

Large tears fell from Lambert's eyes, wrung from him as much by a sense of his offended moral superiority as by the gratuitous insult and betrayal that he had suffered. We gave the accusers a glance of stern reproach: had they not delivered us over to the common enemy? If the common law of school entitled them to thrash us, did it not require them to keep silence as to our misdeeds?

In a moment they were no doubt ashamed of their baseness.

Father Haugoult probably sold the *Treatise on the Will* to a local grocer, unconscious of the scientific treasure, of which the germs thus fell into unworthy hands.

Six months later I left the school, and I do not know whether Lambert ever recommenced his labors. Our parting threw him into a mood of the darkest melancholy.

It was in memory of the disaster that befell Louis' book that, in the tale which comes first in these *Etudes*, I adopted the title invented by Lambert for a work of fiction, and gave the name of a woman who was dear to him to a girl characterized by her self-devotion; but this is not all I have borrowed from him: his character and occupations were of great value to me in writing that book, and the subject arose from some reminiscences of our youthful meditations. This present volume is intended as a modest monument, a broken column, to commemorate the life of the man who bequeathed to me all he had to leave—his thoughts.

In that boyish effort Lambert had enshrined the ideas of a man. Ten years later, when I met some learned men who were devoting serious attention to the phenomena that had struck us and that Lambert had so marvelously analyzed, I understood the value of his work, then already forgotten as childish. I at once spent several months in recalling the principal theories discovered by my poor schoolmate. Having collected my reminiscences, I can boldly state that, by 1812, he had proved, divined, and set forth in his Treatise several important facts of which, as he had declared, evidence was certain to come sooner or later. His philosophical speculations ought undoubtedly to gain him recognition as one of the great thinkers who have appeared at wide intervals among men, to reveal to them the bare skeleton of some science to come, of which the roots spread slowly, but which, in due time, bring forth fair fruit in the intellectual sphere. Thus a humble artisan, Bernard Palissy, searching the soil to find minerals for glazing pottery, proclaimed, in the sixteenth century, with the infallible intuition of genius, geological facts which it is now the glory of Cuvier and

Buffon to have demonstrated.

I can, I believe, give some idea of Lambert's Treatise by stating the chief propositions on which it was based; but, in spite of myself, I shall strip them of the ideas in which they were clothed, and which were indeed their indispensable accompaniment. I started on a different path, and only made use of those of his researches which answered the purpose of my scheme. I know not, therefore, whether as his disciple I can faithfully expound his views, having assimilated them in the first instance so as to color them with my own.

New ideas require new words, or a new and expanded use of old words, extended and defined in their meaning. Thus Lambert, to set forth the basis of his system, had adopted certain common words that answered to his notions. The word Will he used to connote the medium in which the mind moves, or to use a less abstract expression, the mass of power by which man can reproduce, outside himself, the actions constituting his external life. Volition—a word due to Locke—expressed the act by which a man exerts his will. The word Mind, or Thought, which he regarded as the quintessential product of the Will, also represented the medium in which the ideas originate to which thought gives substance. The Idea, a name common to every creation of the brain, constituted the act by which man uses his mind. Thus the Will and the Mind were the two generating forces; the Volition and the Idea were the two products. Volition, he thought, was the Idea evolved from the abstract state to a concrete state, from its generative fluid to a solid expression, so to speak, if such words may be taken to formulate notions so difficult of definition. According to him, the Mind and Ideas are the motion and the outcome of our inner organization, just as the Will and Volition are of our external activity.

He gave the Will precedence over the Mind.

"You must will before you can think," he said. "Many beings live in a condition of Willing without ever attaining to the condition of Thinking. In the North, life is long; in the South, it is shorter; but in the North we see torpor, in the South a constant excitability of the Will, up to the point where from an excess of cold or of heat the organs are almost nullified."

The use of the word "medium" was suggested to him by an observation he had made in his childhood, though, to be sure, he had no suspicion then of its importance, but its singularity naturally struck his delicately alert imagination. His mother, a fragile, nervous woman, all sensitiveness and affection, was one of those beings created to represent womanhood in all the perfection of her attributes, but relegated by a mistaken fate to too low a place in the social scale. Wholly loving, and consequently wholly suffering, she died young, having thrown all her energies into her motherly love. Lambert, a child of six, lying, but not always sleeping, in a cot by his mother's bed, saw the electric sparks from her hair when she combed it. The man of fifteen made scientific application of this fact which had amused the child, a fact beyond dispute, of which there is ample evidence in many instances, especially of women who by a sad fatality are doomed to let unappreciated feelings evaporate in the air, or some superabundant power run to waste.

In support of his definitions, Lambert propounded a variety of problems to be solved, challenges flung out to science, though he proposed to seek the solution for himself. He inquired, for instance, whether the element that constitutes electricity does not enter as a base into the specific fluid whence our Ideas and Volitions proceed? Whether the hair, which loses its color, turns white, falls out, or disappears, in proportion to the decay or crystallization of our thoughts, may not be in fact a capillary system, either absorbent or diffusive, and wholly electrical? Whether the fluid phenomena of the Will, a matter generated within us, and spontaneously reacting under the impress of conditions as yet unobserved, were at all more extraordinary than those of the invisible and intangible fluid produced by a voltaic pile, and applied to the nervous system of a dead man? Whether the formation of Ideas and their constant diffusion was less incomprehensible than evaporation of the atoms, imperceptible indeed, but so violent in their effects, that are given off from a grain of musk without any loss of weight. Whether, granting that the function of the skin is purely protective, absorbent, excretive, and tactile, the circulation of the blood and all its mechanism would not correspond with the transsubstantiation of our Will, as the circulation of the nerve fluid corresponds to that of the Mind? Finally, whether the more or less rapid affluence of these two real substances may not be the result of a certain perfection or imperfection of organs whose conditions require investigation in every manifestation?

Having set forth these principles, he proposed to class the phenomena of human life in two series of distinct results, demanding, with the ardent insistency of conviction, a special analysis for each. In fact, having observed in almost every type of created thing two separate motions, he assumed, nay, he asserted, their existence in our human nature, and designated this vital antithesis Action and Reaction.

"A desire," he said, "is a fact completely accomplished in our will before it is accomplished externally."

Hence the sum total of our Volitions and our Ideas constitutes Action, and the sum total of our external acts he called Reaction.

When I subsequently read the observations made by Bichat on the duality of our external senses, I was really bewildered by my recollections, recognizing the startling coincidences between the views of that celebrated physiologist and those of Louis Lambert. They both died young, and they had with equal steps arrived at the same strange truths. Nature has in every case been pleased to give a twofold purpose to the various apparatus that constitute her creatures; and the twofold action of the human organism, which is now ascertained beyond dispute, proves by a mass of evidence in daily life how true were Lambert's deductions as to Action and Reaction.

The inner Being, the Being of Action—the word he used to designate an unknown specialization—the mysterious nexus of fibrils to which we owe the inadequately investigated powers of thought and will—in short, the nameless entity which sees, acts, foresees the end, and accomplishes everything before expressing itself in any physical phenomenon—must, in conformity with its nature, be free from the physical conditions by which the external Being of Reaction, the visible man, is fettered in its manifestation. From this followed a multitude of logical explanation as to those results of our twofold nature which appear the strangest, and a rectification of various systems in which truth and falsehood are mingled.

Certain men, having had a glimpse of some phenomena of the natural working of the Being of Action, were, like Swedenborg, carried away above this world by their ardent soul, thirsting for poetry, and filled with the Divine Spirit. Thus, in their ignorance of the causes and their admiration of the facts, they pleased their fancy by regarding that inner man as divine, and constructing a mystical universe. Hence we have angels! A lovely illusion which Lambert would never abandon, cherishing it even when the sword of his logic was cutting off their dazzling wings.

"Heaven," he would say, "must, after all, be the survival of our perfected faculties, and hell the void into which our unperfected faculties are cast away."

But how, then, in the ages when the understanding had preserved the religious and spiritualist impressions, which prevailed from the time of Christ till that of Descartes, between faith and doubt, how could men help accounting for the mysteries of our nature otherwise than by divine interposition? Of whom but of God Himself could sages demand an account of an invisible creature so actively and so reactively sensitive, gifted with faculties so extensive, so improvable by use, and so powerful under certain occult influences, that they could sometimes see it annihilate, by some phenomenon of sight or movement, space in its two manifestations—Time and Distance—of which the former is the space of the intellect, the latter is physical space? Sometimes they found it reconstructing the past, either by the power of retrospective vision, or by the mystery of a palingenesis not unlike the power a man might have of detecting in the form, integument, and embryo in a seed, the flowers of the past, and the numberless variations of their color, scent, and shape; and sometimes, again, it could be seen vaguely foreseeing the future, either by its apprehension of final causes, or by some phenomenon of physical presentiment.

Other men, less poetically religious, cold, and argumentative—quacks perhaps, but enthusiasts in brain at least, if not in heart—recognizing some isolated examples of such phenomena, admitted their truth while refusing to consider them as radiating from a common centre. Each of these was, then, bent on constructing a science out of a simple fact. Hence arose demonology, judicial astrology, the black arts, in short, every form of divination founded on circumstances that were essentially transient, because they varied according to men's temperament, and to conditions that are still completely unknown.

But from these errors of the learned, and from the ecclesiastical trials under which fell so many martyrs to their own powers, startling evidence was derived of the prodigious faculties at the command of the Being of Action, which, according to Lambert, can abstract itself completely from the Being of Reaction, bursting its envelope, and piercing walls by its potent vision; a phenomenon known to the Hindus, as missionaries tell us, by the name of *Tokeiad;* or again, by another faculty, can grasp in the brain, in spite of its closest convolutions, the ideas which are formed or forming there, and the whole of past consciousness.

"If apparitions are not impossible," said Lambert, "they must be due to a faculty of discerning the ideas which represent man in his purest essence, whose life, imperishable perhaps, escapes our grosser senses, though they may become perceptible to the inner being when it has reached a high degree of ecstasy, or a great perfection of vision."

I know—though my remembrance is now vague—that Lambert, by following the results of Mind and Will step by step, after he had established their laws, accounted for a multitude of phenomena which, till then, had been regarded with reason as incomprehensible. Thus wizards, men possessed with second sight, and demoniacs of every degree—the victims of the Middle Ages—became the subject of explanations so natural, that their very simplicity often seemed to me the seal of their truth. The marvelous gifts which the Church of Rome, jealous of all mysteries, punished with the stake, were, in Louis' opinion, the result of certain affinities between the constituent elements of matter and those of mind, which proceed from the same source. The man holding a hazel rod when he found a spring of water was guided by some antipathy or sympathy of which he was unconscious; nothing but the eccentricity of these phenomena could have availed to give some of them historic certainty.

Sympathies have rarely been proved; they afford a kind of pleasure which those who are so happy as to possess them rarely speak of unless they are abnormally singular, and even then only in the privacy of intimate intercourse, where everything is buried. But the antipathies that arise from the inversion of affinities have, very happily, been recorded when developed by famous men. Thus, Bayle had hysterics when he heard water splashing, Scaliger turned pale at the sight of watercress, Erasmus was thrown into a fever by the smell of fish. These three antipathies were connected with water. The Duc d'Epernon fainted at the sight of a hare, Tycho-Brahe at that of a fox, Henri III at the presence of a cat, the Maréchal d'Albret at the sight of a wild hog; these antipathies were produced by animal emanations, and often took effect at a great distance. The Chevalier de Guise, Marie de Medici, and many other persons have felt faint at seeing a rose even in a painting. Lord Bacon, whether he were forewarned or no of an eclipse of the moon, always fell into a syncope while it lasted; and his vitality, suspended while the phenomenon lasted was restored as soon as it was over without his feeling any further inconvenience. These effects of antipathy, all well authenticated, and chosen from among many which history has happened to preserve, are enough to give a clue to the sympathies which remain unknown.

This fragment of Lambert's investigations, which I remember from among his essays, will throw a light on the method on which he worked. I need not emphasize the obvious connection between this theory and the collateral sciences projected by Gall and Lavater; they were its natural corollary; and every more or less scientific brain will discern the ramifications by which it is inevitably connected with the phrenological observations of one and the speculations on physiognomy of the other.

Mesmer's discovery, so important, though as yet so little appreciated, was also embodied in a single section of this treatise, though Louis did not know the Swiss doctor's writings—which are few and brief.

A simple and logical inference from these principles led him to perceive that the will might be accumulated by a contractile effort of the inner man, and then, by another effort, projected, or even imparted, to material objects. Thus the whole force of a man must have the property of reacting on other men, and of infusing into them an essence foreign to their own, if they could not protect themselves against such an aggression. The evidence of this theorem of the science of humanity is, of course, very multifarious; but there is nothing to establish it beyond question. We have only the notorious disaster of Marius and his harangue to the Cimbrian commanded to kill him, or the august injunction of a mother to the Lion of Florence, in historic proof of instances of such lightning flashes of mind. To Lambert, then, Will and Thought were *living forces;* and he spoke of them in such a way as to impress his belief on the hearer. To him these two forces were, in a way, visible, tangible. Thought was slow or alert, heavy or nimble, light or dark; he ascribed to it all the attributes of an active agent, and thought of it as rising, resting, waking, expanding, growing old, shrinking, becoming atrophied, or resuscitating; he described its life, and specified all its actions by the strangest words in our language, speaking of its spontaneity, its strength, and all its qualities with a kind of intuition which enabled him to recognize all the manifestations of its substantial existence.

"Often," said he, "in the midst of quiet and silence, when our inner faculties are dormant, when a sort of darkness reigns within us, and we are lost in the contemplation of things outside us, an idea suddenly flies forth, and rushes with the swiftness of lightning across the infinite space which our inner vision allows us to perceive. This radiant idea, springing into existence like a will-o'-the-wisp, dies out never to return; an ephemeral life, like that of babes who give their parents such infinite joy and sorrow; a sort of stillborn blossom in the fields of the mind. Sometimes an idea, instead of springing forcibly into life and dying unembodied, dawns gradually, hovers in the unknown limbo of the organs where it has its birth; exhausts us by long gestation, develops, is itself fruitful, grows outwardly in all the grace of youth and the promising attributes of a long life; it can endure the closest inspection, invites it, and never tires the sight; the investigation it undergoes commands the admiration we give to works slowly elaborated. Sometimes ideas are evolved in a swarm; one brings another; they come linked together; they vie with each other; they fly in clouds, wild and headlong. Again, they rise up pallid and misty, and perish for want of strength or of nutrition; the vital force is lacking. Or again, on certain days, they rush down into the depths to light up that immense obscurity; they terrify us and leave the soul dejected.

"Ideas are a complete system within us, resembling a natural kingdom, a sort of flora, of which the iconography will one day be outlined by some man who will perhaps be accounted a madman.

"Yes, within us and without, everything testifies to the livingness of those exquisite creations, which I compare with flowers in obedience to some unutterable revelation of their true nature!

"Their being produced as the final cause of man is, after all, not more amazing than the production of perfume and color in a plant. Perfumes *are* ideas, perhaps!

"When we consider the line where flesh ends and the nail begins contains the invisible and inexplicable mystery of the constant transformation of a fluid into horn, we must confess that nothing is impossible in the marvelous modifications of human tissue.

"And are there not in our inner nature phenomena of weight and motion comparable to those of physical nature? Suspense, to choose an example vividly familiar to everybody, is painful only as a result of the law in virtue of which the weight of a body is multiplied by its velocity. The weight of the feeling produced by suspense increases by the constant addition of past pain to the pain of the moment.

"And then, to what, unless it be to the electric fluid, are

we to attribute the magic by which the Will enthrones itself
so imperiously in the eye to demolish obstacles at the behest
of genius, thunders in the voice, or filters, in spite of dis-
simulation, through the human frame? The current of that
sovereign fluid, which, in obedience to the high pressure of
thought or of feeling, flows in a torrent or is reduced to a
mere thread, and collects to flash in lightnings, is the occult
agent to which are due the evil or the beneficent efforts
of Art and Passion—intonation of voice, whether harsh or
suave, terrible, lascivious, horrifying or seductive by turns,
thrilling the heart, the nerves, or the brain at our will; the
marvels of the touch, the instrument of the mental trans-
fusions of a myriad artists, whose creative fingers are able,
after passionate study, to reproduce the forms of nature; or,
again, the infinite gradations of the eye from dull inertia to
the emission of the most terrifying gleams.

"By this system God is bereft of none of His rights.
Mind, as a form of matter, has brought me a new conviction of His greatness."

After hearing him discourse thus, after receiving into my
soul his look like a ray of light, it was difficult not to be dazzled by his conviction and carried away by his arguments.
The Mind appeared to me as a purely physical power,
surrounded by its innumerable progeny. It was a new conception of humanity under a new form.

This brief sketch of the laws which, as Lambert maintained, constitute the formula of our intellect, must suffice
to give a notion of the prodigious activity of his spirit feeding on itself. Louis had sought for proofs of his theories in
the history of great men, whose lives, as set forth by their
biographers, supply very curious particulars as to the operation of their understanding. His memory allowed him to
recall such facts as might serve to support his statements;
he had appended them to each chapter in the form of
demonstrations, so as to give to many of his theories an
almost mathematical certainty. The works of Cardan, a
man gifted with singular powers of insight, supplied him
with valuable materials. He had not forgotten that Apollonius of Tyana had, in Asia, announced the death of a tyrant
with every detail of his execution, at the very hour when

it was taking place in Rome; nor that Plotinus, when far away from Porphyrius, was aware of his friend's intention to kill himself, and flew to dissuade him; nor the incident in the last century, proved in the face of the most incredulous mockery ever known—an incident most surprising to men who were accustomed to regard doubt as a weapon against the fact alone, but simple enough to believers—the fact that Alphonzo Maria di Liguori, Bishop of Saint Agatha, administered consolations to Pope Ganganelli, who saw him, heard him, and answered him, while the Bishop himself, at a great distance from Rome, was in a trance at home, in the chair where he commonly sat on his return from Mass. On recovering consciousness, he saw all his attendants kneeling beside him, believing him to be dead: "My friends," said he, "the Holy Father is just dead." Two days later a letter confirmed the news. The hour of the Pope's death coincided with that when the Bishop had been restored to his natural state.

Nor had Lambert omitted the yet more recent adventure of an English girl who was passionately attached to a sailor, and set out from London to seek him. She found him, without a guide, making her way alone in the North American wilderness, reaching him just in time to save his life.

Louis had found confirmatory evidence in the mysteries of the ancients, in the acts of the martyrs—in which glorious instances may be found of the triumph of human will, in the demonology of the Middle Ages, in criminal trials and medical researches; always selecting the real fact, the probable phenomenon, with admirable sagacity.

All this rich collection of scientific anecdotes, culled from so many books, most of them worthy of credit, served no doubt to wrap parcels in; and this work, which was curious, to say the least of it, as the outcome of a most extraordinary memory, was doomed to destruction.

Among the various cases which added to the value of Lambert's *Treatise* was an incident that had taken place in his own family, of which he had told me before he wrote his essay. This fact, bearing on the post-existence of the inner man, if I may be allowed to coin a new word for a phenomenon hitherto nameless, struck me so forcibly that I have never forgotten it. His father and mother were being forced into a lawsuit, of which the loss would leave them with a stain on their good name, the only thing they had in the world. Hence their anxiety was very great when the question first arose as to whether they should yield to the plaintiff's unjust demands, or should defend themselves against him. The matter came under discussion one autumn evening, before a turf fire in the room used by the tanner and his wife. Two or three relations were invited to this family council, and among others Louis' maternal great-grandfather, an old laborer, much bent, but with a venerable and dignified countenance, bright eyes, and a bald, yellow head, on which grew a few locks of thin, white hair. Like the Obi of the Negroes, or the Sagamore of the Indian savages, he was a sort of oracle, consulted on important occasions. His land was tilled by his grandchildren, who fed and served him; he predicted rain and fine weather, and told them when to mow the hay and gather the crops. The barometric exactitude of his forecasts was quite famous, and added to the confidence and respect he inspired. For whole days he would sit immovable in his armchair. This state of rapt meditation often came upon him since his wife's death; he had been attached to her in the truest and most faithful affection.

This discussion was held in his presence, but he did not seem to give much heed to it.

"My children," said he, when he was asked for his opinion, "this is too serious a matter for me to decide on alone. I must go and consult my wife."

The old man rose, took his stick, and went out, to the great astonishment of the others, who thought him daft. He presently came back and said:

"I did not have to go so far as the graveyard; your mother came to meet me; I found her by the brook. She tells me that you will find some receipts in the hands of a notary at Blois, which will enable you to gain your suit."

The words were spoken in a firm tone; the old man's demeanor and countenance showed that such an apparition was habitual with him. In fact, the disputed receipts were found, and the lawsuit was not attempted.

This event, under his father's roof and to his own knowledge, when Louis was nine years old, contributed largely to his belief in Swedenborg's miraculous visions, for in the course of that philosopher's life he repeatedly gave proof of the power of sight developed in his Inner Being. As he grew older, and as his intelligence was developed, Lambert was naturally led to seek in the laws of nature for the causes of the miracle which, in his childhood, had captivated his attention. What name can be given to the chance which brought within his ken so many facts and books bearing on such phenomena, and made him the principal subject and actor in such marvelous manifestations of mind?

If Lambert had no other title to fame than the fact of his having formulated, in his sixteenth year, such a psychological dictum as this:—" The events which bear witness to the action of the human race, and are the outcome of its intellect, have causes by which they are preconceived, as our actions are accomplished in our minds before they are reproduced by the outer man; presentiments or predictions are the perception of these causes"—I think we may deplore in him a genius equal to Pascal, Lavoisier, or Laplace. His chimerical notions about angels perhaps overruled his work too long; but was it not in trying to make gold that the alchemists unconsciously created chemistry? At the same time, Lambert, at a later period, studied comparative anatomy, physics, geometry, and other sciences bearing on his discoveries, and this was undoubtedly with the purpose of collecting facts and submitting them to analysis—the only torch that can guide us through the dark places of the most inscrutable work of nature. He had too much good sense to dwell among the clouds of theories which can all be expressed in a few words. In our day, is not the simplest demonstration based on facts more highly esteemed than the most specious system though defended by more or less ingenious inductions? But as I did not know him at the period of his life when his cogitations were, no doubt, the most productive of results, I can only conjecture that the bent of his work must have been from that of his first efforts of thought.

It is easy to see where his *Treatise on the Will* was faulty. Though gifted already with the powers which characterize superior men, he was but a boy. His brain, though endowed with a great faculty for abstractions, was still full of the delightful beliefs that hover around youth. Thus his conception, while at some points it touched the ripest fruits of his genius, still, by many more, clung to the smaller elements of its germs. To certain readers, lovers of poetry, what he chiefly lacked must have been a certain vein of interest.

But his work bore the stamp of the struggle that was going on in that noble Spirit between the two great principles of Spiritualism and Materialism, round which so many a fine genius has beaten its way without ever daring to amalgamate them. Louis, at first purely Spiritualist, had been irresistibly led to recognize the Material conditions of Mind. Confounded by the facts of analysis at the moment when his heart still gazed with yearning at the clouds which floated in Swedenborg's heaven, he had not yet acquired the necessary powers to produce a coherent system, compactly cast in a piece, as it were. Hence certain inconsistencies that have left their stamp even on the sketch here given of his first attempts. Still, incomplete as his work may have been, was it not the rough copy of a science of which he would have investigated the secrets at a later time, have secured the foundations, have examined, deduced, and connected the logical sequence?

Six months after the confiscation of the *Treatise on the Will* I left school. Our parting was unexpected. My mother, alarmed by a feverish attack which for some months I had been unable to shake off, while my inactive life induced symptoms of coma, carried me off at four or five hours' notice. The announcement of my departure reduced Lambert to dreadful dejection.

"Shall I ever seen you again?" said he in his gentle voice, as he clasped me in his arms. "You will live," he went on, "but I shall die. If I can, I will come back to you."

Only the young can utter such words with the accent of conviction that gives them the impressiveness of prophecy, of a pledge, leaving a terror of its fulfilment. For a long time indeed I vaguely looked for the promised apparition.

Even now there are days of depression, of doubt, alarm, and loneliness, when I am forced to repel the intrusion of that sad parting, though it was not fated to be the last.

When I crossed the yard by which we left, Lambert was at one of the refectory windows to see me pass. By my request my mother obtained leave for him to dine with us at the inn, and in the evening I escorted him back to the fatal gate of the college. No lover and his mistress ever shed more tears at parting.

"Well, goodbye; I shall be left alone in this desert!" said he, pointing to the playground where two hundred boys were disporting themselves and shouting. "When I come back half dead with fatigue from my long excursions through the fields of thought, on whose heart can I rest? I could tell you everything in a look. Who will understand me now?—Goodbye! I could wish I had never met you; I should not know all I am losing."

"And what is to become of me?" said I. "Is not my position a dreadful one? I have nothing here to uphold me!" and I slapped my forehead.

He shook his head with a gentle gesture, gracious and sad, and we parted.

At that time Louis Lambert was about five feet five inches in height; he grew no more. His countenance, which was full of expression, revealed his sweet nature. Divine patience, developed by harsh usage, and the constant concentration needed for his meditative life, had bereft his eyes of the audacious pride which is so attractive in some faces, and which had so shocked our masters. Peaceful mildness gave charm to his face, an exquisite serenity that was never marred by a tinge of irony or satire; for his natural kindliness tempered his conscious strength and superiority. He had pretty hands, very slender, and almost always moist. His frame was a marvel, a model for a sculptor; but our iron-gray uniform, with gilt buttons and knee breeches, gave us such an ungainly appearance that Lambert's fine proportions and firm muscles could only be appreciated in the bath. When we swam in our pool in the Loire, Louis was conspicuous by the whiteness of his skin, which was unlike the different shades of our schoolfellows' bodies mottled

by the cold, or blue from the water. Gracefully formed, ele-
gant in his attitudes, delicate in hue, never shivering after
his bath, perhaps because he avoided the shade and always
ran into the sunshine, Louis was like one of those cautious
blossoms that close their petals to the blast and refuse to
open unless to a clear sky. He ate little, and drank water
only; either by instinct or by choice he was averse to any
exertion that made a demand on his strength; his movements were few and simple, like those of Orientals or of
savages, with whom gravity seems a condition of nature.

As a rule, he disliked everything that resembled any special care for his person. He commonly sat with his head a
little inclined to the left, and so constantly rested his elbows
on the table, that the sleeves of his coats were soon in holes.

To this slight picture of the outer man I must add a
sketch of his moral qualities, for I believe I can now judge
him impartially.

Though naturally religious, Louis did not accept the
minute practices of the Roman ritual; his ideas were more
intimately in sympathy with Saint Theresa and Fenelon,
and several Fathers and certain Saints, who, in our day,
would be regarded as heresiarchs or atheists. He was rig-
idly calm during the services. His own prayers went up in
gusts, in aspirations, without any regular formality; in all
things he gave himself up to nature, and would not pray,
any more than he would think, at any fixed hour. In chapel
he was equally apt to think of God or to meditate on some
problem of philosophy.

To him Jesus Christ was the most perfect type of his
system. *Et Verbum caro factum est* seemed a sublime statement intended to express the traditional formula of the
Will, the Word, and the Act made visible. Christ's uncon-
sciousness of His Death—having so perfected His inner
Being by divine works, that one day the invisible form of it
appeared to His disciples—and the other Mysteries of the
Gospels, the magnetic cures wrought by Christ, and the
gift of tongues, all to him confirmed his doctrine. I remember once hearing him say on this subject, that the greatest
work that could be written nowadays was a History of the
Primitive Church. And he never rose to such poetic heights

as when, in the evening, as we conversed, he would enter on an inquiry into miracles, worked by the power of Will during that great age of faith. He discerned the strongest evidence of his theory in most of the martyrdoms endured during the first century of our era, which he spoke of as *the great era of the Mind.*

"Do not the phenomena observed in almost every instance of the torments so heroically endured by the early Christians for the establishment of the faith, amply prove that Material force will never prevail against the force of Ideas or the Will of man?" he would say. "From this effect, produced by the Will of all, each man may draw conclusions in favor of his own."

I need say nothing of his views on poetry or history, nor of his judgment on the masterpieces of our language. There would be little interest in the record of opinions now almost universally held, though at that time, from the lips of a boy, they might seem remarkable. Louis was capable of the highest flights. To give a notion of his talents in a few words, he could have written *Zadig* as wittily as Voltaire; he could have thought out the dialogue between Sylla and Eucrates as powerfully as Montesquieu. His rectitude of character made him desire above all else in a work that it should bear the stamp of utility; at the same time, his refined taste demanded novelty of thought as well as of form. One of his most remarkable literary observations, which will serve as a clue to all the others, and show the lucidity of his judgment, is this, which has ever dwelt in my memory, "The Apocalypse is written ecstasy." He regarded the Bible as a part of the traditional history of the antediluvian nations which had taken for its share the new humanity. He thought that the mythology of the Greeks was borrowed both from the Hebrew Scriptures and from the sacred Books of India, adapted after their own fashion by the beauty-loving Hellenes.

"It is impossible," said he, "to doubt the priority of the Asiatic Scriptures; they are earlier than our sacred books. The man who is candid enough to admit this historical fact sees the whole world expand before him. Was it not on the Asiatic highland that the few men took refuge who were able to escape the catastrophe that ruined our globe—if, indeed men had existed before that cataclysm or shock? A serious query, the answer to which lies at the bottom of the sea. The anthropogony of the Bible is merely a genealogy of a swarm escaping from the human hive which settled on the mountainous slopes of Tibet between the summits of the Himalaya and the Caucasus.

"The character of the primitive ideas of that horde called by its lawgiver the people of God, no doubt to secure its unity, and perhaps also to induce it to maintain his laws and his system of government—for the Books of Moses are a religious, political, and civil code—that character bears the authority of terror; convulsions of nature are interpreted with stupendous power as a vengeance from on high. In fact, since this wandering tribe knew none of the ease enjoyed by a community settled in a patriarchal home, their sorrows as pilgrims inspired them with none but gloomy poems, majestic but bloodstained. In the Hindus, on the contrary, the spectacle of the rapid recoveries of the natural world, and the prodigious effects of sunshine, which they were the first to recognize, gave rise to happy images of blissful love, to the worship of Fire and of the endless personifications of reproductive force. These fine fancies are lacking in the Book of the Hebrews. A constant need of self-preservation amid all the dangers and the lands they traversed to reach the Promised Land engendered their exclusive race-feeling and their hatred of all other nations.

"These three Scriptures are the archives of an engulfed world. Therein lies the secret of the extraordinary splendor of those languages and their myths. A grand human history lies beneath those names of men and places, and those fables which charm us so irresistibly, we know not why. Perhaps it is because we find in them the native air of renewed humanity."

Thus, to him, this threefold literature included all the thoughts of man. Not a book could be written, in his opinion, of which the subject might not there be discerned in its germ. This view shows how learnedly he had pursued his early studies of the Bible, and how far they had led him. Hovering, as it were, over the heads of society, and knowing it solely from books, he could judge it coldly.

"The law," said he, "never puts a check on the enterprises of the rich and great, but crushes the poor, who, on the contrary, need protection."

His kind heart did not therefore allow him to sympathize in political ideas; his system led rather to the passive obedience of which Jesus set the example. During the last hours of my life at Vendome, Louis had ceased to feel the spur to glory; he had, in a way, had an abstract enjoyment of fame; and having opened it, as the ancient priests of sacrifice sought to read the future in the hearts of men, he had found nothing in the entrails of his chimera. Scorning a sentiment so wholly personal: "Glory," said he, "is but beatified egoism."

Here, perhaps, before taking leave of this exceptional boyhood, I may pronounce judgment on it by a rapid glance.

A short time before our separation, Lambert said to me:

"Apart from the general laws which I have formulated—and this, perhaps, will be my glory—laws which must be those of the human organism, the life of man is Movement determined in each individual by the pressure of some inscrutable influence—by the brain, the heart, or the sinews. All the innumerable modes of human existence result from the proportions in which these three generating forces are more or less intimately combined with the substances they assimilate in the environment they live in."

He stopped short, struck his forehead, and exclaimed: "How strange! In every great man whose portrait I have remarked, the neck is short. Perhaps nature requires that in them the heart should be nearer to the brain!"

Then he went on:

"From that, a sum total of action takes its rise which constitutes social life. The man of sinew contributes action or strength; the man of brain, genius; the man of heart, faith. But," he added sadly, "faith sees only the clouds of the sanctuary; the Angel alone has light."

So, according to his own definitions, Lambert was all brain and all heart. It seems to me that his intellectual life was divided into three marked phases.

Under the impulsion, from his earliest years, of a pre-cocious activity, due, no doubt, to some malady—or to some special perfection—of organism, his powers were concentrated on the functions of the inner senses and a superabundant flow of nerve fluid. As a man of ideas, he craved to satisfy the thirst of his brain, to assimilate every idea. Hence his reading; and from his reading, the reflec-tions that gave him the power of reducing things to their simplest expression, and of absorbing them to study them in their essence. Thus, the advantages of this splendid stage, acquired by other men only after long study, were achieved by Lambert during his bodily childhood: a happy childhood, colored by the studious joys of a born poet.

The point which most thinkers reach at last was to him the starting point, whence his brain was to set out one day in search of new worlds of knowledge. Though as yet he knew it not, he had made for himself the most exacting life possible, and the most insatiably greedy. Merely to live, was he not compelled to be perpetually casting nutriment into the gulf he had opened in himself? Like some beings who dwell in the grosser world, might not he die of inanition for want of feeding abnormal and disappointed cravings? Was not this a sort of debauchery of the intellect which might lead to spontaneous combustion, like that of bodies satu-rated with alcohol?

I had seen nothing of this first phase of his brain devel-opment; it is only now, at a later day, that I can thus give an account of its prodigious fruit and results. Lambert was now thirteen.

I was so fortunate as to witness the first stage of the second period. Lambert was cast into all the miseries of school life—and that, perhaps, was his salvation—it absorbed the superabundance of his thoughts. After passing from concrete ideas to their purest expression, from words to their ideal import, and from that import to principles, after reducing everything to the abstract, to enable him to live he yearned for yet other intellectual creations. Quelled by the woes of school and the critical development of his physical constitution, he became thoughtful, dreamed of feeling, and caught a glimpse of new sciences—positively masses of ideas. Checked in his career, and not yet strong enough to contemplate the higher spheres, he contemplated his inmost self. I then perceived in him the struggle of the Mind reacting on itself, and trying to detect the secrets of its own nature, like a physician who watches the course of his own disease.

At this stage of weakness and strength, of childish grace and superhuman powers, Louis Lambert is the creature who, more than any other, gave me a poetical and truthful image of the being we call an angel, always excepting one woman whose name, whose features, whose identity, and whose life I would fain hide from all the world, so as to be sole master of the secret of her existence, and to bury it in the depths of my heart.

The third phase I was not destined to see. It began when Lambert and I were parted, for he did not leave college till he was eighteen, in the summer of 1815. He had at that time lost his father and mother about six months before. Finding no member of his family with whom his soul could sympathize, expansive still, but, since our parting, thrown back on himself, he made his home with his uncle, who was also his guardian, and who, having been turned out of his benefice as a priest who had taken the oaths, had come to settle at Blois. There Louis lived for some time; but consumed ere long by the desire to finish his incomplete studies, he came to Paris to see Madame de Stael, and to drink of science at its highest fount. The old priest, being very fond of his nephew, left Louis free to spend his whole little inheritance in his three years' stay in Paris, though he lived very poorly. This fortune consisted of but a few thousand francs.

Lambert returned to Blois at the beginning of 1820, driven from Paris by the sufferings to which the impecunious are exposed there. He must often have been a victim to the secret storms, the terrible rage of mind by which artists are tossed to judge from the only fact his uncle recollected, and the only letter he preserved of all those which Louis Lambert wrote to him at that time, perhaps because it was the last and the longest.

To begin with the story. Louis one evening was at the

Theatre-Français, seated on a bench in the upper gallery, near to one of the pillars which, in those days, divided off the third row of boxes. On rising between the acts, he saw a young woman who had just come into the box next him. The sight of this lady, who was young, pretty, well dressed, in a low bodice no doubt, and escorted by a man for whom her face beamed with all the charms of love, produced such a terrible effect on Lambert's soul and senses, that he was obliged to leave the theater. If he had not been controlled by some remaining glimmer of reason, which was not wholly extinguished by this first fever of burning passion, he might perhaps have yielded to the most irresistible desire that came over him to kill the young man on whom the lady's looks beamed. Was not this a reversion, in the heart of the Paris world, to the savage passion that regards women as its prey, an effect of animal instinct combining with the almost luminous flashes of a soul crushed under the weight of thought? In short, was it not the prick of the penknife so vividly imagined by the boy, felt by the man as the thunderbolt of his most vital craving—for love?

And now, here is the letter that depicts the state of his mind as it was struck by the spectacle of Parisian civilization. His feelings, perpetually wounded no doubt in that whirlpool of self-interest, must always have suffered there; he probably had no friend to comfort him, no enemy to give tone to this life. Compelled to live in himself alone, having no one to share his subtle raptures, he may have hoped to solve the problem of his destiny by a life of ecstasy, adopting an almost vegetative attitude, like an anchorite of the early Church, and abdicating the empire of the intellectual world.

This letter seems to hint at such a scheme, which is a temptation to all lofty souls at periods of social reform. But is not this purpose, in some cases, the result of a vocation? Do not some of them endeavor to concentrate their powers by long silence, so as to emerge fully capable of governing the world by word or by deed? Louis must, assuredly, have found much bitterness in his intercourse with men, or have striven hard with Society in terrible irony, without extracting anything from it, before uttering so strident a cry, and expressing, poor fellow, the desire which satiety of power and of all earthly things has led even monarchs to indulge!

And perhaps, too, he went back to solitude to carry out some great work that was floating inchoate in his brain. We would gladly believe it as we read this fragment of his thoughts, betraying the struggle of his soul at the time when youth was ending and the terrible power of production was coming into being, to which we might have owed the works of the man.

This letter connects itself with the adventure at the theater. The incident and the letter throw light on each other, body and soul were tuned to the same pitch. This tempest of doubts and asseverations, of clouds and of lightnings that flash before the thunder, ending by a starved yearning for heavenly illumination, throws such a light on the third phase of his education as enables us to understand it perfectly. As we read these lines, written at chance moments, taken up when the vicissitudes of life in Paris allowed, may we not fancy that we see an oak at that stage of its growth when its inner expansion bursts the tender green bark, covering it with wrinkles and cracks, when its majestic stature is in preparation—if indeed the lightnings of heaven and the axe of man shall spare it?

This letter, then, will close, alike for the poet and the philosopher, this portentous childhood and unappreciated youth. It finishes off the outline of this nature in its germ. Philosophers will regret the foliage frost-nipped in the bud; but they will, perhaps, find the flowers expanding in regions far above the highest places of the earth.

PARIS, *September–October 1819.*

DEAR UNCLE,—I shall soon be leaving this part of the world, where I could never bear to live. I find no one here who likes what I like, who works at my work, or is amazed at what amazes me. Thrown back on myself, I eat my heart out in misery. My long and patient study of Society here has brought me to melancholy conclusions, in which doubt predominates.

Here, money is the mainspring of everything. Money is indispensable, even for going without money. But though that dross is necessary to anyone who wishes to think in peace, I have not courage enough to make it the sole motive power of my thoughts. To make a fortune, I must take up a profession; in two words, I must, by acquiring some privilege of position or of self-advertisement, either legal or ingeniously contrived, purchase the right of taking day by day out of somebody else's purse a certain sum which, by the end of the year, would amount to a small capital; and this, in twenty years, would hardly secure an income of four or five thousand francs to a man who deals honestly. An advocate, a notary, a merchant, any recognized professional, has earned a living for his later days in the course of fifteen or sixteen years after ending his apprenticeship.

"But I have never felt fit for work of this kind. I prefer thought to action, an idea to a transaction, contemplation to activity. I am absolutely devoid of the constant attention indispensable to the making of a fortune. Any mercantile venture, any need for using other people's money would bring me to grief, and I should be ruined. Though I have nothing, at least at the moment, I owe nothing. The man who gives his life to the achievement of great things in the sphere of intellect, needs very little; still, though twenty sous a day would be enough, I do not possess that small income for my laborious idleness. When I wish to cogitate, want drives me out of the sanctuary where my mind has its being. What is to become of me?

I am not frightened at poverty. If it were not that beggars are imprisoned, branded, scorned, I would beg, to enable me to solve at my leisure the problems that haunt me. Still, this sublime resignation, by which I might emancipate my mind, through abstracting it from the body, would not serve my end. I should still need money to devote myself to certain experiments. But for that, I would accept the outward indigence of a sage possessed of both heaven and heart. A man need only never stoop, to remain lofty in poverty. He who struggles and endures, while marching on to a glorious end, presents a noble spectacle; but who can have the strength to fight here? We can climb cliffs, but it is unendurable to remain forever tramping the mud. Everything here checks the flight of the spirit that strives towards the future.

I should not be afraid of myself in a desert cave; I am

afraid of myself here. In the desert I should be alone with myself, undisturbed; here man has a thousand wants which drag him down. You go out walking, absorbed in dreams; the voice of the beggar asking an alms brings you back to this world of hunger and thirst. You need money only to take a walk. Your organs of sense, perpetually wearied by trifles, never get any rest. The poet's sensitive nerves are perpetually shocked, and what ought to be his glory becomes his torment; his imagination is his cruelest enemy. The injured workman, the poor mother in childbed, the prostitute who has fallen ill, the foundling, the infirm and aged—even vice and crime here find a refuge and charity; but the world is merciless to the inventor, to the man who thinks. Here everything must show an immediate and practical result. Fruitless attempts are mocked at, though they may lead to the greatest discoveries; the deep and untiring study that demands long concentrations of every faculty is not valued here. The State might pay talent as it pays the bayonet; but it is afraid of being taken in by mere cleverness, as if genius could be counterfeited for any length of time.

Ah, my dear uncle, when monastic solitude was destroyed, uprooted from its home at the foot of mountains, under green and silent shade, asylums ought to have been provided for those suffering souls who, by an idea, promote the progress of nations or prepare some new and fruitful development of science.

*September 20th.*
The love of study brought me hither, as you know. I have met really learned men, amazing for the most part; but the lack of unity in scientific work almost nullifies their efforts. There is no Head of instruction or of scientific research. At the Museum a professor argues to prove that another in the Rue Saint-Jacques talks nonsense. The lecturer at the College of Medicine abuses him of the College de France. When I first arrived, I went to hear an old Academician who taught five hundred youths that Corneille was a haughty and powerful genius; Racine, elegiac and graceful; Moliere, inimitable; Voltaire, supremely witty; Bossuet and Pascal, incomparable in argument. A professor of philosophy may make a name by explaining how Plato is Platonic. Another discourses

on the history of words, without troubling himself about ideas. One explains Aeschylus, another tells you that communes were communes, and neither more nor less. These original and brilliant discoveries, diluted to last several hours, constitute the higher education which is to lead to giant strides in human knowledge.

If the Government could have an idea, I should suspect it of being afraid of any real superiority, which, once roused, might bring Society under the yoke of an intelligent rule. Then nations would go too far and too fast; so professors are appointed to produce simpletons. How else can we account for a scheme devoid of method or any notion of the future?

The *Institut* might be the central government of the moral and intellectual world; but it has been ruined lately by its subdivision into separate academies. So human science marches on, without a guide, without a system, and floats haphazard with no road traced out.

This vagueness and uncertainty prevails in politics as well as in science. In the order of nature means are simple, the end is grand and marvelous; here in science as in government, the means are stupendous, the end is mean. The force which in nature proceeds at an equal pace, and of which the sum is constantly being added to itself—the A + A from which everything is produced—is destructive in society. Politics, at the present time, place human forces in antagonism to neutralize each other, instead of combining them to promote their action to some definite end.

Looking at Europe alone, from Caesar to Constantine, from the puny Constantine to the great Attila, from the Huns to Charlemagne, from Charlemagne to Leo X, from Leo X, to Philip II, from Philip II to Louis XIV; from Venice to England, from England to Napoleon, from Napoleon to England, I see no fixed purpose in politics; its constant agitation has led to no progress.

Nations leave witnesses to their greatness in monuments, and to their happiness in the welfare of individuals. Are modern monuments as fine as those of the ancients? I doubt it. The arts, which are the direct outcome of the individual, the products of genius or of handicraft, have not advanced much. The pleasures of Lucullus were as good as those of Samuel Bernard, of Beaujon, or of the King of Bavaria. And then human longevity has diminished.

Thus, to those who will be candid, man is still the same; might is his only law, and success his only wisdom.

Jesus Christ, Muhammad, and Luther only lent a different hue to the arena in which youthful nations disport themselves.

No development of politics has hindered civilization, with its riches, its manners, its alliance of the strong against the weak, its ideas, and its delights, from moving from Memphis to Tyre, from Tyre to Baalbek, from Tadmor to Carthage, from Carthage to Rome, from Rome to Constantinople, from Constantinople to Venice, from Venice to Spain, from Spain to England— while no trace is left of Memphis, of Tyre, of Carthage, of Rome, of Venice, or Madrid. The soul of those great bodies has fled. Not one of them has preserved itself from destruction, nor formulated this axiom: When the effect produced ceases to be in a ratio to its cause, disorganization follows.

The most subtle genius can discover no common bond between great social facts. No political theory has ever lasted. Governments pass away, as men do, without handing down any lesson, and no system gives birth to a system better than that which came before it. What can we say about politics when a Government directly referred to God perished in India and Egypt; when the rule of the Sword and of the Tiara are past; when Monarchy is dying; when the Government of the People has never been alive; when no scheme of intellectual power as applied to material interests has ever proved durable, and everything at this day remains to be done all over again, as it has been at every period when man has turned to cry out, "I am in torment!"

The code, which is considered Napoleon's greatest achievement, is the most Draconian work I know of. Territorial subdivision carried out to the uttermost, and its principle confirmed by the equal division of property generally, must result in the degeneracy of the nation and the death of the Arts and Sciences. The land, too much broken up, is cultivated only with cereals and small crops; the forests, and consequently the rivers, are disappearing; oxen and horses are no longer bred. Means are lacking both for attack and for resistance. If we should be invaded, the people must be crushed; it has lost its mainspring—its leaders. This is the history of deserts!

Thus the science of politics has no definite principles, and it can have no fixity; it is the spirit of the hour, the perpetual application of strength proportioned to the necessities of the moment. The man who should foresee two centuries ahead would die on the place of execution, loaded with the imprecations of the mob, or else—which seems worse—would be lashed with the myriad whips of ridicule. Nations are but individuals, neither wiser nor stronger than man, and their destinies are identical. If we reflect on man, is not that to consider mankind?

By studying the spectacle of society perpetually storm-tossed in its foundations as well as in its results, in its causes as well as in its actions, while philanthropy is but a splendid mistake, and progress is vanity, I have been confirmed in this truth: Life is within and not without us; to rise above men, to govern them, is only the part of an aggrandized schoolmaster; and those men who are capable of rising to the level whence they can enjoy a view of the world should not look at their own feet.

*November 4th.*

I am no doubt occupied with weighty thoughts, I am on the way to certain discoveries, an invincible power bears me toward a luminary which shone at an early age on the darkness of my moral life; but what name can I give to the power that ties my hands and shuts my mouth, and drags me in a direction opposite to my vocation? I must leave Paris, bid farewell to the books in the libraries, those noble centres of illumination, those kindly and always accessible sages, and the younger geniuses with whom I sympathize. Who is it that drives me away? Chance or Providence?

The two ideas represented by those words are irreconcilable. If Chance does not exist, we must admit fatalism, that is to say, the compulsory coordination of things under the rule of a general plan. Why then do we rebel? If man is not free, what becomes of the scaffolding of his moral sense? Or, if he can control his destiny, if by his own free will he can interfere with the execution of the general plan, what becomes of God?

Why did I come here? If I examine myself, I find the answer: I find in myself axioms that need developing. But why then have I such vast faculties without being suffered to use them? If my suffering could serve as an example, I could understand it; but no, I suffer unknown.

This is perhaps as much the act of Providence as the fate of the flower that dies unseen in the heart of the virgin forest, where no one can enjoy its perfume or admire its splendor. Just as that blossom vainly sheds its fragrance to the solitude, so do I, here in the garret, give birth to ideas that no one can grasp.

Yesterday evening I sat eating bread and grapes in front of my window with a young doctor named Meyraux. We talked as men do whom misfortune has joined in brotherhood, and I said to him:

"I am going away; you are staying. Take up my ideas and develop them."

"I cannot!" said he, with bitter regret: "my feeble health cannot stand so much work, and I shall die young of my struggle with penury."

We looked up at the sky and grasped hands. We first met at the Comparative Anatomy course, and in the galleries of the Museum, attracted thither by the same study—the unity of geological structure. In him this was the presentiment of genius sent to open a new path in the fallows of intellect; in me it was a deduction from a general system.

My point is to ascertain the real relation that may exist between God and man. Is not this a need of the age? Without the highest assurance, it is impossible to put bit and bridle on the social factions that have been let loose by the spirit of skepticism and discussion, and which are now crying aloud: "Show us a way in which we may walk and find no pitfalls in our way!"

You will wonder what comparative anatomy has to do with a question of such importance to the future of society. Must we not attain to the conviction that man is the end of all earthly means before we ask whether he too is not the means to some end? If man is bound up with everything, is there not something above him with which he again is bound up? If he is the end-all of the explained transmutations that lead up to him, must he not be also the link between the visible and invisible creations?

The activity of the universe is not absurd; it must tend to an end, and that end is surely not a social body constituted as ours is! There is a fearful gulf between us and heaven. In our present existence we can neither be

always happy nor always in torment; must there not be
some tremendous change to bring about Paradise and
Hell, two images without which God cannot exist to the
mind of the vulgar? I know that a compromise was made
by the invention of the Soul; but it is repugnant to me to
make God answerable for human baseness, for our dis-
enchantments, our aversions, our degeneracy.

Again, how can we recognize as divine the principle
within us which can be overthrown by a few glasses of
rum? How conceive of immaterial faculties which matter
can conquer, and whose exercise is suspended by a
grain of opium? How imagine that we shall be able to
feel when we are bereft of the vehicles of sensation? Why
must God perish if matter can be proved to think? Is
the vitality of matter in its innumerable manifestations—
the effect of its instincts—at all more explicable than the
effects of the mind? Is not the motion given to the worlds
enough to prove God's existence, without our plunging
into absurd speculations suggested by pride? And if we
pass, after our trials, from a perishable state of being to
a higher existence, is not that enough for a creature that
is distinguished from other creatures only by more perfect instincts? If in moral philosophy there is not a single
principle which does not lead to the absurd, or cannot be
disproved by evidence, is it not high time that we should
set to work to seek such dogmas as are written in the
innermost nature of things? Must we not reverse philosophical science?

We trouble ourselves very little about the supposed
void that must have pre-existed for us, and we try to
fathom the supposed void that lies before us. We make
God responsible for the future, but we do not expect
Him to account for the past. And yet it is quite as desir-
able to know whether we have any roots in the past as
to discover whether we are inseparable from the future.

We have been Deists or Atheists in one direction only.

Is the world eternal? Was the world created? We can
conceive of no middle term between these two propositions; one, then, is true and the other false! Take your
choice. Whichever it may be, God, as our reason depicts
Him, must be deposed, and that amounts to denial. The
world is eternal: then, beyond question, God has had it
forced upon Him. The world was created: then God is
an impossibility. How could He have subsisted through

an eternity, not knowing that He would presently want to create the world? How could He have failed to foresee all the results?

Whence did He derive the essence of creation? Evidently from Himself. If, then, the world proceeds from God, how can you account for evil? That Evil should proceed from Good is absurd. If evil does not exist, what do you make of social life and its laws? On all hands we find a precipice! On every side a gulf in which reason is lost! Then social science must be altogether reconstructed.

Listen to me, uncle; until some splendid genius shall have taken account of the obvious inequality of intellects and the general sense of humanity, the word God will be constantly arraigned, and Society will rest on shifting sands. The secret of the various moral zones through which man passes will be discovered by the analysis of the animal type as a whole. That animal type has hitherto been studied with reference only to its differences, not to its similitudes; in its organic manifestations, not in its faculties. Animal faculties are perfected in direct transmission, in obedience to laws which remain to be discovered. These faculties correspond to the forces which express them, and those forces are essentially material and divisible.

Material faculties! Reflect on this juxtaposition of words. Is not this a problem as insoluble as that of the first communication of motion to matter—an unsounded gulf of which the difficulties were transposed rather than removed by Newton's system? Again, the universal assimilation of light by everything that exists on earth demands a new study of our globe. The same animal differs in the tropics of India and in the North. Under the angular or the vertical incidence of the sun's rays nature is developed the same, but not the same; identical in its principles, but totally dissimilar in its outcome. The phenomenon that amazes our eyes in the zoological world when we compare the butterflies of Brazil with those of Europe, is even more startling in the world of Mind. A particular facial angle, a certain amount of brain convolutions, are indispensable to produce Columbus, Raphael, Napoleon, Laplace, or Beethoven; the sunless valley produces the cretin—draw your own conclusions. Why such differences, due to the more or less ample diffusion of

light to men? The masses of suffering humanity, more
or less active, fed, and enlightened, are a difficulty to be
accounted for, crying out against God.

Why in great joy do we always want to quit the earth?
whence comes the longing to rise which every creature
has known or will know? Motion is a great soul, and its
alliance with matter is just as difficult to account for as
the origin of thought in man. In these days science is
one; it is impossible to touch politics independent of
moral questions, and these are bound up with scientific
questions. It seems to me that we are on the eve of a
great human struggle; the forces are there; only I do not
see the General.

*November 25.*
Believe me, dear uncle, it is hard to give up the life that
is in us without a pang. I am returning to Blois with a
heavy grip at my heart; I shall die then, taking with me
some useful truths. No personal interest debases my
regrets. Is earthly fame a guerdon to those who believe
that they will mount to a higher sphere?

I am by no means in love with the two syllables *Lam*
and *bert;* whether spoken with respect or with contempt
over my grave, they can make no change in my ultimate destiny. I feel myself strong and energetic; I might
become a power; I feel in myself a life so luminous that
it might enlighten a world, and yet I am shut up in a sort
of mineral, as perhaps indeed are the colors you admire
on the neck of an Indian bird. I should need to embrace
the whole world, to clasp and re-create it; but those who
have done this, who have thus embraced and remolded it
began—did they not?—by being a wheel in the machine.
I can only be crushed. Muhammad had the sword; Jesus
had the cross; I shall die unknown. I shall be at Blois for
a day, and then in my coffin.

Do you know why I have come back to Swedenborg
after vast studies of all religions, and after proving to
myself, by reading all the works published within the last
sixty years by the patient English, by Germany, and by
France, how deeply true were my youthful views about
the Bible? Swedenborg undoubtedly epitomizes all the
religions—or rather the one religion—of humanity.
Though forms of worship are infinitely various, neither
their true meaning nor their metaphysical interpretation

has ever varied. In short, man has, and has had, but one religion.

Sivaism, Vishnuism, and Brahmanism, the three primitive creeds, originating as they did in Tibet, in the valley of the Indus, and on the vast plains of the Ganges, ended their warfare some thousand years before the birth of Christ by adopting the Hindu Trimurti. The Trimurti is our Trinity. From this dogma Magianism arose in Persia; in Egypt, the African beliefs and the Mosaic law; the worship of the Cabiri, and the polytheism of Greece and Rome. While by this ramification of the Trimurti the Asiatic myths became adapted to the imaginations of various races in the lands they reached by the agency of certain sages whom men elevated to be demigods—Mithra, Bacchus, Hermes, Hercules, and the rest—Buddha, the great reformer of the three primeval religions, lived in India, and founded his Church there, a sect which still numbers two hundred million more believers than Christianity can show, while it certainly influenced the powerful Will both of Jesus and of Confucius.

Then Christianity raised her standard. Subsequently Muhammad fused Judaism and Christianity, the Bible and the Gospel, in one book, the Koran, adapting them to the apprehension of the Arab race. Finally, Swedenborg borrowed from Magianism, Brahmanism, Buddhism, and Christian mysticism all the truth and divine beauty that those four great religious books hold in common, and added to them a doctrine, a basis of reasoning, that may be termed mathematical.

Any man who plunges into these religious waters, of which the sources are not all known, will find proofs that Zoroaster, Moses, Buddha, Confucius, Jesus Christ, and Swedenborg had identical principles and aimed at identical ends.

The last of them all, Swedenborg, will perhaps be the Buddha of the North. Obscure and diffuse as his writings are, we find in them the elements of a magnificent conception of society. His Theocracy is sublime, and his creed is the only acceptable one to superior souls. He alone brings man into immediate communion with God, he gives a thirst for God, he has freed the majesty of God from the trappings in which other human dogmas have disguised Him. He left Him where He is, making His myriad creations and creatures gravitate towards

Him through successive transformations which promise a more immediate and more natural future than the Catholic idea of Eternity. Swedenborg has absolved God from the reproach attaching to Him in the estimation of tender souls for the perpetuity of revenge to punish the sin of a moment—a system of injustice and cruelty.

Each man may know for himself what hope he has of life eternal, and whether this world has any rational sense. I mean to make the attempt. And this attempt may save the world, just as much as the cross at Jerusalem or the sword at Mecca. These were both the offspring of the desert. Of the thirty-three years of Christ's life, we only know the history of nine; His life of seclusion prepared Him for His life of glory. And I too crave for the desert!

Notwithstanding the difficulties of the task, I have felt it my duty to depict Lambert's boyhood, the unknown life to which I owe the only happy hours, the only pleasant memories, of my early days. Excepting during those two years I had nothing but annoyances and weariness. Though some happiness was mine at a later time, it was always incomplete.

I have been diffuse, I know; but in default of entering into the whole wide heart and brain of Louis Lambert—two words which inadequately express the infinite aspects of his inner life—it would be almost impossible to make the second part of his intellectual history intelligible—a phase that was unknown to the world and to me, but of which the mystical outcome was made evident to my eyes in the course of a few hours. Those who have not already dropped this volume, will, I hope, understand the events I still have to tell, forming as they do a sort of second existence lived by this creature—may I not say this creation?—in whom everything was to be so extraordinary, even his end.

When Louis returned to Blois, his uncle was eager to procure him some amusement; but the poor priest was regarded as a perfect leper in that godly-minded town. No one would have anything to say to a revolutionary who had taken the oaths. His society, therefore, consisted of a few individuals of what were then called liberal or patriotic, or constitutional opinions, on whom he would call for a rubber of whist or of boston.

At the first house where he was introduced by his uncle, Louis met a young lady, whose circumstances obliged her to remain in this circle, so contemned by those of the fashionable world, though her fortune was such as to make it probable that she might by and by marry into the highest aristocracy of the province. Mademoiselle Pauline de Villenoix was sole heiress to the wealth amassed by her grandfather, a Jew named Salomon, who, contrary to the customs of his nation, had, in his old age, married a Christian and a Catholic. He had only one son, who was brought up in his mother's faith. At his father's death young Salomon purchased what was known at that time as a *savonnette a vilain* (literally *a cake of soap for a serf*), a small estate called Villenoix, which he contrived to get registered with a baronial title, and took its name. He died unmarried, but he left a natural daughter, to whom he bequeathed the greater part of his fortune, including the lands of Villenoix. He appointed one of his uncles, Monsieur Joseph Salomon, to be the girl's guardian. The old Jew was so devoted to his ward that he seemed willing to make great sacrifices for the sake of marrying her well. But Mademoiselle de Villenoix's birth, and the cherished prejudice against Jews that prevails in the provinces, would not allow of her being received in the very exclusive circle which, rightly or wrongly, considers itself noble, notwithstanding her own large fortune and her guardian's.

Monsieur Joseph Salomon was resolved that if she could not secure a country squire, his niece should go to Paris and make choice of a husband among the peers of France, liberal or monarchical; as to happiness, that he believed he could secure her by the terms of the marriage contract.

Mademoiselle de Villenoix was now twenty. Her remarkable beauty and gifts of mind were surer guarantees of happiness than those offered by money. Her features were of the purest type of Jewish beauty; the oval lines, so noble and maidenly, have an indescribable stamp of the ideal, and seem to speak of the joys of the East, its unchangeably blue sky, the glories of its lands, and the fabulous riches of life there. She had fine eyes, shaded by deep eyelids, fringed with thick, curled lashes. Biblical innocence sat on her brow. Her complexion was of the pure whiteness of the Levite's robe. She was habitually silent and thoughtful, but her movements and gestures betrayed a quiet grace, as her speech bore witness to a woman's sweet and loving nature. She had not, indeed, the rosy freshness, the fruit-like bloom which blush on a girl's cheek during her careless years. Darker shadows, with here and there a redder vein, took the place of color, symptomatic of an energetic temper and nervous irritability, such as many men do not like to meet with in a wife, while to others they are an indication of the most sensitive chastity and passion mingled with pride.

As soon as Louis saw Mademoiselle de Villenoix, he discerned the angel within. The richest powers of his soul, and his tendency to ecstatic reverie, every faculty within him was at once concentrated in boundless love, the first love of a young man, a passion which is strong indeed in all, but which in him was raised to incalculable power by the perennial ardor of his senses, the character of his ideas, and the manner in which he lived. This passion became a gulf, into which the hapless fellow threw everything; a gulf whither the mind dare not venture, since his, flexible and firm as it was, was lost there. There all was mysterious, for everything went on in that moral world, closed to most men, whose laws were revealed to him—perhaps to his sorrow.

When an accident threw me in the way of his uncle, the good man showed me into the room which Lambert had at that time lived in. I wanted to find some vestiges of his writings, if he should have left any. There among his papers, untouched by the old man from that fine instinct of grief that characterized the aged, I found a number of letters, too illegible ever to have been sent to Mademoiselle de Villenoix. My familiarity with Lambert's writing enabled me in time to decipher the hieroglyphics of this shorthand, the result of impatience and a frenzy of passion. Carried away by his feelings, he had written without being conscious of the irregularity of words too slow to express his thoughts. He must have been compelled to copy these chaotic attempts, for the lines often ran into each other; but he was also afraid perhaps of not having sufficiently disguised his feelings, and at first, at any rate, he had probably written his love letters twice over.

It required all the fervency of my devotion to his memory, and the sort of fanaticism which comes of such a task, to enable me to divine and restore the meaning of the five letters that here follow. These documents, preserved by me with pious care, are the only material evidence of his overmastering passion. Mademoiselle de Villenoix had no doubt destroyed the real letters that she received, eloquent witnesses to the delirium she inspired.

The first of these papers, evidently a rough sketch, betrays by its style and by its length the many emendations, the heartfelt alarms, the innumerable terrors caused by a desire to please; the changes of expression and the hesitation between the whirl of ideas that beset a man as he indites his first love letter—a letter he never will forget, each line the result of a reverie, each word the subject of long cogitation, while the most unbridled passion known to man feels the necessity of the most reserved utterance, and like a giant stooping to enter a hovel, speaks humbly and low, so as not to alarm a girl's soul.

No antiquary ever handled his palimpsests with greater respect than I showed in reconstructing these mutilated documents of such joy and suffering as must always be sacred to those who have known similar joy and grief.

I.

Mademoiselle, when you have read this letter, if you ever should read it, my life will be in your hands, for I love you; and to me, the hope of being loved is life. Others, perhaps, ere now, have, in speaking of themselves, misused the words I must employ to depict the state of my soul; yet, I beseech you to believe in the truth of my expressions; though weak, they are sincere. Perhaps I ought not thus to proclaim my love. Indeed, my heart counseled me to wait in silence till my passion should touch you, that I might the better conceal it if its silent demonstrations should displease you; or till I could express it even more delicately than in words if I found favor in your eyes. However, after having listened for long to the coy fears that fill a youthful heart with alarms, I write in obedience to the instinct which drags useless lamentations from the dying.

It has needed all my courage to silence the pride of poverty, and to overleap the barriers which prejudice erects
between you and me. I have had to smother many reflections to love you in spite of your wealth; and as I write
to you, am I not in danger of the scorn which women
often reserve for profession of love, which they accept
only as one more tribute of flattery? But we cannot help
rushing with all our might towards happiness, or being
attracted to the life of love as a plant is to the light; we
must have been very unhappy before we can conquer the
torment, the anguish of those secret deliberations when
reason proves to us by a thousand arguments how barren
our yearning must be if it remains buried in our hearts,
and when hopes bid us dare everything.

I was happy when I admired you in silence; I was so
lost in the contemplation of your beautiful soul, that only
to see you left me hardly anything further to imagine.
And I should not now have dared to address you if I
had not heard that you were leaving. What misery has
that one word brought upon me! Indeed, it is my despair
that has shown me the extent of my attachment—it is
unbounded. Mademoiselle, you will never know—at
least, I hope you may never know—the anguish of dread-
ing lest you should lose the only happiness that has
dawned on you on earth, the only thing that has thrown
a gleam of light in the darkness of misery. I understood
yesterday that my life was no more in myself, but in you.
There is but one woman in the world for me, as there is
but one thought in my soul. I dare not tell you to what
a state I am reduced by my love for you. I would have
you only as a gift from yourself; I must therefore avoid
showing myself to you in all the attractiveness of dejection—for is it not often more impressive to a noble soul
than that of good fortune? There are many things I may
not tell you. Indeed, I have too lofty a notion of love to
taint it with ideas that are alien to its nature. If my soul is
worthy of yours, and my life pure, your heart will have a
sympathetic insight, and you will understand me!

It is the fate of man to offer himself to the woman who
can make him believe in happiness; but it is your prerog-
ative to reject the truest passion if it is not in harmony
with the vague voices in your heart—that I know. If my
lot, as decided by you, must be adverse to my hopes,
mademoiselle, let me appeal to the delicacy of your

maiden soul and the ingenuous compassion of a woman to burn my letter. On my knees I beseech you to forget all! Do not mock at a feeling that is wholly respectful, and that is too deeply graven on my heart ever to be effaced. Break my heart, but do not rend it! Let the expression of my first love, a pure and youthful love, be lost in your pure and youthful heart! Let it die there as a prayer rises up to die in the bosom of God!

I owe you much gratitude: I have spent delicious hours occupied in watching you, and giving myself up to the faint dreams of my life; do not crush these long but transient joys by some girlish irony. Be satisfied not to answer me. I shall know how to interpret your silence; you will see me no more. If I must be condemned to know forever what happiness means, and to be forever bereft of it; if, like a banished angel, I am to cherish the sense of celestial joys while bound forever to a world of sorrow—well, I can keep the secret of my love as well as that of my griefs.—And farewell!

Yes, I resign you to God, to whom I will pray for you, beseeching Him to grant you a happy life; for even if I am driven from your heart, into which I have crept by stealth, still I shall ever be near you. Otherwise, of what value would the sacred words be of this letter, my first and perhaps my last entreaty? If I should ever cease to think of you, to love you whether in happiness or in woe, should I not deserve my punishment?

II.

You are not going away! And I am loved! I, a poor, insignificant creature! My beloved Pauline, you do not yourself know the power of the look I believe in, the look you gave me to tell me that you had chosen me—you so young and lovely, with the world at your feet!

To enable you to understand my happiness, I should have to give you a history of my life. If you had rejected me, all was over for me. I have suffered too much. Yes, my love for you, my comforting and stupendous love, was a last effort of yearning for the happiness my soul strove to reach—a soul crushed by fruitless labor, consumed by fears that make me doubt myself, eaten into by despair which has often urged me to die. No one in the world can conceive of the terrors my fateful imagination inflicts on me. It often bears me up to the sky, and suddenly flings me to earth again from prodigious heights. Deep-seated rushes of power, or some rare and subtle instance of peculiar lucidity, assure me now and then that I am capable of great things. Then I embrace the universe in my mind, I knead, shape it, inform it, I comprehend it—or fancy that I do; then suddenly I awake—alone, sunk in blackest night, helpless and weak; I forget the light I saw but now, I find no succor; above all, there is no heart where I may take refuge.

This distress of my inner life affects my physical existence. The nature of my character gives me over to the raptures of happiness as defenseless as when the fearful light of reflection comes to analyze and demolish them. Gifted as I am with the melancholy faculty of seeing obstacles and success with equal clearness, according to the mood of the moment, I am happy or miserable by turns.

Thus, when I first met you, I felt the presence of an angelic nature, I breathed an air that was sweet to my burning breast, I heard in my soul the voice that never can be false, telling me that here was happiness; but perceiving all the barriers that divided us, I understood the vastness of their pettiness, and these difficulties terrified me more than the prospect of happiness could delight me. At once I felt the awful reaction which casts my expansive soul back on itself; the smile you had brought to my lips suddenly turned to a bitter grimace, and I could only strive to keep calm, while my soul was boiling with the turmoil of contradictory emotions. In short, I experienced that gnawing pang to which twenty-three years of suppressed sighs and betrayed affections have not inured me.

Well, Pauline, the look by which you promised that I should be happy suddenly warmed my vitality, and turned all my sorrows into joy. Now, I could wish that I had suffered more. My love is suddenly full-grown. My soul was a wide territory that lacked the blessing of sunshine, and your eyes have shed light on it. Beloved providence! you will be all in all to me, orphan as I am, without a relation but my uncle. You will be my whole family, as you are my whole wealth, nay, the whole world to me. Have you not bestowed on me every gladness man can desire in that chaste—lavish—timid glance?

You have given me incredible self-confidence and

audacity. I can dare all things now. I came back to Blois
in deep dejection. Five years of study in the heart of
Paris had made me look on the world as a prison. I had
conceived of vast schemes, and dared not speak of them.
Fame seemed to me a prize for charlatans, to which a
really noble spirit should not stoop. Thus, my ideas
could only make their way by the assistance of a man
bold enough to mount the platform of the press, and to
harangue loudly the simpletons he scorns. This kind of
courage I have not. I plowed my way on, crushed by the
verdict of the crowd, in despair at never making it hear
me. I was at once too humble and too lofty! I swallowed
my thoughts as other men swallow humiliations. I had
even come to despise knowledge, blaming it for yielding
no real happiness.

But since yesterday I am wholly changed. For your
sake I now covet every palm of glory, every triumph of
success. When I lay my head on your knees, I could wish
to attract to you the eyes of the whole world, just as I
long to concentrate in my love every idea, every power
that is in me. The most splendid celebrity is a possession
that genius alone can create. Well, I can, at my will, make
for you a bed of laurels. And if the silent ovation paid to
science is not all you desire, I have within me the sword
of the Word; I could run in the path of honor and ambition where others only crawl.

Command me, Pauline; I will be whatever you will.
My iron will can do anything—I am loved! Armed with
that thought, ought not a man to sweep everything
before him? The man who wants all can do all. If you
are the prize of success, I enter the lists tomorrow. To
win such a look as that you bestowed on me, I would
leap the deepest abyss. Through you I understand the
fabulous achievements of chivalry and the most fantastic tales of the *Arabian Nights*. I can believe now in the
most fantastic excesses of love, and in the success of a
prisoner's wildest attempt to recover his liberty. You have
aroused the thousand virtues that lay dormant within
me—patience, resignation, all the powers of my heart,
all the strength of my soul. I live by you and—heavenly
thought!—for you. Everything now has a meaning for
me in life. I understand everything, even the vanities of
wealth.

I find myself shedding all the pearls of the Indies at

your feet; I fancy you reclining either on the rarest flowers, or on the softest tissues, and all the splendor of the
world seems hardly worthy of you, for whom I would
I could command the harmony and the light that are
given out by the harps of seraphs and the stars of heaven!
Alas! a poor, studious poet, I offer you in words treasures
I cannot bestow; I can only give you my heart, in which
you reign forever. I have nothing else. But are there no
treasures in eternal gratitude, in a smile whose expressions will perpetually vary with perennial happiness,
under the constant eagerness of my devotion to guess the
wishes of your loving soul? Has not one celestial glance
given us assurance of always understanding each other?

I have a prayer now to be said to God every night—a
prayer full of you: "Let my Pauline be happy!" And will
you fill all my days as you now fill my heart?

Farewell, I can but trust you to God alone!

III.

Pauline! tell me if I can in any way have displeased you
yesterday? Throw off the pride of heart which inflicts on
me the secret tortures that can be caused by one we love.
Scold me if you will! Since yesterday, a vague, unutterable dread of having offended you pours grief on the life
of feeling which you had made so sweet and so rich. The
lightest veil that comes between two souls sometimes
grows to be a brazen wall. There are no venial crimes in
love! If you have the very spirit of that noble sentiment,
you must feel all its pangs, and we must be unceasingly
careful not to fret each other by some heedless word.

No doubt, my beloved treasure, if there is any fault, it
is in me. I cannot pride myself in the belief that I understand a woman's heart, in all the expansion of its tenderness, all the grace of its devotedness; but I will always
endeavor to appreciate the value of what you vouchsafe
to show me of the secrets of yours.

Speak to me! Answer me soon! The melancholy into
which we are thrown by the idea of a wrong done is
frightful; it casts a shroud over life, and doubts on everything.

I spent this morning sitting on the bank by the sunken
road, gazing at the turrets of Villenoix, not daring to go
to our hedge. If you could imagine all I saw in my soul!
What gloomy visions passed before me under the gray

sky, whose cold sheen added to my dreary mood! I had dark presentiments! I was terrified lest I should fail to make you happy.

I must tell you everything, my dear Pauline. There are moments when the spirit of vitality seems to abandon me. I feel bereft of all strength. Everything is a burden to me; every fiber of my body is inert, every sense is flaccid, my sight grows dim, my tongue is paralyzed, my imagination is extinct, desire is dead—nothing survives but my mere human vitality. At such times, though you were in all the splendor of your beauty, though you should lavish on me your subtlest smiles and tenderest words, an evil influence would blind me, and distort the most ravishing melody into discordant sounds. At those times—as I believe—some argumentative demon stands before me, showing me the void beneath the most real possessions. This pitiless demon mows down every flower, and mocks at the sweetest feelings, saying: "Well—and then?" He mars the fairest work by showing me its skeleton, and reveals the mechanism of things while hiding the beautiful results.

At those terrible moments, when the evil spirit takes possession of me, when the divine light is darkened in my soul without my knowing the cause, I sit in grief and anguish, I wish myself deaf and dumb, I long for death to give me rest. These hours of doubt and uneasiness are perhaps inevitable; at any rate, they teach me not to be proud after the flights which have borne me to the skies where I have gathered a full harvest of thoughts; for it is always after some long excursion in the vast fields of the intellect, and after the most luminous speculations, that I tumble, broken and weary, into this limbo. At such a moment, my angel, a wife would double my love for her—at any rate, she might. If she were capricious, ailing, or depressed, she would need the comforting overflow of ingenious affection, and I should not have a glance to bestow on her. It is my shame, Pauline, to have to tell you that at times I could weep with you, but that nothing could make me smile.

A woman can always conceal her troubles; for her child, or for the man she loves, she can laugh in the midst of suffering. And could not I, for you, Pauline, imitate the exquisite reserve of a woman? Since yesterday I have doubted my own power. If I could displease you once, if I failed once to understand you, I dread lest I should often be carried out of our happy circle by my evil demon. Supposing I were to have many of those dreadful moods, or that my unbounded love could not make up for the dark hours of my life—that I were doomed to remain such as I am?—Fatal doubts!

Power is indeed a fatal possession if what I feel within me is power. Pauline, go! Leave me, desert me! Sooner would I endure every ill in life than endure the misery of knowing that you were unhappy through me.

But, perhaps, the demon has had such empire over me only because I have had no gentle, white hands about me to drive him off. No woman has ever shed on me the balm of her affection; and I know not whether, if love should wave his pinions over my head in these moments of exhaustion, new strength might not be given to my spirit. This terrible melancholy is perhaps a result of my isolation, one of the torments of a lonely soul which pays for its hidden treasures with groans and unknown suffering. Those who enjoy little shall suffer little; immense happiness entails unutterable anguish!

How terrible a doom! If it be so, must we not shudder for ourselves, we who are superhumanly happy? If nature sells us everything at its true value, into what pit are we not fated to fall? Ah! the most fortunate lovers are those who die together in the midst of their youth and love! How sad it all is! Does my soul foresee evil in the future? I examine myself, wondering whether there is anything in me that can cause you a moment's anxiety. I love you too selfishly perhaps? I shall be laying on your beloved head a burden heavy out of all proportion to the joy my love can bring to your heart. If there dwells in me some inexorable power which I must obey—if I am compelled to curse when you pray, if some dark thought coerces me when I would fain kneel at your feet and play as a child, will you not be jealous of that wayward and tricky spirit?

You understand, dearest heart, that what I dread is not being wholly yours; that I would gladly forego all the scepters and the palms of the world to enshrine you in one eternal thought, to see a perfect life and an exquisite poem in our rapturous love; to throw my soul into it, drown my powers, and wring from each hour the joys it has to give!

Ah, my memories of love are crowding back upon me,

the clouds of despair will lift. Farewell. I leave you now
to be more entirely yours. My beloved soul, I look for a
line, a word that may restore my peace of mind. Let me
know whether I really grieved my Pauline, or whether
some uncertain expression of her countenance misled
me. I could not bear to have to reproach myself after a
whole life of happiness, forever having met you without
a smile of love, a honeyed word. To grieve the woman
I love—Pauline, I should count it a crime. Tell me the
truth, do not put me off with some magnanimous sub-
terfuge, but forgive me without cruelty.

## FRAGMENT

Is so perfect an attachment happiness? Yes, for years of
suffering would not pay for an hour of love.

Yesterday, your sadness, as I suppose, passed into my
soul as swiftly as a shadow falls. Were you sad or suffering? I was wretched. Whence came my distress? Write
to me at once. Why did I not know it? We are not yet
completely one in mind. At two leagues' distance or at a
thousand I ought to feel your pain and sorrows. I shall
not believe that I love you till my life is so bound up with
yours that our life is one, till our hearts, our thoughts
are one. I must be where you are, see what you feel, feel
what you feel, be with you in thought. Did not I know,
at once, that your carriage had been overthrown and you
were bruised? But on that day I had been with you, I had
never left you, I could see you. When my uncle asked me
what made me turn so pale, I answered at once, "Mademoiselle de Villenoix had has a fall."

Why, then, yesterday, did I fail to read your soul? Did
you wish to hide the cause of your grief? However, I
fancied I could feel that you were arguing in my favor,
though in vain, with that dreadful Salomon, who freezes
my blood. That man is not of our heaven.

Why do you insist that our happiness, which has no
resemblance to that of other people, should conform
to the laws of the world? And yet I delight too much in
your bashfulness, your religion, your superstitions, not
to obey your lightest whim. What you do must be right;
nothing can be purer than your mind, as nothing is love-
lier than your face, which reflects your divine soul.

I shall wait for a letter before going along the lanes

to meet the sweet hour you grant me. Oh! if you could know how the sight of those turrets makes my heart throb when I see them edged with light by the moon, our only confidante.

## IV.

Farewell to glory, farewell to the future, to the life I had dreamed of! Now, my well-beloved, my glory is that I am yours, and worthy of you; my future lies entirely in the hope of seeing you; and is not my life summed up in sitting at your feet, in lying under your eyes, in drawing deep breaths in the heaven you have created for me? All my powers, all my thoughts must be yours, since you could speak those thrilling words, "Your sufferings must be mine!" Should I not be stealing some joys from love, some moments from happiness, some experiences from your divine spirit, if I gave my hours to study—ideas to the world and poems to the poets? Nay, nay, my very life, I will treasure everything for you; I will bring to you every flower of my soul. Is there anything fine enough, splendid enough, in all the resources of the world, or of intellect, to do honor to a heart so rich, so pure as yours—the heart to which I dare now and again to unite my own? Yes, now and again, I dare believe that I can love as much as you do.

And yet, no; you are the angel-woman; there will always be a greater charm in the expression of your feelings, more harmony in your voice, more grace in your smile, more purity in your looks than in mine. Let me feel that you are the creature of a higher sphere than that I live in; it will be your pride to have descended from it; mine, that I should have deserved you; and you will not perhaps have fallen too far by coming down to me in my poverty and misery. Nay, if a woman's most glorious refuge is in a heart that is wholly her own, you will always reign supreme in mine. Not a thought, not a deed, shall ever pollute this heart, this glorious sanctuary, so long as you vouchsafe to dwell in it—and will you not dwell in it forever? Did you not enchant me by the words, "Now and forever?" *Nunc et semper!* And I have written these words of our ritual below your portrait—words worthy of you, as they are of God. He is *nunc et semper,* as my love is.

Never, no, never, can I exhaust that which is immense,

infinite, unbounded—and such is the feeling I have for you; I have imagined its immeasurable extent, as we measure space by the dimensions of one of its parts. I have had ineffable joys, whole hours filled with delicious meditation, as I have recalled a single gesture or the tone of a word of yours. Thus there will be memories of which the magnitude will overpower me, if the reminiscence of a sweet and friendly interview is enough to make me shed tears of joy, to move and thrill my soul, and to be an inexhaustible wellspring of gladness. Love is the life of angels!

I can never, I believe, exhaust my joy in seeing you. This rapture, the least fervid of any, though it never can last long enough, has made me apprehend the eternal contemplation in which seraphs and spirits abide in the presence of God; nothing can be more natural, if from His essence there emanates a light as fruitful of new emotions as that of your eyes is, of your imposing brow, and your beautiful countenance—the image of your soul. Then, the soul, our second self, whose pure form can never perish, makes our love immortal. I would there were some other language than that I use to express to you the ever-new ecstasy of my love; but since there is one of our own creating, since our looks are living speech, must we not meet face to face to read in each other's eyes those questions and answers from the heart, that are so living, so penetrating, that one evening you could say to me, "Be silent!" when I was not speaking. Do you remember it, dear life?

When I am away from you in the darkness of absence, am I not reduced to use human words, too feeble to express heavenly feelings? But words at any rate represent the marks these feelings leave in my soul, just as the word *God* imperfectly sums up the notions we form of that mysterious First Cause. But, in spite of the subtleties and infinite variety of language, I have no words that can express to you the exquisite union by which my life is merged into yours whenever I think of you.

And with what word can I conclude when I cease writing to you, and yet do not part from you? What can *farewell* mean, unless in death? But is death a farewell? Would not my spirit be then more closely one with yours? Ah! my first and last thought; formerly I offered you my heart and life on my knees; now what fresh blossoms of feelings can I discover in my soul that I have not already given you? It would be a gift of a part of what is wholly yours.

Are you my future? How deeply I regret the past! I would I could have back all the years that are ours no more, and give them to you to reign over, as you do over my present life. What indeed was that time when I knew you not? It would be a void but that I was so wretched.

## FRAGMENT

Beloved angel, how delightful last evening was! How full of riches your dear heart is! And is your love endless, like mine? Each word brought me fresh joy, and each look made it deeper. The placid expression of your countenance gave our thoughts a limitless horizon. It was all as infinite as the sky, and as bland as its blue. The refinement of your adored features repeated itself by some inexplicable magic in your pretty movements and your least gestures. I knew that you were all graciousness, all love, but I did not know how variously graceful you could be. Everything combined to urge me to tender solicitation, to make me ask the first kiss that a woman always refuses, no doubt that it may be snatched from her. You, dear soul of my life, will never guess beforehand what you may grant to my love, and will yield perhaps without knowing it! You are utterly true, and obey your heart alone.

The sweet tones of your voice blended with the tender harmonies that filled the quiet air, the cloudless sky. Not a bird piped, not a breeze whispered—solitude, you, and I. The motionless leaves did not quiver in the beautiful sunset hues which are both light and shadow. You felt that heavenly poetry—you who experienced so many various emotions, and who so often raised your eyes to heaven to avoid answering me. You who are proud and saucy, humble and masterful, who give yourself to me so completely in spirit and in thought, and evade the most bashful caress. Dear witcheries of the heart! They ring in my ears; they sound and play there still. Sweet words but half spoken, like a child's speech, neither promise nor confession, but allowing love to cherish its fairest hopes without fear or torment! How pure a memory for life! What a free blossoming of all the flowers that spring from the soul, which a mere trifle can blight, but which, at that moment, everything warmed and expanded.

And it will always be so, will it not, my beloved? As I recall, this morning, the fresh and living delights revealed to me in that hour, I am conscious of a joy which makes me conceive of true love as an ocean of everlasting and ever-new experiences, into which we may plunge with increasing delight. Every day, every word, every kiss, every glance, must increase it by its tribute of past happiness. Hearts that are large enough never to forget must live every moment in their past joys as much as in those promised by the future. This was my dream of old, and now it is no longer a dream! Have I not met on this earth with an angel who had made me know all its happiness, as a reward, perhaps, for having endured all its torments? Angel of heaven, I salute thee with a kiss.

I shall send you this hymn of thanksgiving from my heart, I owe it to you; but it can hardly express my gratitude or the morning worship my heart offers up day by day to her who epitomized the whole gospel of the heart in this divine word: "Believe."


V.

What! no further difficulties, dearest heart! We shall be free to belong to each other every day, every hour, every minute, and forever! We may be as happy for all the days of our life as we now are by stealth, at rare intervals! Our pure, deep feelings will assume the expression of the thousand fond acts I have dreamed of. For me your little foot will be bared, you will be wholly mine! Such happiness kills me; it is too much for me. My head is too weak, it will burst with the vehemence of my ideas. I cry and I laugh—I am possessed! Every joy is an arrow of flame; it pierces and burns me. In fancy you rise before my eyes, ravished and dazzled by numberless and capricious images of delight.

In short, our whole future life is before me—its torrents, its still places, its joys; it seethes, it flows on, it lies sleeping; then again it awakes fresh and young. I see myself and you side by side, walking with equal pace, living in the same thought; each dwelling in each other's heart, understanding each other, responding to each other as an echo catches and repeats a sound across wide distances.

Can life be long when it is thus consumed hour by hour? Shall we not die in a first embrace? What if our souls have already met in that sweet evening kiss which almost overpowered us—a feeling kiss, but the crown of my hopes, the ineffectual expression of all the prayers I breathe while we are apart, hidden in my soul like remorse?

I, who would creep back and hide in the hedge only to hear your footsteps as you went homewards—I may henceforth admire you at my leisure, see you busy, moving, smiling, prattling! An endless joy! You cannot imagine all the gladness it is to me to see you going and coming; only a man can know that deep delight. Your least movement gives me greater pleasure than a mother even can feel as she sees her child asleep or at play. I love you with every kind of love in one. The grace of your least gesture is always new to me. I fancy I could spend whole nights breathing your breath; I would I could steal into every detail of your life, be the very substance of your thoughts—be your very self.

Well, we shall, at any rate, never part again! No human alloy shall ever disturb our love, infinite in its phases and as pure as all things are which are One—our love, vast as the sea, vast as the sky! You are mine! all mine! I may look into the depths of your eyes to read the sweet soul that alternately hides and shines there, to anticipate your wishes.

My best-beloved, listen to some things I have never yet dared to tell you, but which I may confess to you now. I felt a certain bashfulness of soul which hindered the full expression of my feelings, so I strove to shroud them under the garbs of thoughts. But now I long to lay my heart bare before you, to tell you of the ardor of my dreams, to reveal the boiling demands of my senses, excited, no doubt, by the solitude in which I have lived, perpetually fired by conceptions of happiness, and aroused by you, so fair in form, so attractive in manner. How can I express to you my thirst for the unknown rapture of possessing an adored wife, a rapture to which the union of two souls by love must give frenzied intensity. Yes, my Pauline, I have sat for hours in a sort of stupor caused by the violence of my passionate yearning, lost in the dream of a caress as though in a bottomless abyss. At such moments my whole vitality, my thoughts and powers, are merged and united in what I must call desire, for lack of a word to express that nameless delirium.

And I may confess to you now that one day, when I would not take your hand when you offered it so sweetly—an act of melancholy prudence that made you doubt my love—I was in one of those fits of madness when a man could commit a murder to possess a woman. Yes, if I had felt the exquisite pressure you offered me as vividly as I heard your voice in my heart, I know not to what lengths my passion might not have carried me. But I can be silent, and suffer a great deal. Why speak of this anguish when my visions are to become realities? It will be in my power now to make life one long love-making!

Dearest love, there is a certain effect of light on your black hair which could rivet me for hours, my eyes full of tears, as I gazed at your sweet person, were it not that you turn away and say, "For shame; you make me quite shy!"

Tomorrow, then, our love is to be made known! Oh, Pauline! the eyes of others, the curiosity of strangers, weigh on my soul. Let us go to Villenoix, and stay there far from every one. I should like no creature in human form to intrude into the sanctuary where you are to be mine; I could even wish that, when we are dead, it should cease to exist—should be destroyed. Yes, I would fain hide from all nature a happiness which we alone can understand, alone can feel, which is so stupendous that I throw myself into it only to die—it is a gulf!

Do not be alarmed by the tears that have wetted this page; they are tears of joy. My only blessing, we need never part again!

In 1823 I traveled from Paris to Touraine by *diligence*. At Mer we took up a passenger for Blois. As the guard put him into that part of the coach where I had my seat, he said jestingly:

"You will not be crowded, Monsieur Lefebvre!"—I was, in fact, alone.

On hearing this name, and seeing a white-haired old man, who looked eighty at least, I naturally thought of Lambert's uncle. After a few ingenious questions, I discovered that I was not mistaken. The good man had been looking after his vintage at Mer, and was returning to Blois. I then

asked for some news of my old "chum." At the first word,
the old priest's face, as grave and stern already as that of
a soldier who has gone through many hardships, became
more sad and dark; the lines on his forehead were slightly
knit, he set his lips, and said, with a suspicious glance:

"Then you have never seen him since you left the College?"

"Indeed, I have not," said I. "But we are equally to
blame for our forgetfulness. Young men, as you know, lead
such an adventurous and storm-tossed life when they leave
their school-forms, that it is only by meeting that they
can be sure of an enduring affection. However, a reminiscence of youth sometimes comes as a reminder, and it is
impossible to forget entirely, especially when two lads have
been such friends as we were. We went by the name of the
Poet-and-Pythagoras."

I told him my name; when he heard it, the worthy man
grew gloomier than ever.

"Then you have not heard his story?" said he. "My poor
nephew was to be married to the richest heiress in Blois;
but the day before his wedding he went mad."

"Lambert! Mad!" cried I in dismay. "But from what
cause? He had the finest memory, the most strongly constituted brain, the soundest judgment, I ever met with. Really
a great genius—with too great a passion for mysticism perhaps; but the kindest heart in the world. Something most
extraordinary must have happened?"

"I see you knew him well," said the priest.

From Mer, till we reached Blois, we talked only of my
poor friend, with long digressions, by which I learned the
facts I have already related in the order of their interest. I
confessed to his uncle the character of our studies and of
his nephew's predominant ideas; then the old man told me
of the events that had come into Lambert's life since our
parting. From Monsieur Lefebvre's account, Lambert had
betrayed some symptoms of madness before his marriage;
but they were such as are common to men who love passionately, and seemed to me less startling when I knew how
vehement his love had been and when I saw Mademoiselle
de Villenoix. In the country, where ideas are scarce, a man

overflowing with original thought and devoted to a system, as Louis was, might well be regarded as eccentric, to say the least. His language would, no doubt, seem the stranger because he so rarely spoke. He would say, "That man does not dwell in heaven," where anyone else would have said, "We are not made on the same pattern." Every clever man has his own quirks of speech. The broader his genius, the more conspicuous are the singularities which constitute the various degrees of eccentricity. In the country an eccentric man is at once set down as half mad.

Hence Monsieur Lefebvre's first sentences left me doubtful of my schoolmate's insanity. I listened to the old man, but I criticized his statements.

The most serious symptom had supervened a day or two before the marriage. Louis had had some well-marked attacks of catalepsy. He had once remained motionless for fifty-nine hours, his eyes staring, neither speaking nor eating; a purely nervous affection, to which persons under the influence of violent passion are liable; a rare malady, but perfectly well known to the medical faculty. What was really extraordinary was that Louis should not have had several previous attacks, since his habits of rapt thought and the character of his mind would predispose him to them. But his temperament, physical and mental, was so admirably balanced, that it had no doubt been able to resist the demands on his strength. The excitement to which he had been wound up by the anticipation of acute physical enjoyment, enhanced by a chaste life and a highly-strung soul, had no doubt led to these attacks, of which the results are as little known as the cause.

The letters that have by chance escaped destruction show very plainly a transition from pure idealism to the most intense sensualism.

Time was when Lambert and I had admired this phenomenon of the human mind, in which he saw the fortuitous separation of our two natures, and the signs of a total removal of the inner man, using its unknown faculties under the operation of an unknown cause. This disorder, a mystery as deep as that of sleep, was connected with the scheme of evidence which Lambert had set forth in his

*Treatise on the Will.* And when Monsieur Lefebvre spoke to me of Louis' first attack, I suddenly remembered a conversation we had had on the subject after reading a medical book.

"Deep meditation and rapt ecstasy are perhaps the undeveloped germs of catalepsy," he said in conclusion.

On the occasion when he so concisely formulated this idea, he had been trying to link mental phenomena together by a series of results, following the processes of the intellect step by step, from their beginnings as those simple, purely animal impulses of instinct, which are all-sufficient to many human beings, particularly to those men whose energies are wholly spent in mere mechanical labor; then, going on to the aggregation of ideas and rising to comparison, reflection, meditation, and finally ecstasy and catalepsy. Lambert, of course, in the artlessness of youth, imagined that he had laid down the lines of a great work when he thus built up a scale of the various degrees of man's mental powers.

I remember that, by one of those chances which seems like predestination, we got hold of a great Martyrology, in which the most curious narratives are given of the total abeyance of physical life which a man can attain to under the paroxysms of the inner life. By reflecting on the effects of fanaticism, Lambert was led to believe that the collected ideas to which we give the name of feelings may very possibly be the material outcome of some fluid which is generated in all men, more or less abundantly, according to the way in which their organs absorb, from the medium in which they live, the elementary atoms that produce it. We went crazy over catalepsy; and with the eagerness that boys throw into every pursuit, we endeavored to endure pain by thinking of something else. We exhausted ourselves by making experiments not unlike those of the epileptic fanatics of the last century, a religious mania which will some day be of service to the science of humanity. I would stand on Lambert's chest, remaining there for several minutes without giving him the slightest pain; but notwithstanding these crazy attempts, we did not achieve an attack of catalepsy.

This digression seemed necessary to account for my

first doubts, which were, however, completely dispelled by Monsieur Lefebvre.

"When this attack had passed off," said he, "my nephew sank into a state of extreme terror, a dejection that nothing could overcome. He thought himself unfit for marriage. I watched him with the care of a mother for her child, and found him preparing to perform on himself the operation to which Origen believed he owed his talents. I at once carried him off to Paris, and placed him under the care of Monsieur Esquirol. All through our journey Louis sat sunk in almost unbroken torpor, and did not recognize me. The Paris physicians pronounced him incurable, and unanimously advised his being left in perfect solitude, with nothing to break the silence that was needful for his very improbable recovery, and that he should live always in a cool room with a subdued light.—Mademoiselle de Villenoix, whom I had been careful not to apprise of Louis' state," he went on, blinking his eyes, "but who was supposed to have broken off the match, went to Paris and heard what the doctors had pronounced. She immediately begged to see my nephew, who hardly recognized her; then, like the noble soul she is, she insisted on devoting herself to giving him such care as might tend to his recovery. She would have been obliged to do so if he had been her husband, she said, and could she do less for him as her lover?

"She removed Louis to Villenoix, where they have been living for two years."

So, instead of continuing my journey, I stopped at Blois to go to see Louis. Good Monsieur Lefebvre would not hear of my lodging anywhere but at his house, where he showed me his nephew's room with the books and all else that had belonged to him. At every turn the old man could not suppress some mournful exclamation, showing what hopes Louis' precocious genius had raised, and the terrible grief into which this irreparable ruin had plunged him.

"That young fellow knew everything, my dear sir!" said he, laying on the table a volume containing Spinoza's works. "How could so well organized a brain go astray?"

"Indeed, monsieur," said I, "was it not perhaps the result of its being so highly organized? If he really is a victim to the malady as yet unstudied in all its aspects, which is known simply as madness, I am inclined to attribute it to his passion. His studies and his mode of life had strung his powers and faculties to a degree of energy beyond which the least further strain was too much for nature; Love was enough to crack them, or to raise them to a new form of expression which we are maligning perhaps, by ticketing it without due knowledge. In fact, he may perhaps have regarded the joys of marriage as an obstacle to the perfection of his inner man and his flight towards spiritual spheres."

"My dear sir," said the old man, after listening to me with attention, "your reasoning is, no doubt, very sound; but even if I could follow it, would this melancholy logic comfort me for the loss of my nephew?"

Lambert's uncle was one of those men who live only by their affections.

I went to Villenoix on the following day. The kind old man accompanied me to the gates of Blois. When we were out on the road to Villenoix, he stopped me and said:

"As you may suppose, I do not go there. But do not forget what I have said; and in Mademoiselle de Villenoix's presence affect not to perceive that Louis is mad."

He remained standing on the spot where I left him, watching me till I was out of sight.

I made my way to the chateau of Villenoix, not without deep agitation. My thoughts were many at each step on this road, which Louis had so often trodden with a heart full of hopes, a soul spurred on by the myriad darts of love. The shrubs, the trees, the turns of the winding road where little gullies broke the banks on each side, were to me full of strange interest. I tried to enter into the impressions and thoughts of my unhappy friend. Those evening meetings on the edge of the combe, where his lady-love had been wont to find him, had, no doubt, initiated Mademoiselle de Villenoix into the secrets of that vast and lofty spirit, as I had learned them all some years before.

But the thing that most occupied my mind, and gave to my pilgrimage the interest of intense curiosity, in addition to the almost pious feelings that led me onwards, was that glorious faith of Mademoiselle de Villenoix's which

the good priest had told me of. Had she in the course of
time been infected with her lover's madness, or had she so
completely entered into his soul that she could understand
all its thoughts, even the most perplexed? I lost myself
in the wonderful problem of feeling, passing the highest
inspirations of passion and the most beautiful instances of
self-sacrifice. That one should die for the other is an almost
vulgar form of devotion. To live faithful to one love is a
form of heroism that immortalized Mademoiselle Dupuis.
When the great Napoleon and Lord Byron could find suc-
cessors in the hearts of women they had loved, we may well
admire Bolingbroke's widow; but Mademoiselle Dupuis
could feed on the memories of many years of happiness,
whereas Mademoiselle de Villenoix, having known nothing
of love but its first excitement, seemed to me to typify love
in its highest expression. If she were herself almost crazy, it
was splendid; but if she had understood and entered into
his madness, she combined with the beauty of a noble heart
a crowning effort of passion worthy to be studied and honored.

When I saw the tall turrets of the chateau, remembering
how often poor Lambert must have thrilled at the sight of
them, my heart beat anxiously. As I recalled the events of
our boyhood, I was almost a sharer in his present life and
situation. At last I reached a wide, deserted courtyard, and
I went into the hall of the house without meeting a soul.
There the sound of my steps brought out an old woman,
to whom I gave a letter written to Mademoiselle de Villenoix by Monsieur Lefebvre. In a few minutes this woman
returned to bid me enter, and led me to a low room, floored
with black-and-white marble; the Venetian shutters were
closed, and at the end of the room I dimly saw Louis Lambert.

"Be seated, monsieur," said a gentle voice that went to
my heart.

Mademoiselle de Villenoix was at my side before I was
aware of her presence, and noiselessly brought me a chair,
which at first I would not accept. It was so dark that at first
I saw Mademoiselle de Villenoix and Lambert only as two
black masses perceived against the gloomy background. I

presently sat down under the influence of the feeling that comes over us, almost in spite of ourselves, under the obscure vault of a church. My eyes, full of the bright sunshine, accustomed themselves gradually to this artificial night.

"Monsieur is your old school-friend," she said to Louis.

He made no reply. At last I could see him, and it was one of those spectacles that are stamped on the memory forever. He was standing, his elbows resting on the cornice of the low wainscot, which threw his body forward, so that it seemed bowed under the weight of his bent head. His hair was as long as a woman's, falling over his shoulders and hanging about his face, giving him a resemblance to the busts of the great men of the time of Louis XIV. His face was perfectly white. He constantly rubbed one leg against the other, with a mechanical action that nothing could have checked, and the incessant friction of the bones made a doleful sound. Near him was a bed of moss on boards.

"He very rarely lies down," said Mademoiselle de Villenoix; "but whenever he does, he sleeps for several days."

Louis stood, as I beheld him, day and night with a fixed gaze, never winking his eyelids as we do. Having asked Mademoiselle de Villenoix whether a little more light would hurt our friend, on her reply I opened the shutters a little way, and could see the expression of Lambert's countenance. Alas! he was wrinkled, white-headed, his eyes dull and lifeless as those of the blind. His features seemed all drawn upwards to the top of his head. I made several attempts to talk to him, but he did not hear me. He was a wreck snatched from the grave, a conquest of life from death—or of death from life!

I stayed for about an hour, sunk in unaccountable dreams, and lost in painful thought. I listened to Mademoiselle de Villenoix, who told me every detail of this life—that of a child in arms.

Suddenly Louis ceased rubbing his legs together, and said slowly:

"The angels are white."

I cannot express the effect produced upon me by this utterance, by the sound of the voice I had loved, whose

accents, so painfully expected, had seemed to be lost forever. My eyes filled with tears in spite of every effort. An
involuntary instinct warned me, making me doubt whether
Louis had really lost his reason. I was indeed well assured
that he neither saw nor heard me; but the sweetness of his
tone, which seemed to reveal heavenly happiness, gave his
speech an amazing effect. These words, the incomplete revelation of an unknown world, rang in our souls like some
glorious distant bells in the depth of a dark night. I was
no longer surprised that Mademoiselle de Villenoix considered Lambert to be perfectly sane. The life of the soul had
perhaps subdued that of the body. His faithful companion
had, no doubt—as I had at that moment—intuitions of that
melodious and beautiful existence to which we give the
name of Heaven in its highest meaning.

This woman, this angel, always was with him, seated at
her embroidery frame; and each time she drew the needle
out she gazed at Lambert with sad and tender feeling.
Unable to endure this terrible sight—for I could not, like
Mademoiselle de Villenoix, read all his secrets—I went out,
and she came with me to walk for a few minutes and talk of
herself and of Lambert.

"Louis must, no doubt, appear to be mad," said she. "But
he is not, if the term mad ought only to be used in speaking
of those whose brain is for some unknown cause diseased,
and who can show no reason in their actions. Everything
in my husband is perfectly balanced. Though he did not
actively recognize you, it is not that he did not see you.
He has succeeded in detaching himself from his body, and
discerns us under some other aspect—what that is, I know
not. When he speaks, he utters wondrous things. Only it
often happens that he concludes in speech an idea that had
its beginning in his mind; or he may begin a sentence and
finish it in thought. To other men he seems insane; to me,
living as I do in his mind, his ideas are quite lucid. I follow
the road his spirit travels; and though I do not know every
turning, I can reach the goal with him.

"Which of us has not often known what it is to think of
some futile thing and be led on to some serious reflection
through the ideas or memories it brings in its train? Not

unfrequently, after speaking about some trifle, the simple starting point of a rapid train of reflections, a thinker may forget or be silent as to the abstract connection of ideas leading to his conclusion, and speak again only to utter the last link in the chain of his meditations.

"Inferior minds, to whom this swift mental vision is a thing unknown, who are ignorant of the spirit's inner workings, laugh at the dreamer; and if he is subject to this kind of obliviousness, regard him as a madman. Louis is always in this state; he soars perpetually through the spaces of thought, traversing them with the swiftness of a swallow; I can follow him in his flight. This is the whole history of his madness. Some day, perhaps, Louis will come back to the life in which we vegetate; but if he breathes the air of heaven before the time when we may be permitted to do so, why should we desire to have him down among us? I am content to hear his heart beat, and all my happiness is to be with him. Is he not wholly mine? In three years, twice at intervals he was himself for a few days; once in Switzerland, where we went, and once in an island off the wilds of Brittany, where we took some sea-baths. I have twice been very happy! I can live on memory."

"But do you write down the things he says?" I asked.

"Why should I?" said she.

I was silent; human knowledge was indeed as nothing in this woman's eyes.

"At those times, when he talked a little," she added, "I think I have recorded some of his phrases, but I left it off; I did not understand him then."

I asked her for them by a look; she understood me. This is what I have been able to preserve from oblivion.

I.

Everything here on earth is produced by an ethereal substance which is the common element of various phenomena, known inaccurately as electricity, heat, light, the galvanic fluid, the magnetic fluid, and so forth. The universal distribution of this substance, under various forms, constitutes what is commonly known as Matter.

II.

The brain is the alembic to which the Animal conveys what each of its organizations, in proportion to the strength of that vessel, can absorb of that Substance, which returns it transformed into Will.

The Will is a fluid inherent in every creature endowed with motion. Hence the innumerable forms assumed by the Animal, the results of its combinations with that Substance. The Animal's instincts are the product of the coercion of the environment in which it develops. Hence its variety.

III.

In Man the Will becomes a power peculiar to him, and exceeding in intensity that of any other species.

IV.

By constant assimilation, the Will depends on the Substance it meets with again and again in all its transmutations, pervading them by Thought, which is a product peculiar to the human Will, in combination with the modifications of that Substance.

V.

The innumerable forms assumed by Thought are the result of the greater or less perfection of the human mechanism.

VI.

The Will acts through organs commonly called the five senses, which, in fact, are but one—the faculty of Sight. Feeling and tasting, hearing and smelling, are Sight modified to the transformations of the Substance which Man can absorb in two conditions: untransformed and transformed.

VII.

Everything of which the form comes within the cognizance of the one sense of Sight may be reduced to certain simple bodies of which the elements exist in the air, the light, or in the elements of air and light. Sound is a condition of the air; colors are all conditions of light; every smell is a combination of air and light; hence the four aspects of Matter with regard to Man—sound,

color, smell, and shape—have the same origin, for the
day is not far off when the relationship of the phenomena of air and light will be made clear.

Thought, which is allied to Light, is expressed in
words which depend on sound. To man, then, everything
is derived from the Substance, whose transformations
vary only through Number—a certain quantitative dis-
similarity, the proportions resulting in the individuals or
objects of what are classed as Kingdoms.

## VIII.

When the Substance is absorbed in sufficient number (or
quantity) it makes of man an immensely powerful mechanism, in direct communication with the very element
of the Substance, and acting on organic nature in the
same way as a large stream when it absorbs the smaller
brooks. Volition sets this force in motion independently
of the Mind. By its concentration it acquires some of the
qualities of the Substance, such as the swiftness of light,
the penetrating power of electricity, and the faculty of
saturating a body; to which must be added that it appre-
hends what it can do.

Still, there is in man a primordial and overruling phenomenon which defies analysis. Man may be dissected
completely; the elements of Will and Mind may perhaps
be found; but there still will remain beyond apprehension the $x$ against which I once used to struggle. That $x$
is the Word, the Logos, whose communication burns and
consumes those who are not prepared to receive it. The
Word is forever generating the Substance.

## IX.

Rage, like all our vehement demonstrations, is a current
of the human force that acts electrically; its turmoil when
liberated acts on persons who are present even though
they be neither its cause nor its object. Are there not certain men who by a discharge of Volition can sublimate
the essence of the feelings of the masses?

## X.

Fanaticism and all emotions are living forces. These
forces in some beings become rivers that gather in and
sweep away everything.

## XI.

Though Space *is,* certain faculties have the power of traversing it with such rapidity that it is as though it existed not. From your own bed to the frontiers of the universe there are but two steps: Will and Faith.

## XII.

Facts are nothing; they do not subsist; all that lives of us is the Idea.

## XIII.

The realm of Ideas is divided into three spheres: that of Instinct, that of Abstractions, that of Specialism.

## XIV.

The greater part, the weaker part of visible humanity, dwells in the Sphere of Instinct. The *Instinctives* are born, labor, and die without rising to the second degree of human intelligence, namely Abstraction.

## XV.

Society begins in the sphere of Abstraction. If Abstraction, as compared with Instinct, is an almost divine power, it is nevertheless incredibly weak as compared with the gift of Specialism, which is the formula of God. Abstraction comprises all nature in a germ, more virtually than a seed contains the whole system of a plant and its fruits. From Abstraction are derived laws, arts, social ideas, and interests. It is the glory and the scourge of the earth: its glory because it has created social life; its scourge because it allows man to evade entering into Specialism, which is one of the paths to the Infinite. Man measures everything by Abstractions: Good and Evil, Virtue and Crime. Its formula of equity is a pair of scales, its justice is blind. God's justice sees: there is all the difference.

There must be intermediate Beings, then, dividing the sphere of Instinct from the sphere of Abstractions, in whom the two elements mingle in an infinite variety of proportions. Some have more of one, some more of the other. And there are also some in which the two powers neutralize each other by equality of effect.

### XVI.

Specialism consists in seeing the things of the material universe and the things of the spiritual universe in all their ramifications original and causative. The greatest human geniuses are those who started from the darkness of Abstraction to attain to the light of Specialism. (Specialism, *species*, sight; speculation, or seeing everything, and all at once; *Speculum,* a mirror or means of apprehending a thing by seeing the whole of it.) Jesus had the gift of Specialism; He saw each fact in its root and in its results, in the past where it had its rise, and in the future where it would grow and spread; His sight pierced into the understanding of others. The perfection of the inner eye gives rise to the gift of Specialism. Specialism brings with it Intuition. Intuition is one of the faculties of the Inner Man, of which Specialism is an attribute. Intuition acts by an imperceptible sensation of which he who obeys it is not conscious: for instance, Napoleon instinctively moving from a spot struck immediately afterwards by a cannon ball.

### XVII.

Between the sphere of Abstraction and that of Specialism, as between those of Abstraction and Instinct, there are beings in whom the attributes of both combine and produce a mixture; these are men of genius.

### XVIII.

Specialism is necessarily the most perfect expression of man, and he is the link binding the visible world to the higher worlds; he acts, sees, and feels by his inner powers. The man of Abstraction thinks. The man of Instinct acts.

### XIX.

Hence man has three degrees. That of Instinct, below the average; that of Abstraction, the general average; that of Specialism, above the average. Specialism opens to man his true career; the Infinite dawns on him; he sees what his destiny must be.

### XX.

There are three worlds—the Natural, the Spiritual, and the Divine. Humanity passes through the Natural world, which is not fixed either in its essence and unfixed in its faculties. The Spiritual world is fixed in its essence and unfixed in its faculties. The Divine world is necessarily a Material worship, a Spiritual worship, and a Divine worship: three forms expressed in action, speech, and prayer, or, in other words, in deed, apprehension, and love. Instinct demands deed; Abstraction is concerned with Ideas; Specialism sees the end, it aspires to God with presentiment or contemplation.

#### XXI.
Hence, perhaps, some day the converse of *Et Verbum caro factum est* will become the epitome of a new Gospel, which will proclaim that The Flesh shall be made the Word and become the Utterance of God.

#### XXII.
The Resurrection is the work of the Wind of Heaven sweeping over the worlds. The angel borne on the Wind does not say: "Arise, ye dead"; he says, "Arise, ye who live!"

Such are the meditations which I have with great difficulty cast in a form adapted to our understanding. There are some others which Pauline remembered more exactly, wherefore I know not, and which I wrote from her dictation; but they drive the mind to despair when, knowing in what an intellect they originated, we strive to understand them. I will quote a few of them to complete my study of this figure; partly, too, perhaps, because, in these last aphorisms, Lambert's formulas seem to include a larger universe than the former set, which would apply only to zoological evolution. Still, there is a relation between the two fragments, evident to those persons—though they be but few—who love to dive into such intellectual deeps.

#### I.
Everything on earth exists solely by motion and number.

#### II.
Motion is, so to speak, number in action.

#### III.
Motion is the product of a force generated by the Word

and by Resistance, which is Matter. But for Resistance, Motion would have had no results; its action would have been infinite. Newton's gravitation is not a law, but an effect of the general law of universal motion.

IV.
Motion, acting in proportion to Resistance, produces a result which is Life. As soon as one or the other is the stronger, Life ceases.

V.
No portion of Motion is wasted; it always produces number; still, it can be neutralized by disproportionate resistance, as in minerals.

VI.
Number, which produces variety of all kinds, also gives rise to Harmony, which, in the highest meaning of the word, is the relation of parts to the whole.

VII.
But for Motion, everything would be one and the same. Its products, identical in their essence, differ only by Number, which gives rise to faculties.

VIII.
Man looks to faculties; angels look to the Essence.

IX.
By giving his body up to elemental action, man can achieve an inner union with the Light.

X.
Number is intellectual evidence belonging to man alone; by it he acquires knowledge of the Word.

XI.
There is a Number beyond which the impure cannot pass: the Number which is the limit of creation.

XII.
The Unit was the starting point of every product: compounds are derived from it, but the end must be identical with the beginning. Hence this Spiritual formula: the

compound Unit, the variable Unit, the fixed Unit.

XIII.
The Universe is the Unit in variety. Motion is the means;
Number is the result. The end is the return of all things
to the Unit, which is God.

XIV.
Three and Seven are the two chief Spiritual numbers.

XV.
Three is the formula of created worlds. It is the Spiritual Sign of the creation, as it is the Material Sign of
dimension. In fact, God has worked by curved lines only:
the Straight Line is an attribute of the Infinite; and man,
who has the presentiment of the Infinite, reproduces it in
his works. Two is the number of generation. Three is the
number of Life which includes generation and offspring.
Add the sum of four, and you have seven, the formula of
Heaven. Above all is God; He is the Unit.

After going in to see Louis once more, I took leave of
his wife and went home, lost in ideas so adverse to social
life that, in spite of a promise to return to Villenoix, I did
not go.

The sight of Louis had had some mysteriously sinister
influence over me. I was afraid to place myself again in that
heavy atmosphere, where ecstasy was contagious. Any man
would have felt, as I did, a longing to throw himself into the
infinite, just as one soldier after another killed himself in a
certain sentry box where one had committed suicide in the
camp at Boulogne. It is a known fact that Napoleon was
obliged to have the hut burned which had harbored an idea
that had become a mortal infection.

Louis' room had perhaps the same fatal effect as that
sentry box.

These two facts would then be additional evidence in
favor of his theory of the transfusion of Will. I was conscious of strange disturbances, transcending the most
fantastic results of taking tea, coffee, or opium, of dreams
or of fever—mysterious agents, whose terrible action often
sets our brains on fire.

I ought perhaps to have made a separate book of these fragments of thought, intelligible only to certain spirits who have been accustomed to lean over the edge of abysses in the hope of seeing to the bottom. The life of that mighty brain, which split up on every side perhaps, like a too vast empire, would have been set forth in the narrative of this man's visions—a being incomplete for lack of force or of weakness; but I preferred to give an account of my own impressions rather than to compose a more or less poetical romance.

Louis Lambert died at the age of twenty-eight, September 25, 1824, in his true love's arms. He was buried by her desire in an island in the park at Villenoix. His tombstone is a plain stone cross, without name or date. Like a flower that has blossomed on the margin of a precipice, and drops into it, its colors and fragrance all unknown, it was fitting that he too should fall. Like many another misprized soul, he had often yearned to dive haughtily into the void, and abandon there the secrets of his own life.

Mademoiselle de Villenoix would, however, have been quite justified in recording his name on that cross with her own. Since her partner's death, reunion has been her constant, hourly hope. But the vanities of woe are foreign to faithful souls.

Villenoix is falling into ruin. She no longer resides there; to the end, no doubt, that she may the better picture herself there as she used to be. She had said long ago:

"His heart was mine; his genius is with God."

CHATEAU DE SACHE. *June-July 1832.*

# The Exiles

*Almae sorori.*

In the year 1308 few houses were yet standing on the Island formed by the alluvium and sand deposited by the Seine above the Cite, behind the Church of Notre-Dame. The first man who was so bold as to build on this strand, then liable to frequent floods, was a constable of the watch of the City of Paris, who had been able to do some service to their Reverences the Chapter of the Cathedral; and in return the Bishop leased him twenty-five perches of land, with exemptions from all feudal dues or taxes on the buildings he might erect.

Seven years before the beginning of this narrative, Joseph Tirechair, one of the sternest of Paris constables, as his name (Tear Flesh) would indicate, had, thanks to his share of the fines collected by him for delinquencies committed within the precincts of the Cite, had been able to build a house on the bank of the Seine just at the end of the Rue du Port Saint-Landry. To protect the merchandise landed on the strand, the municipality had constructed a sort of breakwater of masonry, which may still be seen on some old plans of Paris, and which preserved the piles of the landing-place by meeting the rush of water and ice at the upper end of the Island. The constable had taken advantage of this for the foundation of his house, so that there were several steps up to his door.

Like all the houses of that date, this cottage was crowned by a peaked roof, forming a gable-end to the front, or half a diamond. To the great regret of historians, but two or three examples of such roofs survive in Paris. A round opening gave light to a loft, where the constable's wife dried the linen of the Chapter, for she had the honor of washing for the Cathedral—which was certainly not a bad customer. On the first floor were two rooms, let to lodgers at a rent, one year with another, of forty sous *Parisis* each, an exorbitant sum, that was however justified by the luxury Tirechair had lavished on their adornment. Flanders tapestry hung on the walls, and a large bed with a top valance of green serge, like a peasant's bed, was amply furnished with mattresses, and covered with good sheets of fine linen. Each room had a stove called a *chauffe-doux*; the floor, carefully polished by Dame Tirechair's apprentices, shone like the woodwork of a shrine. Instead of stools, the lodgers had deep chairs of carved walnut, the spoils probably of some raided castle. Two chests with pewter moldings, and tables on twisted legs, completed the fittings, worthy of the most fastidious knights-banneret whom business might bring to Paris.

The windows of those two rooms looked out on the river. From one you could only see the shores of the Seine, and the three barren islands, of which two were subsequently joined together to form the Île Saint-Louis; the third was the Île de Louviers. From the other could be seen, down a vista of the Port Saint-Landry, the buildings on the Greve, the Bridge of Notre-Dame, with its houses, and the tall towers of the Louvre, but lately built by Philippe-Auguste to overlook the then poor and squalid town of Paris, which suggests so many imaginary marvels to the fancy of modern romancers.

The ground floor of Tirechair's house consisted of a large hall, where his wife's business was carried on, through which the lodgers were obliged to pass on their way to their own rooms up a stairway like a mill-ladder. Behind this were a kitchen and a bedroom, with a view over the Seine. A tiny garden, reclaimed from the waters, displayed at the foot of this modest dwelling its beds of cabbages and onions, and a few rose-bushes, sheltered by palings, forming a sort of hedge. A little structure of lath and mud served as a kennel for a big dog, the indispensable guardian of so lonely a dwelling. Beyond this kennel was a little plot, where the hens cackled whose eggs were sold to the Canons. Here and there on this patch of earth, muddy or dry according to the whimsical Parisian weather, a few trees grew, constantly lashed by the wind, and teased and broken by the passer-by—willows, reeds, and tall grasses.

The Eyot, the Seine, the landing-place, the house, were all overshadowed on the west by the huge basilica of Notre-Dame casting its cold gloom over the whole plot as the sun moved. Then, as now, there was not in all Paris a more deserted spot, a more solemn or more melancholy prospect. The noise of waters, the chanting of priests, or the piping of the wind, were the only sounds that disturbed this wilderness, where lovers would sometimes meet to discuss their secrets when the church-folds and clergy were safe in church at the services.

One evening in April in the year 1308, Tirechair came home in a remarkably bad temper. For three days past everything had been in good order on the King's highway. Now, as an officer of the peace, nothing annoyed him so much as to feel himself useless. He flung down his halbert in a rage, muttered inarticulate words as he pulled off his doublet, half red and half blue, and slipped on a shabby camlet jerkin. After helping himself from the bread-box to a hunch of bread, and spreading it with butter, he seated himself on a bench, looked round at his four whitewashed walls, counted the beams of the ceiling, made a mental inventory of the household goods hanging from the nails, scowled at the neatness which left him nothing to complain of, and looked at his wife, who said not a word as she ironed the albs and surplices from the sacristy.

"By my halidom," he said, to open the conversation, "I cannot think, Jacqueline, where you go to catch your apprenticed maids. Now, here is one," he went on, pointing to a girl who was folding an altar-cloth, clumsily enough, it must be owned, "who looks to me more like a damsel rather free of her person than a sturdy country wench. Her hands are as white as a fine lady's! By the Mass! and her hair smells of essences, I verily believe, and her hose are as find as a queen's. By the two horns of Old Nick, matters please me but ill as I find them here."

The girl colored, and stole a look at Jacqueline, full of alarm not unmixed with pride. The mistress answered her glance with a smile, laid down her work, and turned to her husband.

"Come now," said she, in a sharp tone, "you need not harry me. Are you going to accuse me next of some underhand tricks? Patrol your roads as much as you please, but do not meddle here with anything but what concerns your sleeping in peace, drinking your wine, and eating what I set before you, or else, I warn you, I will have no more to do with keeping you healthy and happy. Let anyone find me a happier man in all the town," she went on, with a scolding grimace. "He has silver in his purse, a gable over the Seine, a stout halbert on one hand, an honest wife on the other, a house as clean and smart as a new pin! And he growls like a pilgrim smarting from Saint Anthony's fire!"

"Hey day!" exclaimed the sergeant of the watch, "do you fancy, Jacqueline, that I have any wish to see my house razed down, my halbert given to another, and my wife standing in the pillory?"

Jacqueline and the dainty journeywoman turned pale.

"Just tell me what you are driving at," said the washer-woman sharply, "and make a clean breast of it. For some days, my man, I have observed that you have some maggot twisting in your poor brain. Come up, then, and have it all out. You must be a pretty coward indeed if you fear any harm when you have only to guard the common council and live under the protection of the Chapter! Their Reverences the Canons would lay the whole bishopric under an interdict if Jacqueline brought a complaint of the smallest damage."

As she spoke, she went straight up to her husband and took him by the arm.

"Come with me," she added, pulling him up and out on to the steps.

When they were down by the water in their little garden, Jacqueline looked saucily in her husband's face.

"I would have you to know, you old gaby, that when my lady fair goes out, a piece of gold comes into our savings-box."

"Oh, ho!" said the constable, who stood silent and meditative before his wife. But he presently said, "Any way, we are done for.—What brings the dame to our house?"

"She comes to see the well-favored young clerk who lives overhead," replied Jacqueline, looking up at the window that opened on to the vast landscape of the Seine valley.

"The Devil's in it!" cried the man. "For a few base crowns you have ruined me, Jacqueline. Is that an honest trade for a sergeant's decent wife to ply? And, be she Countess or Baroness, the lady will not be able to get us out of the trap in which we shall find ourselves caught sooner or later. Shall we not have to square accounts with some puissant and offended husband? for, by the Mass, she is fair to look upon!"

"But she is a widow, I tell you, gray gander! How dare you accuse your wife of foul play and folly? And the lady has never spoken a word to yon gentle clerk, she is content to look on him and think of him. Poor lad! he would be dead of starvation by now but for her, for she is as good as a mother to him. And he, the sweet cherub! it is as easy to cheat him as to rock a newborn babe. He believes his pence will last forever, and he has eaten them through twice over in the past six months."

"Woman," said the sergeant, solemnly pointing to the Place de Greve, "do you remember seeing, even from this spot, the fire in which they burnt the Danish woman the other day?"

"What then?" said Jacqueline, in a fright.

"What then?" echoed Tirechair. "Why, the two men who lodge with us smell of scorching. Neither Chapter nor Countess or Protector can serve them. Here is Easter come round; the year is ending; we must turn our company out of doors, and that at once. Do you think you can teach an old constable how to know a gallows-bird? Our two lodgers were on terms with la Porette, that heretic jade from Denmark or Norway, whose last cries you heard from here. She was a brave witch; she never blenched at the stake, which was proof enough of her compact with the Devil. I saw her as plain as I see you; she preached to the throng, and declared she was in heaven and could see God.

"And since that, I tell you, I have never slept quietly in my bed. My lord, who lodges over us, is of a surety more of a wizard than a Christian. On my word as an officer, I shiver when that old man passes near me; he never sleeps of nights; if I wake, his voice is ringing like a bourdon of bells, and I hear him muttering incantations in the language of hell. Have you ever seen him eat an honest crust of bread or a hearth-cake made by a good Catholic baker? His brown skin has been scorched and tanned by hell-fires. Marry, and I tell you his eyes hold a spell like that of serpents. Jacqueline, I will have none of those two men under my roof. I see too much of the law not to know that it is well to have

nothing to do with it.—You must get rid of our two lodgers; the elder because I suspect him; the youngster, because
he is too pretty. They neither of them seem to me to keep
Christian company. The boy is ever staring at the moon, the
stars, and the clouds, like a wizard watching for the hour
when he shall mount his broomstick; the other old rogue
certainly makes some use of the poor boy for his black art.
My house stands too close to the river as it is, and that
risk of ruin is bad enough without bringing down fire from
heaven, or the love affairs of a countess. I have spoken. Do
not rebel."

In spite of her sway in the house, Jacqueline stood stupefied as she listened to the edict fulminated against his
lodgers by the sergeant of the watch. She mechanically
looked up at the window of the room inhabited by the old
man, and shivered with horror as she suddenly caught sight
of the gloomy, melancholy face, and the piercing eye that
so affected her husband, accustomed as he was to dealing
with criminals.

At that period, great and small, priests and laymen, all
trembled before the idea of any supernatural power. The
word "magic" was as powerful as leprosy to root up feelings, break social ties, and freeze piety in the most generous
soul. It suddenly struck the constable's wife that she had
never, in fact, seen either of her lodgers exercising any
human function. Though the younger man's voice was as
sweet and melodious as the tones of a flute, she so rarely
heard it that she was tempted to think his silence the result
of a spell. As she recalled the strange beauty of that pink-
and-white face, and saw in memory the fine hair and moist
brilliancy of those eyes, she believed that they were indeed
the artifices of the Devil. She remembered that for days at
a time she had never heard the slightest sound from either
room. Where were the strangers during all those hours?

Suddenly the most singular circumstances recurred to
her mind. She was completely overmastered by fear, and
could even discern witchcraft in the rich lady's interest in
the young Godefroid, a poor orphan who had come from
Flanders to study at the University of Paris. She hastily put
her hand into one of her pockets, pulled out four livres of

Tournay in large silver coinage, and looked at the pieces
with an expression of avarice mingled with terror.

"That, at any rate, is not false coin," said she, showing
the silver to her husband. "Besides," she went on, "how
can I turn them out after taking next year's rent paid in
advance?"

"You had better inquire of the Dean of the Chapter,"
replied Tirechair. "Is not it his business to tell us how we
should deal with these extraordinary persons?"

"Ay, truly extraordinary," cried Jacqueline. "To think
of their cunning; coming here under the very shadow of
Notre-Dame! Still," she went on, "or ever I ask the Dean,
why not warn that fair and noble lady of the risk she runs?"

As she spoke, Jacqueline went into the house with
her husband, who had not missed a mouthful. Tirechair,
as a man grown old in the tricks of his trade, affected to
believe that the strange lady was in fact a work-girl; still,
this assumed indifference could not altogether cloak the
timidity of a courtier who respects a royal incognity. At this
moment six was striking by the clock of Saint-Denis du
Pas, a small church that stood between Notre-Dame and
the Port Saint-Landry—the first church erected in Paris,
on the very spot where Saint-Denis was laid on the grid-
iron, as chronicles tell. The hour flew from steeple to tower
all over the city. Then suddenly confused shouts were heard
on the left bank of the Seine, behind Notre-Dame, in the
quarter where the schools of the University harbored their
swarms.

At this signal, Jacqueline's elder lodger began to move
about his room. The sergeant, his wife, and the strange lady
listened while he opened and shut his door, and the old
man's heavy step was heard on the steep stair. The constable's suspicions gave such interest to the advent of this
personage, that the lady was startled as she observed the
strange expression of the two countenances before her.
Referring the terrors of this couple to the youth she was
protecting—as was natural in a lover—the young lady
awaited, with some uneasiness, the event thus heralded by
the fears of her so-called master and mistress.

The old man paused for a moment on the threshold to

scrutinize the three persons in the room, and seemed to be looking for his young companion. This glance of inquiry, unsuspicious as it was, agitated the three. Indeed, nobody, not even the stoutest man, could deny that Nature had bestowed exceptional powers on this being, who seemed almost supernatural. Though his eyes were somewhat deeply shaded by the wide sockets fringed with long eyebrows, they were set, like a kite's eyes, in eyelids so broad, and bordered by so dark a circle sharply defined on his cheek, that they seemed rather prominent. These singular eyes had in them something indescribably domineering and piercing, which took possession of the soul by a grave and thoughtful look, a look as bright and lucid as that of a serpent or a bird, but which held one fascinated and crushed by the swift communication of some tremendous sorrow, or of some super-human power.

Every feature was in harmony with this eye of lead and of fire, at once rigid and flashing, stern and calm. While in this eagle eye earthly emotions seemed in some sort extinct, the lean, parched face also bore traces of unhappy passions and great deeds done. The nose, which was narrow and aquiline, was so long that it seemed to hang on by the nostrils. The bones of the face were strongly marked by the long, straight wrinkles that furrowed the hollow cheeks. Every line in the countenance looked dark. It would suggest the bed of a torrent where the violence of former floods was recorded in the depth of the water-courses, which testified to some terrible, unceasing turmoil. Like the ripples left by the oars of a boat on the waters, deep lines, starting from each side of his nose, marked his face strongly, and gave an expression of bitter sadness to his mouth, which was firm and straight-lipped. Above the storm thus stamped on his countenance, his calm brow rose with what may be called boldness, and crowned it as with a marble dome.

The stranger preserved that intrepid and dignified manner that is frequently habitual with men inured to disaster, and fitted by nature to stand unmoved before a furious mob and to face the greatest dangers. He seemed to move in a sphere apart, where he poised above humanity. His gestures, no less than his look, were full of irresistible

power; his lean hands were those of a soldier; and if your
own eyes were forced to fall before his piercing gaze, you
were no less sure to tremble when by word or action he
spoke to your soul. He moved in silent majesty that made
him seem a king without his guard, a god without his rays.

His dress emphasized the ideas suggested by the peculiarities of his mien and face. Soul, body, and garb were in
harmony, and calculated to impress the coldest imagination.
He wore a sort of sleeveless gown of black cloth, fastened in
front, and falling to the calf, leaving the neck bare with no
collar. His doublet and boots were likewise black. On his
head was a black velvet cap like a priest's, sitting in a close
circle above his forehead, and not showing a single hair.
It was the strictest mourning, the gloomiest habit a man
could wear. But for a long sword that hung by his side from
a leather belt which could be seen where his surcoat hung
open, a priest would have hailed him as a brother. Though
of no more than middle height, he appeared tall; and, looking him in the face he seemed a giant.

"The clock has struck, the boat is waiting; will you not
come?"

At these words, spoken in bad French, but distinctly
audible in the silence, a little noise was heard in the other
top room, and the young man came down as lightly as a
bird.

When Godefroid appeared, the lady's face turned crimson; she trembled, started, and covered her face with her
white hands.

Any woman might have shared her agitation at the sight
of this youth of about twenty, of a form and stature so slender that at a first glance he might have been taken for a
mere boy, or a young girl in disguise. His black cap—like
the *beret* worn by the Basque people—showed a brow as
white as snow, where grace and innocence shone with an
expression of divine sweetness—the light of a soul full of
faith. A poet's fancy would have seen there the star which,
in some old tale, a mother entreats the fairy godmother to
set on the forehead of an infant abandoned, like Moses,
to the waves. Love lurked in the thousand fair curls that
fell over his shoulders. His throat, truly a swan's throat,

was white and exquisitely round. His blue eyes, bright and liquid, mirrored the sky. His features and the mold of his brow were refined and delicate enough to enchant a painter. The bloom of beauty, which in a woman's face causes men such indescribable delight, the exquisite purity of outline, the halo of light that bathes the features we love, were here combined with a masculine complexion, and with strength as yet but half developed, in the most enchanting contrast. His was one of those melodious countenances which even when silent speak and attract us. And yet, on marking it attentively, the incipient blight might have been detected which comes of a great thought or a passion, the faint yellow tinge that made him seem like a young leaf opening to the sun.

No contrast could be greater or more startling than that seen in the companionship of these two men. It was like seeing a frail and graceful shrub that has grown from the hollow trunk of some gnarled willow, withered by age, blasted by lightning, standing decrepit; one of those majestic trees that painters love; the trembling sapling takes shelter there from storms. One was a god, the other was an angel; one the poet that feels, the other the poet that expresses—a prophet in sorrow, a levite in prayer.

They went out together without speaking.

"Did you mark how he called him to him?" cried the sergeant of the watch when the footsteps of the couple were no longer audible on the strand. "Are not they a demon and his familiar?"

"Phooh!" puffed Jacqueline. "I felt smothered! I never marked our two lodgers so carefully. 'Tis a bad thing for us women that the Devil can wear so fair a mien!"

"Ay, cast some holy water on him," said Tirechair, "and you will see him turn into a toad.—I am off to tell the office all about them."

On hearing this speech, the lady roused herself from the reverie into which she had sunk, and looked at the constable, who was donning his red-and-blue jacket.

"Whither are you off to?" she asked.

"To tell the justices that wizards are lodging in our house very much against our will."

The lady smiled.

"I," said she, "am the Comtesse de Mahaut," and she rose with a dignity that took the man's breath away. "Beware of bringing the smallest trouble on your guests. Above all, respect the old man; I have seen him in the company of your Lord the King, who entreated him courteously; you will be ill advised to trouble him in any way. As to my having been here—never breathe a word of it, as you value your life."

She said no more, but relapsed into thought.

Presently she looked up, signed to Jacqueline, and together they went up into Godefroid's room. The fair Countess looked at the bed, the carved chairs, the chest, the tapestry, the table, with a joy like that of the exile who sees on his return the crowded roofs of his native town nestling at the foot of a hill.

"If you have not deceived me," she said to Jacqueline, "I promise you a hundred crowns in gold."

"Behold, madame," said the woman, "the poor angel is confiding—here is all his treasure."

As she spoke, Jacqueline opened a drawer in the table and showed some parchments.

"God of mercy!" cried the Countess, snatching up a document that caught her eye, on which she read, *Gothofredus Comes Gantiacus* (Godefroid, Count of Ghent).

She dropped the parchment, and passed her hand over her brow; then, feeling, no doubt, that she had compromised herself by showing so much emotion, she recovered her cold demeanor.

"I am satisfied," said she.

She went downstairs and out of the house. The constable and his wife stood in their doorway, and saw her take the path to the landing-place.

A boat was moored hard by. When the rustle of the Countess' approach was audible, a boatman suddenly stood up, helped the fair laundress to take her seat in it, and rowed with such strength as to make the boat fly like a swallow down the stream.

"You are a sorry fellow," said Jacqueline, giving the officer's shoulder a familiar slap. "We have earned a hundred gold crowns this morning."

"I like harboring lords no better than harboring wizards. And I know not, of the two, which is the more like to bring us to the gallows," replied Tirechair, taking up his halbert. "I will go my rounds over by Champfleuri; God protect us, and send me to meet some pert jade out in her bravery of gold rings to glitter in the shade like a glow-worm!"

Jacqueline, alone in the house, hastily went up to the unknown lord's room to discover, if she could, some clue to this mysterious business. Like some learned men who give themselves infinite pains to complicate the clear and simple laws of nature, she had already invented a chaotic romance to account for the meeting of these three persons under her humble roof. She hunted through the chest, examined everything, but could find nothing extraordinary. She saw nothing on the table but a writing-case and some sheets of parchment; and as she could not read, this discovery told her nothing. A woman's instinct then took her into the young man's room, and from thence she descried her two lodgers crossing the river in the ferry boat.

"They stand like two statues," said she to herself. "Ah, ha! They are landing at the Rue du Fouarre. How nimble he is, the sweet youth! He jumped out like a bird. By him the old man looks like some stone saint in the Cathedral.— They are going to the old School of the Four Nations. Presto! they are out of sight.—And this is where he lives, poor cherub!" she went on, looking about the room. "How smart and winning he is! Ah! your fine gentry are made of other stuff than we are."

And Jacqueline went down again after smoothing down the bed-coverlet, dusting the chest, and wondering for the hundredth time in six months:

"What in the world does he do all the blessed day? He cannot always be staring at the blue sky and the stars that God has hung up there like lanterns. That dear boy has known trouble. But why do he and the old man hardly ever speak to each other?"

Then she lost herself in wonderment and in thoughts which, in her woman's brain, were tangled like a skein of thread.

The old man and his young companion had gone into one of the schools for which the Rue du Fouarre was at that time famous throughout Europe. At the moment when Jacqueline's two lodgers arrived at the old School des Quatre Nations, the celebrated Sigier, the most noted Doctor of Mystical Theology of the University of Paris, was mounting his pulpit in a spacious low room on a level with the street. The cold stones were strewn with clean straw, on which several of his disciples knelt on one knee, writing on the other, to enable them to take notes from the Master's improvised discourse, in the shorthand abbreviations which are the despair of modern decipherers.

The hall was full, not of students only, but of the most distinguished men belonging to the clergy, the court, and the legal faculty. There were some learned foreigners, too—soldiers and rich citizens. The broad faces were there, with prominent brows and venerable beards, which fill us with a sort of pious respect for our ancestors when we see their portraits from the Middle Ages. Lean faces, too, with burning, sunken eyes, under bald heads yellow from the labors of futile scholasticism, contrasted with young and eager countenances, grave faces, warlike faces, and the ruddy cheeks of the financial class.

These lectures, dissertations, theses, sustained by the brightest geniuses of the thirteenth and fourteenth centuries, roused our forefathers to enthusiasm. They were to them their bull-fights, their Italian opera, their tragedy, their dancers; in short, all their drama. The performance of Mysteries was a later thing than these spiritual disputations, to which, perhaps, we owe the French stage. Inspired eloquence, combining the attractions of the human voice skilfully used, with daring inquisition into the secrets of God, sufficed to satisfy every form of curiosity, appealed to the soul, and constituted the fashionable entertainment of the time. Not only did Theology include the other sciences, it was science itself, as grammar was science to the Ancient Greeks; and those who distinguished themselves in these duels, in which the orators, like Jacob, wrestled with the Spirit of God, had a promising future before them. Embassies, arbitrations between sovereigns, chancellorships, and ecclesiastical dignities were the meed of men whose rhetoric had been schooled in theological controversy. The professor's chair was the tribune of the period.

This system lasted till the day when Rabelais gibbeted dialectics by his merciless satire, as Cervantes demolished chivalry by a narrative comedy.

To understand this amazing period and the spirit which dictated its voluminous, though now forgotten, masterpieces, to analyze it, even to its barbarisms, we need only examine the Constitutions of the University of Paris and the extraordinary scheme of instruction that then obtained. Theology was taught under two faculties—that of Theology properly so called, and that of Canon Law. The faculty of Theology, again, had three sections—Scholastic, Canonical, and Mystic. It would be wearisome to give an account of the attributes of each section of the science, since one only, namely, Mystic, is the subject of this *Etude*.

Mystical Theology included the whole of Divine Revelation and the elucidation of the Mysteries. And this branch of ancient theology has been secretly preserved with reverence even to our own day; Jacob Boehm, Swendenborg, Martinez Pasqualis, Saint-Martin, Molinos, Madame Guyon, Madame Bourignon, and Madame Krudener, the extensive sect of the Ecstatics, and that of the Illuminati, have at different periods duly treasured the doctrines of this science, of which the aim is indeed truly startling and portentous. In Doctor Sigier's day, as in our own, man has striven to gain wings to fly into the sanctuary where God hides from our gaze.

This digression was necessary to give a clue to the scene at which the old man and the youth from the island under Notre-Dame had come to be audience; it will also protect this narrative from all blame on the score of falsehood and hyperbole, of which certain persons of hasty judgment might perhaps suspect me.

Doctor Sigier was a tall man in the prime of life. His face, rescued from oblivion by the archives of the University, had singular analogies with that of Mirabeau. It was stamped with the seal of fierce, swift, and terrible eloquence. But the Doctor bore on his brow the expression of religious faith that his modern double had not. His voice, too, was of persuasive sweetness, with a clear and pleasing ring in it.

At this moment the daylight, that was stintingly diffused through the small, heavily-leaded window-panes, tinted the assembly with capricious tones and powerful contrasts from the chequered light and shade. Here, in a dark corner, eyes shone brightly, their dark heads under the sunbeams gleamed light above faces in shadow, and various bald heads, with only a circlet of white hair, were distinguished among the crowd like battlements silvered by moonlight. Every face was turned towards the Doctor, mute but impatient. The drowsy voices of other lecturers in the adjoining schools were audible in the silent street like the murmuring of the sea; and the steps of the two strangers, as they now came in, attracted general attention. Doctor Sigier, ready to begin, saw the stately senior standing, looked round for a seat for him, and then finding none, as the place was full, came down from his place, went to the newcomer, and with great respect, led him to the platform of his professor's chair, and there gave him his stool to sit upon. The assembly hailed this mark of deference with a murmur of approval, recognizing the old man as the orator of a fine thesis admirably argued not long since at the Sorbonne.

The stranger looked down from his raised position on the crowd below with that deep glance that held a whole poem of sorrow, and those who met his eye felt an indescribable thrill. The lad, following the old man, sat down on one of the steps, leaning against the pulpit in a graceful and melancholy attitude. The silence was now profound, and the doorway and even the street were blocked by scholars who had deserted the other classes.

Doctor Sigier was to-day to recapitulate, in the last of a series of discourses, the views he had set forth in the former lectures on the Resurrection, Heaven, and Hell. His strange doctrine responded to the sympathies of the time, and gratified the immoderate love of the marvelous, which haunts the mind of man in every age. This effort of man to clutch the infinite, which forever slips through his ineffectual grasp, this last tourney of thought against thought, was a task worthy of an assembly where the most stupendous human imagination ever known, perhaps, at that moment shone.

The Doctor began by summing up in a mild and even tone the principal points he had so far established:

"No intellect was the exact counterpart of another. Had man any right to require an account of his Creator for the inequality of powers bestowed on each? Without attempting to penetrate rashly into the designs of God, ought we not to recognize the fact that by reason of their general diversity intelligences could be classed in spheres? From the sphere where the least degree of intelligence gleamed, to the most translucent souls who could see the road by which to ascend to God, was there not an ascending scale of spiritual gift? And did not spirits of the same sphere understand each other like brothers in soul, in flesh, in mind, and in feeling?"

From this the Doctor went on to unfold the most wonderful theories of sympathy. He set forth in Biblical language the phenomena of love, of instinctive repulsion, of strong affinities which transcend the laws of space, of the sudden mingling of souls which seem to recognize each other. With regard to the different degrees of strength of which our affections are capable, he accounted for them by the place, more or less near the centre, occupied by beings in their respective circles.

He gave mathematical expression to God's grand idea in the co-ordination of the various human spheres. "Through man," he said, "these spheres constituted a world intermediate between the intelligence of the brute and the intelligence of the angels." As he stated it, the divine Word nourishes the spiritual Word, the spiritual Word nourishes the living Word, the living Word nourishes the animal Word, the animal Word nourishes the vegetable Word, and the vegetable Word is the expression of the life of the barren Word. These successive evolutions, as of a chrysalis, which God thus wrought in our souls, this infusorial life, so to speak, communicated from each zone to the next, more vivid, more spiritual, more perceptive in its ascent, represented, rather dimly no doubt, but marvelously enough to his inexperienced hearers, the impulse given to Nature by

the Almighty. Supported by many texts from the Sacred
Scriptures, which he used as a commentary on his own
statements to express by concrete images the abstract
arguments he felt to be wanting, he flourished the Spirit
of God like a torch over the deep secrets of creation, with
an eloquence peculiar to himself, and accents that urged
conviction on his audience. As he unfolded his mysterious system and all its consequences, he gave a key to every
symbol and justified the vocation, the special gifts, the
genius, the talent of each human being.

Then, instinctively becoming physiological, he remarked
on the resemblance to certain animals stamped on some
human faces, accounting for them by primordial analogies and the upward tendency of all creation. He showed
his audience the workings of Nature, and assigned a mission and a future to minerals, plants, and animals. Bible
in hand, after thus spiritualizing Matter and materializing
Spirit, after pointing to the Will of God in all things, and
enjoining respect for His smallest works, he suggested the
possibility of rising by faith from sphere to sphere.

This was the first portion of his discourse, and by adroit
digressions he applied the doctrine of his system to feudal-
ism. The poetry—religious and profane—and the abrupt
eloquence of that period had a grand opening in this vast
theory, wherein the Doctor had amalgamated all the philosophical systems of the ancients, and from which he
brought them out again classified, transfigured, purified.
The false dogmas of two adverse principles and of Pantheism were demolished at his word, which proclaimed the
Divine Unity, while ascribing to God and His angels the
knowledge, the ends to which the means shone resplen-
dent to the eyes of man. Fortified by the demonstrations
that proved the existence of the world of Matter, Doctor
Sigier constructed the scheme of a spiritual world dividing
us from God by an ascending scale of spheres, just as the
plant is divided from man by an infinite number of grades.
He peopled the heavens, the stars, the planets, the sun.

Quoting Saint Paul, he invested man with a new power;
he might rise, from globe to globe, to the very Fount of
eternal life. Jacob's mystical ladder was both the religious

formula and the traditional proof of the fact. He soared through space, carrying with him the passionate souls of his hearers on the wings of his word, making them feel the infinite, and bathing them in the heavenly sea. Then the Doctor accounted logically for hell by circles placed in inverse order to the shining spheres that lead to God, in which torments and darkness take the place of the Spirit and of light. Pain was as intelligible as rapture. The terms of comparison were present in the conditions of human life and its various atmospheres of suffering and of intellect. Thus the most extraordinary traditions of hell and purgatory were quite naturally conceivable.

He gave the fundamental *rationale* of virtue with admirable clearness. A pious man, toiling onward in poverty, proud of his good conscience, at peace with himself, and steadfastly true to himself in his heart in spite of the spectacle of exultant vice, was a fallen angel doing penance, who remembered his origin, foresaw his guerdon, accomplished his task, and obeyed his glorious mission. The sublime resignation of Christians was then seen in all its glory. He depicted martyrs at the burning stake, and almost stripped them of their merit by stripping them of their sufferings. He showed their inner angel as dwelling in the heavens, while the outer man was tortured by the executioner's sword. He described angels dwelling among men, and gave tokens by which to recognize them.

He next strove to drag from the very depths of man's understanding the real sense of the word fall, which occurs in every language. He appealed to the most widely-spread traditions in evidence of this one true origin, explaining, with much lucidity, the passion all men have for rising, mounting—an instinctive ambition, the perennial revelations of our destiny.

He displayed the whole universe at a glance, and described the nature of God Himself circulating in a full tide from the center to the extremities, and from the extremities to the center again. Nature was one and homogeneous. In the most seemingly trivial, as in the most stupendous work, everything obeyed that law; each created object reproduced in little an exact image of that nature—the sap in the plant, the blood in man, the orbits of the planets. He piled proof on proof, always completing his idea by a picture musical with poetry.

And he boldly anticipated every objection. He thundered forth an eloquent challenge to the monumental works of science and human excrescences of knowledge, such as those which societies use the elements of the earthly globe to produce. He asked whether our wars, our disasters, our depravity could hinder the great movement given by God to all the globes; and he laughed human impotence to scorn by pointing to their efforts everywhere in ruins. He cried upon the manes of Tyre, Carthage, and Babylon; he called upon Babel and Jerusalem to appear; and sought, without finding them, the transient furrows made by the plowshare of civilization. Humanity floated on the surface of the earth as a ship whose wake is lost in the calm level of ocean.

These were the fundamental notions set forth in Doctor Sigier's address, all wrapped in the mystical language and strange school Latin of the time. He had made a special study of the Scriptures, and they supplied him with the weapons with which he came before his contemporaries to hasten their progress. He hid his boldness under his immense learning, as with a cloak, and his philosophical bent under a saintly life. At this moment, after bringing his hearers face to face with God, after packing the universe into an idea, and almost unveiling the idea of the world, he gazed down on the silent, throbbing mass, and scrutinized the stranger with a look. Then, spurred on, no doubt, by the presence of this remarkable personage, he added these words, from which I have eliminated the corrupt Latinity of the Middle Ages:—

"Where, think you, may a man find these fruitful truths if not in the heart of God Himself?—What am I?—The humble interpreter of a single line left to us by the greatest of the Apostles—a single line out of thousands all equally full of light. Before us, Saint Paul said, '*In Deo vivimus movemur et sumus.*' In our day, less believing and more learned, or better instructed and more skeptical, we should ask the Apostle, 'To what end this perpetual motion? Whither leads this life divided into zones? Wherefore an intelligence that begins with the obscure perfection of marble and proceeds from sphere to sphere up to man, up to the angel, up to God? Where is the Fount, where is the ocean, if life, attaining to God across worlds and stars, through Matter and Spirit, has to come down again to some other goal?'

"You desire to see both aspects of the universe at once. You would adore the Sovereign on condition of being suffered to sit for an instant on His throne. Mad fools that we are! We will not admit that the most intelligent animals are able to understand our ideas and the object of our actions; we are merciless to the creatures of the inferior spheres, and exile them from our own; we deny them the faculty of divining human thoughts, and yet we ourselves would fain master the highest of all ideas—the Idea of the Idea!

"Well, go then, start! Fly by faith up from globe to globe, soar through space! Thought, love, and faith are its mystical keys. Traverse the circles, reach the throne! God is more merciful than you are; He opens His temple to all His creatures. Only, do not forget the pattern of Moses; put your shoes from off your feet, cast off all filth, leave your body far behind; otherwise you shall be consumed; for God— God is Light!"

Just as Doctor Sigier spoke these grand words, his face radiant, his hand uplifted, a sunbeam pierced through an open window, like a magic jet from a fount of splendor, a long triangular shaft of gold that lay like a scarf over the whole assembly. They all clapped their hands, for the audience accepted this effect of the sinking sun as a miracle. There was a universal cry of:

"*Vivant! Vivant!*"

The very sky seemed to shed approval. Godefroid, struck with reverence, looked from the old man to Doctor Sigier; they were talking together in an undertone.

"All honor to the Master!" said the stranger.

"What is such transient honor?" replied Sigier.

"I would I could perpetuate my gratitude," said the older man.

"A line written by you is enough!" said the Doctor. "It would give me immortality, humanly speaking."

"Can I give what I have not?" cried the elder.

Escorted by the crowd, which followed in their footsteps, like courtiers round a king, at a respectful distance,
Godefroid, with the old man and the Doctor, made their
way to the oozy shore, where as yet there were no houses,
and where the ferryman was waiting for them. The Doctor
and the stranger were talking together, not in Latin nor in
any Gallic tongue, but in an unknown language, and very
gravely. They pointed with their hands now to heaven and
now to the earth. Sigier, to whom the paths by the river
were familiar, guided the venerable stranger with particular
care to the narrow planks which here and there bridged the
mud; the following watched them inquisitively; and some
of the students envied the privileged boy who might walk
with these two great masters of speech. Finally, the Doctor
took leave of the stranger, and the ferry-boat pushed off.

At the moment when the boat was afloat on the wide
river, communicating its motion to the soul, the sun pierced
the clouds like a conflagration blazing up on the horizon,
and poured forth a flood of light, coloring slate roof-tops
and humbler thatch with a ruddy glow and tawny reflections, fringed Philippe Auguste's towers with fire, flooded
the sky, dyed the waters, gilded the plants, and aroused the
half-sleeping insects. The immense shaft of light set the
clouds on fire. It was like the last verse of the daily hymn.
Every heart was thrilled; nature in such a moment is sublime.

As he gazed at the spectacle, the stranger's eyes moistened with the tenderest of human tears: Godefroid too was
weeping; his trembling hand touched that of the elder man,
who, looking round, confessed his emotion. But thinking
his dignity as a man compromised, no doubt, to redeem it,
he said in a deep voice:

"I weep for my native land. I am an exile! Young man,
in such an hour as this I left my home. There, at this hour,
the fireflies are coming out of their fragile dwellings and
clinging like diamond sparks to the leaves of the iris. At
this hour the breeze, as sweet as the sweetest poetry, rises
up from a valley bathed in light, bearing on its wings the
richest fragrance. On the horizon I could see a golden city
like the Heavenly Jerusalem—a city whose name I may not

speak. There, too, a river winds. But that city and its buildings, that river of which the lovely vistas, and the pools of
blue water, mingled, crossed, and embraced each other,
which gladdened my sight and filled me with love—where
are they?

"At that hour the waters assumed fantastic hues under
the sunset sky, and seemed to be painted pictures; the stars
dropped tender streaks of light, the moon spread its pleasing snares; it gave another life to the trees, to the color and
form of things, and a new aspect to the sparkling water, the
silent hills, the eloquent buildings. The city spoke, it glit-
tered, it called to me to return!

"Columns of smoke rose up by the side of the ancient
pillars, whose marble sheen gleamed white through the
night; the lines of the horizon were still visible through the
mists of evening; all was harmony and mystery. Nature
would not say farewell; she desired to keep me there. Ah! It
was all in all to me; my mother and my child, my wife and
my glory! The very bells bewailed my condemnation. Oh,
land of marvels! It is as beautiful as heaven. From that hour
the wide world has been my dungeon. Beloved land, why
hast thou rejected me?

"But I shall triumph there yet!" he cried, speaking with
an accent of such intense conviction and such a ringing
tone, that the boatman started as at a trumpet call.

The stranger was standing in a prophetic attitude and
gazing southwards into the blue, pointing to his native
home across the skyey regions. The ascetic pallor of his face
had given place to a glow of triumph, his eyes flashed, he
was as grand as a lion shaking his mane.

"But you, poor child," he went on, looking at Godefroid,
whose cheeks were beaded with glittering tears, "have you,
like me, studied life from bloodstained pages? What can
you have to weep for, at your age?"

"Alas!" said Godefroid, "I regret a land more beautiful
than any land on earth—a land I never saw and yet remember. Oh, if I could but cleave the air on beating wings, I
would fly——"

"Whither?" asked the exile.

"Up there," replied the boy.

On hearing this answer, the stranger seemed surprised; he looked darkly at the youth, who remained silent. They seemed to communicate by an unspeakable effusion of the spirit, hearing each other's yearnings in the teeming silence, and going forth side by side, like two doves sweeping the air on equal wing, till the boat, touching the strand of the island, roused them from their deep reverie.

Then, each lost in thought, they went together to the sergeant's house.

"And so the boy believes that he is an angel exiled from heaven!" thought the tall stranger. "Which of us all has a right to undeceive him? Not I—I, who am so often lifted by some magic spell so far above the earth; I who am dedicate to God; I who am a mystery to myself. Have I not already seen the fairest of the angels dwelling in this mire? Is this child more or less crazed than I am? Has he taken a bolder step in the way of faith? He believes, and his belief no doubt will lead him into some path of light like that in which I walk. But though he is as beautiful as an angel, is he not too feeble to stand fast in such a struggle?"

Abashed by the presence of his companion, whose voice of thunder expressed to him his own thoughts, as lightning expresses the will of Heaven, the boy was satisfied to gaze at the stars with a lover's eyes. Overwhelmed by a luxury of sentiment, which weighed on his heart, he stood there timid and weak—a midge in the sunbeams. Sigier's discourse had proved to them the mysteries of the spiritual world; the tall, old man was to invest them with glory; the lad felt them in himself, though he could in no way express them. The three represented in living embodiment Science, Poetry, and Feeling.

On going into the house, the Exile shut himself into his room, lighted the inspiring lamp, and gave himself over to the ruthless demon of Work, seeking words of the silence and ideas of the night. Godefroid sat down in his window sill, by turns gazing at the moon reflected in the water, and studying the mysteries of the sky. Lost in one of the trances that were frequent to him, he traveled from sphere to sphere, from vision to vision, listening for obscure rustlings and the voices of angels, and believing that he heard them; seeing, or fancying that he saw, a divine radiance in which he lost himself; striving to attain the far-away goal, the source of all light, the fount of all harmony.

Presently the vast clamor of Paris, brought down on the current, was hushed; lights were extinguished one by one in the houses; silence spread over all; and the huge city slept like a tired giant.

Midnight struck. The least noise, the fall of a leaf, or the flight of a jackdaw changing its perching-place among the pinnacles of Notre-Dame, would have been enough to bring the stranger's mind to earth again, to have made the youth drop from the celestial heights to which his soul had soared on the wings of rapture.

And then the old man heard with dismay a groan mingling with the sound of a heavy fall—the fall, as his experienced ear assured him, of a dead body. He hastened into Godefroid's room, and saw him lying in a heap with a long rope tight round his neck, the end meandering over the floor.

When he had untied it, the poor lad opened his eyes.

"Where am I?" he asked, with a hopeful gleam.

"In your own room," said the elder man, looking with surprise at Godefroid's neck, and at the nail to which the cord had been tied, and which was still in the knot.

"In heaven?" said the boy, in a voice of music.

"No; on earth!"

Godefroid rose and walked along the path of light traced on the floor by the moon through the window, which stood open; he saw the rippling Seine, the willows and plants on the island. A misty atmosphere hung over the waters like a smokey floor.

On seeing the view, to him so heartbreaking, he folded his hands over his bosom, and stood in an attitude of despair; the Exile came up to him with astonishment on his face.

"You meant to kill yourself?" he asked.

"Yes," replied Godefroid, while the stranger passed his hand about his neck again and again to feel the place where the rope had tightened on it.

But for some slight bruises, the young man had been

but little hurt. His friend supposed that the nail had given way at once under the weight of the body, and the terrible attempt had ended in a fall without injury.

"And why, dear lad, did you try to kill yourself?"

"Alas!" said Godefroid, no longer restraining the tears that rolled down his cheeks, "I heard the Voice from on high; it called me by name! It had never named me before, but this time it bade me to Heaven! Oh, how sweet is that voice!—As I could not fly to Heaven," he added artlessly, "I took the only way we know of going to God."

"My child! oh, sublime boy!" cried the old man, throwing his arms round Godefroid, and clasping him to his heart. "You are a poet; you can boldly ride the whirlwind! Your poetry does not proceed from your heart; your living, burning thoughts, your creations, move and grow in your soul.—Go, never reveal your ideas to the vulgar! Be at once the altar, the priest, and the victim!

"You know Heaven, do you not? You have seen those myriads of angels, white-winged, and holding golden sistrums, all soaring with equal flight towards the Throne, and you have often seen their pinions moving at the breath of God as the trees of the forest bow with one consent before the storm. Ah, how glorious is unlimited space! Tell me."

The stranger clasped Godefroid's hand convulsively, and they both gazed at the firmament, whence the stars seemed to shed gentle poetry which they could bear.

"Oh, to see God!" murmured Godefroid.

"Child!" said the old man suddenly, in a sterner voice, "have you so soon forgotten the holy teaching of our good master, Doctor Sigier? In order to return, you to your heavenly home, and I to my native land on earth, must we not obey the voice of God? We must walk on resignedly in the stony paths where His almighty finger points the way. Do not you quail at the thought of the danger to which you exposed yourself? Arriving there without being bidden, and saying, 'Here I am!' before your time, would you not have been cast back into a world beneath that where your soul now hovers? Poor outcast cherub! Should you not rather bless God for having suffered you to live in a sphere where you may hear none but heavenly harmonies? Are you not as pure as a diamond, as lovely as a flower?

"Think what it is to know, like me, only the City of Sorrows!—Dwelling there I have worn out my heart.—To search the tombs for their horrible secrets; to wipe hands steeped in blood, counting them over night after night, seeing them rise up before me imploring forgiveness which I may not grant; to mark the writhing of the assassin and the last shriek of his victim; to listen to appalling noises and fearful silence, the silence of a father devouring his dead sons; to wonder at the laughter of the damned; to look for some human form among the livid heaps wrung and trampled by crime; to learn words such as living men may not hear without dying; to call perpetually on the dead, and always to accuse and condemn!—Is that living?"

"Cease!" cried Godefroid; "I cannot see you or hear you any further! My reason wanders, my eyes are dim. You light a fire within me which consumes me."

"And yet I must go on!" said the senior, waving his hand with a strange gesture that worked on the youth like a spell.

For a moment the old man fixed Godefroid with his large, weary, lightless eyes; then he pointed with one finger to the ground. A gulf seemed to open at his bidding. He remained standing in the doubtful light of the moon; it lent a glory to his brow which reflected an almost solar gleam. Though at first a somewhat disdainful expression lurked in the wrinkles of his face, his look presently assumed the fixity which seems to gaze on an object invisible to the ordinary organs of sight. His eyes, no doubt, were seeing then the remoter images which the grave has in store for us.

Never, perhaps, had this man presented so grand an aspect. A terrible struggle was going on in his soul, and reacted on his outer frame; strong man as he seemed to be, he bent as a reed bows under the breeze that comes before a storm. Godefroid stood motionless, speechless, spellbound; some inexplicable force nailed him to the floor; and, as happens when our attention takes us out of ourselves while watching a fire or a battle, he was wholly unconscious of his body.

"Shall I tell you the fate to which you were hastening, poor angel of love? Listen! It has been given to me to see immeasurable space, bottomless gulfs in which all human creations are swallowed up, the shoreless sea whither flows the vast stream of men and of angels. As I made my way through the realms of eternal torment, I was sheltered under the cloak of an immortal—the robe of glory due to genius, and which the ages hand on—I, a frail mortal! When I wandered through the fields of light where the happy souls play, I was borne up by the love of a woman, the wings of an angel; resting on her heart, I could taste the ineffable pleasures whose touch is more perilous to us mortals than are the torments of the worser world.

"As I achieved my pilgrimage through the dark regions below I had mounted from torture to torture, from crime to crime, from punishment to punishment, from awful silence to heartrending cries, till I reached the uppermost circle of Hell. Already, from afar, I could see the glory of Paradise shining at a vast distance; I was still in darkness, but on the borders of day. I flew, upheld by my Guide, borne along by a power akin to that which, during our dreams, wafts us to spheres invisible to the eye of the body. The halo that crowned our heads seared away the shades as we passed, like impalpable dust. Far above us the suns of all the worlds shone with scarce so much light as the twinkling fireflies of my native land. I was soaring towards the fields of air where, round about Paradise, the bodies of light are in closer array, where the azure is easy to pass through, where worlds innumerable spring like flowers in a meadow.

"There, on the last level of the circles where those phantoms dwell that I had left behind me, like sorrows one would fain forget, I saw a vast shade. Standing in an attitude of aspiration, that soul looked eagerly into space; his feet were riveted by the will of God to the topmost point of the margin, and he remained forever in the painful strain by which we project our purpose when we long to soar, as birds about to take wing. I saw the man; he neither looked at us nor heard us; every muscle quivered and throbbed; at each separate instant he seemed to feel, though he did not move, all the fatigue of traversing the infinite that divided him from Paradise where, as he gazed steadfastly, he believed he had glimpses of a beloved image. At this last gate of Hell, as at the first, I saw the stamp of despair even in hope. The hapless creature was so fearfully held by some unseen force, that his anguish entered into my bones and froze my blood. I shrank closer to my Guide, whose protection restored me to peace and silence.

"Suddenly the Shade gave a cry of joy—a cry as shrill as that of the mother bird that sees a hawk in the air, or suspects its presence. We looked where he was looking, and saw, as it were, a sapphire, floating high up in the abysses of light. The glowing star fell with the swiftness of a sunbeam when it flashes over the horizon in the morning and its first rays shoot across the world. The Splendor became clearer and grew larger; presently I beheld the cloud of glory in which the angels move—a shining vapor that emanates from their divine substance, and that glitters here and there like tongues of flame. A noble face, whose glory none may endure that have not won the mantle, the laurel, and the palm—the attribute of the Powers—rose above this cloud as white and pure as snow. It was Light within light. His wings as they waved shed dazzling ripples in the spheres through which he descended, as the glance of God pierces through the universe. At last I saw the archangel in all his glory. The flower of eternal beauty that belongs to the angels of the Spirit shone in him. In one hand he held a green palm branch, in the other a sword of flame: the palm to bestow on the pardoned soul, the sword to drive back all the hosts of Hell with one sweep. As he approached, the perfumes of Heaven fell upon us as dew. In the region where the archangel paused, the air took the hues of opal, and moved in eddies of which he was the centre. He paused, looked at the Shade, and said:

"'To-morrow.'

"Then he turned heavenwards once more, spread his wings, and clove through space as a vessel cuts through the waves, hardly showing her white sails to the exiles left on some deserted shore.

"The Shade uttered appalling cries, to which the damned responded from the lowest circle, the deepest in the immensity of suffering, to the more peaceful zone near the surface on which we were standing. This worst torment of all had appealed to all the rest. The turmoil was swelled by the roar of a sea of fire which formed a bass to the terrific harmony of endless millions of suffering souls.

"Then suddenly the Shade took flight through the doleful city, and down to its place at the very bottom of Hell; but as suddenly it came up again, turned, soared through the endless circles in every direction, as a vulture, confined for the first time in a cage, exhausts itself in vain efforts. The Shade was free to do this; he could wander through the zones of Hell icy, fetid, or scorching without enduring their pangs; he glided into that vastness as a sunbeam makes its way into the deepest dark.

"'God has not condemned him to any torment,' said the Master; 'but not one of the souls you have seen suffering their various punishments would exchange his anguish for the hope that is consuming this soul.'

"And just then the Shade came back to us, brought thither by an irresistible force which condemned him to perch on the verge of Hell. My divine Guide, guessing my curiosity, touched the unhappy Shade with his palm-branch. He, who was perhaps trying to measure the age of sorrow that divided him from that ever-vanishing 'To-morrow,' started and gave a look full of all the tears he had already shed.

"'You would know my woe?' said he sadly. 'Oh, I love to tell it. I am here, Teresa is above; that is all. On earth we were happy, we were always together. When I saw my loved Teresa Donati for the first time, she was ten years old. We loved each other even then, not knowing what love meant. Our lives were one; I turned pale if she were pale, I was happy in her joy; we gave ourselves up to the pleasure of thinking and feeling together; and we learned what love was, each through the other. We were wedded at Cremona; we never saw each other's lips but decked with pearls of a smile; our eyes always shone; our hair, like our desires, flowed together; our heads were always bent over one book when we read, our feet walked in equal step. Life was one long kiss, our home was a nest.

"'One day, for the first time, Teresa turned pale and said, "I am in pain!"—And I was not in pain!

"'She never rose again. I saw her sweet face change, her golden hair fade—and I did not die! She smiled to hide her sufferings, but I could read them in her blue eyes, of which I could interpret the slightest trembling. "Honorino, I love you!" said she, at the very moment when her lips turned white, and she was clasping my hand still in hers when death chilled them. So I killed myself that she might not lie alone in her sepulchral bed, under her marble sheet. Teresa is above and I am here. I could not bear to leave her, but God has divided us. Why, then, did He unite us on earth? He is jealous! Paradise was no doubt so much the fairer on the day when Teresa entered in.

"'Do you see her? She is sad in her bliss; she is parted from me! Paradise must be a desert to her.'

"'Master,' said I with tears, for I thought of my love, 'when this one shall desire Paradise for God's sake alone, shall he not be delivered?' And the Father of Poets mildly bowed his head in sign of assent.

"We departed, cleaving the air, and making no more noise than the birds that pass overhead sometimes when we lie in the shade of a tree. It would have been vain to try to check the hapless shade in his blasphemy. It is one of the griefs of the angels of darkness that they can never see the light even when they are surrounded by it. He would not have understood us."

At this moment the swift approach of many horses rang through the stillness, the dog barked, the constable's deep growl replied; the horsemen dismounted, knocked at the door; the noise was so unexpected that it seemed like some sudden explosion.

The two exiles, the two poets, fell to earth through all the space that divides us from the skies. The painful shock of this fall rushed through their veins like strange blood, hissing as it seemed, and full of scorching sparks. Their pain was like an electric discharge. The loud, heavy step of a man-at-arms sounded on the stairs with the iron clank of his sword, his cuirass, and spurs; a soldier presently stood before the astonished stranger.

"We can return to Florence," said the man, whose bass voice sounded soft as he spoke in Italian.

"What is that you say?" asked the old man.

"The *Bianchi* are triumphant."

"Are you not mistaken?" asked the poet.

"No, dear Dante!" replied the soldier, whose warlike tones rang with the thrill of battle and the exultation of victory.

"To Florence! To Florence! Ah, my Florence!" cried Dante Alighieri, drawing himself up, and gazing into the distance. In fancy he saw Italy; he was gigantic.

"But I—when shall I be in Heaven?" said Godefroid, kneeling on one knee before the immortal poet, like an angel before the sanctuary.

"Come to Florence," said Dante in compassionate tones. "Come! when you see its lovely landscape from the heights of Fiesole you will fancy yourself in Paradise."

The soldier smiled. For the first time, perhaps for the only time in his life, Dante's gloomy and solemn features wore a look of joy; his eyes and brows expressed the happiness he has depicted so lavishly in his vision of Paradise. He thought perhaps that he heard the voice of Beatrice.

A light step, and the rustle of a woman's gown, were audible in the silence. Dawn was now showing its first streaks of light. The fair Comtesse de Mahaut came in and flew to Godefroid.

"Come, my child, my son! I may at last acknowledge you. Your birth is recognized, your rights are under the protection of the King of France, and you will find Paradise in your mother's heart."

"I hear, I know, the voice of Heaven!" cried the youth in rapture.

The exclamation roused Dante, who saw the young man folded in the Countess' arms. He took leave of them with a look, and left his young companion on his mother's bosom.

"Come away!" he cried in a voice of thunder. "Death to the Guelphs!"

PARIS, *October 1831.*

*Seraphita*

TO

MADAME ÉVELINE DE HANSKA,

*née Comtesse Rzewuska.*

—

MADAME,—Here is the work which you asked of me. I am happy, in thus dedicating it, to offer you a proof of the respectful affection you allow me to bear you. If I am reproached for impotence in this attempt to draw from the depths of mysticism a book which seeks to give, in the lucid transparency of our beautiful language, the luminous poesy of the Orient, to you the blame! Did you not command this struggle (resembling that of Jacob) by telling me that the most imperfect sketch of this Figure, dreamed of by you, as it has been by me since childhood, would still be something to you?

Here, then, it is,—that something. Would that this book could belong exclusively to noble spirits, preserved like yours from worldly pettiness by solitude! *They* would know how to give to it the melodious rhythm that it lacks, which might have made it, in the hands of a poet, the glorious epic that France still awaits.

But from me they must accept it as one of those sculptured balustrades, carved by a hand of faith, on which the pilgrims lean, in the choir of some glorious church, to think upon the end of man.

*I am, madame, with respect,*

*Your devoted servant,*

DE BALZAC.

# I. SERAPHITUS

As the eye glances over a map of the coasts of Norway, can the imagination fail to marvel at their fantastic indentations and serrated edges, like a granite lace, against which the surges of the North Sea roar incessantly? Who has not dreamed of the majestic sights to be seen on those beachless shores, of that multitude of creeks and inlets and little bays, no two of them alike, yet all trackless abysses? We may almost fancy that Nature took pleasure in recording by ineffaceable hieroglyphics the symbol of Norwegian life, bestowing on these coasts the conformation of a fish's spine, fishery being the staple commerce of the country, and wellnigh the only means of living of the hardy men who cling like tufts of lichen to the arid cliffs. Here, through fourteen degrees of longitude, barely seven hundred thousand souls maintain existence. Thanks to perils devoid of glory, to year-long snows which clothe the Norway peaks and guard them from profaning foot of traveller, these sublime beauties are virgin still; they will be seen to harmonize with human phenomena, also virgin—at least to poetry—which here took place, the history of which it is our purpose to relate.

If one of these inlets, mere fissures to the eyes of the eider-ducks, is wide enough for the sea not to freeze between the prison-walls of rock against which it surges, the country-people call the little bay a "fjord,"—a word which geographers of every nation have adopted into their respective languages. Though a certain resemblance exists among all these fjords, each has its own characteristics. The sea has everywhere forced its way as through a breach, yet the rocks about each fissure are diversely rent, and their tumultuous precipices defy the rules of geometric law. Here the scarp is dentelled like a saw; there the narrow ledges barely allow the snow to lodge or the noble crests of the Northern pines to spread themselves; farther on, some convulsion of Nature may have rounded a coquettish curve into a lovely valley flanked in rising terraces with black-plumed pines. Truly we are tempted to call this land the Switzerland of Ocean.

Midway between Trondhjem and Christiansand lies an inlet called the Strom-fjord. If the Strom-fjord is not the loveliest of these rocky landscapes, it has the merit of displaying the terrestrial grandeurs of Norway, and of enshrining the scenes of a history that is indeed celestial.

The general outline of the Strom-fjord seems at first sight to be that of a funnel washed out by the sea. The passage which the waves have forced present to the eye an image of the eternal struggle between old Ocean and the granite rock,—two creations of equal power, one through inertia, the other by ceaseless motion. Reefs of fantastic shape run out on either side, and bar the way of ships and forbid their entrance. The intrepid sons of Norway cross these reefs on foot, springing from rock to rock, undismayed at the abyss—a hundred fathoms deep and only six feet wide—which yawns beneath them. Here a tottering block of gneiss falling athwart two rocks gives an uncertain footway; there the hunters or the fishermen, carrying their loads, have flung the stems of fir-trees in guise of bridges, to join the projecting reefs, around and beneath which the surges roar incessantly. This dangerous entrance to the little bay bears obliquely to the right with a serpentine movement, and there encounters a mountain rising some twenty-five hundred feet above sea-level, the base of which is a vertical palisade of solid rock more than a mile and a half long, the inflexible granite nowhere yielding to clefts or undulations until it reaches a height of two hundred feet above the water. Rushing violently in, the sea is driven back with equal violence by the inert force of the mountain to the opposite shore, gently curved by the spent force of the retreating waves.

The fjord is closed at the upper end by a vast gneiss formation crowned with forests, down which a river plunges in cascades, becomes a torrent when the snows are melting, spreads into a sheet of waters, and then falls with a roar into the bay,—vomiting as it does so the hoary pines and the aged larches washed down from the forests and scarce seen amid the foam. These trees plunge headlong into the fjord and reappear after a time on the surface, clinging together and forming islets which float ashore on the beaches, where the inhabitants of a village on the left bank of the Strom-fjord gather them up, split, broken (though sometimes whole), and always stripped of bark and branches. The mountain which receives at its base the assaults of Ocean, and at its summit the buffeting of the wild North wind, is called the Falberg. Its crest, wrapped at all seasons in a mantle of snow and ice, is the sharpest peak of Norway; its proximity to the pole produces, at the height of eighteen hundred feet, a degree of cold equal to that of the highest mountains of the globe. The summit of this rocky mass, rising sheer from the fjord on one side, slopes gradually downward to the east, where it joins the declivities of the Sieg and forms a series of terraced valleys, the chilly temperature of which allows no growth but that of shrubs and stunted trees.

The upper end of the fjord, where the waters enter it as they come down from the forest, is called the Sieg-dahlen,—a word which may be held to mean "the shedding of the Sieg,"—the river itself receiving that name. The curving shore opposite to the face of the Falberg is the valley of Jarvis,—a smiling scene overlooked by hills clothed with firs, birch-trees, and larches, mingled with a few oaks and beeches, the richest coloring of all the varied tapestries which Nature in these northern regions spreads upon the surface of her rugged rocks. The eye can readily mark the line where the soil, warmed by the rays of the sun, bears cultivation and shows the native growth of the Norwegian flora. Here the expanse of the fjord is broad enough to allow the sea, dashed back by the Falberg, to spend its expiring force in gentle murmurs upon the lower slope of these hills,—a shore bordered with finest sand, strewn with mica and sparkling pebbles, porphyry, and marbles of a thousand tints, brought from Sweden by the river floods, together with ocean waifs, shells, and flowers of the sea driven in by tempests, whether of the Pole or Tropics.

At the foot of the hills of Jarvis lies a village of some two hundred wooden houses, where an isolated population lives like a swarm of bees in a forest, without increasing or diminishing; vegetating happily, while wringing their means of living from the breast of a stern Nature. The almost

unknown existence of the little hamlet is readily accounted
for. Few of its inhabitants were bold enough to risk their
lives among the reefs to reach the deep-sea fishing,—the
staple industry of Norwegians on the least dangerous portions of their coast. The fish of the fjord were numerous
enough to suffice, in part at least, for the sustenance of the
inhabitants; the valley pastures provided milk and butter;
a certain amount of fruitful, well-tilled soil yielded rye and
hemp and vegetables, which necessity taught the people to
protect against the severity of the cold and the fleeting but
terrible heat of the sun with the shrewd ability which Norwegians display in the two-fold struggle. The difficulty of
communication with the outer world, either by land where
the roads are impassable, or by sea where none but tiny
boats can thread their way through the maritime defiles
that guard the entrance to the bay, hinder these people
from growing rich by the sale of their timber. It would cost
enormous sums to either blast a channel out to sea or construct a way to the interior. The roads from Christiana to
Trondhjem all turn toward the Strom-fjord, and cross the
Sieg by a bridge some score of miles above its fall into the
bay. The country to the north, between Jarvis and Trondhjem, is covered with impenetrable forests, while to the
south the Falberg is nearly as much separated from Christiana by inaccessible precipices. The village of Jarvis might
perhaps have communicated with the interior of Norway
and Sweden by the river Sieg; but to do this and to be
thus brought into contact with civilization, the Strom-fjord
needed the presence of a man of genius. Such a man did
actually appear there,—a poet, a Swede of great religious
fervor, who died admiring, even reverencing this region as
one of the noblest works of the Creator.

Minds endowed by study with an inward sight, and
whose quick perceptions bring before the soul, as though
painted on a canvas, the contrasting scenery of this universe,
will now apprehend the general features of the Strom-fjord.
They alone, perhaps, can thread their way through the tor-
tuous channels of the reef, or flee with the battling waves
to the everlasting rebuff of the Falberg whose white peaks
mingle with the vaporous clouds of the pearl-gray sky, or

watch with delight the curving sheet of waters, or hear the rushing of the Sieg as it hangs for an instant in long fillets and then falls over a picturesque abatis of noble trees toppled confusedly together, sometimes upright, sometimes half-sunken beneath the rocks. It may be that such minds alone can dwell upon the smiling scenes nestling among the lower hills of Jarvis; where the luscious Northern vegetables spring up in families, in myriads, where the white birches bend, graceful as maidens, where colonnades of beeches rear their boles mossy with the growth of centuries, where shades of green contrast, and white clouds float amid the blackness of the distant pines, and tracts of many-tinted crimson and purple shrubs are shaded endlessly; in short, where blend all colors, all perfumes of a flora whose wonders are still ignored. Widen the boundaries of this limited ampitheater, spring upward to the clouds, lose yourself among the rocks where the seals are lying and even then your thought cannot compass the wealth of beauty nor the poetry of this Norwegian coast. Can your thought be as vast as the ocean that bounds it? as weird as the fantastic forms drawn by these forests, these clouds, these shadows, these changeful lights?

Do you see above the meadows on that lowest slope which undulates around the higher hills of Jarvis two or three hundred houses roofed with "noever," a sort of thatch made of birch-bark,—frail houses, long and low, looking like silk-worms on a mulberry-leaf tossed hither by the winds? Above these humble, peaceful dwellings stands the church, built with a simplicity in keeping with the poverty of the villagers. A graveyard surrounds the chancel, and a little farther on you see the parsonage. Higher up, on a projection of the mountain is a dwelling-house, the only one of stone; for which reason the inhabitants of the village call it "the Swedish Castle." In fact, a wealthy Swede settled in Jarvis about thirty years before this history begins, and did his best to ameliorate its condition. This little house, certainly not a castle, built with the intention of leading the inhabitants to build others like it, was noticeable for its solidity and for the wall that inclosed it, a rare thing in Norway where, notwithstanding the abundance of stone, wood alone is used for all fences, even those of fields. This Swedish house, thus protected against the climate, stood on rising ground in the center of an immense courtyard. The windows were sheltered by those projecting pent-house roofs supported by squared trunks of trees which give so patriarchal an air to Northern dwellings. From beneath them the eye could see the savage nudity of the Falberg, or compare the infinitude of the open sea with the tiny drop of water in the foaming fjord; the ear could hear the flowing of the Sieg, whose white sheet far away looked motionless as it fell into its granite cup edged for miles around with glaciers,—in short, from this vantage ground the whole landscape whereon our simple yet superhuman drama was about to be enacted could be seen and noted.

The winter of 1799-1800 was one of the most severe ever known to Europeans. The Norwegian sea was frozen in all the fjords, where, as a usual thing, the violence of the surf kept the ice from forming. A wind, whose effects were like those of the Spanish levanter, swept the ice of the Strom-fjord, driving the snow to the upper end of the gulf. Seldom indeed could the people of Jarvis see the mirror of frozen waters reflecting the colors of the sky; a wondrous site in the bosom of these mountains when all other aspects of nature are levelled beneath successive sheets of snow, and crests and valleys are alike mere folds of the vast mantle flung by winter across a landscape at once so mournfully dazzling and so monotonous. The falling volume of the Sieg, suddenly frozen, formed an immense arcade beneath which the inhabitants might have crossed under shelter from the blast had any dared to risk themselves inland. But the dangers of every step away from their own surroundings kept even the boldest hunters in their homes, afraid lest the narrow paths along the precipices, the clefts and fissures among the rocks, might be unrecognizable beneath the snow.

Thus it was that no human creature gave life to the white desert where Boreas reigned, his voice alone resounding at distant intervals. The sky, nearly always gray, gave tones of polished steel to the ice of the fjord. Perchance some ancient eider-duck crossed the expanse, trusting to the warm down beneath which dream, in other lands, the luxurious rich, little knowing of the dangers through which their luxury has come to them. Like the Bedouin of the desert who darts alone across the sands of Africa, the bird is neither seen nor heard; the torpid atmosphere, deprived of its electrical conditions, echoes neither the whirr of its wings nor its joyous notes. Besides, what human eye was strong enough to bear the glitter of those pinnacles adorned with sparkling crystals, or the sharp reflections of the snow, iridescent on the summits in the rays of a pallid sun which infrequently appeared, like a dying man seeking to make known that he still lives. Often, when the flocks of gray clouds, driven in squadrons athwart the mountains and among the tree-tops, hid the sky with their triple veils Earth, lacking the celestial lights, lit herself by herself.

Here, then, we meet the majesty of Cold, seated eternally at the pole in that regal silence which is the attribute of all absolute monarchy. Every extreme principle carries with it an appearance of negation and the symptoms of death; for is not life the struggle of two forces? Here in this Northern nature nothing lived. One sole power—the unproductive power of ice—reigned unchallenged. The roar of the open sea no longer reached the deaf, dumb inlet, where during one short season of the year Nature made haste to produce the slender harvests necessary for the food of the patient people. A few tall pine-trees lifted their black pyramids garlanded with snow, and the form of their long branches and depending shoots completed the mourning garments of those solemn heights.

Each household gathered in its chimney-corner, in houses carefully closed from the outer air, and well supplied with biscuit, melted butter, dried fish, and other provisions laid in for the seven-months winter. The very smoke of these dwellings was hardly seen, half-hidden as they were beneath the snow, against the weight of which they were protected by long planks reaching from the roof and fastened at some distance to solid blocks on the ground, forming a covered way around each building.

During these terrible winter months the women spun and dyed the woollen stuffs and the linen fabrics with which they clothed their families, while the men read, or fell into those endless meditations which have given birth to so many profound theories, to the mystic dreams of the North, to its beliefs, to its studies (so full and so complete in one science, at least, sounded as with a plummet), to its manners and its morals, half-monastic, which force the soul to react and feed upon itself and make the Norwegian peasant a being apart among the peoples of Europe.

Such was the condition of the Strom-fjord in the first year of the nineteenth century and about the middle of the month of May.

On a morning when the sun burst forth upon this landscape, lighting the fires of the ephemeral diamonds produced by crystallizations of the snow and ice, two beings crossed the fjord and flew along the base of the Falberg, rising thence from ledge to ledge toward the summit. What were they? human creatures, or two arrows? They might have been taken for eider-ducks sailing in consort before the wind. Not the boldest hunter nor the most superstitious fisherman would have attributed to human beings the power to move safely along the slender lines traced beneath the snow by the granite ledges, where yet this couple glided with the terrifying dexterity of somnambulists who, forgetting their own weight and the dangers of the slightest deviation, hurry along a ridge-pole and keep their equilibrium by the power of some mysterious force.

"Stop me, Seraphitus," said a pale young girl, "and let me breathe. I look at you, you only, while scaling these walls of the gulf; otherwise, what would become of me? I am such a feeble creature. Do I tire you?"

"No," said the being on whose arm she leaned. "But let us go on, Minna; the place where we are is not firm enough to stand on."

Once more the snow creaked sharply beneath the long boards fastened to their feet, and soon they reached the upper terrace of the first ledge, clearly defined upon the flank of the precipice. The person whom Minna had addressed as Seraphitus threw his weight upon his right heel, arresting the plank—six and a half feet long and narrow as the foot of a child—which was fastened to his boot by a double thong of leather. This plank, two inches thick, was covered with reindeer skin, which bristled against the snow when the foot was raised, and served to stop the wearer. Seraphitus drew in his left foot, furnished with another "skee," which was only two feet long, turned swiftly where he stood, caught his timid companion in his arms, lifted her in spite of the long boards on her feet, and placed her on a projecting rock from which he brushed the snow with his pelisse.

"You are safe there, Minna; you can tremble at your ease."

"We are a third of the way up the Ice-Cap," she said, looking at the peak to which she gave the popular name by which it is known in Norway; "I can hardly believe it."

Too much out of breath to say more, she smiled at Seraphitus, who, without answering, laid his hand upon her heart and listened to its sounding throbs, rapid as those of a frightened bird.

"It often beats as fast when I run," she said.

Seraphitus inclined his head with a gesture that was neither coldness nor indifference, and yet, despite the grace which made the movement almost tender, it none the less bespoke a certain negation, which in a woman would have seemed an exquisite coquetry. Seraphitus clasped the young girl in his arms. Minna accepted the caress as an answer to her words, continuing to gaze at him. As he raised his head, and threw back with impatient gesture the golden masses of his hair to free his brow, he saw an expression of joy in the eyes of his companion.

"Yes, Minna," he said in a voice whose paternal accents were charming from the lips of a being who was still adolescent, "Keep your eyes on me; do not look below you."

"Why not?" she asked.

"You wish to know why? then look!"

Minna glanced quickly at her feet and cried out suddenly like a child who sees a tiger. The awful sensation of abysses seized her; one glance sufficed to communicate its contagion. The fjord, eager for food, bewildered her with its loud voice ringing in her ears, interposing between herself and life as though to devour her more surely. From the

crown of her head to her feet and along her spine an icy
shudder ran; then suddenly intolerable heat suffused her
nerves, beat in her veins and overpowered her extremities
with electric shocks like those of the torpedo. Too feeble to
resist, she felt herself drawn by a mysterious power to the
depths below, wherein she fancied that she saw some monster belching its venom, a monster whose magnetic eyes
were charming her, whose open jaws appeared to craunch
their prey before they seized it.

"I die, my Seraphitus, loving none but thee," she said,
making a mechanical movement to fling herself into the
abyss.

Seraphitus breathed softly on her forehead and eyes.
Suddenly, like a traveller relaxed after a bath, Minna forgot
these keen emotions, already dissipated by that caressing
breath which penetrated her body and filled it with bal-
samic essences as quickly as the breath itself had crossed
the air.

"Who art thou?" she said, with a feeling of gentle terror.
"Ah, but I know! thou art my life. How canst thou look into
that gulf and not die?" she added presently.

Seraphitus left her clinging to the granite rock and placed
himself at the edge of the narrow platform on which they
stood, whence his eyes plunged to the depths of the fjord,
defying its dazzling invitation. His body did not tremble,
his brow was white and calm as that of a marble statue,—
an abyss facing an abyss.

"Seraphitus! dost thou not love me? come back!" she
cried. "Thy danger renews my terror. Who art thou to have
such superhuman power at thy age?" she asked as she felt
his arms inclosing her once more.

"But, Minna," answered Seraphitus, "you look fearlessly
at greater spaces far than that."

Then with raised finger, this strange being pointed
upward to the blue dome, which parting clouds left clear
above their heads, where stars could be seen in open day by
virtue of atmospheric laws as yet unstudied.

"But what a difference!" she answered smiling.

"You are right," he said; "we are born to stretch upward
to the skies. Our native land, like the face of a mother,

cannot terrify her children."

His voice vibrated through the being of his companion, who made no reply.

"Come! let us go on," he said.

The pair darted forward along the narrow paths traced back and forth upon the mountain, skimming from terrace to terrace, from line to line, with the rapidity of a barb, that bird of the desert. Presently they reached an open space, carpeted with turf and moss and flowers, where no foot had ever trod.

"Oh, the pretty saeter!" cried Minna, giving to the upland meadow its Norwegian name. "But how comes it here, at such a height?"

"Vegetation ceases here, it is true," said Seraphitus. "These few plants and flowers are due to that sheltering rock which protects the meadow from the polar winds. Put that tuft in your bosom, Minna," he added, gathering a flower,—"that balmy creation which no eye has ever seen; keep the solitary matchless flower in memory of this one matchless morning of your life. You will find no other guide to lead you again to this saeter."

So saying, he gave her the hybrid plant his falcon eye had seen amid the tufts of gentian acaulis and saxifrages,—a marvel, brought to bloom by the breath of angels. With girlish eagerness Minna seized the tufted plant of transparent green, vivid as emerald, which was formed of little leaves rolled trumpet-wise, brown at the smaller end but changing tint by tint to their delicately notched edges, which were green. These leaves were so tightly pressed together that they seemed to blend and form a mat or cluster of rosettes. Here and there from this green ground rose pure white stars edged with a line of gold, and from their throats came crimson anthers but no pistils. A fragrance, blended of roses and of orange blossoms, yet ethereal and fugitive, gave something as it were celestial to that mysterious flower, which Seraphitus sadly contemplated, as though it uttered plaintive thoughts which he alone could understand. But to Minna this mysterious phenomenon seemed a mere caprice of nature giving to stone the freshness, softness, and perfume of plants.

"Why do you call it matchless? can it not reproduce itself?" she asked, looking at Seraphitus, who colored and turned away.

"Let us sit down," he said presently; "look below you, Minna. See! At this height you will have no fear. The abyss is so far beneath us that we no longer have a sense of its depths; it acquires the perspective uniformity of ocean, the vagueness of clouds, the soft coloring of the sky. See, the ice of the fjord is a turquoise, the dark pine forests are mere threads of brown; for us all abysses should be thus adorned."

Seraphitus said the words with that fervor of tone and gesture seen and known only by those who have ascended the highest mountains of the globe,—a fervor so involuntarily acquired that the haughtiest of men is forced to regard his guide as a brother, forgetting his own superior station till he descends to the valleys and the abodes of his kind. Seraphitus unfastened the skees from Minna's feet, kneeling before her. The girl did not notice him, so absorbed was she in the marvellous view now offered of her native land, whose rocky outlines could here be seen at a glance. She felt, with deep emotion, the solemn permanence of those frozen summits, to which words could give no adequate utterance.

"We have not come here by human power alone," she said, clasping her hands. "But perhaps I dream."

"You think that facts the causes of which you cannot perceive are supernatural," replied her companion.

"Your replies," she said, "always bear the stamp of some deep thought. When I am near you I understand all things without an effort. Ah, I am free!"

"If so, you will not need your skees," he answered.

"Oh!" she said; "I who would fain unfasten yours and kiss your feet!"

"Keep such words for Wilfrid," said Seraphitus, gently.

"Wilfrid!" cried Minna angrily; then, softening as she glanced at her companion's face and trying, but in vain, to take his hand, she added, "You are never angry, never; you are so hopelessly perfect in all things."

"From which you conclude that I am unfeeling."

Minna was startled at this lucid interpretation of her thought.

"You prove to me, at any rate, that we understand each other," she said, with the grace of a loving woman.

Seraphitus softly shook his head and looked sadly and gently at her.

"You, who know all things," said Minna, "tell me why it is that the timidity I felt below is over now that I have mounted higher. Why do I dare to look at you for the first time face to face, while lower down I scarcely dared to give a furtive glance?"

"Perhaps because we are withdrawn from the pettiness of earth," he answered, unfastening his pelisse.

"Never, never have I seen you so beautiful!" cried Minna, sitting down on a mossy rock and losing herself in contemplation of the being who had now guided her to a part of the peak hitherto supposed to be inaccessible.

Never, in truth, had Seraphitus shone with so bright a radiance,—the only word which can render the illumination of his face and the aspect of his whole person. Was this splendor due to the luster which the pure air of mountains and the reflections of the snow give to the complexion? Was it produced by the inward impulse which excites the body at the instant when exertion is arrested? Did it come from the sudden contrast between the glory of the sun and the darkness of the clouds, from whose shadow the charming couple had just emerged? Perhaps to all these causes we may add the effect of a phenomenon, one of the noblest which human nature has to offer. If some able physiologist had studied this being (who, judging by the pride on his brow and the lightning in his eyes seemed a youth of about seventeen years of age), and if the student had sought for the springs of that beaming life beneath the whitest skin that ever the North bestowed upon her offspring, he would undoubtedly have believed either in some phosphoric fluid of the nerves shining beneath the cuticle, or in the constant presence of an inward luminary, whose rays issued through the being of Seraphitus like a light through an alabaster vase. Soft and slender as were his hands, ungloved to remove his companion's snow-boots, they seemed possessed of a

strength equal to that which the Creator gave to the diaphanous tentacles of the crab. The fire darting from his vivid
glance seemed to struggle with the beams of the sun, not
to take but to give them light. His body, slim and delicate
as that of a woman, gave evidence of one of those natures
which are feeble apparently, but whose strength equals
their will, rendering them at times powerful. Of medium
height, Seraphitus appeared to grow in stature as he turned
fully round and seemed about to spring upward. His hair,
curled by a fairy's hand and waving to the breeze, increased
the illusion produced by this aerial attitude; yet his bearing,
wholly without conscious effort, was the result far more of
a moral phenomenon than of a corporal habit.

Minna's imagination seconded this illusion, under
the dominion of which all persons would assuredly have
fallen,—an illusion which gave to Seraphitus the appearance of a vision dreamed of in happy sleep. No known
type conveys an image of that form so majestically made to
Minna, but which to the eyes of a man would have eclipsed
in womanly grace the fairest of Raphael's creations. That
painter of heaven has ever put a tranquil joy, a loving sweetness, into the lines of his angelic conceptions; but what soul,
unless it contemplated Seraphitus himself, could have conceived the ineffable emotions imprinted on his face? Who
would have divined, even in the dreams of artists, where
all things become possible, the shadow cast by some mysterious awe upon that brow, shining with intellect, which
seemed to question Heaven and to pity Earth? The head
hovered awhile disdainfully, as some majestic bird whose
cries reverberate on the atmosphere, then bowed itself
resignedly, like the turtledove uttering soft notes of tenderness in the depths of the silent woods. His complexion
was of marvellous whiteness, which brought out vividly the
coral lips, the brown eyebrows, and the silken lashes, the
only colors that trenched upon the paleness of that face,
whose perfect regularity did not detract from the grandeur
of the sentiments expressed in it; nay, thought and emotion were reflected there, without hindrance or violence,
with the majestic and natural gravity which we delight in
attributing to superior beings. That face of purest marble

expressed in all things strength and peace.

Minna rose to take the hand of Seraphitus, hoping thus to draw him to her, and to lay on that seductive brow a kiss given more from admiration than from love; but a glance at the young man's eyes, which pierced her as a ray of sunlight penetrates a prism, paralyzed the young girl. She felt, but without comprehending, a gulf between them; then she turned away her head and wept. Suddenly a strong hand seized her by the waist, and a soft voice said to her: "Come!" She obeyed, resting her head, suddenly revived, upon the heart of her companion, who, regulating his step to hers with gentle and attentive conformity, led her to a spot whence they could see the radiant glories of the polar Nature.

"Before I look, before I listen to you, tell me, Seraphitus, why you repulse me. Have I displeased you? and how? tell me! I want nothing for myself; I would that all my earthly goods were yours, for the riches of my heart are yours already. I would that light came to my eyes only though your eyes just as my thought is born of your thought. I should not then fear to offend you, for I should give you back the echoes of your soul, the words of your heart, day by day,—as we render to God the meditations with which his spirit nourishes our minds. I would be thine alone."

"Minna, a constant desire is that which shapes our future. Hope on! But if you would be pure in heart mingle the idea of the All-Powerful with your affections here below; then you will love all creatures, and your heart will rise to heights indeed."

"I will do all you tell me," she answered, lifting her eyes to his with a timid movement.

"I cannot be your companion," said Seraphitus sadly.

He seemed to repress some thoughts, then stretched his arms towards Christiana, just visible like a speck on the horizon and said:—

"Look!"

"We are very small," she said.

"Yes, but we become great through feeling and through intellect," answered Seraphitus. "With us, and us alone, Minna, begins the knowledge of things; the little that we

learn of the laws of the visible world enables us to apprehend the immensity of the worlds invisible. I know not if
the time has come to speak thus to you, but I would, ah, I
would communicate to you the flame of my hopes! Perhaps
we may one day be together in the world where Love never
dies."

"Why not here and now?" she said, murmuring.

"Nothing is stable here," he said, disdainfully. "The passing joys of earthly love are gleams which reveal to certain
souls the coming of joys more durable; just as the discovery
of a single law of nature leads certain privileged beings to a
conception of the system of the universe. Our fleeting happiness here below is the forerunning proof of another and a
perfect happiness, just as the earth, a fragment of the world,
attests the universe. We cannot measure the vast orbit of
the Divine thought of which we are but an atom as small
as God is great; but we can feel its vastness, we can kneel,
adore, and wait. Men ever mislead themselves in science by
not perceiving that all things on their globe are related and
co-ordinated to the general evolution, to a constant movement and production which bring with them, necessarily,
both advancement and an End. Man himself is not a finished creation; if he were, God would not Be."

"How is it that in thy short life thou hast found the time
to learn so many things?" said the young girl.

"I remember," he replied.

"Thou art nobler than all else I see."

"We are the noblest of God's greatest works. Has He
not given us the faculty of reflecting on Nature; of gathering it within us by thought; of making it a footstool and
stepping-stone from and by which to rise to Him? We love
according to the greater or the lesser portion of heaven our
souls contain. But do not be unjust, Minna; behold the
magnificence spread before you. Ocean expands at your
feet like a carpet; the mountains resemble ampitheaters;
heaven's ether is above them like the arching folds of a
stage curtain. Here we may breathe the thoughts of God, as
it were like a perfume. See! the angry billows which engulf
the ships laden with men seem to us, where we are, mere
bubbles; and if we raise our eyes and look above, all there is

blue. Behold that diadem of stars! Here the tints of earthly
impressions disappear; standing on this nature rarefied by
space do you not feel within you something deeper far than
mind, grander than enthusiasm, of greater energy than will?
Are you not conscious of emotions whose interpretation is
no longer in us? Do you not feel your pinions? Let us pray."

Seraphitus knelt down and crossed his hands upon his
breast, while Minna fell, weeping, on her knees. Thus they
remained for a time, while the azure dome above their
heads grew larger and strong rays of light enveloped them
without their knowledge.

"Why dost thou not weep when I weep?" said Minna, in
a broken voice.

"They who are all spirit do not weep," replied Seraphitus rising; "Why should I weep? I see no longer human
wretchedness. Here, Good appears in all its majesty. There,
beneath us, I hear the supplications and the wailings of
that harp of sorrows which vibrates in the hands of cap-
tive souls. Here, I listen to the choir of harps harmonious.
There, below, is hope, the glorious inception of faith; but
here is faith—it reigns, hope realized!"

"You will never love me; I am too imperfect; you disdain
me," said the young girl.

"Minna, the violet hidden at the feet of the oak whispers
to itself: 'The sun does not love me; he comes not.' The sun
says: 'If my rays shine upon her she will perish, poor flower.'
Friend of the flower, he sends his beams through the oak
leaves, he veils, he tempers them, and thus they color the
petals of his beloved. I have not veils enough, I fear lest
you see me too closely; you would tremble if you knew me
better. Listen: I have no taste for earthly fruits. Your joys,
I know them all too well, and, like the sated emperors of
pagan Rome, I have reached disgust of all things; I have
received the gift of vision. Leave me! abandon me!" he
murmured, sorrowfully.

Seraphitus turned and seated himself on a projecting
rock, dropping his head upon his breast.

"Why do you drive me to despair?" said Minna.

"Go, go!" cried Seraphitus, "I have nothing that you
want of me. Your love is too earthly for my love. Why do

you not love Wilfrid? Wilfrid is a man, tested by passions; he would clasp you in his vigorous arms and make you feel a hand both broad and strong. His hair is black, his eyes are full of human thoughts, his heart pours lava in every word he utters; he could kill you with caresses. Let him be your beloved, your husband! Yes, thine be Wilfrid!"

Minna wept aloud.

"Dare you say that you do not love him?" he went on, in a voice which pierced her like a dagger.

"Have mercy, have mercy, my Seraphitus!"

"Love him, poor child of Earth to which thy destiny has indissolubly bound thee," said the strange being, beckoning Minna by a gesture, and forcing her to the edge of the saeter, whence he pointed downward to a scene that might well inspire a young girl full of enthusiasm with the fancy that she stood above this earth.

"I longed for a companion to the kingdom of Light; I wished to show you that morsel of mud, I find you bound to it. Farewell. Remain on earth; enjoy through the senses; obey your nature; turn pale with pallid men; blush with women; sport with children; pray with the guilty; raise your eyes to heaven when sorrows overtake you; tremble, hope, throb in all your pulses; you will have a companion; you can laugh and weep, and give and receive. I,—I am an exile, far from heaven; a monster, far from earth. I live of myself and by myself. I feel by the spirit; I breathe through my brow; I see by thought; I die of impatience and of longing. No one here below can fulfil my desires or calm my griefs. I have forgotten how to weep. I am alone. I resign myself, and I wait."

Seraphitus looked at the flowery mound on which he had seated Minna; then he turned and faced the frowning heights, whose pinnacles were wrapped in clouds; to them he cast, unspoken, the remainder of his thoughts.

"Minna, do you hear those delightful strains?" he said after a pause, with the voice of a dove, for the eagle's cry was hushed; "it is like the music of those Eolian harps your poets hang in forests and on the mountains. Do you see the shadowy figures passing among the clouds, the winged feet of those who are making ready the gifts of heaven? They bring refreshment to the soul; the skies are about to open and shed the flowers of spring upon the earth. See, a gleam is darting from the pole. Let us fly, let us fly! It is time we go!"

In a moment their skees were refastened, and the pair descended the Falberg by the steep slopes which join the mountain to the valleys of the Sieg. Miraculous perception guided their course, or, to speak more properly, their flight. When fissures covered with snow intercepted them, Seraphitus caught Minna in his arms and darted with rapid motion, lightly as a bird, over the crumbling causeways of the abyss. Sometimes, while propelling his companion, he deviated to the right or left to avoid a precipice, a tree, a projecting rock, which he seemed to see beneath the snow, as an old sailor, familiar with the ocean, discerns the hidden reefs by the color, the trend, or the eddying of the water. When they reached the paths of the Siegdahlen, where they could fearlessly follow a straight line to regain the ice of the fjord, Seraphitus stopped Minna.

"You have nothing to say to me?" he asked.

"I thought you would rather think alone," she answered respectfully.

"Let us hasten, Minette; it is almost night," he said.

Minna quivered as she heard the voice, now so changed, of her guide,—a pure voice, like that of a young girl, which dissolved the fantastic dream through which she had been passing. Seraphitus seemed to be laying aside his male force and the too keen intellect that flames from his eyes. Presently the charming pair glided across the fjord and reached the snow-field which divides the shore from the first range of houses; then, hurrying forward as daylight faded, they sprang up the hill toward the parsonage, as though they were mounting the steps of a great staircase.

"My father must be anxious," said Minna.

"No," answered Seraphitus.

As he spoke the couple reached the porch of the humble dwelling where Monsieur Becker, the pastor of Jarvis, sat reading while awaiting his daughter for the evening meal.

"Dear Monsieur Becker," said Seraphitus, "I have brought Minna back to you safe and sound."

"Thank you, mademoiselle," said the old man, laying his spectacles on his book; "you must be very tired."

"Oh, no," said Minna, and as she spoke she felt the soft breath of her companion on her brow.

"Dear heart, will you come day after tomorrow evening and take tea with me?"

"Gladly, dear."

"Monsieur Becker, you will bring her, will you not?"

"Yes, mademoiselle."

Seraphitus inclined his head with a pretty gesture, and bowed to the old pastor as he left the house. A few moments later he reached the great courtyard of the Swedish villa. An old servant, over eighty years of age, appeared in the portico bearing a lantern. Seraphitus slipped off his snow-shoes with the graceful dexterity of a woman, then darting into the salon he fell exhausted and motionless on a wide divan covered with furs.

"What will you take?" asked the old man, lighting the immensely tall wax-candles that are used in Norway.

"Nothing, David, I am too weary."

Seraphitus unfastened his pelisse lined with sable, threw it over him, and fell asleep. The old servant stood for several minutes gazing with loving eyes at the singular being before him, whose sex it would have been difficult for anyone at that moment to determine. Wrapped as he was in a form-less garment, which resembled equally a woman's robe and a man's mantle, it was impossible not to fancy that the slen-der feet which hung at the side of the couch were those of a woman, and equally impossible not to note how the fore-head and the outlines of the head gave evidence of power brought to its highest pitch.

"She suffers, and she will not tell me," thought the old man. "She is dying, like a flower wilted by the burning sun."

And the old man wept.


## II. SERAPHITA

Later in the evening David re-entered the salon.

"I know who it is you have come to announce," said

Seraphita in a sleepy voice. "Wilfrid may enter."

Hearing these words a man suddenly presented himself, crossed the room and sat down beside her.

"My dear Seraphita, are you ill?" he said. "You look paler than usual."

She turned slowly towards him, tossing back her hair like a pretty woman whose aching head leaves her no strength even for complaint.

"I was foolish enough to cross the fjord with Minna," she said. "We ascended the Falberg."

"Do you mean to kill yourself?" he said with a lover's terror.

"No, my good Wilfrid; I took the greatest care of your Minna."

Wilfrid struck his hand violently on a table, rose hastily, and made several steps towards the door with an exclamation full of pain; then he returned and seemed about to remonstrate.

"Why this disturbance if you think me ill?" she said.

"Forgive me, have mercy!" he cried, kneeling beside her. "Speak to me harshly if you will; exact all that the cruel fancies of a woman lead you to imagine I least can bear; but oh, my beloved, do not doubt my love. You take Minna like an axe to hew me down. Have mercy!"

"Why do you say these things, my friend, when you know that they are useless?" she replied, with a look which grew in the end so soft that Wilfrid ceased to behold her eyes, but saw in their place a fluid light, the shimmer of which was like the last vibrations of an Italian song.

"Ah! no man dies of anguish!" he murmured.

"You are suffering?" she said in a voice whose intonations produced upon his heart the same effect as that of her look. "Would I could help you!"

"Love me as I love you."

"Poor Minna!" she replied.

"Why am I unarmed!" exclaimed Wilfrid, violently.

"You are out of temper," said Seraphita, smiling. "Come, have I not spoken to you like those Parisian women whose loves you tell of?"

Wilfrid sat down, crossed his arms, and looked gloomily

at Seraphita. "I forgive you," he said; "for you know not what you do."

"You mistake," she replied; "every woman from the days of Eve does good and evil knowingly."

"I believe it," he said.

"I am sure of it, Wilfrid. Our instinct is precisely that which makes us perfect. What you men learn, we feel."

"Why, then, do you not feel how much I love you?"

"Because you do not love me."

"Good God!"

"If you did, would you complain of your own sufferings?"

"You are terrible to-night, Seraphita. You are a demon."

"No, but I am gifted with the faculty of comprehending, and it is awful. Wilfrid, sorrow is a lamp which illumines life."

"Why did you ascend the Falberg?"

"Minna will tell you. I am too weary to talk. You must talk to me,—you who know so much, who have learned all things and forgotten nothing; you who have passed through every social test. Talk to me, amuse me, I am listening."

"What can I tell you that you do not know? Besides, the request is ironical. You allow yourself no intercourse with social life; you trample on its conventions, its laws, its customs, sentiments, and sciences; you reduce them all to the proportions such things take when viewed by you beyond this universe."

"Therefore you see, my friend, that I am not a woman. You do wrong to love me. What! am I to leave the ethereal regions of my pretended strength, make myself humbly small, cringe like the hapless female of all species, that you may lift me up? and then, when I, helpless and broken, ask you for help, when I need your arm, you will repulse me! No, we can never come to terms."

"You are more maliciously unkind to-night than I have ever known you."

"Unkind!" she said, with a look which seemed to blend all feelings into one celestial emotion, "no, I am ill, I suffer, that is all. Leave me, my friend; it is your manly right. We women should ever please you, entertain you, be gay in your presence and have no whims save those that amuse you. Come, what shall I do for you, friend? Shall I sing, shall I dance, though weariness deprives me of the use of voice and limbs?—Ah! gentlemen, be we on our deathbeds, we yet must smile to please you; you call that, methinks, your right. Poor women! I pity them. Tell me, you who abandon them when they grow old, is it because they have neither hearts nor souls? Wilfrid, I am a hundred years old; leave me! leave me! go to Minna!"

"Oh, my eternal love!"

"Do you know the meaning of eternity? Be silent, Wilfrid. You desire me, but you do not love me. Tell me, do I not seem to you like those coquettish Parisian women?"

"Certainly I no longer find you the pure celestial maiden I first saw in the church of Jarvis."

At these words Seraphita passed her hands across her brow, and when she removed them Wilfrid was amazed at the saintly expression that overspread her face.

"You are right, my friend," she said; "I do wrong whenever I set my feet upon your earth."

"Oh, Seraphita, be my star! stay where you can ever bless me with that clear light!"

As he spoke, he stretched forth his hand to take that of the young girl, but she withdrew it, neither disdainfully nor in anger. Wilfrid rose abruptly and walked to the window that she might not see the tears that rose to his eyes.

"Why do you weep?" she said. "You are not a child, Wilfrid. Come back to me. I wish it. You are annoyed if I show just displeasure. You see that I am fatigued and ill, yet you force me to think and speak, and listen to persuasions and ideas that weary me. If you had any real perception of my nature, you would have made some music, you would have lulled my feelings—but no, you love me for yourself and not for myself."

The storm which convulsed the young man's heart calmed down at these words. He slowly approached her, letting his eyes take in the seductive creature who lay exhausted before him, her head resting in her hand and her elbow on the couch.

"You think that I do not love you," she resumed. "You

are mistaken. Listen to me, Wilfrid. You are beginning to know much; you have suffered much. Let me explain your thoughts to you. You wished to take my hand just now"; she rose to a sitting posture, and her graceful motions seemed to emit light. "When a young girl allows her hand to be taken it is as though she made a promise, is it not? and ought she not to fulfil it? You well know that I cannot be yours. Two sentiments divide and inspire the love of all the women of the earth. Either they devote themselves to suffering, degraded, and criminal beings whom they desire to console, uplift, redeem; or they give themselves to superior men, sublime and strong, whom they adore and seek to comprehend, and by whom they are often annihilated. You have been degraded, though now you are purified by the fires of repentance, and to-day you are once more noble; but I know myself too feeble to be your equal, and too religious to bow before any power but that On High. I may refer thus to your life, my friend, for we are in the North, among the clouds, where all things are abstractions."

"You stab me, Seraphita, when you speak like this. It wounds me to hear you apply the dreadful knowledge with which you strip from all things human the properties that time and space and form have given them, and consider them mathematically in the abstract, as geometry treats substances from which it extracts solidity."

"Well, I will respect your wishes, Wilfrid. Let the subject drop. Tell me what you think of this bearskin rug which my poor David has spread out."

"It is very handsome."

"Did you ever see me wear this 'doucha greka'?"

She pointed to a pelisse made of cashmere and lined with the skin of the black fox,—the name she gave it signifying "warm to the soul."

"Do you believe that any sovereign has a fur that can equal it?" she asked.

"It is worthy of her who wears it."

"And whom you think beautiful?"

"Human words do not apply to her. Heart to heart is the only language I can use."

"Wilfrid, you are kind to soothe my griefs with such

sweet words—which you have said to others."

"Farewell!"

"Stay. I love both you and Minna, believe me. To me you two are as one being. United thus you can be my brother or, if you will, my sister. Marry her; let me see you both happy before I leave this world of trial and of pain. My God! the simplest of women obtain what they ask of a lover; they whisper 'Hush!' and he is silent; 'Die' and he dies; 'Love me afar' and he stays at a distance, like courtiers before a king! All I desire is to see you happy, and you refuse me! Am I then powerless?—Wilfrid, listen, come nearer to me. Yes, I should grieve to see you marry Minna but—when I am here no longer, then—promise me to marry her; heaven destined you for each other."

"I listen to you with fascination, Seraphita. Your words are incomprehensible, but they charm me. What is it you mean to say?"

"You are right; I forget to be foolish,—to be the poor creature whose weaknesses gratify you. I torment you, Wilfrid. You came to these Northern lands for rest, you, worn-out by the impetuous struggle of genius unrecognized, you, weary with the patient toils of science, you, who well-nigh dyed your hands in crime and wore the fetters of human justice—"

Wilfrid dropped speechless on the carpet. Seraphita breathed softly on his forehead, and in a moment he fell asleep at her feet.

"Sleep! rest!" she said, rising.

She passed her hands over Wilfrid's brow; then the following sentences escaped her lips, one by one,—all different in tone and accent, but all melodious, full of a Goodness that seemed to emanate from her head in vaporous waves, like the gleams the goddess chastely lays upon Endymion sleeping.

"I cannot show myself such as I am to thee, dear Wilfrid,—to thee who art strong.

"The hour is come; the hour when the effulgent lights of the future cast their reflections backward on the soul; the hour when the soul awakes into freedom.

"Now am I permitted to tell thee how I love thee. Dost

thou not see the nature of my love, a love without self-interest; a sentiment full of thee, thee only; a love which follows
thee into the future to light that future for thee—for it is the
one True Light. Canst thou now conceive with what ardor I
would have thee leave this life which weighs thee down, and
behold thee nearer than thou art to that world where Love
is never-failing? Can it be aught but suffering to love for
one life only? Hast thou not felt a thirst for the eternal love?
Dost thou not feel the bliss to which a creature rises when,
with twin-soul, it loves the Being who betrays not love, Him
before whom we kneel in adoration?

"Would I had wings to cover thee, Wilfrid; power to give
thee strength to enter now into that world where all the
purest joys of purest earthly attachments are but shadows
in the Light that shines, unceasing, to illumine and rejoice
all hearts.

"Forgive a friendly soul for showing thee the picture of
thy sins, in the charitable hope of soothing the sharp pangs
of thy remorse. Listen to the pardoning choir; refresh thy
soul in the dawn now rising for thee beyond the night of
death. Yes, thy life, thy true life is there!

"May my words now reach thee clothed in the glorious
forms of dreams; may they deck themselves with images
glowing and radiant as they hover round you. Rise, rise,
to the height where men can see themselves distinctly,
pressed together though they be like grains of sand upon a
sea-shore. Humanity rolls out like a many-colored ribbon.
See the diverse shades of that flower of the celestial gardens. Behold the beings who lack intelligence, those who
begin to receive it, those who have passed through trials,
those who love, those who follow wisdom and aspire to the
regions of Light!

"Canst thou comprehend, through this thought made
visible, the destiny of humanity?—whence it came, whither
to goeth? Continue steadfast in the Path. Reaching the end
of thy journey thou shalt hear the clarions of omnipotence
sounding the cries of victory in chords of which a single
one would shake the earth, but which are lost in the spaces
of a world that hath neither east nor west.

"Canst thou comprehend, my poor beloved Tried-one,

that unless the torpor and the veils of sleep had wrapped thee, such sights would rend and bear away thy mind as the whirlwinds rend and carry into space the feeble sails, depriving thee forever of thy reason? Dost thou understand that the Soul itself, raised to its utmost power can scarcely endure in dreams the burning communications of the Spirit?

"Speed thy way through the luminous spheres; behold, admire, hasten! Flying thus thou canst pause or advance without weariness. Like other men, thou wouldst fain be plunged forever in these spheres of light and perfume where now thou art, free of thy swooning body, and where thy thought alone has utterance. Fly! enjoy for a fleeting moment the wings thou shalt surely win when Love has grown so perfect in thee that thou hast no senses left; when thy whole being is all mind, all love. The higher thy flight the less canst thou see the abysses. There are none in heaven. Look at the friend who speaks to thee; she who holds thee above this earth in which are all abysses. Look, behold, contemplate me yet a moment longer, for never again wilt thou see me, save imperfectly as the pale twilight of this world may show me to thee."

Seraphita stood erect, her head with floating hair inclining gently forward, in that aerial attitude which great painters give to messengers from heaven; the folds of her raiment fell with the same unspeakable grace which holds an artist—the man who translates all things into sentiment—before the exquisite well-known lines of Polyhymnia's veil. Then she stretched forth her hand. Wilfrid rose. When he looked at Seraphita she was lying on the bear's-skin, her head resting on her hand, her face calm, her eyes brilliant. Wilfrid gazed at her silently; but his face betrayed a deferential fear in its almost timid expression.

"Yes, dear," he said at last, as though he were answering some question; "we are separated by worlds. I resign myself; I can only adore you. But what will become of me, poor and alone!"

"Wilfrid, you have Minna."

He shook his head.

"Do not be so disdainful; woman understands all things

through love; what she does not understand she feels; what she does not feel she sees; when she neither sees, nor feels, nor understands, this angel of earth divines to protect you, and hides her protection beneath the grace of love."

"Seraphita, am I worthy to belong to a woman?"

"Ah, now," she said, smiling, "you are suddenly very modest; is it a snare? A woman is always so touched to see her weakness glorified. Well, come and take tea with me the day after tomorrow evening; good Monsieur Becker will be here, and Minna, the purest and most artless creature I have known on earth. Leave me now, my friend; I need to make long prayers and expiate my sins."

"You, can you commit sin?"

"Poor friend! if we abuse our power, is not that the sin of pride? I have been very proud to-day. Now leave me, till tomorrow."

"Till tomorrow," said Wilfrid faintly, casting a long glance at the being of whom he desired to carry with him an ineffaceable memory.

Though he wished to go far away, he was held, as it were, outside the house for some moments, watching the light which shone from all the windows of the Swedish dwelling.

"What is the matter with me?" he asked himself. "No, she is not a mere creature, but a whole creation. Of her world, even through veils and clouds, I have caught echoes like the memory of sufferings healed, like the dazzling vertigo of dreams in which we hear the plaints of generations mingling with the harmonies of some higher sphere where all is Light and all is Love. Am I awake? Do I still sleep? Are these the eyes before which the luminous space retreated further and further indefinitely while the eyes followed it? The night is cold, yet my head is on fire. I will go to the parsonage. With the pastor and his daughter I shall recover the balance of my mind."

But still he did not leave the spot whence his eyes could plunge into Seraphita's salon. The mysterious creature seemed to him the radiating center of a luminous circle which formed an atmosphere about her wider than that of other beings; whoever entered it felt the compelling influence of, as it were, a vortex of dazzling light and all

consuming thoughts. Forced to struggle against this inexplicable power, Wilfrid only prevailed after strong efforts;
but when he reached and passed the inclosing wall of the
courtyard, he regained his freedom of will, walked rapidly
towards the parsonage, and was soon beneath the high
wooden arch which formed a sort of peristyle to Monsieur
Becker's dwelling. He opened the first door, against which
the wind had driven the snow, and knocked on the inner
one, saying:—

"Will you let me spend the evening with you, Monsieur
Becker?"

"Yes," cried two voices, mingling their intonations.

Entering the parlor, Wilfrid returned by degrees to
real life. He bowed affectionately to Minna, shook hands
with Monsieur Becker, and looked about at the picture
of a home which calmed the convulsions of his physical
nature, in which a phenomenon was taking place analogous to that which sometimes seizes upon men who have
given themselves up to protracted contemplations. If some
strong thought bears upward on phantasmal wing a man
of learning or a poet, isolates him from the external circumstances which environ him here below, and leads him
forward through illimitable regions where vast arrays of
facts become abstractions, where the greatest works of
Nature are but images, then woe betide him if a sudden
noise strikes sharply on his senses and calls his errant soul
back to its prison-house of flesh and bones. The shock of
the reunion of these two powers, body and mind,—one of
which partakes of the unseen qualities of a thunderbolt,
while the other shares with sentient nature that soft resistant
force which deifies destruction,—this shock, this struggle,
or, rather let us say, this painful meeting and co-mingling,
gives rise to frightful sufferings. The body receives back the
flame that consumes it; the flame has once more grasped
its prey. This fusion, however, does not take place without
convulsions, explosions, tortures; analogous and visible
signs of which may be seen in chemistry, when two antagonistic substances which science has united separate.

For the last few days whenever Wilfrid entered Seraphita's presence his body seemed to fall away from him into

nothingness. With a single glance this strange being led him in spirit through the spheres where meditation leads the learned man, prayer the pious heart, where vision transports the artist, and sleep the souls of men,—each and all have their own path to the Height, their own guide to reach it, their own individual sufferings in the dire return. In that sphere alone all veils are rent away, and the revelation, the awful flaming certainty of an unknown world, of which the soul brings back mere fragments to this lower sphere, stands revealed. To Wilfrid one hour passed with Seraphita was like the sought-for dreams of Theriakis, in which each knot of nerves becomes the center of a radiating delight. But he left her bruised and wearied as some young girl endeavoring to keep step with a giant.

The cold air, with its stinging flagellations, had begun to still the nervous tremors which followed the reunion of his two natures, so powerfully disunited for a time; he was drawn towards the parsonage, then towards Minna, by the sight of the every-day home life for which he thirsted as the wandering European thirsts for his native land when nostalgia seizes him amid the fairy scenes of Orient that have seduced his senses. More weary than he had ever yet been, Wilfrid dropped into a chair and looked about him for a time, like a man who awakens from sleep. Monsieur Becker and his daughter accustomed, perhaps, to the apparent eccentricity of their guest, continued the employments in which they were engaged.

The parlor was ornamented with a collection of the shells and insects of Norway. These curiosities, admirably arranged on a background of the yellow pine which panelled the room, formed, as it were, a rich tapestry to which the fumes of tobacco had imparted a mellow tone. At the further end of the room, opposite to the door, was an immense wrought-iron stove, carefully polished by the serving-woman till it shone like burnished steel. Seated in a large tapestried armchair near the stove, before a table, with his feet in a species of muff, Monsieur Becker was reading a folio volume which was propped against a pile of other books as on a desk. At his left stood a jug of beer and a glass, at his right burned a smoky lamp fed by some species of fish-oil. The pastor seemed about sixty years of age. His face belonged to a type often painted by Rembrandt; the same small bright eyes, set in wrinkles and surmounted by thick gray eyebrows; the same white hair escaping in snowy flakes from a black velvet cap; the same broad, bald brow, and a contour of face which the ample chin made almost square; and lastly, the same calm tranquillity, which, to an observer, denoted the possession of some inward power, be it the supremacy bestowed by money, or the magisterial influence of the burgomaster, or the consciousness of art, or the cubic force of blissful ignorance. This fine old man, whose stout body proclaimed his vigorous health, was wrapped in a dressing-gown of rough gray cloth plainly bound. Between his lips was a meerschaum pipe, from which, at regular intervals, he blew the smoke, following with abstracted vision its fantastic wreathings,—his mind employed, no doubt, in assimilating through some meditative process the thoughts of the author whose works he was studying.

On the other side of the stove and near a door which communicated with the kitchen Minna was indistinctly visible in the haze of the good man's smoke, to which she was apparently accustomed. Beside her on a little table were the implements of household work, a pile of napkins, and another of socks waiting to be mended, also a lamp like that which shone on the white page of the book in which the pastor was absorbed. Her fresh young face, with its delicate outline, expressed an infinite purity which harmonized with the candor of the white brow and the clear blue eyes. She sat erect, turning slightly toward the lamp for better light, unconsciously showing as she did so the beauty of her waist and bust. She was already dressed for the night in a long robe of white cotton; a cambric cap, without other ornament than a frill of the same, confined her hair. Though evidently plunged in some inward meditation, she counted without a mistake the threads of her napkins or the meshes of her socks. Sitting thus, she presented the most complete image, the truest type, of the woman destined for terrestrial labor, whose glance may piece the clouds of the sanctuary while her thought, humble and charitable, keeps her ever on the level of man.

Wilfrid had flung himself into a chair between the two tables and was contemplating with a species of intoxication this picture full of harmony, to which the clouds of smoke did no despite. The single window which lighted the parlor during the fine weather was now carefully closed. An old tapestry, used for a curtain and fastened to a stick, hung before it in heavy folds. Nothing in the room was picturesque, nothing brilliant; everything denoted rigorous simplicity, true heartiness, the ease of unconventional nature, and the habits of a domestic life which knew neither cares nor troubles. Many a dwelling is like a dream, the sparkle of passing pleasure seems to hide some ruin beneath the cold smile of luxury; but this parlor, sublime in reality, harmonious in tone, diffused the patriarchal ideas of a full and self-contained existence. The silence was unbroken save by the movements of the servant in the kitchen engaged in preparing the supper, and by the sizzling of the dried fish which she was frying in salt butter according to the custom of the country.

"Will you smoke a pipe?" said the pastor, seizing a moment when he thought that Wilfrid might listen to him.

"Thank you, no, dear Monsieur Becker," replied the visitor.

"You seem to suffer more to-day than usual," said Minna, struck by the feeble tones of the stranger's voice.

"I am always so when I leave the chateau."

Minna quivered.

"A strange being lives there, Monsieur Becker," he continued after a pause. "For the six months that I have been in this village I have never yet dared to question you about her, and even now I do violence to my feelings in speaking of her. I began by keenly regretting that my journey in this country was arrested by the winter weather and that I was forced to remain here. But during the last two months chains have been forged and riveted which bind me irrevocably to Jarvis, till now I fear to end my days here. You know how I first met Seraphita, what impression her look and voice made upon me, and how at last I was admitted to her home where she receives no one. From the very first day I have longed to ask you the history of this mysterious being. On that day began, for me, a series of enchantments."

"Enchantments!" cried the pastor shaking the ashes of his pipe into an earthen-ware dish full of sand, "are there enchantments in these days?"

"You, who are carefully studying at this moment that volume of the 'Incantations' of Jean Wier, will surely understand the explanation of my sensations if I try to give it to you," replied Wilfrid. "If we study Nature attentively in its great evolutions as in its minutest works, we cannot fail to recognize the possibility of enchantment—giving to that word its exact significance. Man does not create forces; he employs the only force that exists and which includes all others namely Motion, the breath incomprehensible of the sovereign Maker of the universe. Species are too distinctly separated for the human hand to mingle them. The only miracle of which man is capable is done through the conjunction of two antagonistic substances. Gunpowder for instance is germane to a thunderbolt. As to calling forth a creation, and a sudden one, all creation demands time, and time neither recedes nor advances at the word of command. So, in the world without us, plastic nature obeys laws the order and exercise of which cannot be interfered with by the hand of man. But after fulfilling, as it were, the function of Matter, it would be unreasonable not to recognize within us the existence of a gigantic power, the effects of which are so incommensurable that the known generations of men have never yet been able to classify them. I do not speak of man's faculty of abstraction, of constraining Nature to confine itself within the Word,—a gigantic act on which the common mind reflects as little as it does on the nature of Motion, but which, nevertheless, has led the Indian theosophists to explain creation by a word to which they give an inverse power. The smallest atom of their subsistence, namely, the grain of rice, from which a creation issues and in which alternately creation again is held, presented to their minds so perfect an image of the creative word, and of the abstractive word, that to them it was easy to apply the same system to the creation of worlds. The majority of men content themselves with the grain of rice sown in the

first chapter of all the Geneses. Saint John, when he said
the Word was God only complicated the difficulty. But the
fructification, germination, and efflorescence of our ideas is
of little consequence if we compare that property, shared by
many men, with the wholly individual faculty of communicating to that property, by some mysterious concentration,
forces that are more or less active, of carrying it up to a
third, a ninth, or a twenty-seventh power, of making it thus
fasten upon the masses and obtain magical results by con-
densing the processes of nature.

"What I mean by enchantments," continued Wilfrid
after a moment's pause, "are those stupendous actions
taking place between two membranes in the tissue of the
brain. We find in the unexplorable nature of the Spiritual
World certain beings armed with these wondrous faculties,
comparable only to the terrible power of certain gases in
the physical world, beings who combine with other beings,
penetrate them as active agents, and produce upon them
witchcrafts, charms, against which these helpless slaves are
wholly defenseless; they are, in fact, enchanted, brought
under subjection, reduced to a condition of dreadful vas-
salage. Such mysterious beings overpower others with the
scepter and the glory of a superior nature,—acting upon
them at times like the torpedo which electrifies or paralyzes
the fisherman, at other times like a dose of phosphorous
which stimulates life and accelerates its propulsion; or
again, like opium, which puts to sleep corporeal nature,
disengages the spirit from every bond, enables it to float
above the world and shows this earth to the spiritual eye as
through a prism, extracting from it the food most needed;
or, yet again, like catalepsy, which deadens all faculties for
the sake of one only vision. Miracles, enchantments, incantations, witchcrafts, spells, and charms, in short, all those
acts improperly termed supernatural, are only possible and
can only be explained by the despotism with which some
spirit compels us to feel the effects of a mysterious optic
which increases, or diminishes, or exalts creation, moves
within us as it pleases, deforms or embellishes all things to
our eyes, tears us from heaven, or drags us to hell,—two
terms by which men agree to express the two extremes of

joy and misery.

"These phenomena are within us, not without us," Wilfrid went on. "The being whom we call Seraphita seems to me one of those rare and terrible spirits to whom power is given to bind men, to crush nature, to enter into participation of the occult power of God. The course of her enchantments over me began on that first day, when silence as to her was imposed upon me against my will. Each time that I have wished to question you it seemed as though I were about to reveal a secret of which I ought to be the incorruptible guardian. Whenever I have tried to speak, a burning seal has been laid upon my lips, and I myself have become the involuntary minister of these mysteries. You see me here to-night, for the hundredth time, bruised, defeated, broken, after leaving the hallucinating sphere which surrounds that young girl, so gentle, so fragile to both of you, but to me the cruellest of magicians! Yes, to me she is like a sorcerer holding in her right hand the invisible wand that moves the globe, and in her left the thunderbolt that rends asunder all things at her will. No longer can I look upon her brow; the light of it is insupportable. I skirt the borders of the abyss of madness too closely to be longer silent. I must speak. I seize this moment, when courage comes to me, to resist the power which drags me onward without inquiring whether or not I have the force to follow. Who is she? Did you know her young? What of her birth? Had she father and mother, or was she born of the conjunction of ice and sun? She burns and yet she freeze; she shows herself and then withdraws; she attracts me and repulses me; she brings me life, she gives me death; I love her and yet I hate her! I cannot live thus; let me be wholly in heaven or in hell!"

Holding his refilled pipe in one hand, and in the other the cover which he forgot to replace, Monsieur Becker listened to Wilfrid with a mysterious expression on his face, looking occasionally at his daughter, who seemed to understand the man's language as in harmony with the strange being who inspired it. Wilfrid was splendid to behold at this moment,—like Hamlet listening to the ghost of his father as it rises for him alone in the midst of the living.

"This is certainly the language of a man in love," said the

good pastor, innocently.

"In love!" cried Wilfrid, "yes, to common minds. But, dear Monsieur Becker, no words can express the frenzy which draws me to the feet of that unearthly being."

"Then you do love her?" said Minna, in a tone of reproach.

"Mademoiselle, I feel such extraordinary agitation when I see her, and such deep sadness when I see her no more, that in any other man what I feel would be called love. But that sentiment draws those who feel it ardently together, whereas between her and me a great gulf lies, whose icy coldness penetrates my very being in her presence; though the feeling dies away when I see her no longer. I leave her in despair; I return to her with ardor,—like men of science who seek a secret from Nature only to be baffled, or like the painter who would fain put life upon his canvas and strives with all the resources of his art in the vain attempt."

"Monsieur, all that you say is true," replied the young girl, artlessly.

"How can you know, Minna?" asked the old pastor.

"Ah! my father, had you been with us this morning on the summit of the Falberg, had you seen him praying, you would not ask me that question. You would say, like Monsieur Wilfrid, that he saw his Seraphita for the first time in our temple, 'It is the Spirit of Prayer.'"

These words were followed by a moment's silence.

"Ah, truly!" said Wilfrid, "she has nothing in common with the creatures who grovel upon this earth."

"On the Falberg!" said the old pastor, "how could you get there?"

"I do not know," replied Minna; "the way is like a dream to me, of which no more than a memory remains. Perhaps I should hardly believe that I had been there were it not for this tangible proof."

She drew the flower from her bosom and showed it to them. All three gazed at the pretty saxifrage, which was still fresh, and now shone in the light of the two lamps like a third luminary.

"This is indeed supernatural," said the old man, astounded at the sight of a flower blooming in winter.

"A mystery!" cried Wilfrid, intoxicated with its perfume.

"The flower makes me giddy," said Minna; "I fancy I still hear that voice,—the music of thought; that I still see the light of that look, which is Love."

"I implore you, my dear Monsieur Becker, tell me the history of Seraphita,—enigmatical human flower,—whose image is before us in this mysterious bloom."

"My dear friend," said the old man, emitting a puff of smoke, "to explain the birth of that being it is absolutely necessary that I disperse the clouds which envelop the most obscure of Christian doctrines. It is not easy to make myself clear when speaking of that incomprehensible revelation,— the last effulgence of faith that has shone upon our lump of mud. Do you know Swedenborg?"

"By name only,—of him, of his books, and his religion I know nothing."

"Then I must relate to you the whole chronicle of Swedenborg."

## III. SERAPHITA-SERAPHITUS

After a pause, during which the pastor seemed to be gathering his recollections, he continued in the following words:—

"Emanuel Swedenborg was born at Upsala in Sweden, in the month of January, 1688, according to various authors,—in 1689, according to his epitaph. His father was Bishop of Skara. Swedenborg lived eighty-five years; his death occurred in London, March 29, 1772. I use that term to convey the idea of a simple change of state. According to his disciples, Swedenborg was seen at Jarvis and in Paris after that date. Allow me, my dear Monsieur Wilfrid," said Monsieur Becker, making a gesture to prevent all interruption, "I relate these facts without either affirming or denying them. Listen; afterwards you can think and say what you like. I will inform you when I judge, criticize, and discuss these doctrines, so as to keep clearly in view my own intellectual neutrality between HIM and Reason.

"The life of Swedenborg was divided into two parts,"

continued the pastor. "From 1688 to 1745 Baron Emanuel Swedenborg appeared in the world as a man of vast
learning, esteemed and cherished for his virtues, always
irreproachable and constantly useful. While fulfilling high
public functions in Sweden, he published, between 1709
and 1740, several important works on mineralogy, physics,
mathematics, and astronomy, which enlightened the world
of learning. He originated a method of building docks suitable for the reception of large vessels, and he wrote many
treatises on various important questions, such as the rise of
tides, the theory of the magnet and its qualities, the motion
and position of the earth and planets, and while Assessor in the Royal College of Mines, on the proper system
of working salt mines. He discovered means to construct
canal-locks or sluices; and he also discovered and applied
the simplest methods of extracting ore and of working
metals. In fact he studied no science without advancing it.
In youth he learned Hebrew, Greek, and Latin, also the
oriental languages, with which he became so familiar that
many distinguished scholars consulted him, and he was
able to decipher the vestiges of the oldest known books of
Scripture, namely: 'The Wars of Jehovah' and 'The Enunciations,' spoken of by Moses (Numbers xxi. 14, 15, 27-30),
also by Joshua, Jeremiah, and Samuel,—'The Wars of Jehovah' being the historical part and 'The Enunciations' the
prophetical part of the Mosaical Books anterior to Genesis. Swedenborg even affirms that 'the Book of Jasher,'
the Book of the Righteous, mentioned by Joshua, was in
existence in Eastern Tartary, together with the doctrine
of Correspondences. A Frenchman has lately, so they tell
me, justified these statements of Swedenborg, by the discovery at Bagdad of several portions of the Bible hitherto
unknown to Europe. During the widespread discussion
on animal magnetism which took its rise in Paris, and in
which most men of Western science took an active part
about the year 1785, Monsieur le Marquis de Thome vin-
dicated the memory of Swedenborg by calling attention to
certain assertions made by the Commission appointed by
the King of France to investigate the subject. These gentlemen declared that no theory of magnetism existed, whereas

Swedenborg had studied and promulgated it ever since the year 1720. Monsieur de Thome seizes this opportunity to show the reason why so many men of science relegated Swedenborg to oblivion while they delved into his treasure-house and took his facts to aid their work. 'Some of the most illustrious of these men,' said Monsieur de Thome, alluding to the 'Theory of the Earth' by Buffon, 'have had the meanness to wear the plumage of the noble bird and refuse him all acknowledgment'; and he proved, by masterly quotations drawn from the encyclopaedic works of Swedenborg, that the great prophet had anticipated by over a century the slow march of human science. It suffices to read his philosophical and mineralogical works to be convinced of this. In one passage he is seen as the precursor of modern chemistry by the announcement that the productions of organized nature are decomposable and resolve into two simple principles; also that water, air, and fire are *not elements*. In another, he goes in a few words to the heart of magnetic mysteries and deprives Mesmer of the honors of a first knowledge of them.

"There," said Monsieur Becker, pointing to a long shelf against the wall between the stove and the window on which were ranged books of all sizes, "behold him! here are seventeen works from his pen, of which one, his 'Philosophical and Mineralogical Works,' published in 1734, is in three folio volumes. These productions, which prove the incontestable knowledge of Swedenborg, were given to me by Monsieur Seraphitus, his cousin and the father of Seraphita.

"In 1740," continued Monsieur Becker, after a slight pause, "Swedenborg fell into a state of absolute silence, from which he emerged to bid farewell to all his earthly occupations; after which his thoughts turned exclusively to the Spiritual Life. He received the first commands of heaven in 1745, and he thus relates the nature of the vocation to which he was called: One evening, in London, after dining with a great appetite, a thick white mist seemed to fill his room. When the vapor dispersed a creature in human form rose from one corner of the apartment, and said in a stern tone, 'Do not eat so much.' He refrained. The next night the same man returned, radiant in light, and said to him, 'I am sent of God, who has chosen you to explain to men the meaning of his Word and his Creation. I will tell you what to write.' The vision lasted but a few moments. The *angel* was clothed in purple. During that night the eyes of his *inner man* were opened, and he was forced to look into the heavens, into the world of spirits, and into hell,—three separate spheres; where he encountered persons of his acquaintance who had departed from their human form, some long since, others lately. Thenceforth Swedenborg lived wholly in the spiritual life, remaining in this world only as the messenger of God. His mission was ridiculed by the incredulous, but his conduct was plainly that of a being superior to humanity. In the first place, though limited in means to the bare necessaries of life, he gave away enormous sums, and publicly, in several cities, restored the fortunes of great commercial houses when they were on the brink of failure. No one ever appealed to his generosity who was not immediately satisfied. A skeptical Englishman, determined to know the truth, followed him to Paris, and relates that there his doors stood always open. One day a servant complained of this apparent negligence, which laid him open to suspicion of thefts that might be committed by others. 'He need feel no anxiety,' said Swedenborg, smiling. 'But I do not wonder at his fear; he cannot see the guardian who protects my door.' In fact, no matter in what country he made his abode he never closed his doors, and nothing was ever stolen from him. At Gottenburg—a town situated some sixty miles from Stockholm—he announced, eight days before the news arrived by courier, the conflagration which ravaged Stockholm, and the exact time at which it took place. The Queen of Sweden wrote to her brother, the King, at Berlin, that one of her ladies-in-waiting, who was ordered by the courts to pay a sum of money which she was certain her husband had paid before his death, went to Swedenborg and begged him to ask her husband where she could find proof of the payment. The following day Swedenborg, having done as the lady requested, pointed out the place where the receipt would be found. He also begged the deceased to appear to his wife, and the latter saw her husband in a dream, wrapped in a dressing-gown which he wore just before his death; and he showed her the paper in the place indicated by Swedenborg, where it had been securely put away. At another time, embarking from London in a vessel commanded by Captain Dixon, he overheard a lady asking if there were plenty of provisions on board. 'We do not want a great quantity,' he said; 'in eight days and two hours we shall reach Stockholm,'— which actually happened. This peculiar state of vision as to the things of the earth—into which Swedenborg could put himself at will, and which astonished those about him—was, nevertheless, but a feeble representative of his faculty of looking into heaven.

"Not the least remarkable of his published visions is that in which he relates his journeys through the Astral Regions; his descriptions cannot fail to astonish the reader, partly through the crudity of their details. A man whose scientific eminence is incontestable, and who united in his own person powers of conception, will, and imagination, would surely have invented better if he had invented at all. The fantastic literature of the East offers nothing that can give an idea of this astounding work, full of the essence of poetry, if it is permissible to compare a work of faith with one of oriental fancy. The transportation of Swedenborg by the Angel who served as guide to this first journey is told with a sublimity which exceeds, by the distance which God has placed betwixt the earth and the sun, the great epics of Klopstock, Milton, Tasso, and Dante. This description, which serves in fact as an introduction to his work on the Astral Regions, has never been published; it is among the oral traditions left by Swedenborg to the three disciples who were nearest to his heart. Monsieur Silverichm has written them down. Monsieur Seraphitus endeavored more than once to talk to me about them; but the recollection of his cousin's words was so burning a memory that he always stopped short at the first sentence and became lost in a revery from which I could not rouse him."

The old pastor sighed as he continued: "The baron told me that the argument by which the Angel proved to Swedenborg that these bodies are not made to wander through space puts all human science out of sight beneath the grandeur of a divine logic. According to the Seer, the inhabitants of Jupiter will not cultivate the sciences, which they call darkness; those of Mercury abhor the expression of ideas by speech, which seems to them too material,— their language is ocular; those of Saturn are continually tempted by evil spirits; those of the Moon are as small as six-year-old children, their voices issue from the abdomen, on which they crawl; those of Venus are gigantic in height, but stupid, and live by robbery,—although a part of this latter planet is inhabited by beings of great sweetness, who live in the love of Good. In short, he describes the customs and morals of all the peoples attached to the different globes, and explains the general meaning of their existence as related to the universe in terms so precise, giving explanations which agree so well with their visible evolutions in the system of the world, that some day, perhaps, scientific men will come to drink of these living waters.

"Here," said Monsieur Becker, taking down a book and opening it at a mark, "here are the words with which he ended this work:—

"'If any man doubts that I was transported through a vast number of Astral Regions, let him recall my observation of the distances in that other life, namely, that they exist only in relation to the external state of man; now, being transformed within like unto the Angelic Spirits of those Astral Spheres, I was able to understand them.'

"The circumstances to which we of this canton owe the presence among us of Baron Seraphitus, the beloved cousin of Swedenborg, enabled me to know all the events of the extraordinary life of that prophet. He has lately been accused of imposture in certain quarters of Europe, and the public prints reported the following fact based on a letter written by the Chevalier Baylon. Swedenborg, they said, informed by certain senators of a secret correspondence of the late Queen of Sweden with her brother, the Prince of Prussia, revealed his knowledge of the secrets contained in that correspondence to the Queen, making her believe he had obtained this knowledge by supernatural means. A man worthy of all confidence, Monsieur Charles-Leonhard de Stahlhammer, captain in the Royal guard and knight of the Sword, answered the calumny with a convincing letter."

The pastor opened a drawer of his table and looked through a number of papers until he found a gazette which he held out to Wilfrid, asking him to read aloud the following letter:—

*Stockholm, May 18, 1788.*

I have read with amazement a letter which purports to relate the interview of the famous Swedenborg with Queen Louisa-Ulrika. The circumstances therein stated are wholly false; and I hope the writer will excuse me for showing him by the following faithful narration, which can be proved by the testimony of many distinguished persons then present and still living, how completely he has been deceived.

In 1758, shortly after the death of the Prince of Prussia Swedenborg came to court, where he was in the habit of attending regularly. He had scarcely entered the queen's presence before she said to him: "Well, Mr. Assessor, have you seen my brother?" Swedenborg answered no, and the queen rejoined: "If you do see him, greet him for me." In saying this she meant no more than a pleasant jest, and had no thought whatever of asking him for information about her brother. Eight days later (not twenty-four as stated, nor was the audience a private one), Swedenborg again came to court, but so early that the queen had not left her apartment called the White Room, where she was conversing with her maids-of-honor and other ladies attached to the court. Swedenborg did not wait until she came forth, but entered the said room and whispered something in her ear. The queen, overcome with amazement, was taken ill, and it was some time before she recovered herself. When she did so she said to those about her: "Only God and my brother knew the thing that he has just spoken of." She admitted that it related to her last correspondence with the prince on a subject which was known to them alone. I cannot explain how Swedenborg came to know the contents of that letter, but I can affirm on my honor, that neither Count H—— (as the writer of the article states) nor any other person intercepted, or read, the queen's letters. The senate allowed her to write to her brother in perfect security, considering the correspondence as of no interest to the State. It is evident that the author of the said article is ignorant of the character of Count H——. This honored gentleman, who has done many important services to his country, unites the qualities of a noble heart to gifts of mind, and his great age has not yet weakened these precious possessions. During his whole administration he added the weight of scrupulous integrity to his enlightened policy and openly declared himself the enemy of all secret intrigues and underhand dealings, which he regarded as unworthy means to attain an end. Neither did the writer of that article understand the Assessor Swedenborg. The only weakness of that essentially honest man was a belief in the apparition of spirits; but I knew him for many years, and I can affirm that he was as fully convinced that he met and talked with spirits as I am that I am writing at this moment. As a citizen and as a friend his integrity was absolute; he abhorred deception and led the most exemplary of lives. The version which the Chevalier Baylon gave of these facts is, therefore, entirely without justification; the visit stated to have been made to Swedenborg in the night-time by Count H—— and Count T—— is hereby contradicted. In conclusion, the writer of the letter may rest assured that I am not a follower of Swedenborg. The love of truth alone impels me to give this faithful account of a fact which has been so often stated with details that are entirely false. I certify to the truth of what I have written by adding my signature.

*Charles-Leonhard de Stahlhammer.*

"The proofs which Swedenborg gave of his mission to the royal families of Sweden and Prussia were no doubt the foundation of the belief in his doctrines which is prevalent at the two courts," said Monsieur Becker, putting the gazette into the drawer. "However," he continued, "I shall not tell you all the facts of his visible and material life; indeed his habits prevented them from being fully known. He lived a hidden life; not seeking either riches or fame. He was even noted for a sort of repugnance to making proselytes; he opened his mind to few persons, and never showed his external powers of second-sight to any who were not

eminent in faith, wisdom, and love. He could recognize at a
glance the state of the soul of every person who approached
him, and those whom he desired to reach with his inward
language he converted into Seers. After the year 1745, his
disciples never saw him do a single thing from any human
motive. One man alone, a Swedish priest, named Mathesius, set afloat a story that he went mad in London in 1744.
But a eulogium on Swedenborg prepared with minute care
as to all the known events of his life, was pronounced after
his death in 1772 on behalf of the Royal Academy of Sciences in the Hall of the Nobles at Stockholm, by Monsieur
Sandels, counsellor of the Board of Mines. A declaration
made before the Lord Mayor of London gives the details of
his last illness and death, in which he received the ministrations of Monsieur Ferelius a Swedish priest of the highest
standing, and pastor of the Swedish Church in London,
Mathesius being his assistant. All persons present attested
that so far from denying the value of his writings Swedenborg firmly asserted their truth. 'In one hundred years,'
Monsieur Ferelius quotes him as saying, 'my doctrine will
guide the *Church*.' He predicted the day and hour of his
death. On that day, Sunday, March 29, 1772, hearing the
clock strike, he asked what time it was. 'Five o'clock' was
the answer. 'It is well,' he answered; 'thank you, God bless
you.' Ten minutes later he tranquilly departed, breathing
a gentle sigh. Simplicity, moderation, and solitude were
the features of his life. When he had finished writing any
of his books he sailed either for London or for Holland,
where he published them, and never spoke of them again.
He published in this way twenty-seven different treatises,
all written, he said, from the dictation of Angels. Be it true
or false, few men have been strong enough to endure the
flames of oral illumination.

"There they all are," said Monsieur Becker, pointing to a
second shelf on which were some sixty volumes. "The treatises on which the Divine Spirit casts its most vivid gleams
are seven in number, namely: 'Heaven and Hell'; 'Angelic
Wisdom concerning the Divine Love and the Divine
Wisdom'; 'Angelic Wisdom concerning the Divine Providence'; 'The Apocalypse Revealed'; 'Conjugial Love and

its Chaste Delights'; 'The True Christian Religion'; and
'An Exposition of the Internal Sense.' Swedenborg's explanation of the Apocalypse begins with these words," said
Monsieur Becker, taking down and opening the volume
nearest to him: "'Herein I have written nothing of mine
own; I speak as I am bidden by the Lord, who said, through
the same angel, to John: "Thou shalt not seal the sayings of
this Prophecy."'" (Revelation xxii. 10.)

"My dear Monsieur Wilfrid," said the old man, looking
at his guest, "I often tremble in every limb as I read, during
the long winter evenings the awe-inspiring works in which
this man declares with perfect artlessness the wonders that
are revealed to him. 'I have seen,' he says, 'Heaven and the
Angels. The spiritual man sees his spiritual fellows far better
than the terrestrial man sees the men of earth. In describing the wonders of heaven and beneath the heavens I obey
the Lord's command. Others have the right to believe me
or not as they choose. I cannot put them into the state in
which God has put me; it is not in my power to enable
them to converse with Angels, nor to work miracles within
their understanding; they alone can be the instrument of
their rise to angelic intercourse. It is now twenty-eight years
since I have lived in the Spiritual world with angels, and on
earth with men; for it pleased God to open the eyes of my
spirit as he did that of Paul, and of Daniel and Elisha.'

"And yet," continued the pastor, thoughtfully, "certain
persons have had visions of the spiritual world through
the complete detachment which somnambulism produces
between their external form and their inner being. 'In this
state,' says Swedenborg in his treatise on Angelic Wisdom
(No. 257) 'Man may rise into the region of celestial light
because, his corporeal senses being abolished, the influence
of heaven acts without hindrance on his inner man.' Many
persons who do not doubt that Swedenborg received celestial revelations think that his writings are not all the result
of divine inspiration. Others insist on absolute adherence to
him; while admitting his many obscurities, they believe that
the imperfection of earthly language prevented the prophet
from clearly revealing those spiritual visions whose clouds
disperse to the eyes of those whom faith regenerates; for, to

use the words of his greatest disciple, 'Flesh is but an external propagation.' To poets and to writers his presentation of the marvellous is amazing; to Seers it is simply reality. To some Christians his descriptions have seemed scandalous. Certain critics have ridiculed the celestial substance of his temples, his golden palaces, his splendid cities where angels disport themselves; they laugh at his groves of miraculous trees, his gardens where the flowers speak and the air is white, and the mystical stones, the sard, carbuncle, chrysolite, chrysoprase, jacinth, chalcedony, beryl, the Urim and Thummim, are endowed with motion, express celestial truths, and reply by variations of light to questions put to them ('True Christian Religion,' 219). Many noble souls will not admit his spiritual worlds where colors are heard in delightful concert, where language flames and flashes, where the Word is writ in pointed spiral letters ('True Christian Religion,' 278). Even in the North some writers have laughed at the gates of pearl, and the diamonds which stud the floors and walls of his New Jerusalem, where the most ordinary utensils are made of the rarest substances of the globe. 'But,' say his disciples, 'because such things are sparsely scattered on this earth does it follow that they are not abundant in other worlds? On earth they are terrestrial substances, whereas in heaven they assume celestial forms and are in keeping with angels.' In this connection Swedenborg has used the very words of Jesus Christ, who said, 'If I have told you earthly things and ye believe not, how shall ye believe if I tell you of heavenly things?'

"Monsieur," continued the pastor, with an emphatic gesture, "I have read the whole of Swedenborg's works; and I say it with pride, because I have done it and yet retained my reason. In reading him men either miss his meaning or become Seers like him. Though I have evaded both extremes, I have often experienced unheard-of delights, deep emotions, inward joys, which alone can reveal to us the plenitude of truth,—the evidence of celestial Light. All things here below seem small indeed when the soul is lost in the perusal of these Treatises. It is impossible not to be amazed when we think that in the short space of thirty years this man wrote and published, on the truths of the Spiritual

World, twenty-five quarto volumes, composed in Latin, of which the shortest has five hundred pages, all of them printed in small type. He left, they say, twenty others in London, bequeathed to his nephew, Monsieur Silverichm, formerly almoner to the King of Sweden. Certainly a man who, between the ages of twenty and sixty, had already exhausted himself in publishing a series of encyclopaedical works, must have received supernatural assistance in composing these later stupendous treatises, at an age, too, when human vigor is on the wane. You will find in these writings thousands of propositions, all numbered, none of which have been refuted. Throughout we see method and precision; the presence of the spirit issuing and flowing down from a single fact,—the existence of angels. His 'True Christian Religion,' which sums up his whole doctrine and is vigorous with light, was conceived and written at the age of eighty-three. In fact, his amazing vigor and omniscience are not denied by any of his critics, not even by his enemies.

"Nevertheless," said Monsieur Becker, slowly, "though I have drunk deep in this torrent of divine light, God has not opened the eyes of my inner being, and I judge these writings by the reason of an unregenerated man. I have often felt that the *inspired* Swedenborg must have misunderstood the Angels. I have laughed over certain visions which, according to his disciples, I ought to have believed with veneration. I have failed to imagine the spiral writing of the Angels or their golden belts, on which the gold is of great or lesser thickness. If, for example, this statement, 'Some angels are solitary,' affected me powerfully for a time, I was, on reflection, unable to reconcile this solitude with their marriages. I have not understood why the Virgin Mary should continue to wear blue satin garments in heaven. I have even dared to ask myself why those gigantic demons, Enakim and Hephilim, came so frequently to fight the cherubim on the apocalyptic plains of Armageddon; and I cannot explain to my own mind how Satans can argue with Angels. Monsieur le Baron Seraphitus assured me that those details concerned only the angels who live on earth in human form. The visions of the prophet are often blurred with grotesque figures. One of his spiritual tales, or 'Memorable relations,' as he called them, begins thus: 'I see the spirits assembling, they have hats upon their heads.' In another of these Memorabilia he receives from heaven a bit of paper, on which he saw, he says, the hieroglyphics of the primitive peoples, which were composed of curved lines traced from the finger-rings that are worn in heaven. However, perhaps I am wrong; possibly the material absurdities with which his works are strewn have spiritual significations. Otherwise, how shall we account for the growing influence of his religion? His church numbers to-day more than seven hundred thousand believers,—as many in the United States of America as in England, where there are seven thousand Swedenborgians in the city of Manchester alone. Many men of high rank in knowledge and in social position in Germany, in Prussia, and in the Northern kingdoms have publicly adopted the beliefs of Swedenborg; which, I may remark, are more comforting than those of all other Christian communions. I wish I had the power to explain to you clearly in succinct language the leading points of the doctrine on which Swedenborg founded his church; but I fear such a summary, made from recollection, would be necessarily defective. I shall, therefore, allow myself to speak only of those 'Arcana' which concern the birth of Seraphita."

Here Monsieur Becker paused, as though composing his mind to gather up his ideas. Presently he continued, as follows:—

"After establishing mathematically that man lives eternally in spheres of either a lower or a higher grade, Swedenborg applies the term 'Spiritual Angels' to beings who in this world are prepared for heaven, where they become angels. According to him, God has not created angels; none exist who have not been men upon the earth. The earth is the nursery-ground of heaven. The Angels are therefore not Angels as such ('Angelic Wisdom,' 57), they are transformed through their close conjunction with God; which conjunction God never refuses, because the essence of God is not negative, but essentially active. The spiritual angels pass through three natures of love, because man is only regenerated through successive stages ('True Religion').

First, the *love of self*: the supreme expression of this love is human genius, whose works are worshipped. Next, *love of life*: this love produces prophets,—great men whom the world accepts as guides and proclaims to be divine. Lastly, *love of heaven*, and this creates the Spiritual Angel. These angels are, so to speak, the flowers of humanity, which culminates in them and works for that culmination. They must possess either the love of heaven or the wisdom of heaven, but always Love before Wisdom.

"Thus the transformation of the natural man is into Love. To reach this first degree, his previous existences must have passed through Hope and Charity, which prepare him for Faith and Prayer. The ideas acquired by the exercise of these virtues are transmitted to each of the human envelopes within which are hidden the metamorphoses of the *inner being*; for nothing is separate, each existence is necessary to the other existences. Hope cannot advance without Charity, nor Faith without Prayer; they are the four fronts of a solid square. 'One virtue missing,' he said, 'and the Spiritual Angel is like a broken pearl.' Each of these existences is therefore a circle in which revolves the celestial riches of the inner being. The perfection of the Spiritual Angels comes from this mysterious progression in which nothing is lost of the high qualities that are successfully acquired to attain each glorious incarnation; for at each transformation they cast away unconsciously the flesh and its errors. When the man lives in Love he has shed all evil passions: Hope, Charity, Faith, and Prayer have, in the words of Isaiah, purged the dross of his inner being, which can never more be polluted by earthly affections. Hence the grand saying of Christ quoted by Saint Matthew, 'Lay up for yourselves treasures in Heaven where neither moth nor rust doth corrupt,' and those still grander words: 'If ye were of this world the world would love you, but I have chosen you out of the world; be ye therefore perfect as your Father in heaven is perfect.'

"The second transformation of man is to Wisdom. Wisdom is the understanding of celestial things to which the Spirit is brought by Love. The Spirit of Love has acquired strength, the result of all vanquished terrestrial passions; it loves God blindly. But the Spirit of Wisdom has risen to understanding and knows why it loves. The wings of the one are spread and bear the spirit to God; the wings of the other are held down by the awe that comes of understanding: the spirit knows God. The one longs incessantly to see God and to fly to Him; the other attains to Him and trembles. The union effected between the Spirit of Love and the Spirit of Wisdom carries the human being into a Divine state during which time his soul is *woman* and his body *man*, the last human manifestation in which the Spirit conquers Form, or Form still struggles against the Spirit,—for Form, that is, the flesh, is ignorant, rebels, and desires to continue gross. This supreme trial creates untold sufferings seen by Heaven alone,—the agony of Christ in the Garden of Olives.

"After death the first heaven opens to this dual and purified human nature. Therefore it is that man dies in despair while the Spirit dies in ecstasy. Thus, the *natural*, the state of beings not yet regenerated; the *spiritual*, the state of those who have become Angelic Spirits, and the *divine*, the state in which the Angel exists before he breaks from his covering of flesh, are the three degrees of existence through which man enters heaven. One of Swedenborg's thoughts expressed in his own words will explain to you with wonderful clearness the difference between the *natural* and the *spiritual*. 'To the minds of men,' he says, 'the Natural passes into the Spiritual; they regard the world under its visible aspects, they perceive it only as it can be realized by their senses. But to the apprehension of Angelic Spirits, the Spiritual passes into the Natural; they regard the world in its inward essence and not in its form.' Thus human sciences are but analyses of form. The man of science as the world goes is purely external like his knowledge; his inner being is only used to preserve his aptitude for the perception of external truths. The Angelic Spirit goes far beyond that; his knowledge is the thought of which human science is but the utterance; he derives that knowledge from the Logos, and learns the law of *correspondences* by which the world is placed in unison with heaven. The *word of God* was wholly written by pure Correspondences, and covers an esoteric or spiritual meaning, which according to the science of Correspondences, cannot be understood. 'There exist,' says Swedenborg ('Celestial Doctrine' 26), 'innumerable Arcana within the hidden meaning of the Correspondences. Thus the men who scoff at the books of the Prophets where the Word is enshrined are as densely ignorant as those other men who know nothing of a science and yet ridicule its truths. To know the Correspondences which exist between the things visible and ponderable in the terrestrial world and the things invisible and imponderable in the spiritual world, is to hold heaven within our comprehension. All the objects of the manifold creations having emanated from God necessarily enfold a hidden meaning; according, indeed, to the grand thought of Isaiah, 'The earth is a garment.'

"This mysterious link between Heaven and the smallest atoms of created matter constitutes what Swedenborg calls a Celestial Arcanum, and his treatise on the 'Celestial Arcana' in which he explains the correspondences or significances of the Natural with, and to, the Spiritual, giving, to use the words of Jacob Boehm, the sign and seal of all things, occupies not less than sixteen volumes containing thirty thousand propositions. 'This marvellous knowledge of Correspondences which the goodness of God granted to Swedenborg,' says one of his disciples, 'is the secret of the interest which draws men to his works. According to him, all things are derived from heaven, all things lead back to heaven. His writings are sublime and clear; he speaks in heaven, and earth hears him. Take one of his sentences by itself and a volume could be made of it'; and the disciple quotes the following passages taken from a thousand others that would answer the same purpose.

"'The kingdom of heaven,' says Swedenborg ('Celestial Arcana'), 'is the kingdom of motives. *Action* is born in heaven, thence into the world, and, by degrees, to the infinitely remote parts of earth. Terrestrial effects being thus linked to celestial causes, all things are *correspondent* and *significant*. Man is the means of union between the Natural and the Spiritual.'

"The Angelic Spirits therefore know the very nature

of the Correspondences which link to heaven all earthly things; they know, too, the inner meaning of the prophetic words which foretell their evolutions. Thus to these Spirits everything here below has its significance; the tiniest flower is a thought,—a life which corresponds to certain lineaments of the Great Whole, of which they have a constant intuition. To them Adultery and the excesses spoken of in Scripture and by the Prophets, often garbled by self-styled scholars, mean the state of those souls which in this world persist in tainting themselves with earthly affections, thus compelling their divorce from Heaven. Clouds signify the veil of the Most High. Torches, shew-bread, horses and horsemen, harlots, precious stones, in short, everything named in Scripture, has to them a clear-cut meaning, and reveals the future of terrestrial facts in their relation to Heaven. They penetrate the truths contained in the Revelation of Saint John the divine, which human science has subsequently demonstrated and proved materially; such, for instance, as the following ('big,' said Swedenborg, 'with many human sciences'): 'I saw a new heaven and a new earth, for the first heaven and the first earth were passed away' (Revelation xxi. 1). These Spirits know the supper at which the flesh of kings and the flesh of all men, free and bond, is eaten, to which an Angel standing in the sun has bidden them. They see the winged woman, clothed with the sun, and the mailed man. 'The horse of the Apocalypse,' says Swedenborg, 'is the visible image of human intellect ridden by Death, for it bears within itself the elements of its own destruction.' Moreover, they can distinguish beings concealed under forms which to ignorant eyes would seem fantastic. When a man is disposed to receive the prophetic afflation of Correspondences, it rouses within him a perception of the Word; he comprehends that the creations are transformations only; his intellect is sharpened, a burning thirst takes possession of him which only Heaven can quench. He conceives, according to the greater or lesser perfection of his inner being, the power of the Angelic Spirits; and he advances, led by Desire (the least imperfect state of unregenerated man) towards Hope, the gateway to the world of Spirits, whence he reaches Prayer, which gives him the Key of Heaven.

"What being here below would not desire to render himself worthy of entrance into the sphere of those who live in secret by Love and Wisdom? Here on earth, during their lifetime, such spirits remain pure; they neither see, nor think, nor speak like other men. There are two ways by which perception comes,—one internal, the other external. Man is wholly external, the Angelic Spirit wholly internal. The Spirit goes to the depth of Numbers, possesses a full sense of them, knows their significances. It controls Motion, and by reason of its ubiquity it shares in all things. 'An Angel,' says Swedenborg, 'is ever present to a man when desired' ('Angelic Wisdom'); for the Angel has the gift of detaching himself from his body, and he sees into heaven as the prophets and as Swedenborg himself saw into it. 'In this state,' writes Swedenborg ('True Religion,' 136), 'the spirit of a man may move from one place to another, his body remaining where it is,—a condition in which I lived for over twenty-six years.' It is thus that we should interpret all Biblical statements which begin, 'The Spirit led me.' Angelic Wisdom is to human wisdom what the innumerable forces of nature are to its action, which is one. All things live again, and move and have their being in the Spirit, which is in God. Saint Paul expresses this truth when he says, 'In Deo sumus, movemur, et vivimus,'—we live, we act, we are in God.

"Earth offers no hindrance to the Angelic Spirit, just as the Word offers him no obscurity. His approaching divinity enables him to see the thought of God veiled in the Logos, just as, living by his inner being, the Spirit is in communion with the hidden meaning of all things on this earth. Science is the language of the Temporal world, Love is that of the Spiritual world. Thus man takes note of more than he is able to explain, while the Angelic Spirit sees and comprehends. Science depresses man; Love exalts the Angel. Science is still seeking, Love has found. Man judges Nature according to his own relations to her; the Angelic Spirit judges it in its relation to Heaven. In short, all things have a voice for the Spirit. Spirits are in the secret of the harmony of all creations with each other; they comprehend the spirit of sound, the spirit of color, the spirit of vegetable life; they can question the mineral, and the mineral makes answer to their thoughts. What to them are sciences and the treasures of the earth when they grasp all things by the eye at all moments, when the worlds which absorb the minds of so many men are to them but the last step from which they spring to God? Love of heaven, or the Wisdom of heaven, is made manifest to them by a circle of light which surrounds them, and is visible to the Elect. Their innocence, of which that of children is a symbol, possesses, nevertheless, a knowledge which children have not; they are both innocent and learned. 'And,' says Swedenborg, 'the innocence of Heaven makes such an impression upon the soul that those whom it affects keep a rapturous memory of it which lasts them all their lives, as I myself have experienced. It is perhaps sufficient,' he goes on, 'to have only a minimum perception of it to be forever changed, to long to enter Heaven and the sphere of Hope.'

"His doctrine of Marriage can be reduced to the following words: 'The Lord has taken the beauty and the grace of the life of man and bestowed them upon woman. When man is not reunited to this beauty and this grace of his life, he is harsh, sad, and sullen; when he is reunited to them he is joyful and complete.' The Angels are ever at the perfect point of beauty. Marriages are celebrated by wondrous ceremonies. In these unions, which produce no children, man contributes the *understanding*, woman the *will*; they become one being, one Flesh here below, and pass to heaven clothed in the celestial form. On this earth, the natural attraction of the sexes towards enjoyment is an Effect which allures, fatigues and disgusts; but in the form celestial the pair, now *one* in Spirit find within theirself a ceaseless source of joy. Swedenborg was led to see these nuptials of the Spirits, which in the words of Saint Luke (xx. 35) are neither marrying nor giving in marriage, and which inspire none but spiritual pleasures. An Angel offered to make him witness of such a marriage and bore him thither on his wings (the wings are a symbol and not a reality). The Angel clothed him in a wedding garment and when Swedenborg, finding himself thus robed in light, asked why, the answer was: 'For these events, our garments are illuminated; they shine; they are made nuptial.' ('Conjugial Love,' 19, 20, 21.) Then he saw the two Angels, one coming from the South, the other from the East; the Angel of the South was in a chariot drawn by two white horses, with reins of the color and brilliance of the dawn; but lo, when they were near him in the sky, chariot and horses vanished. The Angel of the East, clothed in crimson, and the Angel of the South, in purple, drew together, like breaths, and mingled: one was the Angel of Love, the other the Angel of Wisdom. Swedenborg's guide told him that the two Angels had been linked together on earth by an inward friendship and ever united though separated in life by great distances. Consent, the essence of all good marriage upon earth, is the habitual state of Angels in Heaven. Love is the light of their world. The eternal rapture of Angels comes from the faculty that God communicates to them to render back to Him the joy they feel through Him. This reciprocity of infinitude forms their life. They become infinite by participating of the essence of God, who generates Himself by Himself.

"The immensity of the Heavens where the Angels dwell is such that if man were endowed with sight as rapid as the darting of light from the sun to the earth, and if he gazed throughout eternity, his eyes could not reach the horizon, nor find an end. Light alone can give an idea of the joys of heaven. 'It is,' says Swedenborg ('Angelic Wisdom,' 7, 25, 26, 27), 'a vapor of the virtue of God, a pure emanation of His splendor, beside which our greatest brilliance is obscurity. It can compass all; it can renew all, and is never absorbed: it environs the Angel and unites him to God by infinite joys which multiply infinitely of themselves. This Light destroys whosoever is not prepared to receive it. No one here below, nor yet in Heaven can see God and live. This is the meaning of the saying (Exodus xix. 12, 13, 21-23) "Take heed to yourselves that ye go not up into the mount—lest ye break through unto the Lord to gaze, and many perish." And again (Exodus xxxiv. 29-35), "When Moses came down from Mount Sinai with the two Tables of testimony in his hand, his face shone, so that he put a veil upon it when he spake with the people, lest any of them die." The Transfiguration of Jesus Christ likewise revealed the light surrounding the Messengers from on high and the ineffable joys of the Angels who are forever imbued with it. "His face," says Saint Matthew (xvii. 1-5), "did shine as the sun and his raiment was white as the light—and a bright cloud overshadowed them.'"

"When a planet contains only those beings who reject the Lord, when his word is ignored, then the Angelic Spirits are gathered together by the four winds, and God sends forth an Exterminating Angel to change the face of the refractory earth, which in the immensity of this universe is to Him what an unfruitful seed is to Nature. Approaching the globe, this Exterminating Angel, borne by a comet, causes the planet to turn upon its axis, and the lands lately covered by the seas reappear, adorned in freshness and obedient to the laws proclaimed in Genesis; the Word of God is once more powerful on this new earth, which everywhere exhibits the effects of terrestrial waters and celestial flames. The light brought by the Angel from On High, causes the sun to pale. 'Then,' says Isaiah, (xix. 20) 'men will hide in the clefts of the rock and roll themselves in the dust of the earth.' 'They will cry to the mountains' (Revelation), 'Fall on us! and to the seas, Swallow us up! Hide us from the face of Him that sitteth on the throne, and from the wrath of the Lamb!' The Lamb is the great figure and hope of the Angels misjudged and persecuted here below. Christ himself has said, 'Blessed are those who mourn! Blessed are the simple-hearted! Blessed are they that love!'—All Swedenborg is there! Suffer, Believe, Love. To love truly must we not suffer? must we not believe? Love begets Strength, Strength bestows Wisdom, thence Intelligence; for Strength and Wisdom demand Will. To be intelligent, is not that to Know, to Wish, and to Will,—the three attributes of the Angelic Spirit? 'If the universe has a meaning,' Monsieur Saint-Martin said to me when I met him during a journey which he made in Sweden, 'surely this is the one most worthy of God.'

"But, Monsieur," continued the pastor after a thoughtful pause, "of what avail to you are these shreds of thoughts taken here and there from the vast extent of a work of which no true idea can be given except by comparing it to a river of light, to billows of flame? When a man plunges into it he is carried away as by an awful current. Dante's poem seems but a speck to the reader submerged in the almost Biblical verses with which Swedenborg renders palpable the Celestial Worlds, as Beethoven built his palaces of harmony with thousands of notes, as architects have reared cathedrals with millions of stones. We roll in soundless depths, where our minds will not always sustain us. Ah, surely a great and powerful intellect is needed to bring us back, safe and sound, to our own social beliefs.

"Swedenborg," resumed the pastor, "was particularly attached to the Baron de Seraphitz, whose name, according to an old Swedish custom, had taken from time immemorial the Latin termination of 'us.' The baron was an ardent disciple of the Swedish prophet, who had opened the eyes of his Inner-Man and brought him to a life in conformity with the decrees from On-High. He sought for an Angelic Spirit among women; Swedenborg found her for him in a vision. His bride was the daughter of a London shoemaker, in whom, said Swedenborg, the life of Heaven shone, she having passed through all anterior trials. After the death, that is, the transformation of the prophet, the baron came to Jarvis to accomplish his celestial nuptials with the observances of Prayer. As for me, who am not a Seer, I have only known the terrestrial works of this couple. Their lives were those of saints whose virtues are the glory of the Roman Church. They ameliorated the condition of our people; they supplied them all with means in return for work,— little, perhaps, but enough for all their wants. Those who lived with them in constant intercourse never saw them show a sign of anger or impatience; they were constantly beneficent and gentle, full of courtesy and loving-kindness; their marriage was the harmony of two souls indissolubly united. Two eiders winging the same flight, the sound in the echo, the thought in the word,—these, perhaps, are true images of their union. Every one here in Jarvis loved them with an affection which I can compare only to the love of a plant for the sun. The wife was simple in her manners, beautiful in form, lovely in face, with a dignity of bearing like that of august personages. In 1783, being then twenty-six years old, she conceived a child; her pregnancy was to the pair a solemn joy. They prepared to bid the earth farewell; for they told me they should be transformed when their child had passed the state of infancy which needed their fostering care until the strength to exist alone should be given to her.

"Their child was born,—the Seraphita we are now concerned with. From the moment of her conception father and mother lived a still more solitary life than in the past, lifting themselves up to heaven by Prayer. They hoped to see Swedenborg, and faith realized their hope. The day on which Seraphita came into the world Swedenborg appeared in Jarvis, and filled the room of the newborn child with light. I was told that he said, 'The work is accomplished; the Heavens rejoice!' Sounds of unknown melodies were heard throughout the house, seeming to come from the four points of heaven on the wings of the wind. The spirit of Swedenborg led the father forth to the shores of the fjord and there quitted him. Certain inhabitants of Jarvis, having approached Monsieur Seraphitus as he stood on the shore, heard him repeat those blissful words of Scripture: 'How beautiful on the mountains are the feet of Him who is sent of God!'

"I had left the parsonage on my way to baptize the infant and name it, and perform the other duties required by law, when I met the baron returning to the house. 'Your ministrations are superfluous,' he said; 'our child is to be without name on this earth. You must not baptize in the waters of an earthly Church one who has just been immersed in the fires of Heaven. This child will remain a blossom, it will not grow old; you will see it pass away. You exist, but our child has life; you have outward senses, the child has none, its being is always inward.' These words were uttered in so strange and supernatural a voice that I was more affected by them than by the shining of his face, from which light appeared to exude. His appearance realized the phantasmal ideas which we form of inspired beings as we read the prophesies of the Bible. But such effects are not rare among our mountains, where the niter of perpetual snows produces extraordinary phenomena in the human organization.

"I asked him the cause of his emotion. 'Swedenborg came to us; he has just left me; I have breathed the air of heaven,' he replied. 'Under what form did he appear?' I said. 'Under his earthly form; dressed as he was the last time I saw him in London, at the house of Richard Shearsmith, Coldbath-fields, in July, 1771. He wore his brown frieze coat with steel buttons, his waistcoat buttoned to the throat, a white cravat, and the same magisterial wig rolled and powdered at the sides and raised high in front, showing his vast and luminous brow, in keeping with the noble square face, where all is power and tranquillity. I recognized the large nose with its fiery nostril, the mouth that ever smiled,—angelic mouth from which these words, the pledge of my happiness, have just issued, "We shall meet soon."'

"The conviction that shone on the baron's face forbade all discussion; I listened in silence. His voice had a contagious heat which made my bosom burn within me; his fanaticism stirred my heart as the anger of another makes our nerves vibrate. I followed him in silence to his house, where I saw the nameless child lying mysteriously folded to its mother's breast. The babe heard my step and turned its head toward me; its eyes were not those of an ordinary child. To give you an idea of the impression I received, I must say that already they saw and thought. The childhood of this predestined being was attended by circumstances quite extraordinary in our climate. For nine years our winters were milder and our summers longer than usual. This phenomenon gave rise to several discussions among scientific men; but none of their explanations seemed sufficient to academicians, and the baron smiled when I told him of them. The child was never seen in its nudity as other children are; it was never touched by man or woman, but lived a sacred thing upon the mother's breast, and it never cried. If you question old David he will confirm these facts about his mistress, for whom he feels an adoration like that of Louis IX for the saint whose name he bore.

"At nine years of age the child began to pray; prayer is

her life. You saw her in the church at Christmas, the only day on which she comes there; she is separated from the other worshippers by a visible space. If that space does not exist between herself and men she suffers. That is why she passes nearly all her time alone in the chateau. The events of her life are unknown; she is seldom seen; her days are spent in the state of mystical contemplation which was, so Catholic writers tell us, habitual with the early Christian solitaries, in whom the oral tradition of Christ's own words still remained. Her mind, her soul, her body, all within her is virgin as the snow on those mountains. At ten years of age she was just what you see her now. When she was nine her father and mother expired together, without pain or visible malady, after naming the day and hour at which they would cease to be. Standing at their feet she looked at them with a calm eye, not showing either sadness, or grief, or joy, or curiosity. When we approached to remove the two bodies she said, 'Carry them away!' 'Seraphita,' I said, for so we called her, 'are you not affected by the death of your father and your mother who loved you so much?' 'Dead?' she answered, 'no, they live in me forever—That is nothing,' she pointed without emotion to the bodies they were bearing away. I then saw her for the third time only since her birth. In church it is difficult to distinguish her; she stands near a column which, seen from the pulpit, is in shadow, so that I cannot observe her features.

"Of all the servants of the household there remained after the death of the master and mistress only old David, who, in spite of his eighty-two years, suffices to wait on his mistress. Some of our Jarvis people tell wonderful tales about her. These have a certain weight in a land so essentially conducive to mystery as ours; and I am now studying the treatise on Incantations by Jean Wier and other works relating to demonology, where pretended supernatural events are recorded, hoping to find facts analogous to those which are attributed to her."

"Then you do not believe in her?" said Wilfrid.

"Oh yes, I do," said the pastor, genially, "I think her a very capricious girl; a little spoilt by her parents, who turned her head with the religious ideas I have just revealed to you."

Minna shook her head in a way that gently expressed contradiction.

"Poor girl!" continued the old man, "her parents bequeathed to her that fatal exaltation of soul which misleads mystics and renders them all more or less mad. She subjects herself to fasts which horrify poor David. The good old man is like a sensitive plant which quivers at the slightest breeze, and glows under the first sun-ray. His mistress, whose incomprehensible language has become his, is the breeze and the sun-ray to him; in his eyes her feet are diamonds and her brow is strewn with stars; she walks environed with a white and luminous atmosphere; her voice is accompanied by music; she has the gift of rendering herself invisible. If you ask to see her, he will tell you she has gone to the *astral regions*. It is difficult to believe such a story, is it not? You know all miracles bear more or less resemblance to the story of the Golden Tooth. We have our golden tooth in Jarvis, that is all. Duncker the fisherman asserts that he has seen her plunge into the fjord and come up in the shape of an eider-duck, at other times walking on the billows of a storm. Fergus, who leads the flocks to the saeters, says that in rainy weather a circle of clear sky can be seen over the Swedish castle; and that the heavens are always blue above Seraphita's head when she is on the mountain. Many women hear the tones of a mighty organ when Seraphita enters the church, and ask their neighbors earnestly if they too do not hear them. But my daughter, for whom during the last two years Seraphita has shown much affection, has never heard this music, and has never perceived the heavenly perfumes which, they say, make the air fragrant about her when she moves. Minna, to be sure, has often on returning from their walks together expressed to me the delight of a young girl in the beauties of our spring-time, in the spicy odors of budding larches and pines and the earliest flowers; but after our long winters what can be more natural than such pleasure? The companionship of this so-called spirit has nothing so very extraordinary in it, has it, my child?"

"The secrets of that spirit are not mine," said Minna. "Near it I know all, away from it I know nothing; near that exquisite life I am no longer myself, far from it I forget all. The time we pass together is a dream which my memory scarcely retains. I may have heard yet not remember the music which the women tell of; in that presence, I may have breathed celestial perfumes, seen the glory of the heavens, and yet be unable to recollect them here."

"What astonishes me most," resumed the pastor, addressing Wilfrid, "is to notice that you suffer from being near her."

"Near her!" exclaimed the stranger, "she has never so much as let me touch her hand. When she saw me for the first time her glance intimidated me; she said: 'You are welcome here, for you were to come.' I fancied that she knew me. I trembled. It is fear that forces me to believe in her."

"With me it is love," said Minna, without a blush.

"Are you making fun of me?" said Monsieur Becker, laughing good-humoredly; "you my daughter, in calling yourself a Spirit of Love, and you, Monsieur Wilfrid, in pretending to be a Spirit of Wisdom?"

He drank a glass of beer and so did not see the singular look which Wilfrid cast upon Minna.

"Jesting apart," resumed the old gentleman, "I have been much astonished to hear that these two mad-caps ascended to the summit of the Falberg; it must be a girlish exaggeration; they probably went to the crest of a ledge. It is impossible to reach the peaks of the Falberg."

"If so, father," said Minna, in an agitated voice, "I must have been under the power of a spirit; for indeed we reached the summit of the Ice-Cap."

"This is really serious," said Monsieur Becker. "Minna is always truthful."

"Monsieur Becker," said Wilfrid, "I swear to you that Seraphita exercises such extraordinary power over me that I know no language in which I can give you the least idea of it. She has revealed to me things known to myself alone."

"Somnambulism!" said the old man. "A great many such effects are related by Jean Wier as phenomena easily explained and formerly observed in Egypt."

"Lend me Swedenborg's theosophical works," said Wilfrid, "and let me plunge into those gulfs of light,—you have given me a thirst for them."

Monsieur Becker took down a volume and gave it to his guest, who instantly began to read it. It was about nine o'clock in the evening. The serving-woman brought in the supper. Minna made tea. The repast over, each turned silently to his or her occupation; the pastor read the Incantations; Wilfrid pursued the spirit of Swedenborg; and the young girl continued to sew, her mind absorbed in recollections. It was a true Norwegian evening—peaceful, studious, and domestic; full of thoughts, flowers blooming beneath the snow. Wilfrid, as he devoured the pages of the prophet, lived by his inner senses only; the pastor, looking up at times from his book, called Minna's attention to the absorption of their guest with an air that was half-serious, half-jesting. To Minna's thoughts the face of Seraphitus smiled upon her as it hovered above the clouds of smoke which enveloped them. The clock struck twelve. Suddenly the outer door was opened violently. Heavy but hurried steps, the steps of a terrified old man, were heard in the narrow vestibule between the two doors; then David burst into the parlor.

"Danger, danger!" he cried. "Come! come, all! The evil spirits are unchained! Fiery mitres are on their heads! Demons, Vertumni, Sirens! they tempt her as Jesus was tempted on the mountain! Come, come! and drive them away."

"Do you not recognize the language of Swedenborg?" said the pastor, laughing, to Wilfrid. "Here it is; pure from the source."

But Wilfrid and Minna were gazing in terror at old David, who, with hair erect, and eyes distraught, his legs trembling and covered with snow, for he had come without snow-shoes, stood swaying from side to side, as if some boisterous wind were shaking him.

"Is he harmed?" cried Minna.

"The devils hope and try to conquer her," replied the old man.

The words made Wilfrid's pulses throb.

"For the last five hours she has stood erect, her eyes raised to heaven and her arms extended; she suffers, she cries to God. I cannot cross the barrier; Hell has posted the Vertumni as sentinels. They have set up an iron wall between her and her old David. She wants me, but what can I do? Oh, help me! help me! Come and pray!"

The old man's despair was terrible to see.

"The Light of God is defending her," he went on, with infectious faith, "but oh! she might yield to violence."

"Silence, David! you are raving. This is a matter to be verified. We will go with you," said the pastor, "and you shall see that there are no Vertumni, nor Satans, nor Sirens, in that house."

"Your father is blind," whispered David to Minna.

Wilfrid, on whom the reading of Swedenborg's first treatise, which he had rapidly gone through, had produced a powerful effect, was already in the corridor putting on his skees; Minna was ready in a few moments, and both left the old men far behind as they darted forward to the Swedish castle.

"Do you hear that cracking sound?" said Wilfrid.

"The ice of the fjord stirs," answered Minna; "the spring is coming."

Wilfrid was silent. When the two reached the courtyard they were conscious that they had neither the faculty nor the strength to enter the house.

"What think you of her?" asked Wilfrid.

"See that radiance!" cried Minna, going towards the window of the salon. "He is there! How beautiful! O my Seraphitus, take me!"

The exclamation was uttered inwardly. She saw Seraphitus standing erect, lightly swathed in an opal-tinted mist that disappeared at a little distance from the body, which seemed almost phosphorescent.

"How beautiful she is!" cried Wilfrid, mentally.

Just then Monsieur Becker arrived, followed by David; he saw his daughter and guest standing before the window; going up to them, he looked into the salon and said quietly, "Well, my good David, she is only saying her prayers."

"Ah, but try to enter, Monsieur."

"Why disturb those who pray?" answered the pastor.

At this instant the moon, rising above the Falberg, cast

its rays upon the window. All three turned round, attracted by this natural effect which made them quiver; when they turned back to again look at Seraphita she had disappeared.

"How strange!" exclaimed Wilfrid.

"I hear delightful sounds," said Minna.

"Well," said the pastor, "it is all plain enough; she is going to bed."

David had entered the house. The others took their way back in silence; none of them interpreted the vision in the same manner,—Monsieur Becker doubted, Minna adored, Wilfrid longed.

Wilfrid was a man about thirty-six years of age. His figure, though broadly developed, was not wanting in symmetry. Like most men who distinguish themselves above their fellows, he was of medium height; his chest and shoulders were broad, and his neck short,—a characteristic of those whose hearts are near their heads; his hair was black, thick, and fine; his eyes, of a yellow brown, had, as it were, a solar brilliancy, which proclaimed with what avidity his nature aspired to Light. Though these strong and virile features were defective through the absence of an inward peace,—granted only to a life without storms or conflicts,—they plainly showed the inexhaustible resources of impetuous senses and the appetites of instinct; just as every motion revealed the perfection of the man's physical apparatus, the flexibility of his senses, and their fidelity when brought into play. This man might contend with savages, and hear, as they do, the tread of enemies in distant forests; he could follow a scent in the air, a trail on the ground, or see on the horizon the signal of a friend. His sleep was light, like that of all creatures who will not allow themselves to be surprised. His body came quickly into harmony with the climate of any country where his tempestuous life conducted him. Art and science would have admired his organization in the light of a human model. Everything about him was symmetrical and well-balanced,—action and heart, intelligence and will. At first sight he might be classed among purely instinctive beings, who give themselves blindly up to the material wants of life; but in the very morning of his days he had flung himself into a higher social world, with which his feelings harmonized; study had widened his mind, reflection had sharpened his power of thought, and the sciences had enlarged his understanding. He had studied human laws,—the working of self-interests brought into conflict by the passions, and he seemed to have early familiarized himself with the abstractions on which societies rest. He had pored over books,—those deeds of dead humanity; he had spent whole nights of pleasure in every European capital; he had slept on fields of battle the night before the combat and the night that followed victory. His stormy youth may have flung him on the deck of some corsair and sent him among the contrasting regions of the globe; thus it was that he knew the actions of a living humanity. He knew the present and the past,—a double history; that of to-day, that of other days. Many men have been, like Wilfrid, equally powerful by the Hand, by the Heart, by the Head; like him, the majority have abused their triple power. But though this man still held by certain outward liens to the slimy side of humanity, he belonged also and positively to the sphere where force is intelligent. In spite of the many veils which enveloped his soul, there were certain ineffable symptoms of this fact which were visible to pure spirits, to the eyes of the child whose innocence has known no breath of evil passions, to the eyes of the old man who has lived to regain his purity.

These signs revealed a Cain for whom there was still hope,—one who seemed as though he were seeking absolution from the ends of the earth. Minna suspected the galley-slave of glory in the man; Seraphita recognized him. Both admired and both pitied him. Whence came their prescience? Nothing could be more simple nor yet more extraordinary. As soon as we seek to penetrate the secrets of Nature, where nothing is secret, and where it is only necessary to have the eyes to see, we perceive that the simple produces the marvellous.

"Seraphitus," said Minna one evening a few days after Wilfrid's arrival in Jarvis, "you read the soul of this stranger while I have only vague impressions of it. He chills me or else he excites me; but you seem to know the cause of this cold and of this heat; tell me what it means, for you know all about him."

"Yes, I have seen the causes," said Seraphitus, lowing his large eyelids.

"By what power?" asked the curious Minna.

"I have the gift of Specialism," he answered. "Specialism is an inward sight which can penetrate all things; you will only understand its full meaning through a comparison. In the great cities of Europe where works are produced by which the human Hand seeks to represent the effects of the moral nature was well as those of the physical nature, there are glorious men who express ideas in marble. The sculptor acts on the stone; he fashions it; he puts a realm of ideas into it. There are statues which the hand of man has endowed with the faculty of representing the noble side of humanity, or the whole evil side; most men see in such marbles a human figure and nothing more; a few other men, a little higher in the scale of being, perceive a fraction of the thoughts expressed in the statue; but the Initiates in the secrets of art are of the same intellect as the sculptor; they see in his work the whole universe of his thought. Such persons are in themselves the principles of art; they bear within them a mirror which reflects nature in her slightest manifestations. Well! so it is with me; I have within me a mirror before which the moral nature, with its causes and effects, appears and is reflected. Entering thus into the consciousness of others I am able to divine both the future and the past. How? do you still ask how? Imagine that the marble statue is the body of a man, a piece of statuary in which we see the emotion, sentiment, passion, vice or crime, virtue or repentance which the creating hand has put into it, and you will then comprehend how it is that I read the soul of this foreigner—though what I have said does not explain the gift of Specialism; for to conceive the nature of that gift we must possess it."

Though Wilfrid belonged to the two first divisions of humanity, the men of force and the men of thought, yet his excesses, his tumultuous life, and his misdeeds had often turned him towards Faith; for doubt has two sides; a side to the light and a side to the darkness. Wilfrid had too closely clasped the world under its forms of Matter and of Mind

not to have acquired that thirst for the unknown, that longing to *go beyond* which lay their grasp upon the men who
know, and wish, and will. But neither his knowledge, nor
his actions, nor his will, had found direction. He had fled
from social life from necessity; as a great criminal seeks the
cloister. Remorse, that virtue of weak beings, did not touch
him. Remorse is impotence, impotence which sins again.
Repentance alone is powerful; it ends all. But in traversing
the world, which he made his cloister, Wilfrid had found no
balm for his wounds; he saw nothing in nature to which he
could attach himself. In him, despair had dried the sources
of desire. He was one of those beings who, having gone
through all passions and come out victorious, have nothing
more to raise in their hot-beds, and who, lacking opportunity to put themselves at the head of their fellow-men to
trample under iron heel entire populations, buy, at the price
of a horrible martyrdom, the faculty of ruining themselves
in some belief,—rocks sublime, which await the touch of a
wand that comes not to bring the waters gushing from their
far-off spring.

Led by a scheme of his restless, inquiring life to the
shores of Norway, the sudden arrival of winter had
detained the wanderer at Jarvis. The day on which, for the
first time, he saw Seraphita, the whole past of his life faded
from his mind. The young girl excited emotions which he
had thought could never be revived. The ashes gave forth
a lingering flame at the first murmurings of that voice.
Who has ever felt himself return to youth and purity after
growing cold and numb with age and soiled with impurity?
Suddenly, Wilfrid loved as he had never loved; he loved
secretly, with faith, with fear, with inward madness. His
life was stirred to the very source of his being at the mere
thought of seeing Seraphita. As he listened to her he was
transported into unknown worlds; he was mute before her,
she magnetized him. There, beneath the snows, among the
glaciers, bloomed the celestial flower to which his hopes,
so long betrayed, aspired; the sight of which awakened
ideas of freshness, purity, and faith which grouped about
his soul and lifted it to higher regions,—as Angels bear to
heaven the Elect in those symbolic pictures inspired by the

guardian spirit of a great master. Celestial perfumes softened the granite hardness of the rocky scene; light endowed
with speech shed its divine melodies on the path of him
who looked to heaven. After emptying the cup of terrestrial love which his teeth had bitten as he drank it, he saw
before him the chalice of salvation where the limpid waters
sparkled, making thirsty for ineffable delights whoever dare
apply his lips burning with a faith so strong that the crystal
shall not be shattered.

But Wilfrid now encountered the wall of brass for which
he had been seeking up and down the earth. He went
impetuously to Seraphita, meaning to express the whole
force and bearing of a passion under which he bounded
like the fabled horse beneath the iron horseman, firm in
his saddle, whom nothing moves while the efforts of the
fiery animal only made the rider heavier and more solid.
He sought her to relate his life,—to prove the grandeur of
his soul by the grandeur of his faults, to show the ruins of
his desert. But no sooner had he crossed her threshold, and
found himself within the zone of those eyes of scintillat-
ing azure, that met no limits forward and left none behind,
than he grew calm and submissive, as a lion, springing on
his prey in the plains of Africa, receives from the wings of
the wind a message of love, and stops his bound. A gulf
opened before him, into which his frenzied words fell and
disappeared, and from which uprose a voice which changed
his being; he became as a child, a child of sixteen, timid and
frightened before this maiden with serene brow, this white
figure whose inalterable calm was like the cruel impassibil-
ity of human justice. The combat between them had never
ceased until this evening, when with a glance she brought
him down, as a falcon making his dizzy spirals in the air
around his prey causes it to fall stupefied to earth, before
carrying it to his eyrie.

We may note within ourselves many a long struggle the
end of which is one of our own actions,—struggles which
are, as it were, the reverse side of humanity. This reverse
side belongs to God; the obverse side to men. More than
once Seraphita had proved to Wilfrid that she knew this
hidden and ever varied side, which is to the majority of

men a second being. Often she said to him in her dove-like voice: "Why all this vehemence?" when on his way to her he had sworn she should be his. Wilfrid was, however, strong enough to raise the cry of revolt to which he had given utterance in Monsieur Becker's study. The narrative of the old pastor had calmed him. Sceptical and derisive as he was, he saw belief like a sidereal brilliance dawning on his life. He asked himself if Seraphita were not an exile from the higher spheres seeking the homeward way. The fanciful deifications of all ordinary lovers he could not give to this lily of Norway in whose divinity he believed. Why lived she here beside this fjord? What did she? Questions that received no answer filled his mind. Above all, what was about to happen between them? What fate had brought him there? To him, Seraphita was the motionless marble, light nevertheless as a vapor, which Minna had seen that day poised above the precipices of the Falberg. Could she thus stand on the edge of all gulfs without danger, without a tremor of the arching eyebrows, or a quiver of the light of the eye? If his love was to be without hope, it was not without curiosity.

From the moment when Wilfrid suspected the ethereal nature of the enchantress who had told him the secrets of his life in melodious utterance, he had longed to try to subject her, to keep her to himself, to tear her from the heaven where, perhaps, she was awaited. Earth and Humanity seized their prey; he would imitate them. His pride, the only sentiment through which man can long be exalted, would make him happy in this triumph for the rest of his life. The idea sent the blood boiling through his veins, and his heart swelled. If he did not succeed, he would destroy her,—it is so natural to destroy that which we cannot possess, to deny what we cannot comprehend, to insult that which we envy.

On the morrow, Wilfrid, laden with ideas which the extraordinary events of the previous night naturally awakened in his mind, resolved to question David, and went to find him on the pretext of asking after Seraphita's health. Though Monsieur Becker spoke of the old servant as falling into dotage, Wilfrid relied on his own perspicacity to discover scraps of truth in the torrent of the old man's rambling talk.

David had the immovable, undecided, physiognomy of an octogenarian. Under his white hair lay a forehead lined with wrinkles like the stone courses of a ruined wall; and his face was furrowed like the bed of a dried-up torrent. His life seemed to have retreated wholly to the eyes, where light still shone, though its gleams were obscured by a mistiness which seemed to indicate either an active mental alienation or the stupid stare of drunkenness. His slow and heavy movements betrayed the glacial weight of age, and communicated an icy influence to whoever allowed themselves to look long at him,—for he possessed the magnetic force of torpor. His limited intelligence was only roused by the sight, the hearing, or the recollection of his mistress. She was the soul of this wholly material fragment of an existence. Any one seeing David alone by himself would have thought him a corpse; let Seraphita enter, let her voice be heard, or a mention of her be made, and the dead came forth from his grave and recovered speech and motion. The dry bones were not more truly awakened by the divine breath in the valley of Jehoshaphat, and never was that apocalyptic vision better realized than in this Lazarus issuing from the sepulchre into life at the voice of a young girl. His language, which was always figurative and often incomprehensible, prevented the inhabitants of the village from talking with him; but they respected a mind that deviated so utterly from common ways,—a thing which the masses instinctively admire.

Wilfrid found him in the antechamber, apparently asleep beside the stove. Like a dog who recognizes a friend of the family, the old man raised his eyes, saw the foreigner, and did not stir.

"Where is she?" inquired Wilfrid, sitting down beside him.

David fluttered his fingers in the air as if to express the flight of a bird.

"Does she still suffer?" asked Wilfrid.

"Beings vowed to Heaven are able so to suffer that suffering does not lessen their love; this is the mark of the true faith," answered the old man, solemnly, like an instrument which, on being touched, gives forth an accidental note.

"Who taught you those words?"

"The Spirit."

"What happened to her last night? Did you force your way past the Vertumni standing sentinel? did you evade the Mammons?"

"Yes"; answered David, as though awaking from a dream.

The misty gleam of his eyes melted into a ray that came direct from the soul and made it by degrees brilliant as that of an eagle, as intelligent as that of a poet.

"What did you see?" asked Wilfrid, astonished at this sudden change.

"I saw Species and Shapes; I heard the Spirit of all things; I beheld the revolt of the Evil Ones; I listened to the words of the Good. Seven devils came, and seven archangels descended from on high. The archangels stood apart and looked on through veils. The devils were close by; they shone, they acted. Mammon came on his pearly shell in the shape of a beautiful naked woman; her snowy body dazzled the eye, no human form ever equalled it; and he said, 'I am Pleasure; thou shalt possess me!' Lucifer, prince of serpents, was there in sovereign robes; his Manhood was glorious as the beauty of an angel, and he said, 'Humanity shall be at thy feet!' The Queen of misers,—she who gives back naught that she has ever received,—the Sea, came wrapped in her virent mantle; she opened her bosom, she showed her gems, she brought forth her treasures and offered them; waves of sapphire and of emerald came at her bidding; her hidden wonders stirred, they rose to the surface of her breast, they spoke; the rarest pearl of Ocean spread its iridescent wings and gave voice to its marine melodies, saying, 'Twin daughter of suffering, we are sisters! await me; let us go together; all I need is to become a Woman.' The Bird with the wings of an eagle and the paws of a lion, the head of a woman and the body of a horse, the Animal, fell down before her and licked her feet, and promised seven hundred years of plenty to her best-beloved daughter. Then came the most formidable of all, the Child, weeping at her knees, and saying, 'Wilt thou leave me, feeble and suffering as I am? oh, my mother, stay!' and he played with her, and shed languor on the air, and the Heavens themselves had pity for his wail. The Virgin of pure song brought forth her choirs to relax the soul. The Kings of the East came with their slaves, their armies, and their women; the Wounded asked her for succor, the Sorrowful stretched forth their hands: 'Do not leave us! do not leave us!' they cried. I, too, I cried, 'Do not leave us! we adore thee! stay!' Flowers, bursting from the seed, bathed her in their fragrance which uttered, 'Stay!' The giant Enakim came forth from Jupiter, leading Gold and its friends and all the Spirits of the Astral Regions which are joined with him, and they said, 'We are thine for seven hundred years.' At last came Death on his pale horse, crying, 'I will obey thee!' One and all fell prostrate before her. Could you but have seen them! They covered as it were a vast plain, and they cried aloud to her, 'We have nurtured thee, thou art our child; do not abandon us!' At length Life issued from her Ruby Waters, and said, 'I will not leave thee!' then, finding Seraphita silent, she flamed upon her as the sun, crying out, 'I am light!' '*The light* is there!' cried Seraphita, pointing to the clouds where stood the archangels; but she was wearied out; Desire had wrung her nerves, she could only cry, 'My God! my God!' Ah! many an Angelic Spirit, scaling the mountain and nigh to the summit, has set his foot upon a rolling stone which plunged him back into the abyss! All these lost Spirits adored her constancy; they stood around her,—a choir without a song,—weeping and whispering, 'Courage!' At last she conquered; Desire—let loose upon her in every Shape and every Species—was vanquished. She stood in prayer, and when at last her eyes were lifted she saw the feet of Angels circling in the Heavens."

"She saw the feet of Angels?" repeated Wilfrid.

"Yes," said the old man.

"Was it a dream that she told you?" asked Wilfrid.

"A dream as real as your life," answered David; "I was there."

The calm assurance of the old servant affected Wilfrid powerfully. He went away asking himself whether these visions were any less extraordinary than those he had read of in Swedenborg the night before.

"If Spirits exist, they must act," he was saying to himself as he entered the parsonage, where he found Monsieur Becker alone.

"Dear pastor," he said, "Seraphita is connected with us in form only, and even that form is inexplicable. Do not think me a madman or a lover; a profound conviction cannot be argued with. Convert my belief into scientific theories, and let us try to enlighten each other. To-morrow evening we shall both be with her."

"What then?" said Monsieur Becker.

"If her eye ignores space," replied Wilfrid, "if her thought is an intelligent sight which enables her to perceive all things in their essence, and to connect them with the general evolution of the universe, if, in a word, she sees and knows all, let us seat the Pythoness on her tripod, let us force this pitiless eagle by threats to spread its wings! Help me! I breathe a fire which burns my vitals; I must quench it or it will consume me. I have found a prey at last, and it shall be mine!"

"The conquest will be difficult," said the pastor, "because this girl is—"

"Is what?" cried Wilfrid.

"Mad," said the old man.

"I will not dispute her madness, but neither must you dispute her wonderful powers. Dear Monsieur Becker, she has often confounded me with her learning. Has she travelled?"

"From her house to the fjord, no further."

"Never left this place!" exclaimed Wilfrid. "Then she must have read immensely."

"Not a page, not one iota! I am the only person who possesses any books in Jarvis. The works of Swedenborg—the only books that were in the chateau—you see before you. She has never looked into a single one of them."

"Have you tried to talk with her?"

"What good would that do?"

"Does no one live with her in that house?"

"She has no friends but you and Minna, nor any servant except old David."

"It cannot be that she knows nothing of science nor of

art."

"Who should teach her?" said the pastor.

"But if she can discuss such matters pertinently, as she has often done with me, what do you make of it?"

"The girl may have acquired through years of silence the faculties enjoyed by Apollonius of Tyana and other pretended sorcerers burned by the Inquisition, which did not choose to admit the fact of second-sight."

"If she can speak Arabic, what would you say to that?"

"The history of medical science gives many authentic instances of girls who have spoken languages entirely unknown to them."

"What can I do?" exclaimed Wilfrid. "She knows of secrets in my past life known only to me."

"I shall be curious if she can tell me thoughts that I have confided to no living person," said Monsieur Becker.

Minna entered the room.

"Well, my daughter, and how is your familiar spirit?"

"He suffers, father," she answered, bowing to Wilfrid. "Human passions, clothed in their false riches, surrounded him all night, and showed him all the glories of the world. But you think these things mere tales."

"Tales as beautiful to those who read them in their brains as the 'Arabian Nights' to common minds," said the pastor, smiling.

"Did not Satan carry our Savior to the pinnacle of the Temple, and show him all the kingdoms of the world?" she said.

"The Evangelists," replied her father, "did not correct their copies very carefully, and several versions are in existence."

"You believe in the reality of these visions?" said Wilfrid to Minna.

"Who can doubt when he relates them."

"He?" demanded Wilfrid. "Who?"

"He who is there," replied Minna, motioning towards the chateau.

"Are you speaking of Seraphita?" he said.

The young girl bent her head, and looked at him with an expression of gentle mischief.

"You too!" exclaimed Wilfrid, "you take pleasure in confounding me. Who and what is she? What do you think of her?"

"What I feel is inexplicable," said Minna, blushing.

"You are all crazy!" cried the pastor.

"Farewell, until tomorrow evening," said Wilfrid.

## IV. THE CLOUDS OF THE SANCTUARY

There are pageants in which all the material splendors that man arrays co-operate. Nations of slaves and divers have searched the sands of ocean and the bowels of earth for the pearls and diamonds which adorn the spectators. Transmitted as heirlooms from generation to generation, these treasures have shone on consecrated brows and could be the most faithful of historians had they speech. They know the joys and sorrows of the great and those of the small. Everywhere do they go; they are worn with pride at festivals, carried in despair to usurers, borne off in triumph amid blood and pillage, enshrined in masterpieces conceived by art for their protection. None, except the pearl of Cleopatra, has been lost. The Great and the Fortunate assemble to witness the coronation of some king, whose trappings are the work of men's hands, but the purple of whose raiment is less glorious than that of the flowers of the field. These festivals, splendid in light, bathed in music which the hand of man creates, aye, all the triumphs of that hand are subdued by a thought, crushed by a sentiment. The Mind can illumine in a man and round a man a light more vivid, can open his ear to more melodious harmonies, can seat him on clouds of shining constellations and teach him to question them. The Heart can do still greater things. Man may come into the presence of one sole being and find in a single word, a single look, an influence so weighty to bear, of so luminous a light, so penetrating a sound, that he succumbs and kneels before it. The most real of all splendors are not in outward things, they are within us. A single secret of science is a realm of wonders to the man of learning. Do the trumpets of Power,

the jewels of Wealth, the music of Joy, or a vast concourse
of people attend his mental festival? No, he finds his glory
in some dim retreat where, perchance, a pallid suffering
man whispers a single word into his ear; that word, like a
torch lighted in a mine, reveals to him a Science. All human
ideas, arrayed in every attractive form which Mystery can
invent surrounded a blind man seated in a wayside ditch.
Three worlds, the Natural, the Spiritual, the Divine, with
all their spheres, opened their portals to a Florentine exile;
he walked attended by the Happy and the Unhappy; by
those who prayed and those who moaned; by angels and by
souls in hell. When the Sent of God, who knew and could
accomplish all things, appeared to three of his disciples it
was at eventide, at the common table of the humblest of
inns; and then and there the Light broke forth, shattering
Material Forms, illuminating the Spiritual Faculties, so
that they saw him in his glory, and the earth lay at their feet
like a cast-off sandal.

Monsieur Becker, Wilfrid, and Minna were all under the
influence of fear as they took their way to meet the extraordinary being whom each desired to question. To them, in
their several ways, the Swedish castle had grown to mean
some gigantic representation, some spectacle like those
whose colors and masses are skilfully and harmoniously
marshalled by the poets, and whose personages, imaginary
actors to men, are real to those who begin to penetrate the
Spiritual World. On the tiers of this Coliseum Monsieur
Becker seated the gray legions of Doubt, the stern ideas,
the specious formulas of Dispute. He convoked the various
antagonistic worlds of philosophy and religion, and they all
appeared, in the guise of a fleshless shape, like that in which
art embodies Time,—an old man bearing in one hand a
scythe, in the other a broken globe, the human universe.

Wilfrid had bidden to the scene his earliest illusions and
his latest hopes, human destiny and its conflicts, religion
and its conquering powers.

Minna saw heaven confusedly by glimpses; love raised a
curtain wrought with mysterious images, and the melodious sounds which met her ear redoubled her curiosity.

To all three, therefore, this evening was to be what that

other evening had been for the pilgrims to Emmaus, what a vision was to Dante, an inspiration to Homer,—to them, three aspects of the world revealed, veils rent away, doubts dissipated, darkness illumined. Humanity in all its moods expecting light could not be better represented than here by this young girl, this man in the vigor of his age, and these old men, of whom one was learned enough to doubt, the other ignorant enough to believe. Never was any scene more simple in appearance, nor more portentous in reality.

When they entered the room, ushered in by old David, they found Seraphita standing by a table on which were served the various dishes which compose a "tea"; a form of collation which in the North takes the place of wine and its pleasures,—reserved more exclusively for Southern climes. Certainly nothing proclaimed in her, or in him, a being with the strange power of appearing under two distinct forms; nothing about her betrayed the manifold powers which she wielded. Like a careful housewife attending to the comfort of her guests, she ordered David to put more wood into the stove.

"Good evening, my neighbors," she said. "Dear Monsieur Becker, you do right to come; you see me living for the last time, perhaps. This winter has killed me. Will you sit there?" she said to Wilfrid. "And you, Minna, here?" pointing to a chair beside her. "I see you have brought your embroidery. Did you invent that stitch? the design is very pretty. For whom is it,—your father, or monsieur?" she added, turning to Wilfrid. "Surely we ought to give him, before we part, a remembrance of the daughters of Norway."

"Did you suffer much yesterday?" asked Wilfrid.

"It was nothing," she answered; "the suffering gladdened me; it was necessary, to enable me to leave this life."

"Then death does not alarm you?" said Monsieur Becker, smiling, for he did not think her ill.

"No, dear pastor; there are two ways of dying: to some, death is victory, to others, defeat."

"Do you think that you have conquered?" asked Minna.

"I do not know," she said, "perhaps I have only taken a step in the path."

The lustrous splendor of her brow grew dim, her eyes were veiled beneath slow-dropping lids; a simple movement which affected the prying guests and kept them silent. Monsieur Becker was the first to recover courage.

"Dear child," he said, "you are truth itself, and you are ever kind. I would ask of you to-night something other than the dainties of your tea-table. If we may believe certain persons, you know amazing things; if this be true, would it not be charitable in you to solve a few of our doubts?"

"Ah!" she said smiling, "I walk on the clouds. I visit the depths of the fjord; the sea is my steed and I bridle it; I know where the singing flower grows, and the talking light descends, and fragrant colors shine! I wear the seal of Solomon; I am a fairy; I cast my orders to the wind which, like an abject slave, fulfils them; my eyes can pierce the earth and behold its treasures; for lo! am I not the virgin to whom the pearls dart from their ocean depths and—"

"—who led me safely to the summit of the Falberg?" said Minna, interrupting her.

"Thou! thou too!" exclaimed the strange being, with a luminous glance at the young girl which filled her soul with trouble. "Had I not the faculty of reading through your foreheads the desires which have brought you here, should I be what you think I am?" she said, encircling all three with her controlling glance, to David's great satisfaction. The old man rubbed his hands with pleasure as he left the room.

"Ah!" she resumed after a pause, "you have come, all of you, with the curiosity of children. You, my poor Monsieur Becker, have asked yourself how it was possible that a girl of seventeen should know even a single one of those secrets which men of science seek with their noses to the earth,—instead of raising their eyes to heaven. Were I to tell you how and at what point the plant merges into the animal you would begin to doubt your doubts. You have plotted to question me; you will admit that?"

"Yes, dear Seraphita," answered Wilfrid; "but the desire is a natural one to men, is it not?"

"You will bore this dear child with such topics," she said, passing her hand lightly over Minna's hair with a caressing gesture.

The young girl raised her eyes and seemed as though she longed to lose herself in him.

"Speech is the endowment of us all," resumed the mysterious creature, gravely. "Woe to him who keeps silence, even in a desert, believing that no one hears him; all voices speak and all ears listen here below. Speech moves the universe. Monsieur Becker, I desire to say nothing unnecessarily. I know the difficulties that beset your mind; would you not think it a miracle if I were now to lay bare the past history of your consciousness? Well, the miracle shall be accomplished. You have never admitted to yourself the full extent of your doubts. I alone, immovable in my faith, I can show it to you; I can terrify you with yourself.

"You stand on the darkest side of Doubt. You do not believe in God,—although you know it not,—and all things here below are secondary to him who rejects the first principle of things. Let us leave aside the fruitless discussions of false philosophy. The spiritualist generations made as many and as vain efforts to deny Matter as the materialist generations have made to deny Spirit. Why such discussions? Does not man himself offer irrefragable proof of both systems? Do we not find in him material things and spiritual things? None but a madman can refuse to see in the human body a fragment of Matter; your natural sciences, when they decompose it, find little difference between its elements and those of other animals. On the other hand, the idea produced in man by the comparison of many objects has never seemed to anyone to belong to the domain of Matter. As to this, I offer no opinion. I am now concerned with your doubts, not with my certainties. To you, as to the majority of thinkers, the relations between things, the reality of which is proved to you by your sensations and which you possess the faculty to discover, do not seem Material. The Natural universe of things and beings ends, in man, with the Spiritual universe of similarities or differences which he perceives among the innumerable forms of Nature,—relations so multiplied as to seem infinite; for if, up to the present time, no one has been able to enumerate the separate terrestrial creations, who can reckon their

correlations? Is not the fraction which you know, in relation to their totality, what a single number is to infinity?
Here, then, you fall into a perception of the infinite which
undoubtedly obliges you to conceive of a purely Spiritual
world.

"Thus man himself offers sufficient proof of the two
orders,—Matter and Spirit. In him culminates a visible finite universe; in him begins a universe invisible and
infinite,—two worlds unknown to each other. Have the
pebbles of the fjord a perception of their combined being?
have they a consciousness of the colors they present to
the eye of man? do they hear the music of the waves that
lap them? Let us therefore spring over and not attempt to
sound the abysmal depths presented to our minds in the
union of a Material universe and a Spiritual universe,—a
creation visible, ponderable, tangible, terminating in a
creation invisible, imponderable, intangible; completely
dissimilar, separated by the void, yet united by indisputable
bonds and meeting in a being who derives equally from the
one and from the other! Let us mingle in one world these
two worlds, absolutely irreconcilable to your philosophies,
but conjoined by fact. However abstract man may suppose the relation which binds two things together, the line
of junction is perceptible. How? Where? We are not now
in search of the vanishing point where Matter subtilizes.
If such were the question, I cannot see why He who has,
by physical relations, studded with stars at immeasurable
distances the heavens which veil Him, may not have created solid substances, nor why you deny Him the faculty of
giving a body to thought.

"Thus your invisible moral universe and your visible
physical universe are one and the same matter. We will
not separate properties from substances, nor objects from
effects. All that exists, all that presses upon us and over-
whelms us from above or from below, before us or in us,
all that which our eyes and our minds perceive, all these
named and unnamed things compose—in order to fit the
problem of Creation to the measure of your logic—a block
of finite Matter; but were it infinite, God would still not be
its master. Now, reasoning with your views, dear pastor, no

matter in what way God the infinite is concerned with this block of finite Matter, He cannot exist and retain the attributes with which man invests Him. Seek Him in facts, and He is not; spiritually and materially, you have made God impossible. Listen to the Word of human Reason forced to its ultimate conclusions.

"In bringing God face to face with the Great Whole, we see that only two states are possible between them,—either God and Matter are contemporaneous, or God existed alone before Matter. Were Reason—the light that has guided the human race from the dawn of its existence—accumulated in one brain, even that mighty brain could not invent a third mode of being without suppressing both Matter and God. Let human philosophies pile mountain upon mountain of words and of ideas, let religions accumulate images and beliefs, revelations and mysteries, you must face at last this terrible dilemma and choose between the two propositions which compose it; you have no option, and one as much as the other leads human reason to Doubt.

"The problem thus established, what signifies Spirit or Matter? Why trouble about the march of the worlds in one direction or in another, since the Being who guides them is shown to be an absurdity? Why continue to ask whether man is approaching heaven or receding from it, whether creation is rising towards Spirit or descending towards Matter, if the questioned universe gives no reply? What signifies theogonies and their armies, theologies and their dogmas, since whichever side of the problem is man's choice, his God exists not? Let us for a moment take up the first proposition, and suppose God contemporaneous with Matter. Is subjection to the action or the co-existence of an alien substance consistent with being God at all? In such a system, would not God become a secondary agent compelled to organize Matter? If so, who compelled Him? Between His material gross companion and Himself, who was the arbiter? Who paid the wages of the six days' labor imputed to the great Designer? Has any determining force been found which was neither God nor Matter? God being regarded as the manufacturer of the machinery of the worlds, is it not as ridiculous to call Him God as to call the slave who turns the grindstone a Roman citizen? Besides, another difficulty, as insoluble to this supreme human reason as it is to God, presents itself.

"If we carry the problem higher, shall we not be like the Hindus, who put the world upon a tortoise, the tortoise on an elephant, and do not know on what the feet of their elephant may rest? This supreme will, issuing from the contest between God and Matter, this God, this more than God, can He have existed throughout eternity without willing what He afterwards willed,—admitting that Eternity can be divided into two eras. No matter where God is, what becomes of His intuitive intelligence if He did not know His ultimate thought? Which, then, is the true Eternity,—the created Eternity or the uncreated? But if God throughout all time did will the world such as it is, this new necessity, which harmonizes with the idea of sovereign intelligence, implies the co-eternity of Matter. Whether Matter be co-eternal by a divine will necessarily accordant with itself from the beginning, or whether Matter be co-eternal of its own being, the power of God, which must be absolute, perishes if His will is circumscribed; for in that case God would find within Him a determining force which would control Him. Can He be God if He can no more separate Himself from His creation in a past eternity than in the coming eternity?

"This face of the problem is insoluble in its cause. Let us now inquire into its effects. If a God compelled to have created the world from all eternity seems inexplicable, He is quite as unintelligible in perpetual cohesion with His work. God, constrained to live eternally united to His creation is held down to His first position as workman. Can you conceive of a God who shall be neither independent of nor dependent on His work? Could He destroy that work without challenging Himself? Ask yourself, and decide! Whether He destroys it some day, or whether He never destroys it, either way is fatal to the attributes without which God cannot exist. Is the world an experiment? is it a perishable form to which destruction must come? If it is, is not God inconsistent and impotent? inconsistent, because He ought to have seen the result before the attempt,—moreover why

should He delay to destroy that which He is to destroy?—
impotent, for how else could He have created an imperfect
man?

"If an imperfect creation contradicts the faculties which
man attributes to God we are forced back upon the question, Is creation perfect? The idea is in harmony with that
of a God supremely intelligent who could make no mistakes; but then, what means the degradation of His work,
and its regeneration? Moreover, a perfect world is, necessarily, indestructible; its forms would not perish, it could
neither advance nor recede, it would revolve in the everlasting circumference from which it would never issue. In
that case God would be dependent on His work; it would
be co-eternal with Him; and so we fall back into one of
the propositions most antagonistic to God. If the world
is imperfect, it can progress; if perfect, it is stationary. On
the other hand, if it be impossible to admit of a progressive God ignorant through a past eternity of the results of
His creative work, can there be a stationary God? would
not that imply the triumph of Matter? would it not be the
greatest of all negations? Under the first hypothesis God
perishes through weakness; under the second through the
Force of his inertia.

"Therefore, to all sincere minds the supposition that
Matter, in the conception and execution of the worlds, is
contemporaneous with God, is to deny God. Forced to
choose, in order to govern the nations, between the two
alternatives of the problem, whole generations have preferred this solution of it. Hence the doctrine of the two
principles of Magianism, brought from Asia and adopted
in Europe under the form of Satan warring with the Eternal Father. But this religious formula and the innumerable
aspects of divinity that have sprung from it are surely crimes
against the Majesty Divine. What other term can we apply
to the belief which sets up as a rival to God a personification of Evil, striving eternally against the Omnipotent Mind
without the possibility of ultimate triumph? Your statics
declare that two Forces thus pitted against each other are
reciprocally rendered null.

"Do you turn back, therefore, to the other side of the

problem, and say that God pre-existed, original, alone?

"I will not go over the preceding arguments (which here return in full force) as to the severance of Eternity into two parts; nor the questions raised by the progression or the immobility of the worlds; let us look only at the difficulties inherent to this second theory. If God pre-existed alone, the world must have emanated from Him; Matter was therefore drawn from His essence; consequently Matter in itself is non-existent; all forms are veils to cover the Divine Spirit. If this be so, the World is Eternal, and also it must be God. Is not this proposition even more fatal than the former to the attributes conferred on God by human reason? How can the actual condition of Matter be explained if we suppose it to issue from the bosom of God and to be ever united with Him? Is it possible to believe that the All-Powerful, supremely good in His essence and in His faculties, has engendered things dissimilar to Himself. Must He not in all things and through all things be like unto Himself? Can there be in God certain evil parts of which at some future day he may rid Himself?—a conjecture less offensive and absurd than terrible, for the reason that it drags back into Him the two principles which the preceding theory proved to be inadmissible. God must be ONE; He cannot be divided without renouncing the most important condition of His existence. It is therefore impossible to admit of a fraction of God which yet is not God. This hypothesis seemed so criminal to the Roman Church that she has made the omnipresence of God in the least particles of the Eucharist an article of faith.

"But how then can we imagine an omnipotent mind which does not triumph? How associate it unless in triumph with Nature? But Nature is not triumphant; she seeks, combines, remodels, dies, and is born again; she is even more convulsed when creating than when all was fusion; Nature suffers, groans, is ignorant, degenerates, does evil; deceives herself, annihilates herself, disappears, and begins again. If God is associated with Nature, how can we explain the inoperative indifference of the divine principle? Wherefore death? How came it that Evil, king of the earth, was born of a God supremely good in His essence and in His faculties, who can produce nothing that is not made in His own image?

"But if, from this relentless conclusion which leads at once to absurdity, we pass to details, what end are we to assign to the world? If all is God, all is reciprocally cause and effect; all is *One* as God is *One*, and we can perceive neither points of likeness nor points of difference. Can the real end be a rotation of Matter which subtilizes and disappears? In whatever sense it were done, would not this mechanical trick of Matter issuing from God and returning to God seem a sort of child's play? Why should God make himself gross with Matter? Under which form is he most God? Which has the ascendant, Matter or Spirit, when neither can in any way do wrong? Who can comprehend the Deity engaged in this perpetual business, by which he divides Himself into two Natures, one of which knows nothing, while the other knows all? Can you conceive of God amusing Himself in the form of man, laughing at His own efforts, dying Friday, to be born again Sunday, and continuing this play from age to age, knowing the end from all eternity, and telling nothing to Himself, the Creature, of what He the Creator, does? The God of the preceding hypothesis, a God so nugatory by the very power of His inertia, seems the more possible of the two if we are compelled to choose between the impossibilities with which this God, so dull a jester, fusillades Himself when two sections of humanity argue face to face, weapons in hand.

"However absurd this outcome of the second problem may seem, it was adopted by half the human race in the sunny lands where smiling mythologies were created. Those amorous nations were consistent; with them all was God, even Fear and its dastardy, even crime and its bacchanals. If we accept pantheism,—the religion of many a great human genius,—who shall say where the greater reason lies? Is it with the savage, free in the desert, clothed in his nudity, listening to the sun, talking to the sea, sublime and always true in his deeds whatever they may be; or shall we find it in civilized man, who derives his chief enjoyments through lies; who wrings Nature and all her resources to put a musket on his shoulder; who employs his intellect to hasten the hour of his death and to create diseases out of pleasures? When the rake of pestilence and the plowshare of war and the demon of desolation have passed over a corner of the globe and obliterated all things, who will be found to have the greater reason,—the Nubian savage or the patrician of Thebes? Your doubts descend the scale, they go from heights to depths, they embrace all, the end as well as the means.

"But if the physical world seems inexplicable, the moral world presents still stronger arguments against God. Where, then, is progress? If all things are indeed moving toward perfection why do we die young? why do not nations perpetuate themselves? The world having issued from God and being contained in God can it be stationary? Do we live once, or do we live always? If we live once, hurried onward by the march of the Great-Whole, a knowledge of which has not been given to us, let us act as we please. If we are eternal, let things take their course. Is the created being guilty if he exists at the instant of the transitions? If he sins at the moment of a great transformation will he be punished for it after being its victim? What becomes of the Divine goodness if we are not transferred to the regions of the blest—should any such exist? What becomes of God's prescience if He is ignorant of the results of the trials to which He subjects us? What is this alternative offered to man by all religions,—either to boil in some eternal cauldron or to walk in white robes, a palm in his hand and a halo round his head? Can it be that this pagan invention is the final word of God? Where is the generous soul who does not feel that the calculating virtue which seeks the eternity of pleasure offered by all religions to whoever fulfils at stray moments certain fanciful and often unnatural conditions, is unworthy of man and of God? Is it not a mockery to give to man impetuous senses and forbid him to satisfy them? Besides, what mean these ascetic objections if Good and Evil are equally abolished? Does Evil exist? If substance in all its forms is God, then Evil is God. The faculty of reasoning as well as the faculty of feeling having been given to man to use, nothing can be more excusable in him than to seek to know the meaning of human suffering and the prospects of the future.

"If these rigid and rigorous arguments lead to such conclusions confusion must reign. The world would have no
fixedness; nothing would advance, nothing would pause,
all would change, nothing would be destroyed, all would
reappear after self-renovation; for if your mind does not
clearly demonstrate to you an end, it is equally impossible
to demonstrate the destruction of the smallest particle of
Matter; Matter can transform but not annihilate itself.

"Though blind force may provide arguments for the
atheist, intelligent force is inexplicable; for if it emanates
from God, why should it meet with obstacles? ought not
its triumph to be immediate? Where is God? If the living
cannot perceive Him, can the dead find Him? Crumble,
ye idolatries and ye religions! Fall, feeble keystones of all
social arches, powerless to retard the decay, the death, the
oblivion that have overtaken all nations however firmly
founded! Fall, morality and justice! our crimes are purely
relative; they are divine effects whose causes we are not
allowed to know. All is God. Either we are God or God is
not!—Child of a century whose every year has laid upon
your brow, old man, the ice of its unbelief, here, here is the
summing up of your lifetime of thought, of your science
and your reflections! Dear Monsieur Becker, you have laid
your head upon the pillow of Doubt, because it is the eas-
iest of solutions; acting in this respect with the majority of
mankind, who say in their hearts: 'Let us think no more of
these problems, since God has not vouchsafed to grant us
the algebraic demonstrations that could solve them, while
He has given us so many other ways to get from earth to
heaven.'

"Tell me, dear pastor, are not these your secret thoughts?
Have I evaded the point of any? nay, rather, have I not
clearly stated all? First, in the dogma of two principles,—
an antagonism in which God perishes for the reason that
being All-Powerful He chose to combat. Secondly, in the
absurd pantheism where, all being God, God exists no
longer. These two sources, from which have flowed all the
religions for whose triumph Earth has toiled and prayed,
are equally pernicious. Behold in them the double-bladed

axe with which you decapitate the white old man whom
you enthrone among your painted clouds! And now, to me
the axe, I wield it!"

Monsieur Becker and Wilfrid gazed at the young girl
with something like terror.

"To believe," continued Seraphita, in her Woman's voice,
for the Man had finished speaking, "to believe is a gift. To
believe is to feel. To believe in God we must feel God. This
feeling is a possession slowly acquired by the human being,
just as other astonishing powers which you admire in great
men, warriors, artists, scholars, those who know and those
who act, are acquired. Thought, that budget of the relations
which you perceive among created things, is an intellectual
language which can be learned, is it not? Belief, the budget
of celestial truths, is also a language as superior to thought
as thought is to instinct. This language also can be learned.
The Believer answers with a single cry, a single gesture;
Faith puts within his hand a flaming sword with which he
pierces and illumines all. The Seer attains to heaven and
descends not. But there are beings who believe and see,
who know and will, who love and pray and wait. Submissive, yet aspiring to the kingdom of light, they have neither
the aloofness of the Believer nor the silence of the Seer;
they listen and reply. To them the doubt of the twilight ages
is not a murderous weapon, but a divining rod; they accept
the contest under every form; they train their tongues to
every language; they are never angered, though they groan;
the acrimony of the aggressor is not in them, but rather the
softness and tenuity of light, which penetrates and warms
and illumines. To their eyes Doubt is neither an impiety,
nor a blasphemy, nor a crime, but a transition through
which men return upon their steps in the Darkness, or
advance into the Light. This being so, dear pastor, let us
reason together.

"You do not believe in God? Why? God, to your thinking, is incomprehensible, inexplicable. Agreed. I will not
reply that to comprehend God in His entirety would be
to be God; nor will I tell you that you deny what seems to
you inexplicable so as to give me the right to affirm that
which to me is believable. There is, for you, one evident

fact, which lies within yourself. In you, Matter has ended in intelligence; can you therefore think that human intelligence will end in darkness, doubt, and nothingness? God may seem to you incomprehensible and inexplicable, but you must admit Him to be, in all things purely physical, a splendid and consistent workman. Why should His craft stop short at man, His most finished creation?

"If that question is not convincing, at least it compels meditation. Happily, although you deny God, you are obliged, in order to establish your doubts, to admit those double-bladed facts, which kill your arguments as much as your arguments kill God. We have also admitted that Matter and Spirit are two creations which do not comprehend each other; that the spiritual world is formed of infinite relations to which the finite material world has given rise; that if no one on earth is able to identify himself by the power of his spirit with the great-whole of terrestrial creations, still less is he able to rise to the knowledge of the relations which the spirit perceives between these creations.

"We might end the argument here in one word, by denying you the faculty of comprehending God, just as you deny to the pebbles of the fjord the faculties of counting and of seeing each other. How do you know that the stones themselves do not deny the existence of man, though man makes use of them to build his houses? There is one fact that appals you,—the Infinite; if you feel it within, why will you not admit its consequences? Can the finite have a perfect knowledge of the infinite? If you cannot perceive those relations which, according to your own admission, are infinite, how can you grasp a sense of the far-off end to which they are converging? Order, the revelation of which is one of your needs, being infinite, can your limited reason apprehend it? Do not ask why man does not comprehend that which he is able to perceive, for he is equally able to perceive that which he does not comprehend. If I prove to you that your mind ignores that which lies within its compass, will you grant that it is impossible for it to conceive whatever is beyond it? This being so, am I not justified in saying to you: 'One of the two propositions under which God is annihilated before the tribunal of our reason must be true, the other is false. Inasmuch as creation exists, you feel the necessity of an end, and that end should be good, should it not? Now, if Matter terminates in man by intelligence, why are you not satisfied to believe that the end of human intelligence is the Light of the higher spheres, where alone an intuition of that God who seems so insoluble a problem is obtained? The species which are beneath you have no conception of the universe, and you have; why should there not be other species above you more intelligent than your own? Man ought to be better informed than he is about himself before he spends his strength in measuring God. Before attacking the stars that light us, and the higher certainties, ought he not to understand the certainties which are actually about him?'

"But no! to the negations of doubt I ought rather to reply by negations. Therefore I ask you whether there is anything here below so evident that I can put faith in it? I will show you in a moment that you believe firmly in things which act, and yet are not beings; in things which engender thought, and yet are not spirits; in living abstractions which the understanding cannot grasp in any shape, which are in fact nowhere, but which you perceive everywhere; which have, and can have, on name, but which, nevertheless, you have named; and which, like the God of flesh upon whom you figure to yourself, remain inexplicable, incomprehensible, and absurd. I shall also ask you why, after admitting the existence of these incomprehensible things, you reserve your doubts for God?

"You believe, for instance, in Number,—a base on which you have built the edifice of sciences which you call 'exact.' Without Number, what would become of mathematics? Well, what mysterious being endowed with the faculty of living forever could utter, and what language would be compact to word the Number which contains the infinite numbers whose existence is revealed to you by thought? Ask it of the loftiest human genius; he might ponder it for a thousand years and what would be his answer? You know neither where Number begins, nor where it pauses, nor where it ends. Here you call it Time, there you call it Space. Nothing exists except by Number. Without it, all would be

one and the same substance; for Number alone differentiates and qualifies substance. Number is to your Spirit what
it is to Matter, an incomprehensible agent. Will you make a
Deity of it? Is it a being? Is it a breath emanating from God
to organize the material universe where nothing obtains
form except by the Divinity which is an effect of Number?
The least as well as the greatest of creations are distinguish-
able from each other by quantities, qualities, dimensions,
forces,—all attributes created by Number. The infinitude
of Numbers is a fact proved to your soul, but of which no
material proof can be given. The mathematician himself
tells you that the infinite of numbers exists, but cannot be
proved.

"God, dear pastor, is a Number endowed with
motion,—felt, but not seen, the Believer will tell you. Like
the Unit, He begins Number, with which He has nothing in
common. The existence of Number depends on the Unit,
which without being a number engenders Number. God,
dear pastor is a glorious Unit who has nothing in common
with His creations but who, nevertheless, engenders them.
Will you not therefore agree with me that you are just as
ignorant of where Number begins and ends as you are of
where created Eternity begins and ends?

"Why, then, if you believe in Number, do you deny God?
Is not Creation interposed between the Infinite of unorganized substances and the Infinite of the divine spheres, just
as the Unit stands between the Cipher of the fractions you
have lately named Decimals, and the Infinite of Numbers
which you call Wholes? Man alone on earth comprehends
Number, that first step of the peristyle which leads to God,
and yet his reason stumbles on it! What! you can neither
measure nor grasp the first abstraction which God deliv-
ers to you, and yet you try to subject His ends to your
own tape-line! Suppose that I plunge you into the abyss of
Motion, the force that organizes Number. If I tell you that
the Universe is naught else than Number and Motion, you
would see at once that we speak two different languages. I
understand them both; you understand neither.

"Suppose I add that Motion and Number are engendered by the Word, namely the supreme Reason of Seers

and Prophets who in the olden time heard the Breath of
God beneath which Saul fell to the earth. That Word, you
scoff at it, you men, although you well know that all visible works, societies, monuments, deeds, passions, proceed
from the breath of your own feeble word, and that without that word you would resemble the African gorilla, the
nearest approach to man, the Negro. You believe firmly in
Number and in Motion, a force and a result both inexplicable, incomprehensible, to the existence of which I may
apply the logical dilemma which, as we have seen, prevents
you from believing in God. Powerful reasoner that you are,
you do not need that I should prove to you that the Infinite
must everywhere be like unto Itself, and that, necessarily,
it is One. God alone is Infinite, for surely there cannot be
two Infinities, two Ones. If, to make use of human terms,
anything demonstrated to you here below seems to you
infinite, be sure that within it you will find some one aspect
of God. But to continue.

"You have appropriated to yourself a place in the
Infinite of Number; you have fitted it to your own proportions by creating (if indeed you did create) arithmetic, the
basis on which all things rest, even your societies. Just as
Number—the only thing in which your self-styled atheists
believe—organized physical creations, so arithmetic, in the
employ of Number, organized the moral world. This numeration must be absolute, like all else that is true in itself; but
it is purely relative, it does not exist absolutely, and no proof
can be given of its reality. In the first place, though Numeration is able to take account of organized substances, it is
powerless in relation to unorganized forces, the ones being
finite and the others infinite. The man who can conceive
the Infinite by his intelligence cannot deal with it in its
entirety; if he could, he would be God. Your Numeration,
applying to things finite and not to the Infinite, is therefore
true in relation to the details which you are able to perceive,
and false in relation to the Whole, which you are unable to
perceive. Though Nature is like unto herself in the organiz-
ing force or in her principles which are infinite, she is not
so in her finite effects. Thus you will never find in Nature
two objects identically alike. In the Natural Order two and

two never make four; to do so, four exactly similar units must be had, and you know how impossible it is to find two leaves alike on the same tree, or two trees alike of the same species. This axiom of your numeration, false in visible nature, is equally false in the invisible universe of your abstractions, where the same variance takes place in your ideas, which are the things of the visible world extended by means of their relations; so that the variations here are even more marked than elsewhere. In fact, all being relative to the temperament, strength, habits, and customs of individuals, who never resemble each other, the smallest objects take the color of personal feelings. For instance, man has been able to create units and to give an equal weight and value to bits of gold. Well, take the ducat of the rich man and the ducat of the poor man to a money-changer and they are rated exactly equal, but to the mind of the thinker one is of greater importance than the other; one represents a month of comfort, the other an ephemeral caprice. Two and two, therefore, only make four through a false conception.

"Again: fraction does not exist in Nature, where what you call a fragment is a finished whole. Does it not often happen (have you not many proofs of it?) that the hundredth part of a substance is stronger than what you term the whole of it? If fraction does not exist in the Natural Order, still less shall we find it in the Moral Order, where ideas and sentiments may be as varied as the species of the Vegetable kingdom and yet be always whole. The theory of fractions is therefore another signal instance of the servility of your mind.

"Thus Number, with its infinite minuteness and its infinite expansion, is a power whose weakest side is known to you, but whose real import escapes your perception. You have built yourself a hut in the Infinite of numbers, you have adorned it with hieroglyphics scientifically arranged and painted, and you cry out, 'All is here!'

"Let us pass from pure, unmingled Number to corporate Number. Your geometry establishes that a straight line is the shortest way from one point to another, but your astronomy proves that God has proceeded by curves. Here, then, we find two truths equally proved by the same science,—one by the testimony of your senses reinforced by the telescope, the other by the testimony of your mind; and yet the one contradicts the other. Man, liable to err, affirms one, and the Maker of the worlds, whom, so far, you have not detected in error, contradicts it. Who shall decide between rectalinear and curvilinear geometry? between the theory of the straight line and that of the curve? If, in His vast work, the mysterious Artificer, who knows how to reach His ends miraculously fast, never employs a straight line except to cut off an angle and so obtain a curve, neither does man himself always rely upon it. The bullet which he aims direct proceeds by a curve, and when you wish to strike a certain point in space, you impel your bombshell along its cruel parabola. None of your men of science have drawn from this fact the simple deduction that the Curve is the law of the material worlds and the Straight line that of the Spiritual worlds; one is the theory of finite creations, the other the theory of the infinite. Man, who alone in the world has a knowledge of the Infinite, can alone know the straight line; he alone has the sense of verticality placed in a special organ. A fondness for the creations of the curve would seem to be in certain men an indication of the impurity of their nature still conjoined to the material substances which engender us; and the love of great souls for the straight line seems to show in them an intuition of heaven. Between these two lines there is a gulf fixed like that between the finite and the infinite, between matter and spirit, between man and the idea, between motion and the object moved, between the creature and God. Ask Love the Divine to grant you his wings and you can cross that gulf. Beyond it begins the revelation of the Word.

"No part of those things which you call material is without its own meaning; lines are the boundaries of solid parts and imply a force of action which you suppress in your formulas,—thus rendering those formulas false in relation to substances taken as a whole. Hence the constant destruction of the monuments of human labor, which you supply, unknown to yourselves, with acting properties. Nature has substances; your science combines only their appearances.

At every step Nature gives the lie to all your laws. Can you find a single one that is not disproved by a fact? Your Static laws are at the mercy of a thousand accidents; a fluid can overthrow a solid mountain and prove that the heaviest substances may be lifted by one that is imponderable.

"Your laws on Acoustics and Optics are defied by the sounds which you hear within yourselves in sleep, and by the light of an electric sun whose rays often overcome you. You know no more how light makes itself seen within you, than you know the simple and natural process which changes it on the throats of tropic birds to rubies, sapphires, emeralds, and opals, or keeps it gray and brown on the breasts of the same birds under the cloudy skies of Europe, or whitens it here in the bosom of our polar Nature. You know not how to decide whether color is a faculty with which all substances are endowed, or an effect produced by an effluence of light. You admit the saltness of the sea without being able to prove that the water is salt at its greatest depth. You recognize the existence of various substances which span what you think to be the void,—substances which are not tangible under any of the forms assumed by Matter, although they put themselves in harmony with Matter in spite of every obstacle.

"All this being so, you believe in the results of Chemistry, although that science still knows no way of gauging the changes produced by the flux and reflux of substances which come and go across your crystals and your instruments on the impalpable filaments of heat or light conducted and projected by the affinities of metal or vitrified flint. You obtain none but dead substances, from which you have driven the unknown force that holds in check the decomposition of all things here below, and of which cohesion, attraction, vibration, and polarity are but phenomena. Life is the thought of substances; bodies are only the means of fixing life and holding it to its way. If bodies were beings living of themselves they would be Cause itself, and could not die.

"When a man discovers the results of the general movement, which is shared by all creations according to their faculty of absorption, you proclaim him mighty in science, as though genius consisted in explaining a thing that is! Genius ought to cast its eyes beyond effects. Your men of science would laugh if you said to them: 'There exist such positive relations between two human beings, one of whom may be here, and the other in Java, that they can at the same instant feel the same sensation, and be conscious of so doing; they can question each other and reply without mistake'; and yet there are mineral substances which exhibit sympathies as far off from each other as those of which I speak. You believe in the power of the electricity which you find in the magnet and you deny that which emanates from the soul! According to you, the moon, whose influence upon the tides you think fixed, has none whatever upon the winds, nor upon navigation, nor upon men; she moves the sea, but she must not affect the sick folk; she has undeniable relations with one half of humanity, and nothing at all to do with the other half. These are your vaunted certainties!

"Let us go a step further. You believe in physics. But your physics begin, like the Catholic religion, with an *act of faith.* Do they not presuppose some external force distinct from substance to which it communicates motion? You see its effects, but what is it? where is it? what is the essence of its nature, its life? has it any limits?—and yet, you deny God!

"Thus, the majority of your scientific axioms, true to their relation to man, are false in relation to the Great Whole. Science is One, but you have divided it. To know the real meaning of the laws of phenomena must we not know the correlations which exist between phenomena and the law of the Whole? There is, in all things, an appearance which strikes your senses; under that appearance stirs a soul; a body is there and a faculty is there. Where do you teach the study of the relations which bind things to each other? Nowhere. Consequently you have nothing positive. Your strongest certainties rest upon the analysis of material forms whose essence you persistently ignore.

"There is a Higher Knowledge of which, too late, some men obtain a glimpse, though they dare not avow it. Such men comprehend the necessity of considering substances not merely in their mathematical properties but also in their entirety, in their occult relations and affinities. The greatest man among you divined, in his latter days, that all was reciprocally cause and effect; that the visible worlds were co-ordinated among themselves and subject to worlds invisible. He groaned at the recollection of having tried to establish fixed precepts. Counting up his worlds, like grape-seeds scattered through ether, he had explained their coherence by the laws of planetary and molecular attraction. You bowed before that man of science—well! I tell you that he died in despair. By supposing that the centrifugal and centripetal forces, which he had invented to explain to himself the universe, were equal, he stopped the universe; yet he admitted motion in an indeterminate sense; but supposing those forces unequal, then utter confusion of the planetary system ensued. His laws therefore were not absolute; some higher problem existed than the principle on which his false glory rested. The connection of the stars with one another and the centripetal action of their internal motion did not deter him from seeking the parent stalk on which his clusters hung. Alas, poor man! the more he widened space the heavier his burden grew. He told you how there came to be equilibrium among the parts, but whither went the whole? His mind contemplated the vast extent, illimitable to human eyes, filled with those groups of worlds a mere fraction of which is all our telescopes can reach, but whose immensity is revealed by the rapidity of light. This sublime contemplation enabled him to perceive myriads of worlds, planted in space like flowers in a field, which are born like infants, grow like men, die as the aged die, and live by assimilating from their atmosphere the substances suitable for their nourishment,—having a center and a principal of life, guaranteeing to each other their circuits, absorbed and absorbing like plants, and forming a vast Whole endowed with life and possessing a destiny.

"At that sight your man of science trembled! He knew that life is produced by the union of the thing and its principle, that death or inertia or gravity is produced by a rupture between a thing and the movement which appertains to it. Then it was that he foresaw the crumbling of the worlds and their destruction if God should withdraw the Breath of

His Word. He searched the Apocalypse for the traces of that Word. You thought him mad. Understand him better! He was seeking pardon for the work of his genius.

"Wilfrid, you have come here hoping to make me solve equations, or rise upon a rain-cloud, or plunge into the fjord and reappear a swan. If science or miracles were the end and object of humanity, Moses would have bequeathed to you the law of fluxions; Jesus Christ would have lightened the darkness of your sciences; his apostles would have told you whence come those vast trains of gas and melted metals, attached to cores which revolve and solidify as they dart through ether, or violently enter some system and combine with a star, jostling and displacing it by the shock, or destroying it by the infiltration of their deadly gases; Saint Paul, instead of telling you to live in God, would have explained why food is the secret bond among all creations and the evident tie between all living Species. In these days the greatest miracle of all would be the discovery of the squaring of the circle,—a problem which you hold to be insoluble, but which is doubtless solved in the march of worlds by the intersection of some mathematical lines whose course is visible to the eye of spirits who have reached the higher spheres. Believe me, miracles are in us, not without us. Here natural facts occur which men call supernatural. God would have been strangely unjust had he confined the testimony of his power to certain generations and peoples and denied them to others. The brazen rod belongs to all. Neither Moses, nor Jacob, nor Zoroaster, nor Paul, nor Pythagoras, nor Swedenborg, not the humblest Messenger nor the loftiest Prophet of the Most High are greater than you are capable of being. Only, there come to nations as to men certain periods when Faith is theirs.

"If material sciences be the end and object of human effort, tell me, both of you, would societies,—those great centres where men congregate,—would they perpetually be dispersed? If civilization were the object of our Species, would intelligence perish? would it continue purely individual? The grandeur of all nations that were truly great was based on exceptions; when the exception ceased their power died. If such were the End-all, Prophets, Seers, and

Messengers of God would have lent their hand to Science
rather than have given it to Belief. Surely they would have
quickened your brains sooner than have touched your
hearts! But no; one and all they came to lead the nations
back to God; they proclaimed the sacred Path in simple
words that showed the way to heaven; all were wrapped in
love and faith, all were inspired by that *word* which hovers
above the inhabitants of earth, enfolding them, inspiriting
them, uplifting them; none were prompted by any human
interest. Your great geniuses, your poets, your kings, your
learned men are engulfed with their cities; while the names
of these good pastors of humanity, ever blessed, have sur-
vived all cataclysms.

"Alas! we cannot understand each other on any point.
We are separated by an abyss. You are on the side of darkness, while I—I live in the light, the true Light! Is this the
word that you ask of me? I say it with joy; it may change
you. Know this: there are sciences of matter and sciences
of spirit. There, where you see substances, I see forces that
stretch one toward another with generating power. To me,
the character of bodies is the indication of their principles
and the sign of their properties. Those principles beget
affinities which escape your knowledge, and which are
linked to centres. The different species among which life is
distributed are unfailing streams which correspond unfailingly among themselves. Each has his own vocation. Man
is effect and cause. He is fed, but he feeds in turn. When
you call God a Creator, you dwarf Him. He did not create,
as you think He did, plants or animals or stars. Could He
proceed by a variety of means? Must He not act by unity
of composition? Moreover, He gave forth principles to
be developed, according to His universal law, at the will
of the surroundings in which they were placed. Hence a
single substance and motion, a single plant, a single animal,
but correlations everywhere. In fact, all affinities are linked
together by contiguous similitudes; the life of the worlds is
drawn toward the centres by famished aspiration, as you
are drawn by hunger to seek food.

"To give you an example of affinities linked to similitudes (a secondary law on which the creations of your

thought are based), music, that celestial art, is the working out of this principle; for is it not a complement of sounds harmonized by number? Is not sound a modification of air, compressed, dilated, echoed? You know the composition of air,—oxygen, nitrogen, and carbon. As you cannot obtain sound from the void, it is plain that music and the human voice are the result of organized chemical substances, which put themselves in unison with the same substances prepared within you by your thought, co-ordinated by means of light, the great nourisher of your globe. Have you ever meditated on the masses of niter deposited by the snow, have you ever observed a thunderstorm and seen the plants breathing in from the air about them the metal it contains, without concluding that the sun has fused and distributed the subtle essence which nourishes all things here below? Swedenborg has said, 'The earth is a man.'

"Your Science, which makes you great in your own eyes, is paltry indeed beside the light which bathes a Seer. Cease, cease to question me; our languages are different. For a moment I have used yours to cast, if it be possible, a ray of faith into your soul; to give you, as it were, the hem of my garment and draw you up into the regions of Prayer. Can God abase Himself to you? Is it not for you to rise to Him? If human reason finds the ladder of its own strength too weak to bring God down to it, is it not evident that you must find some other path to reach Him? That Path is in ourselves. The Seer and the Believer find eyes within their souls more piercing far than eyes that probe the things of earth,—they see the Dawn. Hear this truth: Your science, let it be never so exact, your meditations, however bold, your noblest lights are Clouds. Above, above is the Sanctuary whence the true Light flows."

She sat down and remained silent; her calm face bore no sign of the agitation which orators betray after their least fervid improvisations.

Wilfrid bent toward Monsieur Becker and said in a low voice, "Who taught her that?"

"I do not know," he answered.

"He was gentler on the Falberg," Minna whispered to herself.

Seraphita passed her hand across her eyes and then she said, smiling:—

"You are very thoughtful to-night, gentlemen. You treat Minna and me as though we were men to whom you must talk politics or commerce; whereas we are young girls, and you ought to tell us tales while you drink your tea. That is what we do, Monsieur Wilfrid, in our long Norwegian evenings. Come, dear pastor, tell me some Saga that I have not heard,—that of Frithiof, the chronicle that you believe and have so often promised me. Tell us the story of the peasant lad who owned the ship that talked and had a soul. Come! I dream of the frigate Ellida, the fairy with the sails young girls should navigate!"

"Since we have returned to the regions of Jarvis," said Wilfrid, whose eyes were fastened on Seraphita as those of a robber, lurking in the darkness, fasten on the spot where he knows the jewels lie, "tell me why you do not marry?"

"You are all born widows and widowers," she replied; "but my marriage was arranged at my birth. I am betrothed."

"To whom?" they cried.

"Ask not my secret," she said; "I will promise, if our father permits it, to invite you to these mysterious nuptials."

"Will they be soon?"

"I think so."

A long silence followed these words.

"The spring has come!" said Seraphita, suddenly. "The noise of the waters and the breaking of the ice begins. Come, let us welcome the first spring of the new century."

She rose, followed by Wilfrid, and together they went to a window which David had opened. After the long silence of winter, the waters stirred beneath the ice and resounded through the fjord like music,—for there are sounds which space refines, so that they reach the ear in waves of light and freshness.

"Wilfrid, cease to nourish evil thoughts whose triumph would be hard to bear. Your desires are easily read in the fire of your eyes. Be kind; take one step forward in well-doing. Advance beyond the love of man and sacrifice yourself completely to the happiness of her you love. Obey me; I will lead you in a path where you shall obtain the distinctions which you crave, and where Love is infinite indeed."

She left him thoughtful.

"That soft creature!" he said within himself; "is she indeed the prophetess whose eyes have just flashed lightnings, whose voice has rung through worlds, whose hand has wielded the axe of doubt against our sciences? Have we been dreaming? Am I awake?"

"Minna," said Seraphita, returning to the young girl, "the eagle swoops where the carrion lies, but the dove seeks the mountain spring beneath the peaceful greenery of the glades. The eagle soars to heaven, the dove descends from it. Cease to venture into regions where thou canst find no spring of waters, no umbrageous shade. If on the Falberg thou couldst not gaze into the abyss and live, keep all thy strength for him who will love thee. Go, poor girl; thou knowest, I am betrothed."

Minna rose and followed Seraphita to the window where Wilfrid stood. All three listened to the Sieg bounding out the rush of the upper waters, which brought down trees uprooted by the ice; the fjord had regained its voice; all illusions were dispelled! They rejoiced in Nature as she burst her bonds and seemed to answer with sublime accord to the Spirit whose breath had wakened her.

When the three guests of this mysterious being left the house, they were filled with the vague sensation which is neither sleep, nor torpor, nor astonishment, but partakes of the nature of each,—a state that is neither dusk nor dawn, but which creates a thirst for light. All three were thinking.

"I begin to believe that she is indeed a Spirit hidden in human form," said Monsieur Becker.

Wilfrid, re-entering his own apartments, calm and convinced, was unable to struggle against that influence so divinely majestic.

Minna said in her heart, "Why will he not let me love him!"

## V.  FAREWELL

There is in man an almost hopeless phenomenon for

thoughtful minds who seek a meaning in the march of civilization, and who endeavor to give laws of progression to
the movement of intelligence. However portentous a fact
may be, or even supernatural,—if such facts exist,—however solemnly a miracle may be done in sight of all, the
lightning of that fact, the thunderbolt of that miracle is
quickly swallowed up in the ocean of life, whose surface,
scarcely stirred by the brief convulsion, returns to the level
of its habitual flow.

A Voice is heard from the jaws of an Animal; a Hand
writes on the wall before a feasting Court; an Eye gleams
in the slumber of a king, and a Prophet explains the dream;
Death, evoked, rises on the confines of the luminous sphere
were faculties revive; Spirit annihilates Matter at the foot
of that mystic ladder of the Seven Spiritual Worlds, one
resting upon another in space and revealing themselves in
shining waves that break in light upon the steps of the celestial Tabernacle. But however solemn the inward Revelation,
however clear the visible outward Sign, be sure that on the
morrow Balaam doubts both himself and his ass, Belshaz-
zar and Pharoah call Moses and Daniel to qualify the Word.
The Spirit, descending, bears man above this earth, opens
the seas and lets him see their depths, shows him lost species, wakens dry bones whose dust is the soil of valleys; the
Apostle writes the Apocalypse, and twenty centuries later
human science ratifies his words and turns his visions into
maxims. And what comes of it all? Why this,—that the peoples live as they have ever lived, as they lived in the first
Olympiad, as they lived on the morrow of Creation, and
on the eve of the great cataclysm. The waves of Doubt have
covered all things. The same floods surge with the same
measured motion on the human granite which serves as
a boundary to the ocean of intelligence. When man has
inquired of himself whether he has seen that which he has
seen, whether he has heard the words that entered his ears,
whether the facts were facts and the idea is indeed an idea,
then he resumes his wonted bearing, thinks of his worldly
interests, obeys some envoy of death and of oblivion
whose dusky mantle covers like a pall an ancient Humanity of which the moderns retain no memory. Man never

pauses; he goes his round, he vegetates until the appointed day when his Axe falls. If this wave force, this pressure of bitter waters prevents all progress, no doubt it also warns of death. Spirits prepared by faith among the higher souls of earth can alone perceive the mystic ladder of Jacob.

After listening to Seraphita's answer in which (being earnestly questioned) she unrolled before their eyes a Divine Perspective,—as an organ fills a church with sonorous sound and reveals a musical universe, its solemn tones rising to the loftiest arches and playing, like light, upon their foliated capitals,—Wilfrid returned to his own room, awed by the sight of a world in ruins, and on those ruins the brilliance of mysterious lights poured forth in torrents by the hand of a young girl. On the morrow he still thought of these things, but his awe was gone; he felt he was neither destroyed nor changed; his passions, his ideas awoke in full force, fresh and vigorous. He went to breakfast with Monsieur Becker and found the old man absorbed in the "Treatise on Incantations," which he had searched since early morning to convince his guest that there was nothing unprecedented in all that they had seen and heard at the Swedish castle. With the childlike trustfulness of a true scholar he had folded down the pages in which Jean Wier related authentic facts which proved the possibility of the events that had happened the night before,—for to learned men an idea is a event, just as the greatest events often present no idea at all to them. By the time they had swallowed their fifth cup of tea, these philosophers had come to think the mysterious scene of the preceding evening wholly natural. The celestial truths to which they had listened were arguments susceptible of examination; Seraphita was a girl, more or less eloquent; allowance must be made for the charms of her voice, her seductive beauty, her fascinating motions, in short, for all those oratorical arts by which an actor puts a world of sentiment and thought into phrases which are often commonplace.

"Bah!" said the worthy pastor, making a philosophical grimace as he spread a layer of salt butter on his slice of bread, "the final word of all these fine enigmas is six feet under ground."

"But," said Wilfrid, sugaring his tea, "I cannot image how a young girl of seventeen can know so much; what she said was certainly a compact argument."

"Read the account of that Italian woman," said Monsieur Becker, "who at the age of twelve spoke forty-two languages, ancient and modern; also the history of that monk who could guess thought by smell. I can give you a thousand such cases from Jean Wier and other writers."

"I admit all that, dear pastor; but to my thinking, Seraphita would make a perfect wife."

"She is all mind," said Monsieur Becker, dubiously.

Several days went by, during which the snow in the valleys melted gradually away; the green of the forests and of the grass began to show; Norwegian Nature made ready her wedding garments for her brief bridal of a day. During this period, when the softened air invited every one to leave the house, Seraphita remained at home in solitude. When at last she admitted Minna the latter saw at once the ravages of inward fever; Seraphita's voice was hollow, her skin pallid; hitherto a poet might have compared her luster to that of diamonds,—now it was that of a topaz.

"Have you seen her?" asked Wilfrid, who had wandered around the Swedish dwelling waiting for Minna's return.

"Yes," answered the young girl, weeping; "We must lose him!"

"Mademoiselle," cried Wilfrid, endeavoring to repress the loud tones of his angry voice, "do not jest with me. You can love Seraphita only as one young girl can love another, and not with the love which she inspires in me. You do not know your danger if my jealousy were really aroused. Why can I not go to her? Is it you who stand in my way?"

"I do not know by what right you probe my heart," said Minna, calm in appearance, but inwardly terrified. "Yes, I love him," she said, recovering the courage of her convictions, that she might, for once, confess the religion of her heart. "But my jealousy, natural as it is in love, fears no one here below. Alas! I am jealous of a secret feeling that absorbs him. Between him and me there is a great gulf fixed which I cannot cross. Would that I knew who loves him best, the stars or I! which of us would sacrifice our being most eagerly for his happiness! Why should I not be free to avow my love? In the presence of death we may declare our feelings,—and Seraphitus is about to die."

"Minna, you are mistaken; the siren I so love and long for, she, whom I have seen, feeble and languid, on her couch of furs, is not a young man."

"Monsieur," answered Minna, distressfully, "the being whose powerful hand guided me on the Falberg, who led me to the saeter sheltered beneath the Ice-Cap, there—" she said, pointing to the peak, "is not a feeble girl. Ah, had you but heard him prophesying! His poem was the music of thought. A young girl never uttered those solemn tones of a voice which stirred my soul."

"What certainty have you?" said Wilfrid.

"None but that of the heart," answered Minna.

"And I," cried Wilfrid, casting on his companion the terrible glance of the earthly desire that kills, "I, too, know how powerful is her empire over me, and I will undeceive you."

At this moment, while the words were rushing from Wilfrid's lips as rapidly as the thoughts surged in his brain, they saw Seraphita coming towards them from the house, followed by David. The apparition calmed the man's excitement.

"Look," he said, "could any but a woman move with that grace and langor?"

"He suffers; he comes forth for the last time," said Minna.

David went back at a sign from his mistress, who advanced towards Wilfrid and Minna.

"Let us go to the falls of the Sieg," she said, expressing one of those desires which suddenly possess the sick and which the well hasten to obey.

A thin white mist covered the valleys around the fjord and the sides of the mountains, whose icy summits, sparkling like stars, pierced the vapor and gave it the appearance of a moving milky way. The sun was visible through the haze like a globe of red fire. Though winter still lingered, puffs of warm air laden with the scent of the birch-trees, already adorned with their rosy efflorescence,

and of the larches, whose silken tassels were beginning to
appear,—breezes tempered by the incense and the sighs
of earth,—gave token of the glorious Northern spring, the
rapid, fleeting joy of that most melancholy of Natures. The
wind was beginning to lift the veil of mist which half-ob-
scured the gulf. The birds sang. The bark of the trees where
the sun had not yet dried the clinging hoar-frost shone
gayly to the eye in its fantastic wreathings which trickled
away in murmuring rivulets as the warmth reached them.
The three friends walked in silence along the shore. Wilfrid
and Minna alone noticed the magic transformation that
was taking place in the monotonous picture of the winter
landscape. Their companion walked in thought, as though
a voice were sounding to her ears in this concert of Nature.

Presently they reached the ledge of rocks through which
the Sieg had forced its way, after escaping from the long
avenue cut by its waters in an undulating line through the
forest,—a fluvial pathway flanked by aged firs and roofed
with strong-ribbed arches like those of a cathedral. Looking back from that vantage-ground, the whole extent of the
fjord could be seen at a glance, with the open sea sparkling
on the horizon beyond it like a burnished blade.

At this moment the mist, rolling away, left the sky blue
and clear. Among the valleys and around the trees flitted
the shining fragments,—a diamond dust swept by the fresh-
ening breeze. The torrent rolled on toward them; along its
length a vapor rose, tinted by the sun with every color of his
light; the decomposing rays flashing prismatic fires along
the many-tinted scarf of waters. The rugged ledge on which
they stood was carpeted by several kinds of lichen, forming
a noble mat variegated by moisture and lustrous like the
sheen of a silken fabric. Shrubs, already in bloom, crowned
the rocks with garlands. Their waving foliage, eager for
the freshness of the water, drooped its tresses above the
stream; the larches shook their light fringes and played
with the pines, stiff and motionless as aged men. This lux-
uriant beauty was foiled by the solemn colonnades of the
forest-trees, rising in terraces upon the mountains, and by
the calm sheet of the fjord, lying below, where the torrent
buried its fury and was still. Beyond, the sea hemmed in this

page of Nature, written by the greatest of poets, Chance; to whom the wild luxuriance of creation when apparently abandoned to itself is owing.

The village of Jarvis was a lost point in the landscape, in this immensity of Nature, sublime at this moment like all things else of ephemeral life which present a fleeting image of perfection; for, by a law fatal to no eyes but our own, creations which appear complete—the love of our heart and the desire of our eyes—have but one spring-tide here below. Standing on this breast-work of rock these three persons might well suppose themselves alone in the universe.

"What beauty!" cried Wilfrid.

"Nature sings hymns," said Seraphita. "Is not her music exquisite? Tell me, Wilfrid, could any of the women you once knew create such a glorious retreat for herself as this? I am conscious here of a feeling seldom inspired by the sight of cities, a longing to lie down amid this quickening verdure. Here, with eyes to heaven and an open heart, lost in the bosom of immensity, I could hear the sighings of the flower, scarce budded, which longs for wings, or the cry of the eider grieving that it can only fly, and remember the desires of man who, issuing from all, is none the less ever longing. But that, Wilfrid, is only a woman's thought. You find seductive fancies in the wreathing mists, the light embroidered veils which Nature dons like a coy maiden, in this atmosphere where she perfumes for her spousals the greenery of her tresses. You seek the naiad's form amid the gauzy vapors, and to your thinking my ears should listen only to the virile voice of the Torrent."

"But Love is there, like the bee in the calyx of the flower," replied Wilfrid, perceiving for the first time a trace of earthly sentiment in her words, and fancying the moment favorable for an expression of his passionate tenderness.

"Always there?" said Seraphita, smiling. Minna had left them for a moment to gather the blue saxifrages growing on a rock above.

"Always," repeated Wilfrid. "Hear me," he said, with a masterful glance which was foiled as by a diamond breast-plate. "You know not what I am, nor what I can be, nor what I will. Do not reject my last entreaty. Be mine for the good of that world whose happiness you bear upon your heart. Be mine that my conscience may be pure; that a voice divine may sound in my ears and infuse Good into the great enterprise I have undertaken prompted by my hatred to the nations, but which I swear to accomplish for their benefit if you will walk beside me. What higher mission can you ask for love? what nobler part can woman aspire to? I came to Norway to meditate a grand design."

"And you will sacrifice its grandeur," she said, "to an innocent girl who loves you, and who will lead you in the paths of peace."

"What matters sacrifice," he cried, "if I have you? Hear my secret. I have gone from end to end of the North,— that great smithy from whose anvils new races have spread over the earth, like human tides appointed to refresh the wornout civilizations. I wished to begin my work at some Northern point, to win the empire which force and intellect must ever give over a primitive people; to form that people for battle, to drive them to wars which should ravage Europe like a conflagration, crying liberty to some, pillage to others, glory here, pleasure there!—I, myself, remaining an image of Destiny, cruel, implacable, advancing like the whirlwind, which sucks from the atmosphere the particles that make the thunderbolt, and falls like a devouring scourge upon the nations. Europe is at an epoch when she awaits the new Messiah who shall destroy society and remake it. She can no longer believe except in him who crushes her under foot. The day is at hand when poets and historians will justify me, exalt me, and borrow my ideas, mine! And all the while my triumph will be a jest, written in blood, the jest of my vengeance! But not here, Seraphita; what I see in the North disgusts me. Hers is a mere blind force; I thirst for the Indies! I would rather fight a selfish, cowardly, mercantile government. Besides, it is easier to stir the imagination of the peoples at the feet of the Caucasus than to argue with the intellect of the icy lands which here surround me. Therefore am I tempted to cross the Russian steps and pour my triumphant human tide through Asia to the Ganges, and overthrow the British rule. Seven men have done this thing before me in other epochs of the

world. I will emulate them. I will spread Art like the Sara-
cens, hurled by Mohammed upon Europe. Mine shall be no
paltry sovereignty like those that govern to-day the ancient
provinces of the Roman empire, disputing with their subjects about a customs right! No, nothing can bar my way!
Like Genghis Khan, my feet shall tread a third of the globe,
my hand shall grasp the throat of Asia like Aurung-Zeb.
Be my companion! Let me seat thee, beautiful and noble
being, on a throne! I do not doubt success, but live within
my heart and I am sure of it."

"I have already reigned," said Seraphita, coldly.

The words fell as the axe of a skilful woodman falls at
the root of a young tree and brings it down at a single blow.
Men alone can comprehend the rage that a woman excites
in the soul of a man when, after showing her his strength,
his power, his wisdom, his superiority, the capricious creature bends her head and says, "All that is nothing"; when,
unmoved, she smiles and says, "Such things are known to
me," as though his power were nought.

"What!" cried Wilfrid, in despair, "can the riches of art,
the riches of worlds, the splendors of a court—"

She stopped him by a single inflexion of her lips, and
said, "Beings more powerful than you have offered me far
more."

"Thou hast no soul," he cried,—"no soul, if thou art not
persuaded by the thought of comforting a great man, who
is willing now to sacrifice all things to live beside thee in a
little house on the shores of a lake."

"But," she said, "I am loved with a boundless love."

"By whom?" cried Wilfrid, approaching Seraphita with a
frenzied movement, as if to fling her into the foaming basin
of the Sieg.

She looked at him and slowly extended her arm, pointing
to Minna, who now sprang towards her, fair and glowing
and lovely as the flowers she held in her hand.

"Child!" said Seraphitus, advancing to meet her.

Wilfrid remained where she left him, motionless as the
rock on which he stood, lost in thought, longing to let
himself go into the torrent of the Sieg, like the fallen trees
which hurried past his eyes and disappeared in the bosom

of the gulf.

"I gathered them for you," said Minna, offering the bunch of saxifrages to the being she adored. "One of them, see, this one," she added, selecting a flower, "is like that you found on the Falberg."

Seraphitus looked alternately at the flower and at Minna. "Why question me? Dost thou doubt me?"

"No," said the young girl, "my trust in you is infinite. You are more beautiful to look upon than this glorious nature, but your mind surpasses in intellect that of all humanity. When I have been with you I seem to have prayed to God. I long—"

"For what?" said Seraphitus, with a glance that revealed to the young girl the vast distance which separated them.

"To suffer in your stead."

"Ah, dangerous being!" cried Seraphitus in his heart. "Is it wrong, oh my God! to desire to offer her to Thee? Dost thou remember, Minna, what I said to thee up there?" he added, pointing to the summit of the Ice-Cap.

"He is terrible again," thought Minna, trembling with fear.

The voice of the Sieg accompanied the thoughts of the three beings united on this platform of projecting rock, but separated in soul by the abysses of the Spiritual World.

"Seraphitus! teach me," said Minna in a silvery voice, soft as the motion of a sensitive plant, "teach me how to cease to love you. Who could fail to admire you; love is an admiration that never wearies."

"Poor child!" said Seraphitus, turning pale; "there is but one whom thou canst love in that way."

"Who?" asked Minna.

"Thou shalt know hereafter," he said, in the feeble voice of a man who lies down to die.

"Help, help! he is dying!" cried Minna.

Wilfrid ran towards them. Seeing Seraphita as she lay on a fragment of gneiss, where time had cast its velvet mantle of lustrous lichen and tawny mosses now burnished in the sunlight, he whispered softly, "How beautiful she is!"

"One other look! the last that I shall ever cast upon this nature in travail," said Seraphitus, rallying her strength and rising to her feet.

She advanced to the edge of the rocky platform, whence
her eyes took in the scenery of that grand and glorious
landscape, so verdant, flowery, and animated, yet so lately
buried in its winding-sheet of snow.

"Farewell," she said, "farewell, home of Earth, warmed
by the fires of Love; where all things press with ardent force
from the center to the extremities; where the extremities
are gathered up, like a woman's hair, to weave the mysterious braid which binds us in that invisible ether to the
Thought Divine!

"Behold the man bending above that furrow moistened
with his tears, who lifts his head for an instant to question
Heaven; behold the woman gathering her children that she
may feed them with her milk; see him who lashes the ropes
in the height of the gale; see her who sits in the hollow of
the rocks, awaiting the father! Behold all they who stretch
their hands in want after a lifetime spent in thankless toil.
To all peace and courage, and to all farewell!

"Hear you the cry of the soldier, dying nameless and
unknown? the wail of the man deceived who weeps in the
desert? To them peace and courage; to all farewell!

"Farewell, you who die for the kings of the earth! Farewell, ye people without a country and ye countries without
a people, each, with a mutual want. Above all, farewell to
Thee who knew not where to lay Thy head, Exile divine!
Farewell, mothers beside your dying sons! Farewell, ye
Little Ones, ye Feeble, ye Suffering, you whose sorrows I
have so often borne! Farewell, all ye who have descended
into the sphere of Instinct that you may suffer there for
others!

"Farewell, ye mariners who seek the Orient through the
thick darkness of your abstractions, vast as principles! Farewell, martyrs of thought, led by thought into the presence
of the True Light. Farewell, regions of study where mine
ears can hear the plaint of genius neglected and insulted,
the sigh of the patient scholar to whom enlightenment
comes too late!

"I see the angelic choir, the wafting of perfumes, the
incense of the heart of those who go their way consoling,

praying, imparting celestial balm and living light to suffering souls! Courage, ye choir of Love! you to whom the peoples cry, 'Comfort us, comfort us, defend us!' To you courage! and farewell!

"Farewell, ye granite rocks that shall bloom a flower; farewell, flower that becomes a dove; farewell, dove that shalt be woman; farewell, woman, who art Suffering, man, who art Belief! Farewell, you who shall be all love, all prayer!"

Broken with fatigue, this inexplicable being leaned for the first time on Wilfrid and on Minna to be taken home. Wilfrid and Minna felt the shock of a mysterious contact in and through the being who thus connected them. They had scarcely advanced a few steps when David met them, weeping. "She will die," he said, "why have you brought her hither?"

The old man raised her in his arms with the vigor of youth and bore her to the gate of the Swedish castle like an eagle bearing a white lamb to his mountain eyrie.


## VI. THE PATH TO HEAVEN

The day succeeding that on which Seraphita foresaw her death and bade farewell to Earth, as a prisoner looks round his dungeon before leaving it forever, she suffered pains which obliged her to remain in the helpless immobility of those whose pangs are great. Wilfrid and Minna went to see her, and found her lying on her couch of furs. Still veiled in flesh, her soul shone through that veil, which grew more and more transparent day by day. The progress of the Spirit, piercing the last obstacle between itself and the Infinite, was called an illness, the hour of Life went by the name of death. David wept as he watched her sufferings; unreasonable as a child, he would not listen to his mistress's consolations. Monsieur Becker wished Seraphita to try remedies; but all were useless.

One morning she sent for the two beings whom she loved, telling them that this would be the last of her bad days. Wilfrid and Minna came in terror, knowing well that they were about to lose her. Seraphita smiled to them as one departing to a better world; her head drooped like a flower heavy with dew, which opens its calyx for the last time to waft its fragrance on the breeze. She looked at these friends with a sadness that was for them, not for herself; she thought no longer of herself, and they felt this with a grief mingled with gratitude which they were unable to express. Wilfrid stood silent and motionless, lost in thoughts excited by events whose vast bearings enabled him to conceive of some illimitable immensity.

Emboldened by the weakness of the being lately so powerful, or perhaps by the fear of losing him forever, Minna bent down over the couch and said, "Seraphitus, let me follow thee!"

"Can I forbid thee?"

"Why will thou not love me enough to stay with me?"

"I can love nothing here."

"What canst thou love?"

"Heaven."

"Is it worthy of heaven to despise the creatures of God?"

"Minna, can we love two beings at once? Would our beloved be indeed our beloved if he did not fill our hearts? Must he not be the first, the last, the only one? She who is all love, must she not leave the world for her beloved? Human ties are but a memory, she has no ties except to him! Her soul is hers no longer; it is his. If she keeps within her soul anything that is not his, does she love? No, she loves not. To love feebly, is that to love at all? The voice of her beloved makes her joyful; it flows through her veins in a crimson tide more glowing far than blood; his glance is the light that penetrates her; her being melts into his being. He is warm to her soul. He is the light that lightens; near to him there is neither cold nor darkness. He is never absent, he is always with us; we think in him, to him, by him! Minna, that is how I love him."

"Love whom?" said Minna, tortured with sudden jealousy.

"God," replied Seraphitus, his voice glowing in their souls like fires of liberty from peak to peak upon the mountains,—"God, who does not betray us! God, who will never abandon us! who crowns our wishes; who satisfies His creatures with joy—joy unalloyed and infinite! God, who never wearies but ever smiles! God, who pours into the soul fresh treasures day by day; who purifies and leaves no bitterness; who is all harmony, all flame! God, who has placed Himself within our hearts to blossom there; who hearkens to our prayers; who does not stand aloof when we are His, but gives His presence absolutely! He who revives us, magnifies us, and multiplies us in Himself; *God!* Minna, I love thee because thou mayst be His! I love thee because if thou come to Him thou wilt be mine."

"Lead me to Him," cried Minna, kneeling down; "take me by the hand; I will not leave thee!"

"Lead us, Seraphita!" cried Wilfrid, coming to Minna's side with an impetuous movement. "Yes, thou hast given me a thirst for Light, a thirst for the Word. I am parched with the Love thou hast put into my heart; I desire to keep thy soul in mine; thy will is mine; I will do whatsoever thou biddest me. Since I cannot obtain thee, I will keep thy will and all the thoughts that thou hast given me. If I may not unite myself with thee except by the power of my spirit, I will cling to thee in soul as the flame to what it laps. Speak!"

"Angel!" exclaimed the mysterious being, enfolding them both in one glance, as it were with an azure mantle, "Heaven shall by thine heritage!"

Silence fell among them after these words, which sounded in the souls of the man and of the woman like the first notes of some celestial harmony.

"If you would teach your feet to tread the Path to heaven, know that the way is hard at first," said the weary sufferer; "God wills that you shall seek Him for Himself. In that sense, He is jealous; He demands your whole self. But when you have given Him yourself, never, never will He abandon you. I leave with you the keys of the kingdom of His Light, where evermore you shall dwell in the bosom of the Father, in the heart of the Bridegroom. No sentinels guard the approaches, you may enter where you will; His palaces, His treasures, His scepter, all are free. 'Take them!' He says. But—you must *will* to go there. Like one preparing for a journey, a man must leave his home, renounce his projects, bid farewell to friends, to father, mother, sister,

even to the helpless brother who cries after him,—yes, farewell to them eternally; you will no more return than did the
martyrs on their way to the stake. You must strip yourself of
every sentiment, of everything to which man clings. Unless
you do this you are but half-hearted in your enterprise.

"Do for God what you do for your ambitious projects,
what you do in consecrating yourself to Art, what you have
done when you loved a human creature or sought some
secret of human science. Is not God the whole of science,
the all of love, the source of poetry? Surely His riches are
worthy of being coveted! His treasure is inexhaustible, His
poem infinite, His love immutable, His science sure and
darkened by no mysteries. Be anxious for nothing, He will
give you all. Yes, in His heart are treasures with which the
petty joys you lose on earth are not to be compared. What
I tell you is true; you shall possess His power; you may use
it as you would use the gifts of lover or mistress. Alas! men
doubt, they lack faith, and will, and persistence. If some
set their feet in the path, they look behind them and presently turn back. Few decide between the two extremes,—to
go or stay, heaven or the mire. All hesitate. Weakness leads
astray, passion allures into dangerous paths, vice becomes
habitual, man flounders in the mud and makes no progress
towards a better state.

"All human beings go through a previous life in the
sphere of Instinct, where they are brought to see the worth-
lessness of earthly treasures, to amass which they gave
themselves such untold pains! Who can tell how many
times the human being lives in the sphere of Instinct
before he is prepared to enter the sphere of Abstractions,
where thought expends itself on erring science, where
mind wearies at last of human language? for, when Matter
is exhausted, Spirit enters. Who knows how many fleshly
forms the heir of heaven occupies before he can be brought
to understand the value of that silence and solitude whose
starry plains are but the vestibule of Spiritual Worlds? He
feels his way amid the void, makes trial of nothingness, and
then at last his eyes revert upon the Path. Then follow other
existences,—all to be lived to reach the place where Light
effulgent shines. Death is the post-house of the journey. A

lifetime may be needed merely to gain the virtues which annul the errors of man's preceding life. First comes the life of suffering, whose tortures create a thirst for love. Next the life of love and devotion to the creature, teaching devotion to the Creator,—a life where the virtues of love, its martyrdoms, its joys followed by sorrows, its angelic hopes, its patience, its resignation, excite an appetite for things divine. Then follows the life which seeks in silence the traces of the Word; in which the soul grows humble and charitable. Next the life of longing; and lastly, the life of prayer. In that is the noonday sun; there are the flowers, there the harvest!

"The virtues we acquire, which develop slowly within us, are the invisible links that bind each one of our existences to the others,—existences which the spirit alone remembers, for Matter has no memory for spiritual things. Thought alone holds the tradition of the bygone life. The endless legacy of the past to the present is the secret source of human genius. Some receive the gift of form, some the gift of numbers, others the gift of harmony. All these gifts are steps of progress in the Path of Light. Yes, he who possesses a single one of them touches at that point the Infinite. Earth has divided the Word—of which I here reveal some syllables—into particles, she has reduced it to dust and has scattered it through her works, her dogmas, her poems. If some impalpable grain shines like a diamond in a human work, men cry: 'How grand! how true! how glorious!' That fragment vibrates in their souls and wakes a presentiment of heaven: to some, a melody that weans from earth; to others, the solitude that draws to God. To all, whatsoever sends us back upon ourselves, whatsoever strikes us down and crushes us, lifts or abases us,—*that* is but a syllable of the Divine Word.

"When a human soul draws its first furrow straight, the rest will follow surely. One thought borne inward, one prayer uplifted, one suffering endured, one echo of the Word within us, and our souls are forever changed. All ends in God; and many are the ways to find Him by walking straight before us. When the happy day arrives in which you set your feet upon the Path and begin your pilgrimage, the world will know nothing of it; earth no longer understands

you; you no longer understand each other. Men who attain
a knowledge of these things, who lisp a few syllables of the
Word, often have not where to lay their head; hunted like
beasts they perish on the scaffold, to the joy of assembled
peoples, while Angels open to them the gates of heaven.
Therefore, your destiny is a secret between yourself and
God, just as love is a secret between two hearts. You may be
the buried treasure, trodden under the feet of men thirsting
for gold yet all-unknowing that you are there beneath them.

"Henceforth your existence becomes a thing of ceaseless activity; each act has a meaning which connects you
with God, just as in love your actions and your thoughts are
filled with the loved one. But love and its joys, love and its
pleasures limited by the senses, are but the imperfect image
of the love which unites you to your celestial Spouse. All
earthly joy is mixed with anguish, with discontent. If love
ought not to pall then death should end it while its flame
is high, so that we see no ashes. But in God our wretchedness becomes delight, joy lives upon itself and multiplies,
and grows, and has no limit. In the Earthly life our fleeting
love is ended by tribulation; in the Spiritual life the tribula-
tions of a day end in joys unending. The soul is ceaselessly
joyful. We feel God with us, in us; He gives a sacred savor
to all things; He shines in the soul; He imparts to us His
sweetness; He stills our interest in the world viewed for ourselves; He quickens our interest in it viewed for His sake,
and grants us the exercise of His power upon it. In His
name we do the works which He inspires, we act for Him,
we have no self except in Him, we love His creatures with
undying love, we dry their tears and long to bring them
unto Him, as a loving woman longs to see the inhabitants
of earth obey her well-beloved.

"The final life, the fruition of all other lives, to which the
powers of the soul have tended, and whose merits open the
Sacred Portals to perfected man, is the life of Prayer. Who
can make you comprehend the grandeur, the majesty, the
might of Prayer? May my voice, these words of mine, ring in
your hearts and change them. Be now, here, what you may
be after cruel trial! There are privileged beings, Prophets,
Seers, Messengers, and Martyrs, all those who suffer for

the Word and who proclaim it; such souls spring at a bound across the human sphere and rise at once to Prayer. So, too, with those whose souls receive the fire of Faith. Be one of those brave souls! God welcomes boldness. He loves to be taken by violence; He will never reject those who force their way to Him. Know this! desire, the torrent of your will, is so all-powerful that a single emission of it, made with force, can obtain all; a single cry, uttered under the pressure of Faith, suffices. Be one of such beings, full of force, of will, of love! Be conquerors on the earth! Let the hunger and thirst of God possess you. Fly to Him as the hart panting for the water-brooks. Desire shall lend you its wings; tears, those blossoms of repentance, shall be the celestial baptism from which your nature will issue purified. Cast yourself on the breast of the stream in Prayer! Silence and meditation are the means of following the Way. God reveals Himself, unfailingly, to the solitary, thoughtful seeker.

"It is thus that the separation takes place between Matter, which so long has wrapped its darkness round you, and Spirit, which was in you from the beginning, the light which lighted you and now brings noon-day to your soul. Yes, your broken heart shall receive the light; the light shall bathe it. Then you will no longer feel convictions, they will have changed to certainties. The Poet utters; the Thinker meditates; the Righteous acts; but he who stands upon the borders of the Divine World prays; and his prayer is word, thought, action, in one! Yes, prayer includes all, contains all; it completes nature, for it reveals to you the mind within it and its progression. White and shining virgin of all human virtues, ark of the covenant between earth and heaven, tender and strong companion partaking of the lion and of the lamb, Prayer! Prayer will give you the key of heaven! Bold and pure as innocence, strong, like all that is single and simple, this glorious, invincible Queen rests, nevertheless, on the material world; she takes possession of it; like the sun, she clasps it in a circle of light. The universe belongs to him who wills, who knows, who prays; but he must will, he must know, he must pray; in a word, he must possess force, wisdom, and faith.

"Therefore Prayer, issuing from so many trials, is the

consummation of all truths, all powers, all feelings. Fruit of the laborious, progressive, continued development of natural properties and faculties vitalized anew by the divine breath of the Word, Prayer has occult activity; it is the final worship—not the material worship of images, nor the spiritual worship of formulas, but the worship of the Divine World. We say no prayers,—prayer forms within us; it is a faculty which acts of itself; it has attained a way of action which lifts it outside of forms; it links the soul to God, with whom we unite as the root of the tree unites with the soil; our veins draw life from the principle of life, and we live by the life of the universe. Prayer bestows external conviction by making us penetrate the Material World through the cohesion of all our faculties with the elementary substances; it bestows internal conviction by developing our essence and mingling it with that of the Spiritual Worlds. To be able to pray thus, you must attain to an utter abandonment of flesh; you must acquire through the fires of the furnace the purity of the diamond; for this complete communion with the Divine is obtained only in absolute repose, where storms and conflicts are at rest.

"Yes, Prayer—the aspiration of the soul freed absolutely from the body—bears all forces within it, and applies them to the constant and perseverant union of the Visible and the Invisible. When you possess the faculty of praying without weariness, with love, with force, with certainty, with intelligence, your spiritualized nature will presently be invested with power. Like a rushing wind, like a thunderbolt, it cuts its way through all things and shares the power of God. The quickness of the Spirit becomes yours; in an instant you may pass from region to region; like the Word itself, you are transported from the ends of the world to other worlds. Harmony exists, and you are part of it! Light is there and your eyes possess it! Melody is heard and you echo it! Under such conditions, you feel your perceptions developing, widening; the eyes of your mind reach to vast distances. There is, in truth, neither time nor place to the Spirit; space and duration are proportions created for Matter; spirit and matter have naught in common.

"Though these things take place in stillness, in silence,

without agitation, without external movement, yet Prayer is all action; but it is spiritual action, stripped of substantiality, and reduced, like the motion of the worlds, to an invisible pure force. It penetrates everywhere like light; it gives vitality to souls that come beneath its rays, as Nature beneath the sun. It resuscitates virtue, purifies and sanctifies all actions, peoples solitude, and gives a foretaste of eternal joys. When you have once felt the delights of the divine intoxication which comes of this internal travail, then all is yours! once take the lute on which we sing to God within your hands, and you will never part with it. Hence the solitude in which Angelic Spirits live; hence their disdain of human joys. They are withdrawn from those who must die to live; they hear the language of such beings, but they no longer understand their ideas; they wonder at their movements, at what the world terms policies, material laws, societies. For them all mysteries are over; truth, and truth alone, is theirs. They who have reached the point where their eyes discern the Sacred Portals, who, not looking back, not uttering one regret, contemplate worlds and comprehend their destinies, such as they keep silence, wait, and bear their final struggles. The worst of all those struggles is the last; at the zenith of all virtue is Resignation,—to be an exile and not lament, no longer to delight in earthly things and yet to smile, to belong to God and yet to stay with men! You hear the voice that cries to you, 'Advance!' Often celestial visions of descending Angels compass you about with songs of praise; then, tearless, uncomplaining, must you watch them as they reascent the skies! To murmur is to forfeit all. Resignation is a fruit that ripens at the gates of heaven. How powerful, how glorious the calm smile, the pure brow of the resigned human creature. Radiant is the light of that brow. They who live in its atmosphere grow purer. That calm glance penetrates and softens. More eloquent by silence than the prophet by speech, such beings triumph by their simple presence. Their ears are quick to hear as a faithful dog listening for his master. Brighter than hope, stronger than love, higher than faith, that creature of resignation is the virgin standing on the earth, who holds for a moment the conquered palm, then, rising heavenward, leaves behind her the imprint of her white, pure feet. When she has passed away men flock around and cry, 'See! See!' Sometimes God holds her still in sight,—a figure to whose feet creep Forms and Species of Animality to be shown their way. She wafts the light exhaling from her hair, and they see; she speaks, and they hear. 'A miracle!' they cry. Often she triumphs in the name of God; frightened men deny her and put her to death; smiling, she lays down her sword and goes to the stake, having saved the Peoples. How many a pardoned Angel has passed from martyrdom to heaven! Sinai, Golgotha are not in this place nor in that; Angels are crucified in every place, in every sphere. Sighs pierce to God from the whole universe. This earth on which we live is but a single sheaf of the great harvest; humanity is but a species in the vast garden where the flowers of heaven are cultivated. Everywhere God is like unto Himself, and everywhere, by prayer, it is easy to reach Him."

With these words, which fell from the lips of another Hagar in the wilderness, burning the souls of the hearers as the live coal of the word inflamed Isaiah, this mysterious being paused as though to gather some remaining strength. Wilfrid and Minna dared not speak. Suddenly HE lifted himself up to die:—

"Soul of all things, oh my God, thou whom I love for Thyself! Thou, Judge and Father, receive a love which has no limit. Give me of thine essence and thy faculties that I be wholly thine! Take me, that I no longer be myself! Am I not purified? then cast me back into the furnace! If I be not yet proved in the fire, make me some nurturing plowshare, or the Sword of victory! Grant me a glorious martyrdom in which to proclaim thy Word! Rejected, I will bless thy justice. But if excess of love may win in a moment that which hard and patient labor cannot attain, then bear me upward in thy chariot of fire! Grant me triumph, or further trial, still will I bless thee! To suffer for thee, is not that to triumph? Take me, seize me, bear me away! nay, if thou wilt, reject me! Thou art He who can do no evil. Ah!" he cried, after a pause, "the bonds are breaking.

"Spirits of the pure, ye sacred flock, come forth from the hidden places, come on the surface of the luminous waves! The hour now is; come, assemble! Let us sing at the gates of the Sanctuary; our songs shall drive away the final clouds. With one accord let us hail the Dawn of the Eternal Day. Behold the rising of the one True Light! Ah, why may I not take with me these my friends! Farewell, poor earth, Farewell!"

## VII. THE ASSUMPTION

The last psalm was uttered neither by word, look, nor gesture, nor by any of those signs which men employ to communicate their thoughts, but as the soul speaks to itself; for at the moment when Seraphita revealed herself in her true nature, her thoughts were no longer enslaved by human words. The violence of that last prayer had burst her bonds. Her soul, like a white dove, remained for an instant poised above the body whose exhausted substances were about to be annihilated.

The aspiration of the Soul toward heaven was so contagious that Wilfrid and Minna, beholding those radiant scintillations of Life, perceived not Death.

They had fallen on their knees when *he* had turned toward his Orient, and they shared his ecstasy.

The fear of the Lord, which creates man a second time, purging away his dross, mastered their hearts.

Their eyes, veiled to the things of Earth, were opened to the Brightness of Heaven.

Though, like the Seers of old called Prophets by men, they were filled with the terror of the Most High, yet like them they continued firm when they found themselves within the radiance where the Glory of the *Spirit* shone.

The veil of flesh, which, until now, had hidden that glory from their eyes, dissolved imperceptibly away, and left them free to behold the Divine substance.

They stood in the twilight of the Coming Dawn, whose feeble rays prepared them to look upon the True Light, to hear the Living Word, and yet not die.

In this state they began to perceive the immeasurable differences which separate the things of earth from the things of Heaven.

*Life*, on the borders of which they stood, leaning upon each other, trembling and illuminated, like two children standing under shelter in presence of a conflagration, That Life offered no lodgment to the senses.

The ideas they used to interpret their vision to themselves were to the things seen what the visible senses of a man are to his soul, the material covering of a divine essence.

The departing *spirit* was above them, shedding incense without odor, melody without sound. About them, where they stood, were neither surfaces, nor angles, nor atmosphere.

They dared neither question him nor contemplate him; they stood in the shadow of that Presence as beneath the burning rays of a tropical sun, fearing to raise their eyes lest the light should blast them.

They knew they were beside him, without being able to perceive how it was that they stood, as in a dream, on the confines of the Visible and the Invisible, nor how they had lost sight of the Visible and how they beheld the Invisible.

To each other they said: "If he touches us, we can die!" But the *spirit* was now within the Infinite, and they knew not that neither time, nor space, nor death, existed there, and that a great gulf lay between them, although they thought themselves beside him.

Their souls were not prepared to receive in its fulness a knowledge of the faculties of that Life; they could have only faint and confused perceptions of it, suited to their weakness.

Were it not so, the thunder of the *Living Word*, whose far-off tones now reached their ears, and whose meaning entered their souls as life unites with body,—one echo of that Word would have consumed their being as a whirlwind of fire laps up a fragile straw.

Therefore they saw only that which their nature, sustained by the strength of the *spirit*, permitted them to see; they heard that only which they were able to hear.

And yet, though thus protected, they shuddered when the Voice of the anguished soul broke forth above them—the prayer of the *Spirit* awaiting Life and imploring it with a cry.

That cry froze them to the very marrow of their bones.

The *Spirit* knocked at the *sacred portal*. "What wilt thou?" answered a *choir*, whose question echoed among the worlds. "To go to God." "Hast thou conquered?" "I have conquered the flesh through abstinence, I have conquered false knowledge by humility, I have conquered pride by charity, I have conquered the earth by love; I have paid my dues by suffering, I am purified in the fires of faith, I have longed for Life by prayer: I wait in adoration, and I am resigned."

No answer came.

"God's will be done!" answered the *Spirit*, believing that he was about to be rejected.

His tears flowed and fell like dew upon the heads of the two kneeling witnesses, who trembled before the justice of God.

Suddenly the trumpets sounded,—the last trumpets of Victory won by the *Angel* in this last trial. The reverberation passed through space as sound through its echo, filling it, and shaking the universe which Wilfrid and Minna felt like an atom beneath their feet. They trembled under an anguish caused by the dread of the mystery about to be accomplished.

A great movement took place, as though the Eternal Legions, putting themselves in motion, were passing upward in spiral columns. The worlds revolved like clouds driven by a furious wind. It was all rapid.

Suddenly the veils were rent away. They saw on high as it were a star, incomparably more lustrous than the most luminous of material stars, which detached itself, and fell like a thunderbolt, dazzling as lightning. Its passage paled the faces of the pair, who thought it to be *the Light* Itself.

It was the Messenger of good tidings, the plume of whose helmet was a flame of Life.

Behind him lay the swath of his way gleaming with a flood of the lights through which he passed.

He bore a palm and a sword. He touched the *Spirit* with the palm, and the *Spirit* was transfigured. Its white wings noiselessly unfolded.

This communication of *the Light*, changing the *Spirit* into a *Seraph* and clothing it with a glorious form, a celestial armor, poured down such effulgent rays that the two Seers were paralyzed.

Like the three apostles to whom Jesus showed himself, they felt the dead weight of their bodies which denied them a complete and cloudless intuition of *the Word* and *the True Life*.

They comprehended the nakedness of their souls; they were able to measure the poverty of their light by comparing it—a humbling task—with the halo of the *Seraph*.

A passionate desire to plunge back into the mire of earth and suffer trial took possession of them,—trial through which they might victoriously utter at the *sacred gates* the words of that radiant *Seraph*.

The *Seraph* knelt before the *Sanctuary*, beholding it, at last, face to face; and he said, raising his hands thitherward, "Grant that these two may have further sight; they will love the Lord and proclaim His word."

At this prayer a veil fell. Whether it were that the hidden force which held the Seers had momentarily annihilated their physical bodies, or that it raised their spirits above those bodies, certain it is that they felt within them a rending of the pure from the impure.

The tears of the *Seraph* rose about them like a vapor, which hid the lower worlds from their knowledge, held them in its folds, bore them upwards, gave them forgetfulness of earthly meanings and the power of comprehending the meanings of things divine.

The True Light shone; it illumined the Creations, which seemed to them barren when they saw the source from which all worlds—Terrestrial, Spiritual, and Divine-derived their Motion.

Each world possessed a center to which converged all points of its circumference. These worlds were themselves the points which moved toward the center of their system. Each system had its center in great celestial regions which communicated with the flaming and quenchless *motor of all that is*.

Thus, from the greatest to the smallest of the worlds,

and from the smallest of the worlds to the smallest portion
of the beings who compose it, all was individual, and all
was, nevertheless, One and indivisible.

What was the design of the Being, fixed in His essence
and in His faculties, who transmitted that essence and
those faculties without losing them? who manifested them
outside of Himself without separating them from Himself?
who rendered his creations outside of Himself fixed in their
essence and mutable in their form? The pair thus called to
the celestial festival could only see the order and arrangement of created beings and admire the immediate result.
The Angels alone see more. They know the means; they
comprehend the final end.

But what the two Elect were granted power to contemplate, what they were able to bring back as a testimony
which enlightened their minds forever after, was the proof
of the action of the Worlds and of Beings; the consciousness
of the effort with which they all converge to the Result.

They heard the divers parts of the Infinite forming one
living melody; and each time that the accord made itself felt
like a mighty respiration, the Worlds drawn by the concor-
dant movement inclined themselves toward the Supreme
Being who, from His impenetrable centre, issued all things
and recalled all things to Himself.

This ceaseless alternation of voices and silence seemed
the rhythm of the sacred hymn which resounds and pro-
longs its sound from age to age.

Wilfrid and Minna were enabled to understand some
of the mysterious sayings of Him who had appeared on
earth in the form which to each of them had rendered
him comprehensible,—to one Seraphitus, to the other
Seraphita,—for they saw that all was homogeneous in the
sphere where he now was.

Light gave birth to melody, melody gave birth to light;
colors were light and melody; motion was a Number
endowed with Utterance; all things were at once sonorous,
diaphanous, and mobile; so that each interpenetrated the
other, the whole vast area was unobstructed and the Angels
could survey it from the depths of the Infinite.

They perceived the puerility of human sciences, of which

he had spoken to them.

The scene was to them a prospect without horizon, a boundless space into which an all-consuming desire prompted them to plunge. But, fastened to their miserable bodies, they had the desire without the power to fulfil it.

The *Seraph*, preparing for his flight, no longer looked towards them; he had nothing now in common with Earth.

Upward he rose; the shadow of his luminous presence covered the two Seers like a merciful veil, enabling them to raise their eyes and see him, rising in his glory to Heaven in company with the glad Archangel.

He rose as the sun from the bosom of the Eastern waves; but, more majestic than the orb and vowed to higher destinies, he could not be enchained like inferior creations in the spiral movement of the worlds; he followed the line of the Infinite, pointing without deviation to the One Centre, there to enter his eternal life,—to receive there, in his faculties and in his essence, the power to enjoy through Love, and the gift of comprehending through Wisdom.

The scene which suddenly unveiled itself to the eyes of the two Seers crushed them with a sense of its vastness; they felt like atoms, whose minuteness was not to be compared even to the smallest particle which the infinite of divisibility enabled the mind of man to imagine, brought into the presence of the infinite of Numbers, which God alone can comprehend as He alone can comprehend Himself.

Strength and Love! what heights, what depths in those two entities, whom the *Seraph's* first prayer placed like two links, as it were, to unite the immensities of the lower worlds with the immensity of the higher universe!

They comprehended the invisible ties by which the material worlds are bound to the spiritual worlds. Remembering the sublime efforts of human genius, they were able to perceive the principle of all melody in the songs of heaven which gave sensations of color, of perfume, of thought, which recalled the innumerable details of all creations, as the songs of earth revive the infinite memories of love.

Brought by the exaltation of their faculties to a point that cannot be described in any language, they were able to cast their eyes for an instant into the Divine World. There all was Rejoicing.

Myriads of angels were flocking together, without confusion; all alike yet all dissimilar, simple as the flower of the fields, majestic as the universe.

Wilfrid and Minna saw neither their coming nor their going; they appeared suddenly in the Infinite and filled it with their presence, as the stars shine in the invisible ether.

The scintillations of their united diadems illumined space like the fires of the sky at dawn upon the mountains. Waves of light flowed from their hair, and their movements created tremulous undulations in space like the billows of a phosphorescent sea.

The two Seers beheld the *Seraph* dimly in the midst of the immortal legions. Suddenly, as though all the arrows of a quiver had darted together, the Spirits swept away with a breath the last vestiges of the human form; as the *Seraph* rose he became yet purer; soon he seemed to them but a faint outline of what he had been at the moment of his transfiguration,—lines of fire without shadow.

Higher he rose, receiving from circle to circle some new gift, while the sign of his election was transmitted to each sphere into which, more and more purified, he entered.

No voice was silent; the hymn diffused and multiplied itself in all its modulations:—

"Hail to him who enters living! Come, flower of the Worlds! diamond from the fires of suffering! pearl without spot, desire without flesh, new link of earth and heaven, be Light! Conquering spirit, Queen of the world, come for thy crown! Victor of earth, receive thy diadem! Thou art of us!"

The virtues of the *Seraph* shone forth in all their beauty.

His earliest desire for heaven re-appeared, tender as childhood. The deeds of his life, like constellations, adorned him with their brightness. His acts of faith shone like the Jacinth of heaven, the color of sidereal fires. The pearls of Charity were upon him,—a chaplet of garnered tears! Love divine surrounded him with roses; and the whiteness of his Resignation obliterated all earthly trace.

Soon, to the eyes of the Seers, he was but a point of flame, growing brighter and brighter as its motion was lost in the melodious acclamations which welcomed his entrance into heaven.

The celestial accents made the two exiles weep.

Suddenly a silence as of death spread like a mourning veil from the first to the highest sphere, throwing Wilfrid and Minna into a state of intolerable expectation.

At this moment the *Seraph* was lost to sight within the *sanctuary*, receiving there the gift of Life Eternal.

A movement of adoration made by the Host of heaven filled the two Seers with ecstasy mingled with terror. They felt that all were prostrate before the Throne, in all the spheres, in the Spheres Divine, in the Spiritual Spheres, and in the Worlds of Darkness.

The Angels bent the knee to celebrate the *Seraph's* glory; the Spirits bent the knee in token of their impatience; others bent the knee in the dark abysses, shuddering with awe.

A mighty cry of joy gushed forth, as the spring gushes forth to its millions of flowering herbs sparkling with diamond dewdrops in the sunlight; at that instant the *Seraph* reappeared, effulgent, crying, "*Eternal! Eternal! Eternal!*"

The universe heard the cry and understood it; it penetrated the spheres as God penetrates them; it took possession of the infinite; the Seven Divine Worlds heard the Voice and answered.

A mighty movement was perceptible, as though whole planets, purified, were rising in dazzling light to become Eternal.

Had the *Seraph* obtained, as a first mission, the work of calling to God the creations permeated by His Word?

But already the sublime *hallelujah* was sounding in the ear of the desolate ones as the distant undulations of an ended melody. Already the celestial lights were fading like the gold and crimson tints of a setting sun. Death and Impurity recovered their prey.

As the two mortals re-entered the prison of flesh, from which their spirit had momentarily been delivered by some priceless sleep, they felt like those who wake after a night of brilliant dreams, the memory of which still lingers in their soul, though their body retains no consciousness of them, and human language is unable to give utterance to them.

The deep darkness of the sphere that was now about them was that of the sun of the visible worlds.

"Let us descend to those lower regions," said Wilfrid.

"Let us do what he told us to do," answered Minna. "We have seen the worlds on their march to God; we know the Path. Our diadem of stars is There."

Floating downward through the abysses, they re-entered the dust of the lesser worlds, and saw the Earth, like a subterranean cavern, suddenly illuminated to their eyes by the light which their souls brought with them, and which still environed them in a cloud of the paling harmonies of heaven. The sight was that which of old struck the inner eyes of Seers and Prophets. Ministers of all religions, Preachers of all pretended truths, Kings consecrated by Force and Terror, Warriors and Mighty men apportioning the Peoples among them, the Learned and the Rich standing above the suffering, noisy crowd, and noisily grinding them beneath their feet,—all were there, accompanied by their wives and servants; all were robed in stuffs of gold and silver and azure studded with pearls and gems torn from the bowels of Earth, stolen from the depths of Ocean, for which Humanity had toiled throughout the centuries, sweating and blaspheming. But these treasures, these splendors, constructed of blood, seemed worn-out rags to the eyes of the two Exiles. "What do you there, in motionless ranks?" cried Wilfrid. They answered not. "What do you there, motionless?" They answered not. Wilfrid waved his hands over them, crying in a loud voice, "What do you there, in motionless ranks?" All, with unanimous action, opened their garments and gave to sight their withered bodies, eaten with worms, putrefied, crumbling to dust, rotten with horrible diseases.

"You lead the nations to Death," Wilfrid said to them. "You have depraved the earth, perverted the Word, prostituted justice. After devouring the grass of the fields you have killed the lambs of the fold. Do you think yourself justified because of your sores? I will warn my brethren who have ears to hear the Voice, and they will come and drink of the spring of Living Waters which you have hidden."

"Let us save our strength for Prayer," said Minna.

"Wilfrid, thy mission is not that of the Prophets or the Avenger or the Messenger; we are still on the confines of the lowest sphere; let us endeavor to rise through space on the wings of Prayer."

"Thou shalt be all my love!"

"Thou shalt be all my strength!"

"We have seen the Mysteries; we are, each to the other, the only being here below to whom Joy and Sadness are comprehensible; let us pray, therefore: we know the Path, let us walk in it."

"Give me thy hand," said the Young Girl, "if we walk together, the way will be to me less hard and long."

"With thee, with thee alone," replied the Man, "can I cross the awful solitude without complaint."

"Together we will go to Heaven," she said.

The clouds gathered and formed a darksome dais. Suddenly the pair found themselves kneeling beside a body which old David was guarding from curious eyes, resolved to bury it himself.

Beyond those walls the first summer of the nineteenth century shone forth in all its glory. The two lovers believed they heard a Voice in the sun-rays. They breathed a celestial essence from the newborn flowers. Holding each other by the hand, they said, "That illimitable ocean which shines below us is but an image of what we saw above."

"Where are you going?" asked Monsieur Becker.

"To God," they answered. "Come with us, father."

Also available from Antipodes Press

*Journey to the Orient* BY GÉRARD DE NERVAL

More than just an account of his travels in Cairo, Beirut, and Constantinople in 1842, Gérard de Nerval's *Journey to the Orient* is a quest for the unknown. If his narrator seems credulous in his retelling of legends of the origins of the pyramids and the mysteries of the Druzes, it is with this purpose in mind. While the Orientalists of his day were confident of having, in the words of Edward Said, "grasped, appropriated, reduced, and codified" the Orient, Nerval's Orient remains elusive, impossible to grasp. Poignantly dramatized in the thematic centerpieces of the tales of the Queen of Sheba and the Caliph Hakim, what takes shape in this visionary travelogue, as the author's hopes are alternately disappointed and rapturously renewed, is the story of the artist's search for the ideal.

Paperback: 464 pages. ISBN 978-0-9882026-0-3

*Very Woman (Sixtine)* BY REMY DE GOURMONT

Hubert Entragues, aesthete and litterateur, conceives a passion for the ethereal Sixtine in this "cerebral novel" of 1890. The romance remains largely imaginary, a pursuit localized in the skull of the intellectual Entragues. Alone with his thoughts and his literature, his baroque reflections careen from lyrical exaltation to sullen despondency according to the inscrutable actions of his elusive inamorata. In his refined loneliness, his lucid and sensual daydreams develop into a story within the story, mirroring and embellishing the inner experience of their author.

*Very Woman* is a masterpiece of the symbolist movement of fin de siècle literature. A brilliant stylist, Gourmont's luxurious, poetic prose is full of erudition, irony, and eroticism, creating an atmosphere all its own.

Paperback: 224 pages. ISBN 978-0-9882026-8-9